What You Can Do For Your Country

To Pete -

a novel by
Warner Dixon

A good shooter
and a good man.
Hope you enjoy!

Other books by Warner Dixon, Available July 2010,
from Arizona Adventures Publishing

County Law and Cowboy Coffee
The Mantis

Published by Arizona Adventures Publishing, LLC.
P. O. Box 405
Prescott, Arizona, 86302

azadventurespublish@cableone.net

Additional copies may be ordered from the publisher.
Copyright © 2010 by Warner Dixon

International Standard Book Number
978-0-615-34083-8

Library of Congress Cataloging-in-Publication
Preassigned Control Number
2009913568

Dedicated to my mother and father, Mildred E. Dixon, and Warner B. Dixon, Sr., who would have been pleased to see this book published. To Susan Lange, whose Creative Writing classes and individual help made it possible, and to Barbara Sassone for her valuable help. Special thanks to Bonnie Daniel for her time and insights.

CONTENTS

We sleep soundly in our beds because rough men stand ready in the night to visit violence on those who would do us harm.

Winston Churchill

"...torn and bleeding, he flung himself over the bank. Captain, there are four more lads out there, two wounded, he said. I saw the captains anguished face. I cannot send a party after them, he said, and looked up at him. Realizing their fate, he turned back to the bank. Give me a leg up, mate, he asked. Where are you going, asked the captain. He turned his eyes on Captain Evers. Back, he said. You will be killed, said Evers. He nodded imperceptibly, straightened his bloody tunic. He turned to each of us, then back to Rawlins, who gave him a leg up. He disappeared over the bank.

The next day we found their bodies. Remembering his last words I felt as if struck a physical blow.

These are my men, he had said. I love them like brothers. I will live with them, or I will die with them.

At the time, I could not understand. Now, I am one of the few who do."

I am grateful for the access I was given to the yellowed, handwritten manuscript from which the above is quoted, as written, in the trenches of World War I. Permission to use it was given on the condition that neither the author nor the owner be identified.

Introduction

I remember only a few of the sermons I have ever heard in church. One that I do remember was about the traditional Christmas story. The minister read the story from the Bible, then asked, "Did this really happen?" She paused and looked out across the silent congregation. "Every year, millions of people read this story," she said. "They believe it happened. They re-live it. In their minds, in their belief, it happened just this way."

In some respects, Vietnam happened the same way.

This book is a novel—a work of fiction based on fact.

I have written about the interaction of a group of soldiers, their lives and their missions, before what is known as the Tet Offensive. Some names are not real. Some names will not be found. Some missions were clandestine. All took place without benefit of armored personnel carriers, tanks, or sometimes, even without trucks. These soldiers used weapons that were standard and basic, nothing a foot soldier couldn't carry.

If the reader finds my geography to be in conflict with a map, it probably is. I took liberties with some of the dates. Some geographical locations I moved. Or did not name. Or mention. Some, I remembered wrong. I do not like acronyms because they become confusing, so I used very few.

The American military presence in Vietnam existed far earlier than generally known. The Army Special Forces performed a multitude of tasks in southeast Asia. If some of the military conventions I write about seem unusual—they were.

Mostly I have written about Doug Walker, who is very much a part of me.

At one of the junior colleges I attended, the instructor of a history class asked three Vietnam veterans to give a short talk about their experiences in 'Nam. One vet had been assigned to relocation, and spoke about persuading whole villages to move from an area where their people had lived for generations. Another spoke about the fighting and ambushes, the marches, the terrible food and worse weather. The third had been involved in clandestine operations. He told of storybook missions, insertions from helicopters, sometimes outside the borders of Vietnam.

Had the audience not known the speakers' experiences were from the same war, they could easily have believed they fought in three different wars.

Such was 'Nam.

J. R.'s Flag

BY WARNER DIXON

rigid at attention I salute
and through eyes tear-blurred your form I see,
colors faded by the jungle sun,
graced with rips and dirt and blood and tears.
my friend, my comrade, rescued you
when shrapnel snapped the flagpole
where you flew above our base,
brought you safe into our digs—was killed that very day,
and so you journeyed home with me.
his wife, despite official protests asked
that with the dignity of your battle scars,
you lie atop his casket,
for she knew he would be pleased.
folded with great reverence, they placed you in her hands,
and beside the other warriors, laid him in the ground.
she stood and held you softly to her cheek, and with her tears recalled
the vow he took to fight for what you stand—for which he gave his all.
afterward she said to me to take you back,
that you belong with us, to every fighting man.
goddamn the fools to everlasting hell, she said,
who sent you there to fight without what it would take to win.
new flagpole at the firebase,
with reveille you greet the sun.
at dusk when we retire the colors,
it is as we have known, the ideals
that we fight for, transcend what we must do.
you are the embodiment of our country,
a tattered flag,
    red, white, and blue.

CHAPTER ONE

As American As Apple Pie

I slithered silently over the bank, taking advantage of every stalk and blade of grass I could use to conceal me from the hawkish scrutiny of the riflemen in the foxhole. The rest of my platoon had been wiped out. But I couldn't think about that. It was up to me now. I raised my rifle, holding the sights on the closest enemy, the pressure on the trigger a breath away from vengeance for Matt and the others. But especially Dan. I'd really make them suffer for him.

Then I heard the voice. "Doug? Douglas!" It belonged to my mother. "Come in now! Dinner's ready!" I smelled the peppery spice she put in hamburger, and that greasy frying smell. One of my favorites. But small compensation for defeat.

The enemy riflemen still crouched behind the shallow breastworks of the hastily dug foxhole in Mr. McIntyre's field, itching for victory. They pointed their rifles in my direction, then at the top of their lungs they yelled "Bang! Bang! Brr-rr-rippp! Brr-rr-ipp!"

"Got you, Doug, you're dead!" yelled Byron Hollister, who lived across the street from me.

"Yeah, I got you, too!" Eric Ballard called, when he saw where Byron was looking. He leaned forward, squinted, giving away that he didn't see me in the weeds.

"Aw, you didn't either! You didn't even see me until *Mom* started hollering about dinner." I said the word with disgust, to let everyone know what I thought of a mother who would interrupt a crucial battle. I didn't feel quite right about that, though. After all, Mom had given me Uncle Frank's Korean War army helmet. Everyone else had a plastic toy helmet. Although plastic helmets, being much lighter, didn't give them headaches like my steel helmet did.

I still got headaches from my helmet, but this one was issued to me by the U. S. Army. I only wanted to sit still and let the pain go away. Then an elbow dug into my ribs, precariously rocking the ammo case I had perched on. My eyes popped open and I heard Dan's voice. "Hey! Wake up! You're snoring loud enough to rouse Charlie from his tunnels!"

"Yeah, yeah, no way," I said. "I wasn't really asleep. I was thinking of when we used to play army in McIntyre's field."

Dan smiled. "Yeah. I remember that. You had a real G. I. helmet. Now we all got gen-you-wine G. I. helmets. You think if we'd known what 'Nam is really like, we'd be here now?"

"We were dumb kids," I said, still remembering. "I was about to get revenge because they got you..." A finger of fear traced my spine and stood my hair on end. Dan frowned. Talking about death—even pretend death—could break our run of luck in this world of real death. And luck could be the only explanation for our survival after a whole year in 'Nam. We both looked away.

I scratched at my side. It hurt. The pain kept me from ignoring that particular leech-bitten spot. Leech saliva contains a pain killer that keeps the victim from feeling a leech chewing through the skin to suck blood. I didn't know the thing had crawled under my shirt until I leaned against a tree and felt it squash. Usually we held a match or a cigarette next to them so they'd pull in their teeth and back out. Killing one, the way I unknowingly did, meant I had all its miserable teeth imbedded in my skin. Now the wound had turned into an oozy red pouch of infection. The tube of antibiotic cream our medic, Mack, gave me didn't work.

I rubbed the useless cream on it anyway as everybody waited for Lieutenant Jaimeson. Late as usual, he would give us a briefing on our next mission. Everything felt like bad joss. Maybe we'd run out of luck.

Dan stared off into space. A mask of fear. He saw me watching him and smiled, just a brittle movement around his mouth. He ran shaky fingers through his filthy hair.

The heavy air in the underground digs made it hard to breathe. I had to get out from under the dirt-covered log ceiling. The log stairs were slick with moisture under my boots. When I stuck my head out, a faint whup-whup-whup of chopper blades got louder as a speck against the deep blue sky got bigger. Lieutenant Jaimeson's chopper set down, and I got a whiff of exhaust. I retreated back inside.

As the lieutenant came down the steps, he stubbed his toe on a knot sticking up from one of the logs and took the last two all at once. His khaki uniform, so heavily starched I expected to hear him crackle, had sweat rings under the arms. He would have been tall and willowy, except that he stooped. His soft hands and pink skin pegged him as someone who worked inside, in air conditioned comfort, neatly removed from dirt, sweat and blood. Here, the smell of damp earth, rot and unwashed bodies made him edgy. Lieutenant Jaimeson hadn't "seen the elephant." Our two worlds made us seem alien to each other.

Jaimeson always sucked on antacids. Maybe he felt guilty sending men to do things that got them killed. He knew from the debriefings how well we accomplished our tasks, and he stayed out of our way. I wondered if he assuaged his conscience by procuring almost anything we asked for.

"O-o-o-h," Dan said, watching Jaimeson extract a rolled-up map from a long, tubular case and spread it out on the field desk. "We gonna have visual aids! See Dick run!"

Jaimeson turned to set up his tripod and the map rolled itself off the desk, as if trying to escape. As he turned back for the map, a renegade latch on one leg of the tripod slipped, and it sagged to one side. Retrieving the map, the lieutenant caught the tripod just as it toppled. The team erupted in snorts and laughter. Red-faced, he draped the map over the tripod.

"Okay! Listen up!" he yelled over the buzz of chatter. "I'm going to tell you what your next mission is going to be, so pay attention!" he said.

"Real leadership," Dan whispered. "Che-rist, am I glad we don't have to take him with us!"

"Yeah," I said. "It would take three men and a boy to carry his map and tripod."

"You're the one who's gonna need three men and a boy to pack your arsenal," Dan said.

"You think you're the three men, Foster?" I said. "Or the boy?"

"She-e-e-it, you couldn't keep up with me even if you didn't have anything to carry."

"Sh-h-h, he's looking at us."

"I have a bad feeling about this one," Dan whispered.

"Yeah," I said, frowning. "The dark side of bad."

Suddenly Jaimeson wrinkled his nose. Murdo, who sat in the front row, had yanked off his boot to scratch his foot. Jaimeson gagged, pulled out his handkerchief, and covered his face. More snorts and laughter at his expense. He hadn't experienced "jungle foot," the fungus we got. The smell radiated like a stinking corpse from last week's firefight mixed with cooked cabbage.

Murdo shoved his foot back in his boot and the briefing settled down as Jaimeson began explaining the objectives. This time we would be looking for regular NVA troops, well-trained and armed, that were supposed to be in the area, not just a few locals with limited arms and ammunition. Charlie at his most challenging. If we found them without being detected, I would attempt to take out certain officers. Getting out after that could be especially difficult.

I carried a Thompson sub-machine gun and a load of stick magazines for firefights, even though the army deemed it obsolete. I had asked Lieutenant Jaimeson to find one for me. His knack of trading for the hard-to-get would have made a supply sergeant envious. The Thompson and the .45 Government Model pistols we carried used the same ammo. I also carried my Winchester bolt-action rifle, custom tuned to hit a quarter two football fields away. It had a long barrel and a telescopic sight, which made it heavy and almost useless in dense foliage, but superb for long-range work. For close range, I relied on the Thompson. Carrying it had become a labor of love.

My body and my dreams told me something would change. Our luck had been too good. Scary. I had been counting on it to carry Dan and me through this endless jungle nightmare. I prayed it would. Dan had been my best friend for as long as I could remember. Whatever had lured us away from the peace and beauty of the mountain pine forests of Arizona, the boy games of McIntyre's field, to this shell-pocked hill, months of ceaseless monsoon rain, sickness and death, I could no longer remember. Dreams of our childhood and our living nightmares merged into a ferocious misery for me, a monster Asian leech sucking on my chest.

CHAPTER TWO

Shooting and Hunting

Shooting had been my passion since the sixth grade. The spring of that year my parents gave me a rifle for my birthday, a brand new J. C. Higgins .22 cal. bolt action rifle with a five shot magazine. It was the same spring Eric and his friends filled in the foxhole in McIntyre's field and built it up as a pitcher's mound. They played softball and football in the field, and basketball at Mickey's house. His father had installed regulation-sized basketball hoops on both sides of the driveway. I felt deserted.

Then one day Dan Foster announced his parents had also given him a .22 rifle. After school, while our classmates learned to hit a ball with a bat, we took to the mountains and learned to hit tin cans with bullets. Atop cliffs and mountaintops we sat, rifles across our laps, absorbing scenes and sunsets, the smell of pine needles, damp earth and mountain air. Sometimes we sat so still the blue jays and squirrels ventured close. When we rose to leave, they started, scolding us as they scattered.

I spent all my allowance on .22 ammo that summer. I did every odd job I could to earn money to buy more Winchester Copper-Klad Lubaloy ammunition—words like that tasted as good as chocolate pudding as they fell from my tongue, good as the lightly sweet solvent-smell of powder smoke when I opened the bolt of my .22 rifle after firing a round. Out in the woods, Dan and I shot tin cans and various sticks and rocks at long and short range. A box of fifty cartridges didn't last long, although we made every shot count.

That autumn, my dad gave me a brick of .22's—ten boxes, five hundred rounds. I'd never felt so rich, or so grown up.

The following year I made the rifle team at my junior high school.

My early shooting career had almost been curtailed by my mother. I was going out in the forest where Dan lived one Saturday when she stopped me.

"Doug, I want you to start leaving you rifle at home for a while," she said.

I couldn't believe what she said. "Why?" I asked. "I've always taken my twenty-two. I've never hurt anyone or gotten in trouble. How could you ask me to leave it? I'm supposed to go meet Dan!"

She hesitated, looked at me, looked away, then looked back. "I don't know," she said. "I just don't think it's a good idea. Go ahead and take it, this time. Tonight I'll talk to your father."

When I got to Dan's, I told him what Mom had said. "She didn't even tell you why?" he asked, equally mystified

"No. I think I'd better go talk to my dad before he gets home." My dad taught at the high school.

"It's gotta be three miles to the school. I'll walk with you," Dan said.

My father's decision about my forays into the woods with my rifle would carry the weight of the head of a 1950's family. I knew he understood my fascination with forest lore and with shooting, although he never went with me. While he and Mom talked, I waited in the garage, cleaning my rifle. I had just cleaned it for the third time when he came out. I looked up, apprehensively.

"Doug, we've decided you can keep going on your trips with Dan. You can take your twenty-two as long as you keep your grades up. If you don't, you and your rifle will stay home until they improve."

I felt relieved beyond words. "Thanks, Dad. Did I do something wrong that got Mom all upset?"

He looked thoughtful for a few minutes, rubbed his chin the way he did when someone asked him a tough question. "No, not as far as being safe, or shooting at something you shouldn't. I think she just feels something will happen to you. Women think differently than men. You'll find that out later on."

That made no sense at all to me.

7

When winter blew in with a series of snowstorms, it kept me out of the forest for several months. Or that was my mother's excuse. She was afraid I'd get lost and be found frozen solid. Instead, Dan and I went to the Elk's Theater and agonized with John Wayne in *The Sands of Iwo Jima*. We watched with rapt fascination movies like *The Red Badge of Courage* with Audie Murphy.

With the coming of spring, my adventures with Dan became more frequent than ever. One time we hiked to the top of a ridge where the view stretched for miles, both north and south.

"This is the Tritle Ridge, isn't it?" I asked. The air smelled fresher than my mother's clean sheets.

Dan nodded, absorbed in the view, the elevation high enough the snow hadn't all melted.

"How come the snow turns into little granules?" I asked, scooping up a patch of snow to quench my thirst. "It tastes like pine needles...ahhhhh! It hurts my teeth!"

"Its cooling off fast," Doug said, pointing to the sun as dusk approached. Usually we raced the sun for home. "We better get going. Got something I want to show you when we get back." He started down the mountain.

"What is it?" I asked. He smiled mysteriously. I asked again a dozen times before we got to Dan's home. He didn't say a word.

Dan's family's one-room home had a huge wood stove for cooking and heating. I wished my home was like it.

Dan reached into a corner next to the couch and pulled out a lever action rifle. "It's a deer rifle, a Marlin .30-30. Here," he said. I took it from his hand with awe and reverence. "It belonged to my grandfather."

I checked the chamber and magazine. It was unloaded. The rifle showed wear from its many hunting trips. It seemed to be mechanically sound, though. The action felt smooth, and it had a full buckhorn sight. "Ah, man, this is beautiful!" I said, green with envy.

Our excursions took on new life, a quest for big game. Ever since we had been roaming the forest, Dan had been shooting rabbits or squirrels. It pained me to feel their anguish, kicking in their death throes as life faded, eyes dimming from bright and alive to dull and dead. Now I conspired with Dan to kill the soft-eyed deer we tracked and sneaked up on. I didn't know for sure if I could go through with it when deer season came, but I'd never admit it. Not even under torture.

One day we got back to Dan's after dark and his mother asked if I wanted to stay for dinner. "I've got rabbit cooked with potatoes, carrots and onions" she said.

The aroma, rich with spices, made my stomach growl.

"I'd love to," I said without a thought. The stew tasted delicious, and I almost inhaled it from the speckled enamel bowl Mrs. Foster set in front of me.

She asked if I wanted more. I said yes, but when I heard the ladle scrape the bottom of the pot, I realized she'd already spooned out most of it. "Just about half as much," I added hastily. "It's very filling. Very good, but filling." I could see the vegetables outweighed the meat from the small rabbit Dan killed the day before—all the meat the family had for him, his sister, mother and father—and me. I looked around their one-room home and the big wood cook stove as if seeing it for the first time. The cabin had been built on patented land, whatever that meant.

Suddenly I realized Dan's family was poor. I was touched that they would share what little they had, and somehow I felt ashamed. I'd never really been hungry before. It dawned on me that if Dan shot a deer, it would provide meat for the family for a long time.

I joined Dan in shooting meat for his table, learning to gut and skin the animals and tan the hides. We never shot anything Dan's family couldn't eat. Dan knew where to sell the pelts. With my share of the money, I splurged and bought hollow-point ammo, twenty cents more per box. I believed the hollow points made a quicker kill.

On one hunt Dan tapped my arm and pointed. "Rabbit," he said. "We gotta get closer."

"No, I can get him."

Dan raised his eyebrows. I nodded, leaned against a tree, and made the shot.

"Seventy-one long paces," he said as he picked up the rabbit. "Good shooting."

It surprised me I could make shots Dan couldn't. I thought maybe I could shoot better since I had a better rifle and could afford more ammo for practice.

9

When he ran out, Dan's pride kept him from shooting my ammo if I offered to share. I reminded him that showing me how to prepare the game and tan the hides made it a good trade for me. He decided that made it okay. The extra ammo helped his marksmanship, but I still made the most difficult shots.

"You're really good with a rifle," Dan told me, after I made another long shot. "You just have a natural ability."

"I hope you're right," I said. I wanted to believe it.

The first time Dan brought his Marlin .30-30 on one of our practice sessions, he handed it to me. "Want to shoot it?" he asked proudly. I knew it kicked a lot, and I didn't think I wanted to try it, but I couldn't say no. Anyway, I told myself, I'll have to learn how if I'm going to get my own.

"Sure," I said. I held it the way I'd been holding my .22, lined up the sights and squeezed the trigger. The can flew up in the air, but I didn't notice. I felt like someone had punched me in the nose and cheek, and smacked my shoulder with a hammer.

"Hey! You got it!" Dan said. He looked at me and his smile faded.

"Here's your rifle," I said, handing it back before he could suggest I shoot it again. I sniffed.

His smile disappeared. "Uh...I think you have a bloody nose," he said.

A metallic taste filled my mouth. "Yeah. I bit my lip, too." He looked at me kind of funny. I realized I couldn't bluff my way out of this one. Might as well come clean. "That really kicked me. My cheek hurts, and my shoulder, too."

Dan shook his head. "I'm sorry, I had my eye on the can. You're such a good shot I never thought..." He stopped short of saying I didn't know how to hold the rifle.

"Here's how I do it," he said. "I put the butt plate on the soft fleshy part inside my shoulder, my right hand on the grip and my cheek tight against the stock. Your thumb is what hit your nose," he said while I wiped my face on my sleeve, leaving a bloody trail. "Now, all I have to do is put my left hand on the forestock and pull back with both hands." He squeezed the trigger and missed the can by an inch or two.

Dan taught me the finer points of holding his .30-30. I taught him sight alignment, drawing diagrams on notebook paper. I showed him how to snap the hammer on an empty chamber to learn not to jerk the trigger, or flinch. I didn't know the experts called it dry-firing. I just knew how to do it.

Dan's meager supply of .30-30 cartridges didn't last long. His family had no money to spare, and his dad didn't believe in shooting for shooting's sake. "You got a whole box of shells to learn to shoot the gun," Mr. Foster told us. "Next time you shoot, ought to be a deer in the sights. There was times when we got down to three or four rounds apiece."

"You mean when you were hunting?" I asked him.

"Well, then, too. Two shots to sight it in, one shot for a deer, and an extra just in case. But I meant the Great War. We got ahead of our supply lines several times, and once our trenches almost got overrun."

I didn't know when the Great War happened, but before I could ask, he dropped another bombshell.

"I fought in the Spanish American War, too, you know."

Mr. Foster had always been someone to be polite and courteous to, like most parents, and equally uninteresting. I told Dan once that his father looked a hundred years old. "Nah," he said. "He's eighty. But that's so old he'd already joined the army before we fought with Spain. In the eighteen-hundreds!"

Mr. Foster told us stories about cavalry charges, shooting, heroism, and hardship. And about his disability from mustard gas. Honor, flag and country oozed from his tales. Accounts of gallantry, blood, and guts percolated into our young minds like water into dry ground. We listened for hours. It was just like John Wayne, but for real.

"I didn't know he did all that stuff either," Dan said. "It's kind of neat."

That school year we were assigned a research project in our history class. I laboriously wrote down Mr. Foster's first-hand accounts of different battles in both wars and verified them from reference books in the library. Knowing Mr. Foster had been there brought history alive, gave it an air of patriotism. I got an A-plus.

After Mom and Dad came home one afternoon, I showed them my paper. "You know if I'd never gone out shooting with Dan and met his dad, I'd never have had such a great source—and got such a good grade." Dad seemed to be trying not to laugh, and Mom got red-faced and didn't say much. I decided

I'd never understand parents.

That year we studied Southeast Asia, and a place with the strange name of French Indo-China. The pictures of that far-away land showed a smiling Oriental man in an almost flat, cone-shaped hat working in muddy water up to his knees. A dozen others bent over the muddy water, planting something. There was a picture of a mansion, much like the ones in Georgia or Alabama that survived the Civil War. It belonged to a French plantation owner. I thought it was a little like slavery. No wonder they were fighting.

Different countries had fought in French Indo-China for centuries and lost. Now the French were losing. Nuts, I thought. Give John Wayne a small band of leathernecks, he'd win the war and fly home to his girl on the weekend.

Except for school, Dan and I saw the neighborhood kids only occasionally, and talked to them less and less. When we did, we told them tales of the woods, of shooting and hunting. Some of the guys were impressed, but none had an inclination to participate, any more than we wanted to join the sports games they talked about.

Dan and I grew more isolated, resentful of the popularity of the school "sports heroes" as we called them. They had the means to achieve their goals, even if we thought they were superficial. We didn't have any way to fulfill our dreams, like Mr. Foster had done.

We kept on shooting and hunting, content with the assurance of its importance. We didn't waste our time trying to carry a ball over a line on the ground. We were *real* Americans.

One Sunday afternoon we sat in a grassy clearing without a care in the world. Dan tossed his apple core into the brush where some critter would find it. "I wonder if we'll ever have another war," he said.

The possibility gave me goose bumps.

With hunting season still months away, we followed all kinds of animal tracks. We were mostly interested in the deer, and found their water holes and salt licks, where they bedded down, where and what they ate. We learned to sneak up from downwind. Nothing was important enough to interrupt our lessons in stealth and marksmanship.

Then, at the beginning of our Sophomore year, we discovered girls.

CHAPTER THREE

Girls

Less than a month after high school classes started, our weekends had evolved into a pattern. I was going steady with Sarah Stern. We usually double-dated with Dan and his girlfriend, Marty. Mom and Dad helped me finance a used four-wheel drive truck. We would go to a drive-in movie, then drive my truck out into the forest, build a campfire, and drink beer. We traveled some of the remote four-wheel drive logging roads Dan and I found on our deer hunts, places where the Sheriff couldn't find us. My truck and I would have been grounded if Mom and Dad had found out.

Dan and Marty started going out with the kids whose families had money, and could afford new cars and hard liquor. Their so-called new friends treated them like dirt. Our foursome no longer existed, but worse, Dan's pursuit of this crowd took all his time. Alone, I hiked by myself, long, exhausting treks. I felt abandoned, angry at his blindness.

Sarah and I had gone steady for almost a year, a record of sorts in our high school. We had been making plans for summer vacation, only a few weeks away, when her parents announced they would take her with them on out-of-state business for the summer. They did not approve of me. After all, my father taught school. We did not belong to the country club. I wouldn't be headed for a fancy college. To them, I looked like a dead end, not a suitable prospect for their daughter. Sarah and I loved each other and thought nothing else mattered. The Top 40's songs told us so.

We vowed we would be together again in the fall when school started. That summer I spent even more time alone in the wilderness with my rifle, hiking, hunting, honing my skills. Over Mom's token objection, Dad let me take his revolver, a .22 caliber Smith and Wesson with a six-inch barrel. Of course, I also took my rifle. I think Dad knew I'd find the challenge of learning to shoot the revolver a distraction from losing my friends.

With Sara constantly on my mind, I counted the days until she came home. She wrote a few letters on the sly, and called collect several times from pay phones. One letter bore the bad news that her parents had forbidden her to see me.

I didn't think it could get worse, but it did. She wrote that her parents were forcing her to attend the Catholic academy her senior year. Frantic to figure out how to see her when school started, I devised daring plans, got a job and started saving money so we could go to Las Vegas and be married in one of the wedding chapels.

I yearned to talk to Dan, to have his understanding and counsel. Now and then I saw him and his new crowd. He and Marty broke up shortly after Sarah left. His new friends told jokes at his expense and laughed about Marty's infidelities before they split up. He continued to try to be acceptable to them, and when their cutting comments withered his self-esteem, he pretended it didn't matter. I could only watch and hope, let him fight his inner battle.

When Sarah came home, I couldn't wait to see her. At our first meeting she flung herself into my arms and started crying.

"It's all right," I said. "We're together now. Everything's okay." As I held her, I realized the tears had not been prompted by the joy of our reunion.

"No...nothing is okay. Nothing! We're moving. To Florida."

I felt a sudden queasiness. "When?" I asked.

"In two months," she said in a wavery voice. Her eyes met mine. As her tears fell, I felt my own spill down my cheeks.

I went through the motions of my daily routine, living in hope that somehow we could find a way to be together. Her parents did everything they could to keep us apart. When her father went on business trips, her mother usually went with him. Now she stayed home with Sarah. They took her to school and picked her up. They allowed her attend the dances at the Catholic Academy, driving her there and picking her up afterwards. We would leave the dance, spend the time in secluded places, and return before her parents came.

Two nights before the move to Florida, Sarah's parents gave her permission to spend the night with Mary Lou, her best friend and confidante. With her help, she sneaked out. We had to be back before dawn so Mary Lou's parents wouldn't know.

We drove into the forest and made a bed of pine needles and blankets under a big ponderosa. Our love-making came fast and hungry the first time, then slow and tender, and we held each other the rest of the night. Neither of us had slept when my old wind-up alarm rang in the pre-dawn. We kissed, clung to each other, then dressed.

"You can write to me. Give your letters to Mary Lou. She'll get them to me," she said, her voice flat.

I parked the truck several blocks from Mary Lou's house. On the radio Johnny Mathis sang *It's Not For Me To Say*. I turned it off and walked with her. We stopped and faced each other. She looked pale and drawn, her eyes red and swollen. The face of a child from whom something has been torn away. She stood on her toes and kissed me.

"I love you," she whispered, and ran.

I drove away, still feeling her in my arms, driving without direction. I went back where we'd spent the night and sat, mindless of time.

Without Sarah, school became more foreign than ever. I didn't care what happened. A few of my more sadistic classmates made the unfortunate decision to suggest I'd gotten Sarah pregnant and she had to leave. I flew into a boiling rage. Ensuing fistfights left me with stitches on my knuckles and an occasional black eye or split lip. To keep the peace and quell the talk of lawsuits, my mom and dad had to pay one offender's dental bill. After two more fights—costly victories over big, beefy football heroes—Mom, Dad and I met with the principal, the boys, and their parents. I would not be kicked out of school for fighting. My antagonists agreed to leave me alone, not much of a concession since I'd already convinced them with my fists.

Two months after Sarah left, Dan traded in his old car for a new, flashy red convertible with a big engine. A last, desperate attempt to impress his friends. He wrecked it the first night he had it. Totaled it. No serious injuries, fortunately, except to Dan's self image. The scare brought him to his senses.

The next weekend Dan and I drove to our favorite viewpoint in the forest. He had paid for a case of beer. "I want to celebrate," he said.

"Celebrate what?" I asked, wondering if he'd cracked his head in the wreck.

"No more car payments," he said. "But now I can afford to buy gas."

"Bad humor, Foster." But it sounded good to hear him laugh about it.

Even though the lookout had become a popular place, the usual cars with steamed-up windows and groping, passionate occupants had parked elsewhere tonight. I pulled another bottle from the case of Coors and fumbled for the church key.

"So how long now since you broke up with Marty? Four months?" I asked.

"No, about five." He frowned. "Did you hear what happened?" I shook my head.

"I caught her in the back seat of a car, necking with one of the football jocks. He had her blouse unbuttoned, her skirt up around her waist. He rolled on top of her just as she saw me.

"She told everyone I broke up with her because I found out she got pregnant. Now it's obvious she is, her belly's starting to show, and she's trying to make everyone think she doesn't know how it happened, that it's mine, crying about how I treated her. The trouble is, no one believes she slept with half the guys in town after I broke up with her. It's been five months, but she's not five months gone."

"What did your old man and your old lady say about it?"

He took a pull on his beer. "They never even asked if I did it," he said. "They just started chewing my ass for it, yelling at me about 'my obligations' and 'doing the right thing.' If it had been mine, I'd be doing the 'right thing.' I know how to take care of my responsibilities. They don't have to tell me what to do."

"You mean you'd marry her?"

"I would. If I knew it was mine. But it's not. She got knocked up way too long after we broke up for it to be mine. Okay?"

"Yeah, yeah, okay. I know you'd do what's right. You always do."

"Well, so do you. So do both of us. What's it gotten us?"

Gazing out the windshield into the velvety night, I thought of Sarah. The sliver of a moon strove to light the valley below, casting soft shadows. It could be comforting or frightening, depending on one's state of mind. Tonight it bordered on the demonic.

"Thank your lucky charms you didn't have to worry about that," he said, hesitantly. He knew I didn't talk about my intimacy with Sarah with him or anyone else. I'd shared almost everything in my life with Dan—except that.

"You're wondering how we did it without her getting pregnant."

Dan shrugged.

"She has a diaphragm," I volunteered, wondering why I allowed myself to venture into this sacred ground, but glad to have the closeness of our friendship back.

"A diaphragm isn't foolproof."

For a moment I felt fear slicing away my certainty that Sarah hadn't been pregnant, that an abortion hadn't been the reason for her parents' trip last summer. Surely she'd have told me, I thought. I understood more about how Dan felt.

Dan drank the last of his beer and launched the bottle into space past the guard rail. His anger gave it extended flight, and it took several seconds before we heard it crash at the bottom of the cliff. "It just isn't fair," he said, opening another. "Marty screwed half the guys in our class after we broke up. She couldn't even *know* who knocked her up."

He chugged half the bottle. "What am I gonna do about school?"

"You mean about what they think? You gotta quit caring about that. None of them matter."

"Remember when Rob took us riding?" he asked. His angry words gushed out without pausing long enough for me to answer. "He asked us if we wanted to ride in his new car. As long as he didn't see anyone else, he let us ride with him. Then he saw Brian and his friends and told us to get out. They drove off, leaving us standing there on the street."

"Yeah, I remember," I said. "I was there, too, okay?"

"But he got put down when Tommy bought a new Chevy Impala. The cheerleaders and the good-lookin' girls didn't want to ride with him any more."

"That's when we should have made our move," I said.

"Oh hell yes," he said. "As if the downers are going to even know we exist." It had become his pet name for the society girls who allegedly spread their legs for the athletes.

"Yeah, you're right." None of them would have paid any attention to us, I thought.

"Why are people always doing mean things?"

"I don't know," I said. I knew Dan was more vulnerable to what others thought, more easily wounded by their slings and arrows. Among other things, our friendship had been a shield, although more his than mine.

Once again we kept our own company. The last semester of our senior year flashed by in a blur. Neither of us went to our graduation. We had nothing to celebrate, except the end of an ordeal.

Sarah wrote, but only a short letter every week or ten days. I agonized over finding the mailbox empty and sometimes wished I could end our struggle. It seemed hopeless.

Dan found a new girl, Janice Livingston. She had dropped out of high school to work after her junior year and was starting back. She had been moved to tears over my situation with Sarah, and found our tragedy romantic. She and Dan wouldn't let me sit home alone. They insisted on taking me with them to movies and swimming, even to a couple of dances. Afterwards we usually drove the streets and the back roads. Janice kept us talking, and we all started to heal.

Dan and I usually ate lunch at the Canario Café, our high school hangout. The worn tables and linoleum floor attested to the traffic the place had seen over the years. The county health department's "A" rating, according to a yellowed certificate thumb-tacked to a greasy wall, could only have been awarded after a stretch of judgement. Yet we'd never heard of anyone who suffered from eating there.

"Hey, Bessie, anyone leave a Phoenix paper?" I asked our waitress.

"What do you want a paper for?" asked Dan.

"We've seen the movies at the drive-in and the Elks Theater. Let's see if we can find a decent flick in Phoenix." As I leafed through the entertainment section, the Palms Theater ad leaped out at me. "Well, son of a gun," I said. "They finally made it into a movie." I shoved the movie listing across the table.

"*Lawrence of Arabia*? What's that about?" asked Dan.

"That's about T. E. Lawrence. He wrote a book called *Seven Pillars of Wisdom*. I found my father's copy when I needed a project for history class. It's about World War I, fighting the Turks, armored cars, traveling across the desert on camels. It should be a really good flick."

"Might as well go," Dan said. "Janice is grounded. She got a D on her mid-term."

We left for Phoenix that evening, dining on Mc Donald's hamburgers for twenty-five cents apiece, shakes for the same price. Two dollars bought a feast.

I expected the movie to be a thriller, but I had no idea of the direction it would take us. In one part of the film, the Arabs looted a train they had derailed. After they killed the Turkish soldiers on board, Anthony Quinn, playing an Arab chieftain, looked for "something honorable" to take home to his people. He found several bolts of embroidered material. Then, realizing he had only some fancy cloth, he threw them down. He found a clock, ran to Lawrence to show it to him, discovered it didn't work, and threw it down, too. In despair, he looked up and down the wreckage, seeing for the first time the open railroad cars filled with horses. In one car, by himself, the Turks had tied a white horse, an Arabian stallion. Taking the horse with him, he led his men home. The white horse made a suitable prize. Something of honor.

The movie ended just before midnight. Dan didn't say a word as we walked back to my truck. "Want to stop for coffee?" I asked, wondering what bothered him.

"Nah," he said.

We left the city in silence. At the town of Black Canyon, half-way home,

I pulled over for coffee. Dan broke the silence. "That Arab chieftain got it right," he said.

"What do you mean?" I asked.

"Well, he found something honorable, " Dan mused, "Even if it's just a movie."

"It really happened," I said.

"The white horse. Something of honor." He let out a long breath. "How about some coffee?"

"Isn't that why we stopped?"

We almost didn't make it to our usual lookout point the following Saturday. A January storm dumped enough snow on the mountains to turn the road into serious four-wheel driving. We sat in the truck, drinking beer, running the engine so the heater would keep us warm. Usually we wondered how the Sheriff could be so dumb not to find us. But tonight we were sure no one else would make it to the lookout.

"Where's Janice?" I asked. "Still grounded?"

"Babysitting her older sister's baby," he said. "Her mom decided to make an exception to being grounded. As if any of it mattered."

"You know, that's what's wrong with everything. None of it matters. Remember Kennedy's Inaugural Address?" I asked him.

Dan frowned. "You mean the part about doing what the country needs?"

"Yeah. 'Ask not what your country can do for you, ask what you can do for your country.' That's what he said. It reminded me of your dad's war stories. Something that mattered."

Dan kept staring out through the windshield. He had registered for the draft, and this year I would register after my birthday—but neither of us wanted to be drafted.

"Shall we sign up?" he asked.

I felt like I'd swallowed a Roman candle. I pictured Lawrence on his white horse. A host of feelings, adventure and escape made me feel giddy. I nodded. "Yeah. Let's do it."

"Don't forget, you've got to get your mom or dad to sign for you, you're still seventeen."

"They're not going to like it, but I think they'll do it." I thought of Sarah. Am I just running away, I wondered? It didn't matter. I couldn't stay home.

"Janice isn't going to like it either," Dan said.

"You two are getting pretty serious. You don't have to go. I could go by myself," I said, hoping fervently that Dan would go with me.

"I think this is what we've been looking for. It's something worthwhile," he said, giving me a serious look. "We're best friends. We'll go together."

We visited the U. S. Army Recruiting Office and found out about the Buddy Plan that would ensure we could stay together. The recruiter gave me a form for my parents to sign. The final obstacle.

When I told my Mom and Dad what I wanted to do, they acted as if I'd told a bad joke.

"This is not something to take lightly! It's not something you have to do, so don't even talk about it!" my father said. I knew my parents didn't believe in war or compulsory service in the armed forces. The hurt in my father's voice, sounding as if I had betrayed him, was so strong it surprised me. Another control trip, I decided.

"Look, it's my life. And if I don't go, I'll get drafted. I won't have a choice about anything then," I countered. The conversation, which had rapidly escalated into a confrontation, pre-empted Mom's removal of the dinner dishes from the table, something she had done immediately after dinner for as long as I could remember. She sat on the edge of her chair, staring wordlessly, twisting a paper napkin back and forth.

"You won't get drafted," Dad said. "You can get a deferment for going to college."

"Oh yeah? What's changed? Last time we talked about it, I couldn't get enough scholarships for college. Working full-time and going to school full-time will be too much. And if I did go, I'd get drafted anyway."

"We'll find a way," he said, sounding desperate. "We can get a second mortgage or..."

I thought I had found the extreme my parents would go to—mostly my father—to keep from turning my own life over to me. "If you won't sign for me, I'll just leave and not tell you where I am. Then on my birthday I'll do it anyway!"

"Fine!" Dad yelled, "You do that! Don't bother to let us know!"

I glared at him, my face burning. I wanted him to take back his words, wanted to take back my own. But our pride stood between us. I jumped up from the table, and striding off into my room, I jammed sox, underwear and a some shirts into a shoulder bag. On the way out the door, my mother stopped me, her eyes round like a scared cat's.

"Call me tomorrow after your Dad's at work," she whispered. She pressed something into my hand and pushed the door shut behind me. I looked down to see that she had slipped me a twenty-dollar bill and some ones.

Three days later, with parental permission and without further communication with my father, the recruiter swore me and Dan into the United States Army. I had taken the first step down the path to one particular corner of hell. A place of agony far worse than first love lost.

Little did I know I that I would buy my next love. That Doe-eyed Li waited for me on the other side of the world.

CHAPTER FOUR

You Just Might Be Good Enough

Dan and I tackled the challenges of the U. S. Army boot camp with unflagging determination. We had staked our measure of success on the notion we would not just excel in the craft of soldiery. We would be the best. Our long forays into the mountains had given us an edge over almost everyone when it came to long marches. And marksmanship with our lever-action rifles transferred easily to Uncle Sam's semi-automatic M-1 rifle. Still, we suffered from a variety of fears.

We had just completed a thirty mile hike, two of the four who made it within the twenty-four hour time limit. "Jeezus, that was no damn hike. That was a fuckin' forced march," Dan said. He offered me his canteen to rinse my mouth. I'd had to push myself past any imaginable limits of my endurance. As soon as my body realized it was over, I fell to my knees and threw up.

The rest began to straggle in. Most wouldn't make it for hours. Some hobbled back on feet blistered and bleeding. Some had passed out and had to be carried or dragged, arms thrown loosely over the shoulders of others, who were on the last of their reserves. One sweat stained member of our team staggered and fell. He'd been carrying two field packs. He stood, staggered across the finish line dragging the second pack, and collapsed.

"You know, we did pretty well," I said.

"God, I don't know if I could do that again," Dan said.

I looked up from where I'd sprawled out, leaning against the wall of the barracks. Dan frowned, his lips turned down, glassy-eyed with fatigue and stress.

"Whaddaya talkin' about?" I asked. "You made it better than I did. If I hadn't held you back, you would have been the first one. And the first hike like this is the worst."

"Yeah, but we didn't beat Chapman and Baines."

"Christ, Dan, the four of us staggered in together. At worst, we tied them."

"Yeah, I guess so," he said.

I struggled to my feet, unsure if my legs would support me. "C'mon, we gotta go welcome the rest of the guys."

"Yeah," he said. "Let them know we got here before they did." He'd quit worrying, at least for the moment.

"Naturally." I grinned. "Gotta let 'em know who's top dog."

"Dogs," he said. "We're a team."

Two days later we had recovered enough to go to the rifle range. We'd just started firing when we were summoned off of the line by Drill Sergeant Powell.

"Foster! Walker!" he yelled. Get your asses down here on the double! Report to Captain MacKenzie's office!"

"Now what?" Dan asked. "We in trouble?"

"Hell, I don't know. Guess we'll find out."

We checked our rifles back in, along with our remaining ammo and empty cases. We had to have the same total number of cases and unfired ammo as the number of live rounds we checked out.

"Christ, what a bunch of idiots. Do they think we're gonna smuggle some ammo out of here?" Dan grumped.

We got to Captain MacKenzie's office at the administration building less than fifteen minutes from the time Powell summoned us.

"Man, this guy must be important," I said.

"Of course, shithead, he's a captain!"

"Yeah, a captain with a receptionist and two clerks."

We stopped at the desk of a sergeant whose face made me think he might have poured sour milk on his cereal this morning.

"WHAT?" he bellowed, neither slowing down nor looking up from his typing.

"Private Walker and Private Foster, reporting as ordered," I said.

He turned from his typewriter, scanned us from head to toe. We had been shooting prone, and had dirt from our knees to our elbows, scrapes on the toes of our boots. "You look like shit," he said.

"We were ordered here double time from the rifle range," Dan said. "If there's not some big hurry after all, we can go shit, shave, shower, change into clean uniforms, and come back after chow."

This brought the sergeant out of his chair so fast it fell over backwards. "Don't be a smartass with me! You'll live to regret it!" he yelled.

I frowned, felt the heat of anger in my face. Dan's quick temper had come to the boiling point. Right now we were the lowest life in the army. Privates. Sub-human. Little more important than pond algae. We were treated accordingly, and it didn't set well with Dan. Two weeks from now, when boot camp ended, we would be privates first class. One step up from pond algae.

"Look," I said. "Someone summoned us here, ASAP. We don't know why or..."

A lieutenant came out of the captain's office and we started to come to attention. "At ease," he said. He gave the sergeant a look which, if prolonged, would have produced frostbite. Turning on his heel, he said, "Follow me."

Inside Captain MacKenzie's large office, rather than the standard issue battleship grey metal desk, stood a large hardwood beauty with a mirror-finish top. Around it were four chairs. A major with a silly looking beret sat in one, his back against the window. The lieutenant sat down next to him. We stood at attention. Captain MacKenzie looked us over, then motioned to the remaining two chairs. "Sit," he barked.

"Yessir," I said, Dan echoing my response.

I looked at the major with the beret. He sat straight, almost at attention on the hard, wooden chair, as did the lieutenant. Both, I noticed, looked lean and in superb physical condition. The Major closed the manila folder he had been reading and tossed it on the only thing on MacKenzie's desk—another identical folder. Then he nodded at MacKenzie.

"Major Baker, this is Private Walker and Private Foster." He turned to us. "Lieutenant Lehman is the Major's administrative assistant," MacKenzie said. He leaned back in his chair, steepled his hands, and rested his chin on his fingers. He looked unsure that his part in whatever he and Major Baker were up to, had been wise.

"I've been looking over your records," Major Baker said. It appears you both have some abilities that might qualify you to serve in my outfit." He looked back and forth from Dan to me. "I'm going to tell you a little about what kind of men we need and what we do. Then, if you think you want to be considered for an invitation to join us, we'll take a closer look at each other." He scooped the folders off the desk. Mine and Dan's. He opened one, then the other. "You two joined up on the buddy plan, so whatever you decide, you both have to agree. Questions?"

We looked at each other. I knew the mystique appealed to Dan. A lot. He shrugged, nodded an affirmative. I smiled and nodded. "Yes, sir. I would like to hear more."

"In our outfit you must accept conditions that are considered by some to be not only dangerous, but unorthodox," he said. "You will run a higher risk of capture and torture. You could disappear and no one would ever know what happened to you." He gave us both a searching stare. "You probably will not have the security of a large force with you. You or your team could be on your own for days at a time. If this bothers you, we should go our separate ways now, no regrets, nothing derogatory on your records."

He laid his hand on our folders. I felt a weight press on my chest. Then McIntyre's field played before my eyes, the missions as kids we dared to brave for our country. Spending long days and nights by myself in the woods. Or with Dan. We could do what he asked—so far. Then I felt cold goose bumps. Unlike anything we'd done, this had the feel of life and death.

"Yeah, sure," Dan said. "I can accept that." His answer sounded shallow, almost flip.

I looked Major Baker in the eye.

"You have something to say, Walker?"

"Yes sir. We used to dream of something like this when we were kids. I have no illusions that what you offer us will be easy or without risk. Nevertheless, I would like to hear more about it." He held my eyes with an iron stare, but I didn't look away.

The Major stood and paced the small room. "All right," he said. "We are Army Special Forces. We have a long and varied history, actually starting with the Office of Strategic Services during World War II. The OSS was a precursor to the CIA as well as Army Special Forces. Another World War II outfit, the First Special Service Force, known as the Devil's Brigade, had a lot of influence on the structure of our current Army Special Forces."

He turned and looked out the window. When he turned back, he stood at a rigid parade rest. We listened to his rehearsed recitation as he emphasized its importance.

"We fought in French Indo-China—Vietnam—throughout World War II. Army Special Forces worked side by side with Ho Chi Minh, fighting the Japanese. We're still there, and so is Uncle Ho. Due to the change in the winds of politics, he is now on the other side.

"In 1952, at Fort Bragg, 10th Special Forces Group was formed. There were no 1st Special Forces Group thru 9th Special Forces Group. As part of the cold war, the Army wanted the USSR to think there were nine other units. This was the real birth of the United States Army Special Forces. The deception to any perceived enemy was in keeping with the way we operated then and now. Our purpose was, and still is, to train insurgents behind the lines. We use whatever weapons we can get our hands on. We favor the Johnson light machine gun. However, we've trained our indigenous with everything from civilian firearms to AK-47s, M-1s, and M-14s.

"Many of our missions are classified. Sometimes we don't understand their purpose. We accomplish them anyway, simply because we follow orders without asking questions. We're old hands at clandestine operations and guerilla warfare. Lately, we've had some assignments that are relatively new to us. We are considered to be advisors to the Army of the Republic of Vietnam—the ARVN. And we continue to do extensive training with them.

"As the President has told our country, there are no American combat personnel in southeast Asia, although our advisors now take an active role with the ARVN in combat missions. What we used to call 'mobile strike forces' are now clandestine combat missions in Laos and Cambodia. A few in North Vietnam. In other words, we accomplish our missions without being there."

I looked at Dan. The faint smile on his face must have been a reflection of the one on mine.

Major Baker spent the next hour telling us about the role of Army Special Forces. I was surprised at the variety of overt and covert missions. I drank in every word, for I believed that as part of his outfit, I could fulfill the desire I'd had to serve my country since McIntyre's field. The look on Dan's face was a mixture of the same and an urgency that somehow, if he didn't hang on to it, this opportunity would slip away.

The Major turned to Lieutenant Lehman. "Stan, did I leave anything out?"

"Sir, did you want to mention schools?"

"Oh, yes. I almost forgot," said the Major. "You will have to go to some schools. Particularly, Escape and Evasion, Survival, and Unarmed Combat. That's what they used to call hand-to-hand combat. Since you're on the 'buddy' program, you both will have to graduate, or neither of you goes to Special Forces Camp." He looked thoughtful for a moment. "You should take the Airborne training too. We do some insertions by air."

I felt the grip of fear squeeze my guts. I was afraid of heights. Dan watched me out of the corner of his eye, then turned to me and said, "Nah, that won't be any problem. We can ace those schools, no sweat. Right Doug?"

"Right," I said. "No sweat. Ace those schools." I felt queasy already. Major Baker hadn't missed my reaction to the mention of Airborne training. Not at all.

"Questions, Private Walker?" he asked.

"No, sir. We'll do it." I didn't care how scared I was or might be. The fear of someone finding out was far worse.

Lieutenant Lehman stood. "Okay. Walker, we'll want to see your talents on the rifle range. And Foster—we'll see just how stealthy you really are.

About two days before graduation. You guys just might be good enough. Dismissed."

Smart-ass bastard, I thought. *Might* be good enough? *Dismissed?* Fine. I stood, came to attention. "Yes Sir," I said. Dan took my cue and we executed a marvelously crisp salute.

Lieutenant Lehman had picked up his briefcase and our files. We stood there, waiting for him to return our salutes. Our files slipped out of his grasp and fell to the floor as he tried to free up his hand to salute.

"At ease, Stan," Major Baker said. He snapped us a salute as Lieutenant Lehman bent over to pick up our files. The Major looked fierce as anything I'd ever seen. Still, I couldn't help but feel that he had been mildly amused at our antics. He had the feel of a compressed spring, ready to come unglued. Not a man to trifle with.

As we walked down the hallway, our breathing came easier. The air didn't seem to have such an electric charge.

"Jeezus," I said to Dan. "You told him, 'Yeah, sure, I can accept that?' Are you nuts? That sounded like you didn't give a tinker's damn."

Unfazed, Dan smiled at me. "And I suppose you thought you might be able to stare down that uh..."

"Major, Dan. His rank is major. No. I didn't think so. Well, we gonna do it?"

"Sure," he said. "No doubt. Ace those schools. Jump out of airplanes. Yeah. Are *we* gonna do it?"

I looked to see if anyone had been listening. "Listen, asshole, you tell anyone I'm afraid of heights, I'll kick your ass."

Dan threw his arm over my shoulders. "You wouldn't even if you could. And you won't even sweat it. Cause I'll be there. I'll jump with you. We've always been there—together."

CHAPTER FIVE

Special Forces Camp

From the air, 'Nam looked innocuous, a judgment immediately overturned once we were on the ground.

The axiom of the jungle is that the entire body is always hot and wet. Our damp tobacco burned, not by normal combustion, but by will power. Scrapes, abrasions, bites, infections, and fevers were background noise to the daily terror. We were infested with a thousand varieties of insects, making it unusual to find a patch of healthy skin. Men who would be considered too sick to walk back in the World would go out on patrols and might end up running miles if Charlie chased them, knowing death, or worse, would result if they were captured. A common joke concerned the soldier who felt strange but couldn't pinpoint his malady. They sent him to the rear, to a hospital, where he explained it to a doctor. The doctor checked him over, then told him he'd discovered the problem. At the moment, the soldier had nothing wrong with him. It had been such a long time he just didn't recognize the symptoms.

The driver who delivered us to our base camp— after bouncing us around for several hours in the back of a deuce-and-a-half truck—didn't even turn off the engine or get out. Almost before we could unload our gear and some crates, he left like he needed a head start in case someone came in pursuit. I looked at Dan. He shrugged his shoulders. We watched the ridge where the truck disappeared into the jungle, wondering what immediacy he felt to confront its shadows. A corporal, frowning over a list of the contents of the crates we'd unloaded, didn't even look up.

"You FNGs report to the lieutenant," he said, pointing with his thumb. I was mildly piqued by his insult, but since I was on new ground, I wasn't about to make an issue of it.

We walked down the row of identical tents. Sweat trickled down my back, soaking my shirt. The air smelled like a locker room with a tinge of stale, sweaty socks. Like a recently-turned compost pile, leaves mixed with garbage, the jungle perfume invaded my sinuses and lungs. The humidity seemed high enough to slice and stack.

I could feel everyone watching us, giving us a thorough sizing up. It got worse when we reported to the lieutenant, who just stared for the longest time. After all, we were FNGs— fuckin' new guys—unknown quantities, and in our ignorance we might get someone hurt or killed.

The tent we were assigned to had four cots. Inside, the temperature felt one degree short of spontaneous combustion. The odor of waterproofed canvas competed with the rotting garbage smell.

That first night, the new conditions made sleep impossible. Mosquitos buzzed around my face and hands. The lumps they left itched, then bled when scratched. The scent of fresh blood drew new clouds of winged pestilence. Welcoming us to our new home, I thought.

For the next two days and nights we marched all over the countryside, finding nothing. When we got back to camp, I felt so exhausted, sleep seemed possible anywhere. Still, I tossed and turned into the night.

Dan's voice penetrated the darkness of the tent. "You awake?"

"Hell no, I'm groaning in my sleep."

"You been doing that all night."

"You get any sleep?"

"A few snatches."

I swung my feet off the cot, sat up slowly, shoulders and back in painful protest from the weight of rucksack straps and ammo bandoliers that had rubbed my skin raw. I couldn't find my flashlight, which I'd left under my cot. "Where the fuck's the goddam flashlight?" I muttered as I searched in the darkness. My foot hit it and knocked it farther under the cot. Dan's flashlight lit up and I retrieved it.

"What the goddam hell are you two cherries doin' now? You got so much energy you gonna have a midnight tea party? It's hard enough to sleep without you fuckin' pansies bangin' around, so sweet Jesus, shut up and turn those lights off or I'll shove 'em up your ass!"

The speaker was Lash, our tent mate.

Dan's light went off and I cupped a hand over mine, opening my fingers to let out only a small slit of light. I found the anti-fungal cream our medic had given me. Lash rolled over against the tent wall and started to snore. How, I wondered, could he sleep in this hell-hole?

The cream stung. The light pressure of my fingers seared my skin like hot steel rods. A groan escaped through my gritted teeth. "Ah-h-h-gh!" The snoring from Lash's cot stopped. I froze. Goddammit, I thought, scared shitless of Charlie all day, and now I gotta worry about that asshole at night. Lash—Larry Schumacher—a mass of muscle and endurance, undoubtedly could make good on his threat about the flashlights.

His snoring resumed.

The pain pills the medic gave me were next to the leg of the cot. One at a time, he'd said. I shook three of them out of the bottle. Unable to find my canteen, I crushed them between my teeth and swallowed. For a few minutes the bitterness took my mind off the pain. So that's how they work. Taste so goddam awful you don't think about the pain. My stomach rumbled, threatening to heave them up. The burning subsided, and I slept.

After what seemed like only a few minutes, Dan shook me awake. Another hot, muggy day had begun, and I had a pain-pill hangover.

Each night was a repeat of the one before. We slept fitfully, not feeling rested the next morning. At the mess tent, everyone devoured the chow like it might be their last meal. We didn't understand how they could eat the slop.

"The incredible, *in*edible egg," Dan said one morning, poking at a lumpy yellow mass oozing pale liquid. "How can they eat this?"

Too late, I shushed his criticism. Lash, sitting at the table next to us, nudged the fierce-looking, dark-complected diner sitting next to him. "Listen to the goddamn fuckin' new guys," he said. "They don't appreciate our gourmet menu. Wait till they been eatin' cold C-rats and havin' to heat their own coffee—or go without." The other occupants of his table turned and gave us a contemptuous look.

"What the hell's the matter with everyone?" Dan asked as we walked away from the mess tent. "This is the most uncaring bunch of bastards I ever met."

"Yeah. We're outsiders. No one wants to talk to us or even to be in the same vicinity."

"Well, you're wrong," a voice behind us said. We turned, discovered the voice belonged to a second lieutenant who looked like he'd just spent the night at the Hilton. He looked so clean I almost forgot to salute. Almost.

"Get those hands down! What the hell do you think you're doing?" He yelled and ducked, giving a quick glance around the tree-line. "You trying to get me killed? " We lowered our hands. "Don't you *ever* salute an officer out here! There could be snipers!" He looked nervously out past the wire.

Dressed like you are, asshole, you don't need a salute to be recognized as an officer, I thought. You couldn't be anything else.

"When you go out, listen up, do what you're told," he said. "You'll have a good chance of coming back alive, and not getting someone else killed. New replacements are more likely to be killed the first two weeks they're here. Just shape up and don't cause anyone else any problems." He brushed past us, full of self importance, leaving his own little cloud of dust.

"Don't pay too much attention to him," another voice said. Again we turned. A lanky soldier, unshaven, a cigarette dangling from his lips had materialized behind us. He reminded me of a character out of my book of World War II Sad Sack cartoons. He was our other tent mate.

"That's Lieutenant Jaimeson," he said. "An' he don't know shit. He ain't 'seen the elephant.' But he's right about one thing. You pay attention and do what you're told. Fuckin' new guys like you are not just likely to get killed, they're likely to get someone else killed along with them. That's why you ain't made friends. You're bad luck while you're so goddam green."

He brushed past, and I couldn't help watching, admiring the smoothness in his gait. He moved like a tiger stalking dinner. By comparison the lieutenant was a parade with a brass band.

"Jeezus, these guys give me the creeps," Dan said.

"You know, that lieutenant said something about going out. Wonder if that's why he's here, to give us some kind of orders. Maybe we should go get our gear shaped up."

"When we move out, if we don't hold anyone up, at least we're doin' something right."

"For a change," I said.

We hauled our gear outside the oven our tent had became by mid-morning. We sorted it, packed it in our rucksacks as if our lives depended on it, trying to keep things arranged so the corners wouldn't poke us in the back. Dan looked up from the task as our tent-mate approached. "Well, well. Lash the giant, the bone-crusher. Bet he pulls the wings off of flies."

I looked up. Christ, he *is* a giant, I thought.

"You better learn how to pack that shit, you candy asses. Your momma's not here to take care of your ass and pat you on the head whenever you got a boo-boo. Fuckin' new guys. You make me wanna puke."

"Well, so says Lash fuckin' LaRue," quipped Dan.

Lash who? I thought. Twenty-five cent movies when I was ten. A man on a white horse. White hat. Six-guns. A big bullwhip tied to the saddle. Lash LaRue.

Lash moved as fast as his namesake's whip. Dan's carefully arranged pack went flying from a size twelve boot. A hairy hand fastened itself in the front of Dan's shirt. The pack hit the ground and Dan rose in the air. "Listen, you little cocksucker, you ever call me that again, you'll be wondering how you got in a body bag. You got that?" One-handed, Lash gave Dan a toss like a bag of dirty laundry. He flew through the air, following the trail of gear from his pack, and hit the ground. His breath blew out of his lungs like he'd swallowed a chunk of C4.

"You bastard!" I spit at Lash. I stepped past him, expecting at any moment to feel a hairy, ham-size hand grab me by the back of the neck. I knelt next to Dan, wondering if Lash-la-mountain of muscle would descend on me.

"Hey, you okay?" Dan lay very still. His eyes were glassy and half closed. I put my finger to his neck to see if he had a pulse.

"Goddammit, I'm not dead yet," he wheezed. I leaned forward so my shadow shaded his eyes. "Help me up," he said. He put an arm around my shoulders, bore down where my skin was chafed. I gasped. Together we staggered into the shade of the tent.

When some grunt stuck his head inside our tent the next morning before sunrise, I had been awake long enough to discover I still hurt. "Come on, goddammit, everyone's gonna be waitin' on you guys, he said." I started lacing my boots and grabbed my gear.

We left in the dark, admonished to say nothing and make no noise. I could barely see the man in front of me, who I'd been instructed to follow. Several times I tripped on roots or branches, and finally fell flat on my face. "Shit!" I muttered, then felt myself being hauled to my feet by the scruff of my neck.

Someone stuck his face close to mine. "Shut yer fuckin' mouth!" he whispered, then released me so fast I almost fell again. I felt around in the darkness for my rifle, wondering how anyone could see in the murky black.

When we stopped, the sergeant positioned us along the trail and soundlessly faded away. In the eerie pre-dawn light, I began to make out details. I could see Dan next to me, about fifteen feet on my left. I could see the others just off the trail and remembered from basic training the text-book L-shaped ambush. I caught Dan's eye, traced the shape of an L with one finger in the air. He nodded.

My legs were beginning to cramp when I saw them. They were moving at a dog-trot, and without making a sound. All three were carrying AK-47 rifles. Suddenly my belly cramped up. I thought my bladder would refuse to hold. I brought my rifle up so I could fire as soon as someone else did. The ghost figures came closer. A flash of flame and the crack of Dan's rifle. One of the child-size figures dropped to the ground. As he fell, fire shot out into the darkness from his AK-47. The other two ran toward us. I shouldered my rifle and had my finger on the trigger. I couldn't see my sights. Everyone seemed to be shooting now. I found my sights and by the light of the muzzle flashes fired at the silhouette. I saw it go down. I heard Dan's rifle bark again. The other form charged past us through the jungle. I swung around, fired a long burst at him.

For a moment I couldn't understand why my rifle had quit. Then I realized

I'd emptied the magazine. I slapped a full mag into it, but could see nothing more to shoot at. My heart thumped and my breath came as if I'd been running. I sat still until my breathing and heart rate slowed down a little.

In the dawn light we found them. All three were dead. Of course, we couldn't tell whose bullets had done the job. Less than an hour before they had been running and shooting. Somehow that shocked me. Staring at the torn, bloody bodies made me queasy. I sat next to Dan while the others rifled their pockets for intelligence and souvenirs. We looked up to see our other tent-mate, the one who moved like a tiger. He sat down next to us, leaned his rifle against his shoulder.

"Got 'em." He looked at us and grinned. "I'm Joe," he said, sticking out his hand. "Joe Allison. I go by Rat Man. You guys did okay."

I realized Joe—Rat Man—knew Dan and I had got the young soldier running down the trail and the one that took off through the jungle. I knew we'd have to do a lot more than that before we were no longer considered FNGs. But something had changed.

I looked back at the bodies. I had some responsibility for those wounds, for taking their lives. I didn't know what to think about it. I always pictured my first kill as a face-to-face confrontation, firing a single round that made a single, neat hole. A clean death. Something neutral, not sickening. It happened differently than I expected—the first of many expectations to die with equal finality.

We survived more missions, insect bites, chafed skin, and sore muscles. Every day we swallowed handfuls of pills dished out by our medic. The big ones, called green weenies, were for endurance, we knew, but that they were amphetamines, we did not know. No one doubted they were safe and good for us since they were issued by the U.S. Army. We ate cold, tasteless meals in all sorts of weather—raining a little, raining a lot. Extremely humid all the time. The food at base camp began to look better and better. We were no longer regarded as contemptible, but still not as assets. Four more days before we made the magic two week mark.

Once again the brass flew in.

"Bet we're goin' out tomorrow," Dan speculated.

That night Lieutenant Jaimeson briefed our sergeants on the operation we would undertake the next morning. Sergeant Shay briefed our team. We would be inserted by chopper into a valley, close to the location our military intelligence determined Charlie had established a supply center and bunkers.

"So why are we gonna leave at 0300 hours?" Dan asked as we walked back to our tent.

"Doesn't much matter," I said.

"You out of your mind? Since when do we get up at 0300?"

"And how much sleep you been getting from midnight on?" I asked.

Dan laughed. "Yeah. Midnight seems to be the wake-up hour for mosquitos. Shall we turn in?"

Sprawled on his cot, Lash had already started snoring. We tiptoed in, trying not to wake him. He was still unconvinced that we were worth our salt. Out of his sight, out of his mind, he wanted us.

We lay down, fully dressed, which provided some protection from the mosquitos. I stared into the darkness, trying to sleep. I thought I'd just drifted off when something grabbed me by the shoulder and shook me.

"Get up, you fuckin' pussies. If I gotta wait for you, I'm gonna kick your ass all the way to Saigon." Lash made an effective, if unpleasant, alarm clock.

"We'll be there," I said.

We grabbed our gear and headed for the LZ and our chopper. With some satisfaction I noted that we were the first ones aboard. How you like that, Lash fuckin' LaRue? I thought. Where the hell are *you*? My thoughts were interrupted by the sound of Sergeant DeMerse's voice. I looked out both doors of the chopper. No one. The chopper jockey climbed into the pilot's seat and the engine began to whine.

"Where is everyone?" Dan asked.

I leaned out the door for another look. Just past the tail rotor, out of the prop wash, Sergeant DeMerse was bent over a map with First Team. "Ah, shit. We're in trouble. Big-time. This is First's chopper. Let's get the hell out of here."

We jumped out and almost landed on Sergeant DeMerse, who had come to get us. He grabbed Dan with both hands and started to shake him. "Why the hell can't you assholes pay attention?" he screamed over the roar. "This ain't your chopper. Now get out of my sight!"

I stifled the urge to scream at him that we knew it wasn't our chopper. Instead, I ran, looking for Second Team. My gear, which I thought I had so carefully packed and strapped onto my body shifted and flopped around. I adjusted my web belt and looked up just as I collided with Sergeant Shay. He straight-armed me and I fell backwards. Dan stopped and started to help me up when Sergeant Shay went off like a five-hundred pound bomb.

"You fuckin' shitbirds! Why the hell can't you get your shit together? What are you trying to do, get us killed? You assholes get the hell on board or I'm gonna just leave you here, which is what I should have done to begin with! You're gonna pay for bein' a couple 'a slackers. Goddamn if you aren't gonna pay—if, that is, you make it back from our little picnic!"

He stood with fists on hips, glaring at us, then turned on his heel and marched off, his pace barely short of a run. Dan helped me up and we ran after him. We had to scramble into the chopper by ourselves as it seemed everyone else was too busy to give us a hand. When we lifted off, I pulled myself back from the open door and brushed against someone's legs. I felt a boot in my back, shoving me away so hard I almost slid out the door. Dan grabbed my pack, which stopped me from sliding out into space. We turned to see who had shoved me. Lash, of course.

"You better be careful. Fuckin' new guys have been known to fall clean out." His evil smile turned into a teeth-clenched, brow-furrowed threat. "You get someone hurt today..."

I looked at Dan. His face had turned pasty-white, his eyes open wide with fear. A look of what-do-we-do-now passed between us. Jeezus, I thought, watching the trees race past. I only wanted to help my country. How the hell did I get into such a mess?

Dan and I had been fired up with excitement until we discovered no one else shared our enthusiasm—or even believed the digs we would be looking for even existed. Everyone felt more edgy than usual. No one wanted to get shot up looking for something that did not exist.

We fast-roped down into an open, cratered area. Downed, cris-crossed tree trunks and branches, casualties of artillery, made an obstacle course. We were the first off the chopper and the last to the tree line. I got dizzy, my shoulders already sore from the weight on the shoulder straps. I'd banged my shins half a dozen times.

"Get yer asses down an' be quiet," a familiar voice hissed. Lash. Lash fuckin' LaRue. Great. Just great. Where'd he come from? Dan and I dropped in our tracks. The trees and sky spun around. Clockwise, I noticed. As I tried to make it stop, something slammed into my helmet. Dirt rained down under my collar. I swung my rifle around just as Lash threw another clod of dirt. He motioned us to move out.

We moved at a half-walk, half-trot. I wanted to slow down. I thought I felt miserable before—now I must be dying. Then Lash jabbed me in the ribs with the muzzle of his rifle. "Move, goddammit," he hissed. "You two fuck-ups gonna get someone killed. I could see to it you come back in a body bag. Wouldn't be the first time I did it, either."

That son-of-a-bitch, I thought. The energy of anger gave me strength. Fear had a lot to do with it, too. I got my feet to move faster, thinking of how I'd kick the shit out of Lash when I got the chance. Well, maybe I would if I could catch him asleep.

I stared at a clump of leaves on a tree trunk up ahead of us. It moved up the tree. That can't be right, I thought, and stopped. I saw an arm reach out of the clump of leaves and grab a limb. When Lash careened into me from behind, he knocked me down. Cautiously I raised my head and looked over the tree trunk in front of me. Another arm appeared out of the leaves, its hand holding a rifle.

I put my finger to my lips. "Sniper!" I whispered in a barely audible voice. Lash just stood there, looking at the trees. "Get down, get down!" I hissed. He dropped beside me, disbelief in his eyes.

"I don't see nothin'," he said.

"I don't give a goddam what you see or don't see! Keep your voice down, or he's going to hear you! You don't believe me, you stand up and yell and see what happens. And then you'll wonder how *you* got in a body bag." The anger I felt prompted my words. I didn't know how Lash would react.

"Okay, okay. But you better be right. Can you still see him?"

I slowly peered over the trunk and strained my eyes. The clump of leaves had moved onto a thick branch. It didn't look like it belonged to the tree. The arm with its rifle moved into view. "He's still there. Higher up. That tree that's got a double-curve in the trunk. About two hundred yards.

"I still don't see nothin'," he said.

"Fine. You go on ahead. We'll follow. Bring back your body. In a body bag."

Lash's face turned red. His eyes looked ready to pop out of his head. He squinted, covered one eye, then the other. "The tree with curves in the trunk?" he asked.

"Double curves. Bends one way, then back."

"You still see him?"

"Yeah." I looked over his helmet at Dan. "You see him?" Dan nodded.

"Okay. You both see somethin'. Let's circle around and find out."

"What the hell you want to circle around for?" I asked. The idea seemed foolish—and dangerous.

"Arright, smart-ass. It's a long way. I suppose you can take him out from here?"

"Yes." The word fell out of my mouth. Shit, could I make the shot? I'd hit smaller targets from a greater distance before, but on a range, under ideal conditions. I peeked at the tree again. Confidence replaced the doubt. "I can take him. From here."

"Then do it," he said.

I crawled around Dan to a place where I could lean into a log and support my rifle. When I looked through the sights, I realized what the consequences of my actions would be. If I hit him, I would probably kill another human being. Me. Deliberately. For a moment, a giant python squeezed my chest. I ducked down. Lash watched me and shrugged his shoulders, raised his eyebrows. "Well?" the gesture said. I looked at Dan. He nodded, winked.

"It's just another rabbit," Dan said. A smile appeared on his face and he hid his hand, jabbed a thumb toward Lash, rolled his eyes. *Asshole*, he mouthed.

I rested my rifle over a tree trunk and carefully lined up my sights. The leaves hadn't moved. The still air left no wind to compensate for. I estimated

40

where the torso would be in the mass of leaves, and gently squeezed the trigger. The shot broke the silence like Armageddon. My ears rang, and I watched as nothing happened. I put my sights on the leaves again, ready to fire. I started to squeeze the trigger. Then the arm with the rifle began to sag. The rifle fell, the arm went out of sight behind the limb. The mass of leaves spit out a human form, which fell to the ground.

I felt dizzy, like I'd pass out. I moved from the log and lay flat. Semi-auto rifle fire cracked from the direction beyond the tree. AK-47s? I asked myself. Then the familiar voices of our M-14s predominated and bullets cracked over our heads as they broke the sound barrier. Fear and adrenaline took over. I looked at Dan. He, too, lay flat behind the log. Beyond him, Lash motioned us to stay down. For once, we agreed on something.

I heard more firing from both sides. Then Lash looked over the log. "Two of em!" he yelled at us, "comin' our way! Wait a minute, then we get 'em!" He looked up. "Now!" he yelled. "Now!"

When I raised up, I could see two diminutive soldiers. They ran for their lives, straight for us. I put the front sight on the chest of the soldier on my side, and squeezed the trigger. I expected the rifle to fire a burst, but it quit after one round. *Now what?* I hadn't moved the selector switch after I shot the sniper. It was set to fire one round at a time. Dan and Lash fired at the same time, making one long, single burst. I thumbed the selector switch and looked up. Both NVA had disappeared.

"Stay down!" Lash yelled. I could barely hear him, my ears ringing from the reports of our rifles. "Hey–uhm..." he pointed to Dan.

"Dan. My name is Dan."

"Uh, Dan. See if you can turn around and watch our rear. There may be more of those little bastards out there." He looked at me, disbelief plain on his face. "Nice shooting," he said.

We lay there for what seemed hours, long after the firing had ended. Bugs crawled on us, buzzed around us. We had good cover and concealment, and I guessed Lash decided to play it safe, letting our outfit come to us. My muscles were cramping, my neck hurt from the weight of my helmet.

"Here! Over here!" Lash yelled, suddenly.

"Lash?" someone answered.

"Yeah! I got—uh—Dan, and uh, Shooter, here with me!"

The lieutenant motioned us to the top of a knoll, established a perimeter, and we broke out our C-rats. Dan and I were trying to force down the pasty substance in one of the cans. "Says right here you can eat it," Dan said.

"I don't care. I'm not *that* hungry." I flung the can with its mystery contents into the brush. Lash watched the can disappear. He got up, fished it out of a bush and dropped down beside us. Another ass-chewing, I thought.

"You don't ever want to toss a can without smashing it. Then Charlie can't use it for a booby-trap," he said, crunching it under his heel. "And here. I had been hoarding these. But you guys can have em.'" He handed me two cans of peaches and two cans of coffee cake. We didn't fully appreciate the value of the gift—the best of all the selections our C-rats offered. We did recognize the gesture.

"Thanks," I said, baffled by the peace offering.

"Yeah, thanks!" Dan said.

Lash sat down next to us. "Hey, you guys, you ain't gonna believe this," he said to some of the others. "That sniper?" Everyone nodded. "These two got that sniper. Probably some of us wouldn't be here if they hadn't got him!"

No shit, sherlock, I thought. So what's the point?

Several guys in our team ambled over, along with a few from First Team. Lash told them about the sniper. He seemed to have forgotten that we'd fallen behind, that he'd threatened to kill us, and a few other details. For the most part, though, I recognized the story.

"Old, ah –" Lash waved an arm at me, as if trying to decide something. "Yeah, ol' Shooter, here, he's the one who got the little bastard. And Dan, he spotted him climbin' that tree, when I couldn't see a goddam thing.

Rightfully, I thought, Dan got some of the credit.

The others' silent stares held an element of interest, of reevaluation.

"So Dan spotted him. Spotter?" asked the fierce-looking, dark complected soldier from the mess tent.

"Naw," someone else said, "That's too long a handle. Spots. Fits better."

"Shooter and Spots," Lash said. Everyone nodded.

"Shooter got one of those three." Lash pointed in the direction of the three bodies. "One shot. Same as the sniper."

Everyone looked at me as if they'd never seen me before. "Then Shooter's a good name for him," said the soldier from the mess tent.

We'd just been given our new names. Our handles.

Sergeant Shay interrupted our gathering. "Jeezus H. Christ on roller skates, you tryin' to get half the outfit killed? You know better than to cluster around where a single mortar round could take you all out! Now break it up!"

"Sure, Sarge," Lash said. "I just had to tell about Shooter an' Spots an' how they got that sniper."

"Shooter? And Spots?" asked Shay, obviously surprised. He stood and stared as the others walked off. "Sometimes I wonder what the hell..." he muttered as he followed them, but he looked relieved.

"Shooter and Spots?" Dan asked.

"Beats fuckin' new guys," I said.

I learned early on the value of souvenirs, the personal effects of the enemy. Rifles, pistols, letters, photos—all had a monetary value, especially to those who were never close enough to collect them first-hand. They were also valuable as trade goods for things money can't buy. For an AK-47 and a half-full ammo belt, I arranged space for Dan and myself on a Military Air Transport System cargo flight to Hawaii. It was our first leave since boot camp.

We went to the bar in the hotel we'd checked into, and proceeded to get so drunk we had to have help finding our room. We didn't wake up until the next afternoon. After coffee-by-the-gallon and some hair of the dog, we demolished the seafood buffet and started drinking again. The first night had taken the edge off of our nerves, our drinking now slower-paced and more meditative.

Dan had that restless look in his eyes, and I knew he wrestled with the same old demons.

"Let it go, man," I said. "Relax. You've aced out all the training schools we've gone to, from basic to survival, jump school, demolitions, even escape and evasion. You're better than I am at everything—except shooting. And you're pushing me on that."

"Yeah, you beat everyone in the whole damn division," he said.

"Yeah, Foster, but you beat me hands down on everything else. When it comes to moving through jungle or bush, even open ground, you're invisible. I've watched you sit for hours without moving, then suddenly you appear from behind a tree a hundred yards away. You keep trying to be the best—you don't realize you already are."

He looked out the big windows of the bar at the panorama of beach and ocean, swirling his Scotch around in the glass.

"Are you listening to me?" I asked. He was listening, but not hearing, I thought. Dan still put himself at the mercy of a legion of self-created demons, the spawn of his own self-judgment, his notion of his own acceptability. Whenever they sensed a weakness, they attacked, spurring him on to a new wave of effort and accomplishments.

"You're still trying to convince yourself you're good enough to fit into that group in high school," I said.

He scowled.

"What you're trying to find is right under your nose. Look at our team. We're seasoned and trained, there isn't a man who wouldn't do anything for any of us. Or for all of us. Even if he might get killed doing it. Risking our lives for each other is routine. When it comes right down to it, that's what we're fighting for. Each other." Although I knew it was true, saying it out loud gave me goose bumps.

"We've made what the army calls 'unit integrity' so real you could slice it like C-rations. If that's not meaningful and honorable, what is?"

He looked thoughtful, then smiled. "Yeah. Sure," he said.

"I give up," I told him. "I hope you find what you're looking for. I hope you discover what it *is* you're looking for."

"Yeah. Sure," he repeated, looking out at the water.

After another night of drinking in a dozen bars, we were ready to cut our leave short. We hadn't been able to pick up any women. Actually, we hadn't given finding female companionship much more than a token effort. We checked out of our hotel, headed for the air base to try to catch an earlier flight, back to the world of demons that could be stopped with bullets and hot shrapnel.

44

CHAPTER SIX

Candlelight

Rain pattered on the canvas roof of the big army tent. The sound, along with the canvas smell, felt comforting. Like Boy Scout camp. The white cross on the platform stood almost six feet tall and evoked memories of peace, love, and forgiveness. Its incongruous contrast with the time and place translated as hope for the future. Water leaked through a small tear in the tent wall, darkening the canvas as it dribbled down to the floor. It looked a lot like the sniper's blood from this morning's skirmish.

Someone drew back the tent flap. Cold air swirled around my boots, leaching away the little bit of body warmth left in my feet. It was Dan. He stood for a moment, his eyes adjusting from the pitch black of the fog-bound village to the dim light inside the tent. He stepped around an old man and a young woman holding a baby. His M-14 in one hand, the folds of his poncho in the other, he tried to keep from dripping on them. Unsuccessfully.

Dan doffed his helmet, pulled his poncho over his head, and thrust his hands toward the oil drum-heater. He rolled his eyes. "It's a dry heat."

"Yeah, yeah," I said, trying not to smile. "I just lit all three heaters. Let's stoke these things up," I said, reaching for another chunk of wood. "I don't remember the last time I was warm. It should be cozy in here pretty quick."

Tomorrow would be Christmas day. Lieutenant Jaimeson assigned us and the ARVNs our team was training to guard this Christmas Eve candle lighting service for the church mission.

About a dozen Vietnamese civilians had come early and sat on the plywood floor, cushioned by an assortment of clothing and bundles.

"So how many of our outfit are coming?" I asked.

"Looks like everyone except Willie and Johnny. I won't be surprised if Willie stays out there. Don't know about Johnny. They're on the perimeter with most of the ARVNs." We pronounced ARVN, which stood for Army of the Republic of Vietnam, like a name. Arvin. We didn't believe most of the ARVNs could fight their way out of a paper sack.

"Maybe Willie's gonna turn out to be a loner," I said.

Perez and Cardwell entered the tent as I jammed a branch into the stove. They were carrying their ponchos. Must have quit drizzling. Neither one spoke.

I watched as they settled themselves, Perez perched on his steel pot. In between them they dumped their bandoliers, packs and gear, M-14s perched on top.

"Sort that shit out," I told them. "If you need it in a hurry 'cause Charlie hits us, you'll be old and grey, but mostly dead, before you can unscramble your goddam gear!"

"Tch, tch. Such swearing. And after all, we *are* in church. Ever since you made corporal you've been a pain in the ass," Dan said. "I can't imagine what you're going to be like when you officially make sergeant."

I knew Lieutenant Jaimeson had gotten me promoted to sergeant, and would make the announcement next time he was here. It was supposed to be a surprise. After seven months, Dan and I had gone from FNGs to old hands. We made corporal at the same time, and he would have made sergeant when I did, but he couldn't keep his mouth shut. I was finding out there was a lot of nonsense went with the third chevron—politics and even diplomacy. They were not my strong points.

"You didn't want to do this, did you?" Dan asked.

"Huh?"

"This service. You didn't want to do it."

"I guess I'm not quite comfortable with some of this shit they expect me to do. Or what I think they expect. It's not that long ago we were FNGs. Now we got a new bunch of guys that aren't much more than that. Jaimeson's treating us like we're a bunch of goddam rent-a-cops," I muttered. "We lose someone doing this, I'm not gonna be happy."

"Who's a bunch of goddam rent-a-cops?" Perez asked.

So much for not swearing in church. "It just doesn't seem like Christmas," I said.

Dan gave me a funny look, blinked.

"You too, huh?" I asked.

He looked down, rubbed something with the toe of his boot. "Yeah. Me too. Doesn't seem like Christmas."

"I don't even remember what kind'a church this is," I said.

"I don't either."

"Guess it don't matter."

A group of ARVNs came in, followed by Tony, Hoagie, and three others. Then Lash.

"Wow. Didn't expect the ARVNs," I said.

"Didn't expect Lash, either."

We fed the last of the firewood into the drum-heaters and sat against the wall. Cold canvass slapped against my back as the wind blew.

"We gonna get weather?" Dan asked.

"Hundred percent chance," I said.

"Of what?"

"Weather," I said.

"Real fuckin' funny."

"Hey, you're in church."

"Sorry."

Cold air from the tent flap wrapped itself around my feet again. A tall, slender man wearing a black suit and a priest's collar stepped inside.

"This the sky pilot?" I asked.

Dan frowned. "Must be, ain't a gook. Maybe French."

He wove his way through the small crowd, touching everyone in his reach, squeezing their upraised hands. Others he greeted with a smile. Stepping up on the platform before the white cross, he lit a solitary candle. The platform,

47

devoid of any Christmas decoration, filled with light. When he raised his arms, no four-star could have commanded more attention. He spoke first in Vietnamese, then in English.

"Welcome to all on this holy night," he said, his welcome so real I could feel it. Unbidden, my dispirited feelings loosened their grip. My vulnerability alarm rang. I scowled. "Who is this guy, anyway?" I whispered to Dan.

He shrugged. "Dunno. He for real?"

I listened warily as the man—priest or minister—began to speak again in Vietnamese. His voice sounded soothing, even though I didn't understand any of the words. I looked around the crowd. Our whole outfit was listening. Then he spoke in English.

At length he stopped, motioned to two women who brought baskets to the platform. After he blessed the contents, they turned to the congregation and handed everyone a small candle.

Alternating again from Vietnamese to English, the man with the white collar recited the Christmas story, first in Vietnamese, then in English. "To you is born a savior..." I heard him say. "... the Prince of Peace...that man shall not die, but is born to eternal life." The familiar words ricocheted through my heart. Memories of Christmas past taunted me. Mom and dad, sitting in their rockers, a fire in the fireplace, looking hopeful they had been able to provide gifts us kids would like. The Christmas tree with familiar ornaments, presents piled underneath. Does that home still exist? I wondered. It seemed like decades ago, not just a half-dozen years.

The voice of the man in black overlaid the scene like an English subtitle. He spoke again in Vietnamese. His voice held the conviction and certainty of one who has been there, one who knows—one who's "seen the elephant"— the Christmas elephant. It filled me with terrible doubts. I didn't know if I believed in that world any more, or even if it existed outside this tent. What if he had done what we did this morning? Would he still sound so certain?

He faced the large candle on the platform, touched his small candle to its flame. Turning to a woman in the front row, he lit her candle. She turned to a man sitting next to her who lit his own, and then lit the one held by a girl seated next to him. The two feeble light bulbs in the tent dimmed and went

48

out, perhaps recognizing the futility of their competition with the golden warmth spreading from the candles. Or maybe the generator ran out of gas.

Vietnamese civilians, ARVNs, and American soldiers sat intermingled on the floor. "Don't think we ever had a mix like this before," Dan said with a frown. "I just hope one of the civilians don't pull an AK out of a bundle..."

"It's Christmas Eve," I said.

"Yeah. Even more likely."

I watched the candles spring to life. A young woman shyly turned to an ARVN soldier, her tiny frame lost in a coat several sizes too big, her feet tucked up under her. The soldier smiled, lit his candle, then turned to his comrades. Bare-headed, rifles held clumsily in their laps, one by one they tipped their candles to the flame. The last ARVN turned to an old woman behind him, who hesitated, then with an air of defiance, held out her candle.

I saw Tony, seated on his helmet, gear neatly stacked, web belt and pouches next to him. Neat and organized as always. An exceptional soldier. He watched reverently as the flame passed to him, lit his candle, and passed it on. Then he sat still, mesmerized. The colors of his camouflage uniform blended together. Bandoliers of ammunition—missiles of death—took on a golden cast, disguising their olive drab. The shape of his rifle across his lap seemed to soften and mellow, its sharp edges blurred. A look of wonder appeared on his face.

Most of our outfit, similarly seated on helmets or packs, cradled M-14s in their arms or across their laps. Johnny, kneeling behind Tony, still wore all his gear. So he'd made it after all. Only his helmet had been removed and lay next to him. With a look of wonder, he lit his candle and held it out to an old man.

Lash sat cross-legged on the floor, rifle on his lap. His wide shoulders relaxed forward, his head bent down. I looked closer, wondering if I could believe my eyes. Holding his candle in his big hands, he closed his eyes. I'd never seen him like that.

Dan nudged me out of my thoughts. I touched my candle's wick to his burning light, and watched the small miracle as it caught and grew bright. No one sat next to me, no one to offer the gift of my flame. I rose and walked toward Willie and Parkhurst, who stood just inside the tent. They had come from the perimeter and still wore their combat gear. Hand grenades and extra magazines hung protruding like some lethal fruit. Their M-14s were slung across their bodies. Willie held his candle in his right hand, along with his helmet. Parkhurst's pot remained clamped firmly on his head. Somehow I didn't think God would care if he still wore it.

I held out my guttering candle to Willie. His eyes held mine for a moment, then he growled and lit his own. A candle had materialized in Parkhurst's hand. I watched the two warriors, their aura softened by the pure, bright flame as Willie lit Parkhurst's candle. The soft flame lit his features, and he looked across the tent, through the galaxy of lights. Slowly he removed his helmet.

The tent had been transformed. Each point of light stood out singly, yet together cast the room in a glow of life and beauty. Our implements of war had grown muted, their threat lessened. For a silent moment, vigilance and fear and the quest to arms surrendered to peace declared, hope renewed. The priest spoke again, then translated, asking us to stand. We sang two verses of Silent Night, in English and Vietnamese at the same time. After the second verse we stood quietly, not wanting to break the spell. We had been separated, mostly by language, but now some ethereal strand, finer than cobwebs, bound us in time.

No one wanted to be the first to leave. Finally, someone started toward the door, and the rest slowly followed. A bucket had been placed by the tent flap for the used candles. I slipped mine into my pocket.

CHAPTER SEVEN

Hoagie's Bullet

Lieutenant Jaimeson hitched a ride to our digs on our supply chopper. His second lieutenant's butter-bars had been replaced by silver. A lieutenant first class.

"Well, he got promoted," Dan said. "Probably for penmanship and typing skills. At this rate, if he stays in the rear, he'll be a general by the time we go home."

"You know how he got promoted," I said.

"Yeah. We did a damn good job for him."

The lieutenant pulled me aside and handed me two rolled up shoulder insignia. Three chevrons with one rocker.

"What's this?" I asked, playing the game.

"You been promoted," he said. "Now get everyone together. I have some changes to talk about."

"Nice surprise," I said. "Thanks." I didn't sound very convincing, but it didn't matter. He wasn't paying attention.

Jaimeson announced—which everyone knew already—that Dan and I, under Lieutenant Beltz' supervision, would run the team until Beltz finished his current assignment and went home, back to the World. Then Lieutenant Jaimeson would take over again. This brought a mixed reaction from our team, since Beltz and Jaimeson could hardly be more different.

"I've got a couple of other things," Jaimeson said. "You're moving, about thirty miles north to existing digs closer to the Ho Chi Minh Trail. The facility needs extensive repair."

He didn't say who built the digs.

"Gotta be some other outfit doing black ops. Who could that be?" I asked, wondering how they could have gotten so close without us finding out.

Dan shrugged. "Not anyone around here. But if these digs are old, they're probably French, and Charlie's booby trapped everything."

"Sounds about right," I said.

The team grumbled so loud it almost drowned out Lieutenant Jaimeson's second announcement. "Since we're under strength, we're getting two replacements," he continued. Everyone groaned. On top of having to move, the prospect of looking out for two FNGs would be a real pain.

Lieutenant Jaimeson made his exit without another word.

"Guess he didn't want to answer any questions," I said.

"Of course not. He hasn't even seen the place, I'll bet," Dan said.

"Can't expect him to stay too long," Tony said, watching the lieutenant as he ran to his chopper. "He must believe the devil's one step behind him."

"He's partial to his air-conditioned office where no one kills anyone," Dan said.

I caught Dan's eye. We had no problems jointly running the team. I would need Dan's input and support, but as senior NCO, I would have the last word. "I had no idea I'd ever get more stripes," I said, lamely. 'I don't know why you didn't."

Dan shrugged. "Doesn't matter," he said. We both knew it was Dan's temper, and regardless, it did matter.

"I'll need your input," I said. "Whenever possible, we'll discuss the options and figure out what to do. Can I count on you?"

"As always," he said, without hesitation, with a smile that didn't cover all the hurt.

"Hey," I said, "Want to make any bets on the FNGs?"

"Maybe we'll get someone adept in the art of soldiering," he said. "I'll flip you for the first one. Call it." He tossed a coin in the air. I won. "Well, we'll see. Maybe you'll luck out."

We'd been at the new digs for two days when the first of the FNGs arrived. Private First Class William Harrison Bender, tall and lanky, would have looked at home riding on a tractor and wearing a straw hat. When he spoke, the words started slowly and took a long time to finish. He's worse than Willie, I thought.

"Speak up, Bender," I told him when he reported. Jesus, I thought, he's more like Strider, our point-man-of-few-words. Maybe they're related.

"Sorry, Sarge," he drawled slowly. "I got in trouble in boot camp 'cause I couldn't speak up fast enough. My voice jus' don't want to move faster."

Exasperated, I stood there studying my FNG, wondering if Dan might trade. Bender's mop of curly hair, the most unlikely copper red, stood out like a signal flare. A veritable beacon. He went by the nickname of Hoagie, he told me. Over the next few days Hoagie threw himself into the renovation of our new digs as if the project belonged to him. He earned the respect of everyone for his ability to spot and deactivate the booby traps Charlie had left. It looked like I'd lucked out after all.

Hoagie's brand of gung-ho thundered like a battery of howitzers. He'd volunteered to come to Vietnam. He knew and recited the nomenclature of his rifle while he put it together blindfolded, after cleaning it antiseptically. Strong and eager to help out, Hoagie would carry an extra field pack or rifle and ammo if someone got hurt. He thrived on C-rations, made by the lowest bidder and only marginally fit for human consumption. He smiled as he ate the meat-like substance, and would give away his canned peaches or pears, truly a sacrifice.

No one would have thought that Hoagie would have frozen up under fire. We'd gone out on patrol, checking out the trails, looking for any sign of NVA traffic. All of a sudden Willie, our point man, reappeared, crouching, looking back over his shoulder. I made the hand signal for everyone to get down, off the trail.

"Charlie," he signed with his fingers, pointing.

"How many?" I replied in the same manner.

A shake of the head. "Don't know."

I motioned for him to come closer.

"How the hell you know it's Charlie?" I gave him my best sergeant's scowl.

"Smelled 'em. That goddam fish smell. Heard someone giving orders."

We skirted the trail where we thought they would be. I wanted to come up behind them. A rifle cracked, the sharper report of an M-14. Then bullets flew everywhere and someone screamed out a string of Vietnamese words. I motioned two men forward on their flank left. "C'mon, Hoagie, let's get to the right side." I had started to move out when I looked back. It was Skeeter who followed me, not Hoagie.

We were too late. Charlie had slipped off into the jungle. We found bloody drag marks where they had dragged off their dead or injured comrades. There were four or five others, judging from their tracks. I stopped Skeeter as he started after them. "We could walk into an ambush," I said. Tony collected the weapons their casualties had dropped, and we got ready to move out.

"Where's Hoagie?" I asked. No one answered. I found him leaning up against a tree, head in his hands, shaking as if he had a fever.

"What the hell. Is Hoagie hit? We need a dustoff?" I asked. Everyone suddenly found it necessary to adjust their pack straps or bandoliers and not look at me. "Mack? What's wrong?"

Mack gestured to me, and we walked off a few steps. "I found him lying there after the shooting stopped, face down, scared to death. The magazine in his rifle's still full."

"Great. Just fucking great. Let's get out of here. They might get help and come back."

Hoagie, my FNG, had turned out to be a liability.

We were half-way home when Corporal Alvin "Skeeter" Johnson caught up with me. "Sarge, we gonna stop where they called in that arty strike?" Skeeter referred to an area that we would pass by on the way back to our digs, cratered and burned from artillery.

"All I want is to get back to the comfort of my cot. That place doesn't seem like a good place to stop."

"It's a spooky one. Maybe it has spirits of the dead," Strider said.

Most soldiers fell into two categories—very superstitious or extremely superstitious. Most of us carried some kind of talisman. It could be anything from a pocket-sized New Testament to a rabbit's foot. My commercial model of the 1911A1 Army .45 would make a great talisman, except that I didn't have any superstitions, and everyone knew it. As I thought about stopping at the arty strike, I fingered the grip of the big pistol. I would have denied the habit had anything in common with rubbing a rabbit's foot.

"I want to find a dud arty round, so I can use it for an ashtray," Skeeter said. Artillery rounds sometimes exploded only enough to split open the shell of steel that encased the charge. The twisted, sharp steel arms that were left looked something like a work of modern art growing out of the flat base of the projectile.

"You gonna carry it back?" I asked. Skeeter grinned and nodded. I knew he'd get the others to help him.

A few miles farther up the trail, we arrived at the site of the artillery strike. I placed the team in defensive positions behind some trees on a small rise. Charlie could be watching.

"You smell it?" Skeeter suddenly asked.

I breathed deeply through my nose several times, detected the faint odor of rotting human flesh. "Yeah," I said. "Goddammit anyway. Let's go." I caught Strider's eye and pointed at him and Skeeter, then in the general direction of the odor. Strider wrinkled his nose and nodded. The three of us headed upwind, into the smell of death.

"Who could be missing people?" whispered Skeeter.

"Probably no one. Let's check it out, just in case. Maybe it's Charlie." The odds were long that we would find a body from one of our outfits, but I'd be worrying about it if we didn't go look. The area had been pocked with craters, the tree trunks splintered and criss-crossed on the ground. We had to negotiate the uneven terrain, always watching for booby traps and unexploded ordnance.

"Fuckin' artillery. What a mess," Skeeter mumbled.

"You're the one who wanted to stop here," I said. Then I saw him. "There. In that tree, the big one. Jeezus, he's ripe," I muttered, as I doused my handkerchief with bug juice. It didn't repel bugs very well, but breathing through it dulled the stench of rotting flesh. Cautiously we made our way forward, circumventing the craters. We checked every branch, every leaf and vine for trip wires and booby traps.

We came face to skull with the body, hanging upside-down. One foot had caught in a tree branch. The other leg was doubled forward, ankle next to the head. The face had been mostly eaten away. Vacant eye sockets stared, pleading with us.

"From the looks of what's left of his uniform, he was NVA," I said.

"He must've been up there sniping at someone when they called in the strike," Skeeter said. "But what's the North Vietnamese Army doing here?"

The corpse's left side had been ripped open by shrapnel, probably as he tried to climb down the tree. "He's half-gutted!" Skeeter poked the gas-swollen body with a stick, and the flies, still crazed for carrion, buzzed out in a black cloud.

"Look out!" I yelled, and leaped into the closest crater, tumbling head over heels. Strider landed next to me. We lay there, waiting through a long silence for an explosion. When I looked up, Skeeter grinned down at us.

"Why're you guys so twitchy?" he asked.

"You think that's funny, asshole? You goddamn know better than to do something like that! If he'd been booby trapped, you would've gotten all three of us killed!" I glared at him from the bottom of the crater. He offered me a hand up, which I took. "*Always* look to see if there are booby traps. *First.* Got it?"

"Yeah, yeah. I know. I just didn't think."

"'I didn't think' can get us dead. Let's get outta here."

"Hey, wait a minute, there's his AK!" Skeeter looked thoughtful. "Sarge, I think I got a way to cure Hoagie. But I need this AK, because it's different." The rifle had been fitted with a sniper scope. The sling had tangled itself in a branch next to the body. Fortunately, the rifle hung on the opposite side of the dark, oozing wound, its trailing entrails moving slightly in the breeze. With extreme caution we probed the ground for booby traps, checked the rifle for wires. Slowly, carefully, Skeeter pulled the rifle off the branch and we followed our tracks away from the stench.

Skeeter pulled back the bolt and a round popped out of the chamber. Not surprisingly, it had been loaded with the standard 7.62x39mm full metal jacket military ammunition. "Great!" he exclaimed with a grin. "I'm gonna make ol' Hoagie feel one hell of a lot better."

"How you gonna do that?" I asked.

"Gimme a couple minutes."

I watched him as he removed the thirty-round magazine. He flipped the rounds out, grabbed a handful and flung them away. He pulled out his knife and laboriously scratched something on each of the others.

I looked around, nervous at the quiet, but not feeling any danger. A gut-hunch with no logical way to explain it.

"Hurry up!" I whispered to Skeeter as he carved.

"Just a few more," Skeeter said. He reloaded the magazine with the ones he had marked with his knife.

"For Christ's sake, what are you doing?" I asked.

He smiled. "I'm gonna give Hoagie something he needs. A good-luck piece." Standing up, he slung the AK-47 over his shoulder. "Ready?"

"More than ready," I said. We moved out, heading back to where we left the team.

We called the small bar in our digs The Well. We made furniture and a counter of sorts from wooden ammo cases, our universal building material. We kept The Well generously stocked through the efforts of Lieutenant Jaimeson and his highly developed art of quarter-mastering. If he failed to provide, we stocked the bar by trading Charlie's rifles, pistols and other paraphernalia to the REMFs, the guys we called the rear-echelon mother-fuckers. Most REMFs were never in a firefight. They were somewhere safe and out of danger in roles of non-combatants. We provided them with "souvenirs," so they could brag about how they'd captured them from Charlie. We despised them, but tolerated them because we took their money and other essentials in exorbitant quantities.

I started to leave my digs for The Well to have a couple of drinks when Skeeter stepped through the door carrying his newly acquired AK-47.

"Don't you guys ever knock? What if I had one of those nurses in here?" I asked.

"Yeah. Only in your wildest fucking dreams. And if you did, I'd be here because you would call me."

"I'm going to have some alcohol before I take a long winter's nap. To guard against frostbite, of course," I said.

"Will you see if Hoagie's at The Well?" Skeeter asked. "If not, come back and tell me. If I don't see you in five minutes, I'll head that way."

"What are you up to?"

"Trust me. This is gonna make Hoagie into a different man."

I decided this was something I should know about. So much for a nap.

Hoagie sat inside The Well, slouched in an ammo-crate chair. He had a lazy smile on his face, the tension of the patrol eased with the aid of a few beers. Slumped down with his legs stretched out, he looked like he might be eight feet tall. Mack, Lieutenant Beltz, and a some of the other guys nursed drinks in the tiny, crowded room that was beginning to take on the aroma of unwashed bodies.

"Any more of that single-malt Scotch?" I asked. Mack held out the bottle. I poured a generous slug and sat, waiting for Skeeter.

"Well, Hoagie, I guess we can sleep well tonight. ARVN is awake," I said.

Hoagie smiled a slow, wide smile. "Wel-l-l-l, I reckon they'll be there for us, Sarge."

We all looked up as Skeeter made his entrance with a shout, waving the AK-47 in front of him.

"Waa-hoo! You're not gonna believe it, you're not gonna be-*leeve* it!" he yelled. He yanked the magazine out of the AK-47 and plopped it and the rifle on the ammo-case table.

Reaching into the ice chest, Skeeter grabbed a beer. "Hot-damn, they're cold this time!" He started to gulp one down. We used an insulated container made for shipping blood for an ice chest. When we got ice.

"So what are you so excited about?" Mack asked.

Skeeter chugged his beer and reached for another. "Well suppose, just suppose, that you knew—absolutely knew—that you would leave this wonderful land, return to the World..." He paused and looked us in the eye one by one, Hoagie last. "Suppose you knew beyond a doubt that you would go home all in one piece?"

Hoagie focused on Skeeter, but said nothing. Neither did anyone else.

"Okay, okay," Mack said. "So how the hell are we gonna come by this precious little piece of information?"

"Right here." Skeeter pointed to the AK-47 magazine. "You won't be-*leeve* what I got here!"

"Okay, so give," Mack said. "What's so special about it? It looks like a million AK mags I've seen." I suspected Mack might be in on Skeeter's scheme.

"Well, I thought I'd clean this so we could trade it off." Skeeter held up the AK with its telescopic sight. "You guys might not know, me and Sarge, an' Stryder took this off a sniper in a tree this morning." He paused for effect. I wondered if anyone would realize no shots had been fired on the way home.

"This guy could'a taken us out," Skeeter continued. "But not any more. And there's a bunch of guys won't get taken out."

Hoagie sat up, listening carefully.

Skeeter stood and held out the magazine, as if it was infused with a mystical power. Hoagie shrank back as Skeeter waved it past him. "This magazine has twelve rounds left in it. And there's something special about each one of them." Skeeter paused again, looked around dramatically.

Hoagie leaned forward in his chair, cleared his throat. "What's so special about 'em?" he asked.

Skeeter slipped a round out of the magazine, and holding it carefully between thumb and forefinger, brought it close enough for Hoagie to see.

"They have names on them," Skeeter announced. "All of them."

Mack's voice sliced into the silence. "Whose names?"

"I don't know. I just saw there were names. I wanted you guys to see them when I took them out."

"Well, let's take a look," I said, not too sure how much I liked this game. I glanced back at Hoagie. His eyes were open so wide under his thatch of red hair he looked like a clown.

"All right," Skeeter said. He sat at the table and everyone crowded around. "The first one," he said, still holding it between thumb and forefinger. "The name on it is Gordon Weit." He looked up. "Who the hell is that?"

Hoagie cleared his throat. "Whose name is on the next one?" he asked, his voice small and forced.

Skeeter gently removed another round from the magazine. "Dennis Howard?" No one said a word. He removed the third round. "Albert Trebles?"

I looked at Hoagie. He was flushed, his skin and hair the same hue.

"The next one?" he said. Skeeter removed another round.

"Bill Davis? Is that the guy in artillery?"

"Nah, that's Johnny Davis," Mack said.

"Try another one," croaked Hoagie.

"Yeah, just start takin' 'em out, don't be so slow!" Mack leaned over the table.

Skeeter pulled out another round. "Howard Innsburt. That's five. Jordan Jones. Six. Arturo Sanchez. Seven."

Skeeter froze as he looked at the next round. "Oh, my God, my God!" He looked at Hoagie, whose breathing had become rapid and audible, then turned to Mack.

"Mack! It's got your name on it!" Skeeter handed it over. I thought I could detect the faintest smile on Mack's face. Hoagie sat back, deflated.

Mack's eyes widened as he took the round. "Wow! It *is* my name!" With something akin to a rebel yell, Mack jumped up from the table. Waving the round with his name on it over his head and yelling at the top of his lungs, he ran up the steps. Hoagie strode around the table and sat in Mack's chair, next to Skeeter.

"Number nine," Skeeter called out. "Morrey Steinmetz." He looked at Hoagie. "There's three left."

Hoagie leaned forward. "Number ten. Benny Brown. Eleven is..." Skeeter gaped at the round as if he could not believe his eyes. He looked at Hoagie, smiled, and reverently held the round out to him. "It's got your name on it, Hoagie!" Hoagie sat frozen, staring down at the cartridge. "Take it, Hoagie. It's your passport out of here in one piece!" Skeeter said with a smile. "You lucky bastard!"

Hoagie stretched out his hand. Skeeter dropped the round into it and Hoagie sat up straight, like a balloon-character that had leaked and was getting pumped up again. He stood, his eyes fastened on the 7.62x39mm cartridge that had his name crudely scratched on the case, and ran up the stairs after Mack.

I felt uncomfortable, glad the deception had come to an end. Or has it just started, I wondered. We looked at each other. No one said anything.

Lieutenant Beltz had solemnly watched the proceedings. "Is my name on the last one?" he asked.

When we realized Beltz had not been in on the deception, we laughed until we were weak. The lieutenant gave us a wounded look and left with a growl.

"Boy, he musta' been shit-faced!" Skeeter said.

"Ahh-h, you know officers can't hold their liquor," said Skeeter.

"Either way, let's not cook up anything else that's meant to encourage Hoagie," I said.

I stumbled back to my cot and fell into oblivion.

Hoagie had a knack for catching fish. His gear included line impossible to see three feet away, stretched across a trail. His new talisman, having made fishing seem tame, elevated the use of it to trip exotic booby traps. Flares that fired into cans of gasoline. Flechettes, small bomb-shaped projectiles, rigged to explode from cut-off artillery casings. His new confidence spurred his thrill of blowing things to bits, whether by an ingeniously detonated hand grenade or a modified Claymore. He'd begun to get on everyone's nerves.

Several days after Skeeter gave Hoagie his bullet, we received a report from some of the Montagnards who worked with us. They had word of a cache of arms and food, and Viet Cong recruiting activity in a nearby village. The VC recruited Montagnards by threatening to kill their families or wiping out their villages. Our source had proven good in the past, so Dan took out a patrol, including Hoagie, to see what they could find.

Vegetation on the steep slopes in that area grew so thick that we could climb on branches and tree trunks without touching the ground. A step ladder designed by a sadist. Because of the undergrowth and the changes in elevation, a distance of two or three miles on a map could turn into a day's travel.

When they returned the next day, Dan stopped by my digs. It had taken the patrol most of the day by trail to reach the village where the VC had been reported. "After talking to the headman, I decided to look for the cache,"

Dan said. "He said it should be close by, but off the trail. We hacked our way through the vegetation and decided to stay for the night on top of a knoll that looked defendable.

"I felt uneasy about the place," Dan told me. "One of those things where the hair stood up on the back of my neck. Well, that night Charlie found us and tried to slip in. Hoagie had set out a bunch of homemade booby traps. When the VC tripped his creations, Hoagie laughed and taunted Charlie. Like a lunatic. He began firing at the VC, who were silhouetted by his fireworks. I had to order him to leave for our rendezvous point. He kept saying, 'Man, some cool demolition derby!' Like he'd gone into the ozone."

"Hey, Dan, it sounds like he saved your asses."

"Maybe. But he's freaked out," he said. "He's gonna get someone hurt."

As time went on, Hoagie conducted a series of bigger and bigger explosions. I began to worry he would rain down in pieces. It would take just one premature explosion. One day I found him outside the perimeter playing with some of his toys. I'd never seen someone so excited by a new batch of detonators.

"Hey, Hoagie!" I hollered. "I need to talk to you for a minute." He looked up and frowned, annoyed at the for interruption.

"Yeah. Just a minute."

"Meet me at The Well, okay?"

"Yeah," he murmured, already re-immersed in his latest lethal toe-popper.

I waited impatiently. I had just got up to go get him when he came through the door. "I got something to show you," he said, pointing outside.

"Sit down. I want to talk to you first."

"But Sarge..."

"Sit! Now!"

He sat.

"How about a drink?" I asked. "We got some ice left. Beer's cold." Hoagie nodded, and opened the ice chest. He pulled out a beer and sat on the edge of his ammo case chair.

"Hoagie, I'm just a little bit worried about you." Hoagie said nothing.

"Foster said you've really been taking some chances. Y'know, if you get your ass shot off, you make us sergeants look real bad. You get blown up by one of your own concoctions, we look worse."

Hoagie smiled. He took a pull on his beer. "Sarge, if that's all you're worried about, you can forget it."

"How's that?" I asked.

Hoagie reached inside his shirt and pulled out a piece of olive drab nylon webbing. He had doubled it over and stitched the sides together, making a pouch that hung around his neck on a piece of parachute cord.

"Don't you remember, Sarge? The day Skeeter found that sniper rifle?" He took the 7.62x39 round out of the pouch and held it up. "See? It's got my name on it. I already got my bullet. You don't gotta worry about me. I'm gonna walk to that freedom bird on my own, with all my parts. Go back to the World."

His eyes expressed absolute belief. Written in stone, not just on a cartridge case. He gulped down the rest of his beer.

"Anything else, Sarge?"

"No, that's it. Just be more careful, goddammit!" He looked surprised.

"Okay, Sarge. Sure. I will."

"Get outta here." I pointed at the door with my thumb.

"Sarge, I wanna show you..."

"I said, get the hell out of here. I don't want to see your fireworks."

Now he looked hurt.

"Look, Hoagie, some of the guys think you're a loose cannon. They worry you may get hurt because of the way you act, or maybe you'll get someone else hurt. Don't act like you're invincible. None of us are. Okay?" He nodded. "Now go on."

Four days later Dan and I were in The Well. "Come by my digs when you got a chance?" Dan said. He had come back from another patrol with Hoagie. He thought he had located Charlie's cache and wanted to move on it. I had a hunch Dan didn't want Hoagie along.

Foster's digs, on the high side of our hill, looked down steeply at the jungle below. I liked the location better than mine. I stuck my head in the door. "Anyone home?" Dan sat at his ammo-crate desk, cleaning a .45.

"Come in. Park it."

"Bet I know what you want to talk to me about," I said. "Hoagie."

"Right. I don't want him along when we go after this one."

"Okay by me," I said.

"Look, you're gonna have to do something about him. He's gonna get wasted, and he's gonna take some of us with him."

"I've tried. Any suggestions?"

"Did you tell him Skeeter is the one who carved his name on that bullet?"

"Think I should?"

"Gotta do something."

I groaned. I didn't look forward to telling Hoagie the invincibility he believed in was a lie. I wished I hadn't gone along with Skeeter's story in the first place. Now I didn't know how to get out of it.

The next day I sent for Hoagie. "Sit down," I said. "Look, I know you believe that you're immune from harm because of that bullet with your name on it, but..."

"No, Sarge, not really," he said.

"Okay, then...what *do* you think?" I asked, surprised.

"Well, I know the sniper intended this bullet for me." He pulled it out from under his shirt and stared at it. "And now that I've got it, I'm not gonna get shot up." He held up his hand as I started to interrupt him. "But Sarge, I know that even so, I gotta watch out that I don't accidentally catch a bullet meant for someone else. Or a mine, or shrapnel that's not intended for me."

"Look, Hoagie. I gotta tell you what really happened. How your name got on that bullet." I told him how Skeeter had scratched the names on the cartridges.

Hoagie sat in the ammo-crate chair for several minutes, his face blank, eyes unfocused. I began to wonder if I'd have to call Father Dennis, the Sky-pilot, when Hoagie got up and smiled. "Y'know, Sarge, I don't guess that makes any difference. It don't seem to matter who put my name on that bullet. It happened. No coincidence my name got on it. It don't change nothin'. That all you wanted, Sarge?"

"Yes. I just wanted you to know the whole story. Go back to your fireworks."

"Thanks, Sarge. Don't worry none about me," he said on the way out.

I found Dan at The Well and told him about my talk with Hoagie. "He's still convinced that bullet had been for him. His bullet. His passport back to the world. It's what he believes. Y' know, Foster, it could be a lot worse if we hadn't convinced him that bullet's his." Dan grunted, shook his head, and reached for another beer.

"Okay," he said. "We'll try him again."

That night I dreamed about Hoagie going home, joking all the way to the chopper that had come for him. He was smiling, having a good time kidding us that we had to stay. "I told you, Sarge," he said, "I'm goin' home, all in one piece!" His playful remarks didn't stop, even when the chopper revved up and we could no longer hear him. His ear-to-ear grin beamed down at us as the chopper gained elevation. He leaned out so far I thought he would fall. Then a single shot rang out from the tree line and caught him in the chest. His smile faded and surprise took its place. He fell back into the cargo bay as the chopper lifted up over the treetops.

I awoke in a sweat, and couldn't get back to sleep.

Hoagie's antics, which had made everyone uneasy, began to gain some acceptability, mainly because of his air of confidence. Hoagie obviously believed he would come back unharmed, regardless of what happened. His conviction became contagious. Rather than feeling ill at ease with Hoagie, the team had begun to think of him as a walking, talking, good-luck charm.

A few days later, we took another patrol out after the cache and came up empty-handed again. No Charlie. And Hoagie's behavior had settled down to almost sane. But I had the same dream about Hoagie every night. Smiling, waving, then catching a bullet in the chest.

One afternoon I was tossing on my cot, competing against the bugs, temperature, and mid-afternoon humidity for some sleep. I heard the familiar whop-whop-whop that announced a chopper setting down inside our wire.

"Hey, Sarge, we got a chopper settin' down!" Skeeter hollered through the doorway.

"No shit. Your powers of observation are fine-tuned," I said, irritated at the interruption.

The chopper's only passenger, a shave-tail lieutenant, had a fist-full of papers, and he looked brand new. Right out of the box. Skeeter and I watched as he made a bee-line for the trench next to our .50 cal. machine gun. Corporal Thomas gawked at him. Lieutenant Clean started yelling. Thomas snapped to attention. He and the groomed lieutenant took off in the direction of Beltz's digs, Thomas in the lead. I went back to my cot. I didn't care what the spit 'n polish lieutenant wanted.

A few minutes later Dan stuck his head through the doorway.

"Beltz wants to see you. On the double," he said, smiling big.

"Oh, shit. What gives?" I asked.

"Dunno, but we got us one spit-and-polish, store-bought lieutenant who wants something." I grabbed my web belt, rifle and helmet, and trotted down to our command post. I burst through the doorway, almost knocking down our visitor.

"Lieutenant, you wanted..." I blurted out, then my jaw dropped in amazement as I surveyed the bantam rooster of a second lieutenant up close. His khakis had been starched and pressed, and in spite of the dark sweat-stains under his arms, still looked creased. His brass shone so brightly that a sniper could have used it for an aiming point at midnight in a thick fog. When I saw his boots, my eyes went wide at the sight of the spit-shined mirror surface. One boot had gotten scuffed, probably where he had jumped into the trench by the .50 cal. I wondered if we should apologize.

"Do any of your goddam people salute an officer any more?" He spit the words out at Lieutenant Beltz.

I looked at Beltz. He'd pushed his helmet back on his head, the strap swinging free. His hair, in greasy spikes, stuck out over his ears. He hadn't had the chance to shave or bathe for a long time. His uniform looked like he had been rolling in the dirt, which he might have been, probably while dodging incoming. I didn't look at his boots, but I would have bet six months pay that they hadn't seen polish for a long time. He gave the lieutenant a sharp look, then smiled at me.

"So, do you 'goddam people' salute an officer any more?" Beltz asked.

"Yes, SIR!" I said. With exaggerated motions, I dropped my web belt with its three canteens, two M-14 ammo pouches, each with two grenades attached, and some other gear on it. The pile landed on top of the papers I had seen Spic-and-Span lay on Beltz's desk. I laid my M-14 across the pile. I came to attention and saluted. The store-bought lieutenant started to protest, but I held my salute, determined not to move until he returned it or left. Begrudgingly, he saluted.

"Sergeant, I have…" the Lieutenant Spick and Span started to say to me.

"Where's Hoagie?" Beltz interrupted.

"I think he's still tinkering with his booby traps, sir. Want me to find him?"

"Yes. He's to leave with…this…lieutenant," he said, his lip curling. "ASAP."

"Problems, sir?" I asked.

Lieutenant Spick-and-Span piped up. "That's for me to…"

"It's his dad," Beltz interrupted again, glowering at the lieutenant. "Hoagie's brother got killed last year. Hoagie's a sole surviving son, and his dad's had a heart attack. He's going home."

Everything slowed, became dreamlike as in a nightmare. My nightmare. "I'll go get him, sir," I said, my legs having to work hard, as if I was walking through knee-high water.

I heard Lieutenant Beltz's voice, the one he used when outsiders interfered. "Lieutenant, I don't give a damn where the hell you came from, even if you came straight from General HQ. I will overlook your supercilious attitude, but I *will not tolerate your…*"

When I returned with Hoagie, Beltz told him about his father and sent him to gather his gear. I stood helplessly, the dream about to unfold. I wondered if somehow I made it happen.

Hoagie joked all the way to the helipad, smiling, having a good time, kidding us about having to stay. "I told you, Sarge," he said, "I'm goin' home, walkin' onto that freedom bird with all my parts intact!"

The store-bought lieutenant strapped himself into the chopper. His face had turned white. His eyes were big and round, and he stared straight ahead.

Hoagie's horsing around didn't stop, even when the pilot revved up the chopper and we could no longer hear him. His flaming hair blew in the rotor wash. His mouthful of glistening teeth shown down on us from his manic grin as the chopper gained elevation. He leaned so far out I thought he would fall.

Frozen with fear I watched, bracing myself for the sound of the shot. The chopper cleared the trees with Hoagie still waving insanely. Soon the wopp-wopp-wopp of the blades faded and Hoagie left the jungle behind.

"The goddam chopper must have his name on it, too," I muttered. Grinning like an idiot, I headed for The Well. I was ready for a beer. Or six.

CHAPTER EIGHT

Love And The White Horse

Lieutenant Jaimeson briefed us on the area where our brass expected us to find a North Vietnamese Army outfit. Seasoned regulars. The next night we made our insertion by chopper, roping down through the trees. We formed a perimeter and waited for dawn. Everything felt wrong. The hair on the back of my neck felt prickly, as if someone was watching me. I felt itchy and stinky hot. On and off I thought I heard voices beyond the trees, which added to my restlessness.

That morning we made our way along a creek, each man moving as quietly as possible, eyes sweeping the jungle, back and forth. I carried my long-range Winchester bolt-action rifle, and my Thompson sub-machine gun for close work. Only a labor of love could justify carrying all that weight, I thought, as the slings and rucksack straps began to chafe my shoulders.

Several hours past sunup, we reached the rice paddies on our maps, about two miles from where Charlie was supposed to be. Here, the stream forked, making an upside-down "Y." And here, our intelligence went bad. We'd run smack into the seasoned regulars we were trying to find.

The first enemy fire killed two of our team and wounded another. I saw Dan circle to the right to get to the wounded man. If someone already had picked up him up, Dan would take one of the bodies. Charlie mutilated the bodies if we didn't bring them back. We always brought back our dead.

We began our retreat. The wounded, who could not walk, and the dead were carried in the lead. I slung the Thompson across my chest. I could fire with my right hand and still help if someone else was wounded. We stopped at the perimeter of the rice paddies to consider our next move. They outnumbered us. The banks of the stream were too steep to climb. We would have to take to the ridge at the center of the fork of the creek. Crossing the paddies to get there would mean at least a hundred yards of open water and mud, all of it under enemy fire. We had no choice.

Someone would have to stay below, keep their riflemen from picking us off as we scrambled up through the brush. I knew Dan would stay, watched his stiff, nervous smile tell me it was the hand he had drawn. And I would stay with him. We worked together. We had to give the rest of the team a chance.

We laid down a covering fire. One by one the men moved out along the sides of the paddy, broke for a rocky spot in the middle, then disappeared into the brush and up the ridge. Only Dan and I were left. I emptied several magazines at heads and silhouettes. With the bullets still cracking around us, I heard him call to me.

"My white horse, Doug," he said in a voice I can still hear. An eternity passed in that split second as I understood. Our eyes communicated wordlessly. "Go! Go! Go!" he said, and turned away, firing to cover my retreat.

I ran as I have never run in my life, bullets tearing at my pouches, piercing my plastic canteens. One nicked the side of my helmet with a clang so loud it almost disoriented me. I heard Dan firing. As I started up the ridge, I knew he hadn't been killed.

The team had gathered on top, almost two hundred yards above Dan's position. As soon as I knew my lungs weren't going to burst, I unslung the big Winchester rifle, checked it and the scope sight. Nothing was damaged. I dug out the ammunition. Fifty rounds. Just like a box of .22s, I thought, and I can make every shot count. I wouldn't leave until Dan got out. I had a clear view of the paddy where we were a few minutes ago, and the area between it and the foliage where Charlie was hiding. They would have to pass through there to get to him. I could see the creek to the left, but not to the right, and that worried me.

I throttled the voice that told me how hopeless it looked, and began to fire.

At that range, I could hit a target the size of a quarter. It only took a few shots for them to discover they were well within in my range.

I poured out sweat and tears as I lay on my belly, placing the death dot in the scope on a torso, then on a head, always gently squeezing the light, crisp trigger. I worked the bolt of the rifle again and again. Reloaded.

A spasm of loss wracked me, and I missed, then steadied myself. I couldn't lose Dan. We had been through the humiliations and glories of our lives together. Our joint histories defined us, made us something no one else knew of. He liked to eat rabbit, liked the color red, laughed with his head back, cleaned his fingernails with his antler-handled knife. I couldn't let him die because of bad intelligence. "*Goddam* army intelligence!" I swore as I slammed the bolt home again.

I let the tears fall, knowing that no one would be able to tell them from the sweat and the dirt and bugs. No one but us. I clenched my jaw so tight I thought the ivory would chip off my teeth. With all the sureness of my training, I put body and soul into my marksmanship. I worked the bolt, acquired a target, and squeezed the trigger. Chamber another round. Acquire. Squeeze. Again and again, with deadly sureness. Bullets began to plow into the ground around me. My rifle barrel heated up, and the point of impact changed. I held the dot over my target to compensate for it, the way Dan had taught me to "hold over" for a long shot with his 30-30. Take that, you bastard. I worked the bolt, chambered another round, squeezed, watched a human form fall and twitch. They wanted him so much they were willing to sacrifice a lot of their men to get him.

Once again, someone was trying to mess with us. I forced the words from between my clenched teeth. "Don't-you-*fuck* with us!"

My shoulder felt sore from recoil. I checked my ammo, surprised that I had only seven rounds left. How could I have fired over forty rounds, I wondered. Oh well. Lucky seven, I thought, unwilling to give up. Suddenly full-auto fire came from the right side of the canyon, where I couldn't see. I jumped up and ran forward, oblivious of the target I had become. Looking down on the paddies I saw Dan crouch and run. His feet mired in the muck and he slowed. The full-auto fire sounded again. Dan staggered, fell to one knee. I knew he had been hit.

"No! No!" I yelled, "Get up! Get up!"

As if my will power hoisted him back on his feet, he slowly stood. "Move, goddammit, Dan, run!" I screamed, so loud I tasted blood in my mouth. He lurched forward. I heard a long burst from an AK-47, and he twirled halfway around. I saw him topple and fall face-down into the water.

I stood there in the open, unable to move. Someone kept slapping my face, yelling, "C'mon! C'mon, we gotta go!"

After Dan's death I could only get a few days' leave, which took the combined efforts of Lieutenant Jaimeson, the American Red Cross, a great many threats and much bluster on my part. My leave approved, I called Janice, Dan's fiancee for some time now. I took a Military Air Transport flight to Hawaii, and she would fly from the States to meet me. Dan and I had agreed that if one of us didn't make it back, the other would do this.

As I came through the tunnel from the plane to the gate, I saw Janice. Tall and slender, her light brown hair framed her face. My heart felt a jolt, realizing that Dan would never see her again.

We hugged, our emotions bridging out to each other. I realized I held a woman in my arms, and how good it felt. Dan's woman.

Janice drove me to her hotel. She had a letter from Sarah. I carefully folded it and put it in my pocket. I would read it later. Now, I had to be strong for Janice. I gave her Dan's personal things and a sealed envelope, her name written out in his jerky handwriting. I touched the writing, as if I might feel him there.

"You've changed, Doug," she said.

I nodded. Forced a smile. "You have, too. You're more beautiful than ever." My words sounded strained, but she smiled.

As we talked about Dan, I felt as if someone had parked a truck on my chest. She stepped into the kitchenette, brought back a pot of coffee and a bottle of good whiskey. A couple of Irish coffees took the starch out of me. I felt the tears, and tried to hold them back. Suddenly they erupted, and she put her arms around me.

"I couldn't even bring his body back," I sobbed. I had no idea all those tears were inside, but I couldn't stop them, even though I had thought I had come to comfort her.

"You loved him, Doug," she said, after my waterworks had quit. I squirmed a bit, thinking of him, knowing she was right, I did love him. But it didn't seem like she thought we were queer or something.

"No," she said, reading my thoughts, "You just loved him."

I felt that half of me had been lost. The good half. The Dan Foster half. The one of us who hunted the white horse, looking for something honorable to take home to his people.

CHAPTER NINE

KABAR

I made Sergeant First Class. As I adapted to the routine my new rank required, I moved into a protective shell. I split my life into before I lost Dan and after. My dreams taunted me with endless variations of rescue. Dan still alive in some. I scrambled to recover his body in others. Always, I failed. My dreams reminded me I'd found my Achilles' heel on that patrol.

The day I lost Dan, I wouldn't have made it out If it hadn't been for Tony. He carried my big scope-sighted rifle and my Thompson. He kept talking to me, leading me by the arm, as we plodded out to our extraction point. He talked about everything and nothing, a calm, quiet voice that kept my attention.

I vowed I'd never get close to anyone else, ever. I felt a terrible rage inside, a large part of it directed at Dan for dying and leaving me. Then I felt guilty for my anger toward him.

I settled in, getting used to our new base camp. JR, one of the rookies who had lived past the REMF stage, traded for a big American flag. We cut a tree for a flagpole. For some reason we were not supposed to fly the flag, but that only encouraged us to fly it. It gave us a sense of purpose, of belonging. Of home.

I made some lucrative trades for the trophies we scavenged from Charlie. We sold them as war souvenirs or traded with REMFs for things we couldn't get through regular channels. I kept track of what the REMFs wanted, cleaning all the guns and blades, and made repairs as needed. For myself, I traded for liquor and ammo for my .45 Government Model pistol and my Thompson.

It kept my mind occupied.

Our team had been ordered to participate in joint CIA/Army operations in Laos and Cambodia. We were to be given the new army rifle, the M-16, before we went with the spooks. Our whole team was flown to a base somewhere in the middle of nowhere to be trained. Our first day on the range brought some surprises—some pleasant, some not.

On a range newly scraped out of the jungle, firing positions had been set up for us. A black rifle, ammo, and magazines were spread on small ground cloths at each position. Tony and I walked over to the firing line and picked up one of the new rifles.

"Jeezus, it's light," Tony said. "Must not weigh half as much as the M-14."

"Looks kind of awkward," I said. The rifle had a pistol grip that stuck down behind the magazine. I wrapped my hand around it and put the rifle to my shoulder. The rear peep sight, mounted on a carry handle over the receiver, was easy to see. The front sight stuck up much farther than I was used to. I aimed at the target downrange.

"What do you think?" asked Tony, bringing one of the other rifles up to his shoulder.

"It's comfortable. Might be better, but I don't know if I like the little bullet it shoots."

Three spooks, dressed in camouflage uniforms without any insignia, appeared and started yelling orders.

"Instructors?" asked Tony.

"I don't know. Why the hell is it that they seem to think we're some kind of green FNGs? I haven't heard yelling like that since boot camp."

"Maybe spooks like to yell a lot," Tony said.

The spooks yelled some orders at us. Tony and I paid no attention to them. The team followed our example. The one who appeared to be the chief spook strode up to me, looking indignant, angry, and impatient, all at once.

"Are you Walker?" he yelled.

I took my time looking him up and down. "No," I said.

"Well who the hell is in charge of this bunch?" he asked.

"I am."

That slowed him down some. He took a paper from his pocket and studied it. "It says here that Sergeant Douglas Walker is in charge of this bunch."

"I'm Sergeant First Class Walker," I said. He turned red and angry all over again.

"I just asked you if you are Walker and you told me..."

"I told you I am Sergeant First Class Walker," I said once more, leaning into his face. "You may call me Sergeant Walker. These men are part of an Army Special Forces A Team. All of them are experienced, all of them are blooded. They are my men. And neither you nor you associates, whoever the hell you are, may yell at any of them again. Now if you don't understand that, I'll say it for you one more time." I watched him struggle with his temper. He said nothing for several minutes.

"We are charged with training your squad..."

"We are an A Team," I said, wondering if his blood pressure would cause him to have a stroke. "Not a squad."

"All right, your A Team—with the 5.56 mm M-16 rifle," he said. He turned and faced the team, who were thoroughly enjoying our exchange. "All right. I want you to pick a firing position. Remember the number. You will return to the same position tomorrow."

No one moved. We stood there in silence. Finally, he looked back at me.

"I have a couple of other things to tell you," I said. "First, you will give no orders to these men. None. You will tell me what you want, and I will give them the orders I deem fit. Do you understand that?"

"We can't operate without—" he started to say.

"Furthermore, you will identify yourselves in some way so that we know what to call you. You may tell us to call you A, B, and C, or one, two, and three. You may give us names. Or we may decide which one of you we will call Larry, Curly, or Moe. It's up to you."

Our training with the new rifle, despite its rocky start, was intense and inclusive. Except for cleaning and maintaining the rifle. Our spooks knew how to take it down and reassemble it, but were vague on oiling and cleaning some of the internal parts. We applied common sense, cleaned our rifles after every three or four hundred rounds fired, and had no malfunctions. We were winding down our last range session when Tony came out of the big tent they used for an office.

"Sarge," he said, "take a look at this." Looking around to be sure none of the spooks saw us, he pulled a booklet out of his fatigue pocket. It was a manual for our new M-16 rifles.

"Find that in their office?" I asked.

"Yeah. I got lost, ended up behind their field desk. Clumsy of me."

"Wonderfully clumsy. Why do you suppose they didn't tell us they had these?"

"Because they're assholes?" asked Tony.

As far as our Team was concerned, the jury was still out on the new rifle. The 5.56 mm cartridge pushed the lighter bullet to a higher velocity than our old 7.62 round. We were not sold on the velocity in place of bullet weight, but since we were not ballisticians, we reserved our judgment until we used it in the field.

"Your training is completed," our gracious host spook told us the next day. "If you will line up at the supply tent, we will issue your magazines, pouches, and rifles. When your transport arrives this afternoon, you will be issued ammunition and spare magazines," he said.

When we entered the supply tent, our eyes bulged out at the huge supply of ammunition, magazines, and other unidentified wooden cases.

"Jeezus," Tony said, "they gotta have half a million rounds of ammo. Wonder how much they're going to give us?"

"Probably a case each. You thinking what I am?" I asked Tony.

"Yup. Why take one when each of us will need three or four?"

"And magazines," Tony said.

When our chopper landed, one of the big flying bananas, our spooks let us back in to the supply tent. Each man was to take one case of a little over one thousand rounds of the new ammo to the chopper. Tony, the first in, moved to the back of the tent and cut a slit up the side. The next man took two cases and carried it out through the slit to the chopper. Then he got back in line for another case, checking it out with the assistant spook at the front of the tent. We ended up with about sixty thousand rounds of ammo. It worked so well we did the same thing with magazines, but the assistant spook got wise to us and we got only twenty-eight cases of magazines.

"Let's get out of here," I yelled.

Everyone piled into the chopper and we lifted off. When I looked down, the spooks were shaking their fists at us. We couldn't hear them, of course.

"Can you guys get them on your radio?" I asked.

"No," the pilot yelled over the rotor noise. "They're some kind of secret club that don't like us grunts. Why, you forget something?"

"Nah," I said. "I forgot to say thanks. They were very generous."

The pilot raised his eyebrows.

"They just didn't know how generous."

When we got back, we stashed what was left of our booty after filling up magazines for the new rifles. It dawned on us that pound for pound we could carry a lot more ammo. A point in favor of the new rifle.

We finished two clandestine missions, staged across the DMZ, in North Vietnam. The next, estimated to last about two weeks, required us to live off the land for the last week or so. We would cross a line on a map that meant we couldn't get resupply.

The cloak-and-dagger, spook-man aura of this CIA group became tiring. The complete lack of insignia or rank or unit seemed unnecessary and confusing. The spooks proved to be good fighters, although they had an inflated opinion of their abilities. If they were good, we must have been superb. We had to pull their bacon out of the fire more than once.

A few of their outfit had a wildness that bordered on insanity. Whether it resulted from spending long periods in the heat and humidity, fighting leeches and insects, or using drugs, we didn't know. Purportedly, they could creep into an enemy camp at night and dispatch their human targets with a knife —or their bare hands—then fade back into the jungle, their work undetected until the camp awakened at dawn. I thought about Dan and how he could do the same thing.

Our mission didn't seem to amount to much. We surprised some NVA

78

and some Chinese soldiers, killed five of them, and blew up their cache of rice, ammo, and some explosives like our own C-4. The spookies were beside themselves with the paperwork they'd found, and the mission was declared a success. I declared it a success because none of our team was injured or killed.

Two days after we returned to our digs from what we were promised would be the end of our joint venture, another mystery outfit showed up. Lieutenant Jaimeson ordered us to give them anything they asked for, since they had come to re-supply. We resented their cart-blanc claim on our goodies. Suddenly our supply shack became bare of the goodies of war. Boxes and crates ended up under cots. Some got buried inside the perimeter. Some fifty cases of 5.56mm ammo and two dozen cases of magazines disappeared overnight. I had no idea there were that many hidey-holes in our digs.

I watched one of the spooks come out of our supply shack empty-handed. I noticed he carried a worn-looking Fairbairn-Sykes knife. Used by the British during World War II, its slender, double-sided blade tapered to a lethal point—a killing knife. I had a new one like it, but only for trading stock.

According to Army legend, the Kabar had proven itself from Wake to Bataan in World War II, and from Seoul to the Yalu in Korea. Proclaimed as the GI's knife. Preferred by 98 out of 100 GIs surveyed. And as the saying went, the other two would change their minds. It had a blade almost two inches wide, six inches long, made of good, thick, American steel. It could be used as a crowbar, to dig a foxhole, or polished and used as a signal mirror. It held a razor edge, ideal for an easy, quiet kill. Or so they said.

We had only one issue knife, the bayonet for the M-14, which we found to be worthless. Replacing the issue bayonet with a Kabar on one's belt identified the wearer, like a badge, as an insider, the bearer of Knowledge of the Knife. It said: Beware—Deadly. Had there been a list of the ten best-dressed enlisted men in clandestine operations in Southeast Asia, undoubtedly all would have a Kabar on their belts.

Eventually, most of the guys in our team had been equipped with Kabars, largely through my trading abilities. I, too, wore a Kabar.

The wearer of the worn Fairbairn-Sykes, a giant of a man, loomed over me when I walked up to him. His eyes looked not at me, but through me, as if I hadn't been standing there. Or more likely, as if he wasn't all there. He had black hair, braided in seven strands that reached a few inches below his ears. His brown skin looked so dark that at first he didn't appear to be Caucasian. He took first place as the hairiest human being I have ever seen. His shirt, unbuttoned to the waist, sleeves cut off at the shoulder, showed well-muscled biceps and forearms, dark brown under their cover of thick, black fur. A full and luxurious beard started almost under his eyes, and flowed down past his throat where it met with the hair growing on his chest. I couldn't tell where his uniform came from. I had never seen the camouflage pattern before, and it was without insignia.

Always one for a profitable trade, I pointed out his lack of preferred cutlery. "I see you don't have a Kabar. I know where I can you get you one, but it will cost you," I said.

In two strides he glided up to me, looked directly into my eyes, wrapped a gargantuan hand around each shoulder, and held me at arm's length. He moved smoothly and rapidly, surprising for such a mountain of muscle. A mouth appeared in the midst of his black whiskers. "What?" he asked. His straight, even teeth, which were very white, seemed oddly out of place. "What did you say?"

"I can get you a Kabar," I croaked, thoroughly uncomfortable at his touch. "But it will cost you. They...they're hard to get...you know?" Talking to the man gave me the impression of someone whose attention is fractured in several directions. Then, like a movie that has been spliced, leaving out a piece of the action, the Fairbairn-Sykes knife he wore upside-down on his left shoulder strap materialized in his hand, inches from my face. He moved it slowly back and forth.

"See this? You know how many goddam gooks I've stuck this into? A lot. A lot more than you have," he said accusingly.

"Ah-h-h, okay," I said. I allowed this to be true, since I had never "stuck any gooks."

"That thing you got there," he indicated the highly prized Kabar I wore, "is too damn big to stick in a gook. Or anyone else. Blade's too wide. Too thick. You ain't strong enough to push it in without him makin' noise. You want to

80

take him out quietly? Get him here—with this."

Before I knew what was happening, he flipped me around and I felt the smelly pelt of his arm slither under my chin. The point of his Fairbairn-Sykes pricked my back, over my right kidney. Involuntarily my back arched, and before I could recover, he spun me back like I was standing on ball-bearings. I felt too astonished to be angry. And too scared.

"I have a knife like yours," I said with a croak.

"Then what the hell you wearin' *that* for? Unless you want a crowbar–or a hatchet. This," he patted the Fairbairn-Sykes, now back in the upside-down sheath on his shoulder strap, "this is for silent killing. Take a man out like I showed you, right in the kidney. No sound. I don't want your goddam Kabar, wouldn't take it if you give me the fuckin' thing."

"Sh-show me again where you stick it in," I choked, still dizzy from the spin. I didn't really want to know, but I had to show some interest, I thought, or this gorilla would realize how badly he scared me. He showed me again, then had me demonstrate on him with his knife. He must have been one of the most trusting people I'd ever met, or so tough he could turn around and pinch my head off even if I stuck him. I decided it was the latter.

"Thanks," I said, handing him back the knife.

He brushed past me without a word and disappeared. Only the lingering feeling of the sharp point of his knife outside my kidney kept me from wondering if I hadn't imagined the whole thing.

Later that night we got word through the grapevine we would soon go on another mission, and the following afternoon Lieutenant Jaimeson scheduled a briefing. As if in preview of the mischief the Fates had in store, it started to rain. I sat next to Private Willie Davis, the only man I ever met in 'Nam who actually looked forward to, even enjoyed, going down into Charlie's tunnels. Willie, a bean-pole just over six feet tall, didn't weigh much more than a hundred and ten pounds. He'd been assigned to my team about two months before Dan died. He always got into trouble when he went on leave, and he was still a private first class after almost a year. Usually he got drunk and picked a fight with someone who proceeded to beat him senseless. Once he hid in the nurses' showers. His ear-to-ear smile persisted even after we got him back to our digs and patched up his multiple claw marks. "You should'a seen 'em, guys," he kept saying. "They was just pink all over!"

Much to our annoyance and trepidation, Lieutenant Jaimeson announced he had decided to lead this patrol. We'll be lucky if he doesn't get someone killed, I thought. Then, for some reason known only to him, and disregarding everything we knew about small-squad tactics, he split us up into pairs. We would be less likely to be detected that way, he said.

We did a carabineer wrap rappel out of the choppers and down through the trees, some seventy feet below. Our insertion point turned out to be a jungle hell so thick with trees the chopper jockeys couldn't get us anywhere close to the ground. It seemed like it took forever to get down through the racket of drops pelting the leaves, our helmets, ponchos. The discordant roar sounded like snow on a TV set with the volume turned up high. It hissed and popped like a thousand pounds of frying bacon. The rain gushed down so heavy we couldn't see anything, trees or branches, and couldn't tell until we landed in pools of rainwater that we had reached the ground. We hovered in the pre-dawn darkness, cursing military intelligence as an evil oxymoron.

"All these trees, so much for gettin' a dustoff if we get our asses in a sling," Willie yelled over the noise. "We better play it cautious." I waited for him to make a crack about the rain keeping the dust down, but for once his voice sounded serious.

"Yeah," I hollered. "Once on the ground, we'll be a long way from the only extraction point. Hey, Willie. You, ah...still got a strange feeling on this one?"

He frowned. "Somethin' weird's gonna happen."

The rain continued to cascade through the canopy in buckets. I could feel the thick darkness press against me. Then flashlights with red filters, like giant fireflies, feebly winked on one by one as the men disentangled themselves from the ropes.

"Jeezus, that's too much light," Willie said, making me jump. "I hope Luke the Gook ain't anywhere around here."

"Sh-h-h!" I whispered back at him.

"I'm soaked, in spite of this damn poncho," Willie went on, still too loud. "Wet with rain outside, sweat underneath. It's times like this what makes me wonder why I joined up. Could have a cushy job in the World right now instead of slogging through this fuckin' muck, lookin' for the goddamn North Vee-etnamese Army."

"Okay, okay. Me, too. Now quit bitchin' and shaddup!" I hissed at him.

The NVA supposedly had camped somewhere in the valley over the ridge where we rapelled in. We had to find them and assess their strength and equipment. At least the rain would make it easier to move undetected. But a whole lot more miserable.

When Lieutenant Jaimeson showed up, he was accompanied by another sergeant, a new guy no one had seen before. Maybe it's his idea to split us up, I thought. So much for the lieutenant's confidence in my ability as his sergeant. And if it doesn't go down the way he thinks it should, he's still gonna expect me to pull his chestnuts out of the fire.

"Who's the new guy?" I asked Willie.

"Dunno," he said. "Whadda ya think? This one gonna be a major cluster fuck?"

When Willie talked, his soft, Arkansas drawl eventually became irritating. If I listened for too long, I wanted to speed him up—wind his spring a little tighter. Maybe he's related to Hoagie, I thought.

"I think you're right," I said. "I got a bad feeling about this." I frowned, Dan vividly on my mind. "Shit, here we go again."

We huddled under ponchos as the lieutenant made last minute changes, showing us on his waterproof army map that got soggy anyway, taking compass readings and explaining how he wanted us to get there. The new sergeant, listening to his briefing, looked completely baffled. We'd gotten used to it.

"Nothing more dangerous than a second lieutenant with a map and a compass," whispered Willie. "Why the hell'd he have to decide he'd lead this one?"

"Probably means there won't be any shooting," I said.

We split into our two-man teams and moved out. After several hours of sliding and slipping in the mud, pulling ourselves up with branches and vines, Willie and I made it over the ridge and started into the valley.

Lieutenant Jaimeson had designated a big rock outcropping that stuck out from the side of the slope as our rendezvous point. We navigated by compass and map, locating it before dawn. Crawling under the ledge didn't give us much shelter. At least the rain no longer came down on us like a sluice.

We napped in fifteen minute intervals, taking turns shivering in wet ponchos, trying to sleep, watching for the others. Pair by pair the team showed up and we rotated the watch. I noted with some satisfaction Jaimeson, leading Sergeant Kennelley, arrived last. Kennelley had been in-country for a year, and had a feel for what we were doing. But at the moment, he had a case of lockjaw and looked exasperated. I turned away so he wouldn't see my smile.

"Ah, cut Jaimeson some slack," Willie said. "Lootennant can't help it if he's just a green-ass shavetail."

One last time we reviewed our plan to find the camp that military intelligence located barely a click from our rendezvous point. The heavy clouds and rain would provide us with cover, if the Lieutenant would shut up and move us out. Finally he announced he and Sergeant Kennelley would wait for us here. As we left I caught Kennelley's eye and winked. He put a hand over his eyes and shook his head.

After we'd covered half the distance, Willie and I stopped for a breather. "Ya know, Willie, if I camped in the valley so close to these rocks, I'd have some kind of observation post close by."

"Yeah, but in this rain we could walk within fifteen feet of a damn truck and never know it," he said.

"Works both ways. They'll never know we're here unless we make a lot of noise, or step on 'em."

Then we almost did. We came up on a small clearing, Willie in the lead. Suddenly he dropped to his belly in the mud and brought his M-16 up to his shoulder. He turned to signal to me, his eyes wide. Startled, I tripped and fell, and rolled over on my side. I expected to hear him open fire. Nothing. I raised my head, peeked out from under my helmet. Willie had moved up behind a log and motioned me forward. I crawled up behind the log into a depression where rainwater had collected.

"There's your OP," Willie whispered. "Dug in, about fifty yards—across the clearing." I could see what appeared to be a fox hole.

"You sure?" I said.

"I saw an arm come out, bailing water. Those guys must be takin' a mud bath by now."

"Yeah. It's good for the skin," I offered nervously.

We lay there and watched. The arm made another appearance with a can in its hand, throwing water out of the hole. A left hand, I noticed. Then we heard their voices. Arguing. A poncho-clad head and torso rose out of the hole, and immediately a taller, similarly clad figure rose next to it. Willie's head settled down over his rifle sights, and I saw him slip his finger into the trigger guard. I tugged on his sleeve and shook my head. Our shots might be heard in their camp in spite of the rain, and we had no idea how big a force we faced. We had to take these two out quietly.

I lay there thoroughly soaked and plastered with mud. I kept hearing noises. What if we'd been discovered and the whole camp moved stealthily toward us? Surrounded us? I calmed my breathing. I could hear nothing but the rain, which filled my imagination with fear. Willie's eyes had the same wild look they got when he went into a tunnel. A rictus grin turned his skinny face into a death's head.

Cautiously I peeked over the log. The argument apparently resolved, the legless torsos had disappeared back into the hole. Only the tops of two hooded ponchos could be seen. As I watched, first one, then the other, fell forward. They had fallen asleep.

The pelting rain began to let up. Soon, if they looked, they could see us across the clearing. "Shit," I whispered. "We're running out of time. We gotta do it, now or never." I drew my Kabar. Willie drew his. We moved out.

I had gone only a few feet from behind the log when it became obvious how clumsy it was trying to keep my rifle out of the mud as I crawled forward with my Kabar in one hand. An old John Wayne movie played in my mind. I remembered the scene where he crept up on the enemy with his knife in his teeth. I'd crack my chattering teeth, I thought, fumbling with the scabbard, trying to ease the Kabar back in. I thought about the upside-down, left-shoulder-strap-sheath arrangement I had seen the hairy giant wearing. Right now it made a lot of sense.

As I crawled closer to the hole, the purpose of my Kabar suddenly became frighteningly clear. How much easier it would have been to accomplish this with a rifle. More distant. Impersonal. Fear stood my hair on end. My experience hadn't prepared me for the closeness of this killing. Could I do it? My heart pounded out an insane morse code. Blood roared in my ears, and bladder control became almost impossible. The Gordian knot in my stomach tightened.

Willie motioned, then circled around their hole to the left. He stopped about ten feet away, waiting for me to crawl closer. Covered with their hooded ponchos, foolishly, they slept. I looked at Willie and he nodded. We drew our Kabars and inched our way to the edge of the hole. The rain muffled the noises we made—or so I hoped. My breathing sounded like the whoosh of a bellows, my heartbeat thundered like artillery. If they wake up, I thought, they'll get one, maybe both of us. I should have my rifle in both hands, not a Kabar.

Breaking the paralysis of fear, I moved closer to the soldier on my side. I could see all the little details, things about people that are always there, but go unnoticed. He appeared to be a detached head, floating on a sea of tan poncho. He had a scar on his chin, on the right side, crescent shaped. A ringlet of his black hair had crept out from under the poncho. Water pasted it to the skin of his forehead. Hair covered his ears, as if he had been in the field for a long time without a haircut. The wrinkles on his face converged on lashes so short his eyes vaguely looked as if something had been left out. His face showed strain and exhaustion.

His sleep would cost him his life.

I clung to my Kabar and inched forward. Then, in less than an arm's reach, the soldier's eyes opened and he stared at me. His worst nightmare had come true. I stared back, trapped with him in a time warp which slowed to allow predator and prey to evaluate each other. His pupils and iris, which I'd almost expected to be oval like a monster's, looked completely black, macabre, supernatural. Then he blinked, and he looked like a scared young kid about my age. Water beaded on the hood of his poncho and dripped off in front of his face, into the puddle of his foxhole.

For a moment, a disturbing understanding passed between us. We both suffered from the same woes. Rain. Cold. Heat. Bugs. Bad food. Cold meals.

Pawns in a game beyond our control. Acting as enemies. The strange feeling of kinship with him frightened me more than my personal danger.

He knew he would die. I knew I would take his life. Fear, then anger, tightened his face. His hands reached for the AK-47 that lay across his lap. His movement metamorphosed our time of understanding. Once again he became my enemy who would kill me if I didn't kill him. I lunged and jammed the Kabar into the side of his neck as hard as I could. His skin felt rubbery as the tip of the blade sliced through it. The big knife slowed, hit some cartilage, scraped a vertebrae. I shoved harder, ramming it in, mesmerized by the horror of the moment. Adrenalin burst into my system and gave me strength to shove the knife in to the hilt.

His mouth formed a little "O," as if, vaguely surprised, he questioned my aggression. Blood, mixed with his last breath, gurgled up and drowned out any last words. It gushed out in red rivulets over his poncho. He dropped the rifle, his hands flew up to tear at mine, trying desperately to staunch the flow. I held fast to the Kabar. The few seconds it took for him to bleed to death ticked by slowly. Robbed of strength, slippery with his own blood, his hands fell away. He leaned forward, still looking at me. The flow, now unconfined, cascaded from his mouth. I shoved him away, repulsed. The realization I had "stuck a gook" leaked into my consciousness as the bloody stickiness soaked into my shirt sleeve. I stared at the too-short eyelashes as they blinked for the last time, then stilled. His head fell back at a grotesque angle, rebuking the heavens. Falling raindrops splattered on his face and ran like tears from lifeless eyes.

Willie had come up behind the comrade of the man I had just killed. Although mortally wounded by Willie's knife-thrust, the soldier grabbed his arm and managed to pull him half way into the hole. I broke out of my mesmerized state and started to grab Willie just as the dying soldier's hands surrendered. His arterial fount pulsed upward, painting Willie's face, blinding him.

We sat on the edge of the hole for what seemed hours. I felt violated. So this is what sticking a gook is like. Way too personal. I found myself blaming him for being here, blaming Charlie for making us kill them. Knowing that wasn't right. Wondering what was. I could feel my mind surrounding what had happened with a barricade, as if to keep this awful thing hidden from myself.

"Let's go," I said.

"Yeah," Willie said. "God, yes." His helmet lay next to him on the ground, and he, too, looked up into the heavens–but only to let the rain wash away the blood.

I had to put my boot on the soldier's neck and pull with both hands to get my Kabar out of his body. When I pulled it out, it grated on something. Chalk-on-a-blood-red-blackboard, magnified. The earth shook and the horizon dipped. I dropped to my hands and knees and my empty stomach heaved. When the internal quake subsided, I rubbed my uniform against the muddy ground, into the mixture of rain and rotting vegetation, trying to rid myself of his blood.

"We would 'a had their whole goddam camp on our asses if we'd shot these two," Willie said.

I shoved my Kabar back into its scabbard.

The brass called the mission a success. We located the NVA, determined their strength and location, made it back without casualties. I put out the word that I had a blooded Kabar for sale.

A few days later, Sergeant Kennelley, Willie, Tony and I sat outside my sweltering tent where it felt slightly less sweltering. We had a bottle of good Scotch set out on an ammo case with real glasses we'd stolen from somewhere.

Kennelley and I had spent a lot of time talking about the biggest success of the mission. It appeared that Lieutenant Jaimeson found his latest taste of field work to be unpalatable. He decided to go back to his "administrative role," as he called it. He would be our liaison with the upper echelon and also act as our quartermaster. Kennelley and I would have to manage our missions without him for the meantime, he'd said. We assured him emphatically that we could.

"You think Jaimeson's going to be able to get us what we need?" asked Kennelley.

"He's been pretty good at it so far," I said. "What he can't get we can trade for with other outfits."

"Who the hell is this?" Willie interrupted, pointing to a short, stocky stranger, standing off a ways, eyeballing us. He looked like a chopper jockey. "You Sergeant Walker?" he asked.

"Why you wanna know?" asked Willie. "You a bill collector?"

"Heard you got a Kabar," he said. "What do you want for it?"

"That your chopper?" I asked. He nodded and looked back at Willie.

"I'm Walker," I said. "Have a drink. Pull up an ammo case." He eagerly helped himself to a generous glassful. I went and got the Kabar. "Be careful. It's sharp," I said. He pulled the knife out of the scabbard and his eyes opened wide at the dried blood. "Shit, I forgot to clean it!" I said. Obviously the blood didn't diminish its value.

"What you want for it?" he asked again, so eager I knew he'd trade for far more than its real value.

"Well, I kinda favor you guys. You get our asses out of trouble once in a while." I thought for a moment. "You know any of the navy pukes?"

"Yeah, I do."

"We haven't had a good steak dinner for...how long, guys?"

"A hunnert years," Willie said. "Way too long."

The chopper jockey nodded his head. "I know some navy guys. They eat real well."

"Sirloins. Rib-eyes. T-bones. Some good steaks. And potatoes. Butter, a couple of pounds of it."

"How many steaks?" the chopper jockey asked, looking worried.

"A dozen. No, fifteen. Five pounds of butter."

"I'll get it for you. That's no big deal, gimme three or four days." He held out the Kabar.

Now that it had been out of my possession, I didn't want it back. It might be bad luck.

"Nah," I said. "I'll trust you."

"I won't let you down," he said. He walked back to his chopper, smiling, examining the blood on the knife.

"Hey, you two," I said to Mike and Willie. The promise of steaks had sent them into a state of gastronomical ecstacy. "You're gonna slobber all over yourselves."

Tony laughed. "Man, I haven't had a good old American steak since...I don't know when.

"There's one more thing we need to do before that," I said to Willie. "We need to go get falling-down drunk. We'll initiate Kennelley, see if can hold his own."

Mike smiled. "My daddy always told me to bet on a sure thing."

When we hitched a ride into Saigon several days later, I had a cobbler make a sheath for my Fairbairn-Sykes, rigged to be carried upside-down on my left shoulder strap.

CHAPTER TEN

Point Man

"Hey, Sarge," Tony called from outside my digs. "Lieutenant's comin' in, 'bout ten minutes out." Hesitantly, he stuck his head in the door.

I'd been irritable off and on since Dan bought it. Without him, I had to work more closely with some of the other guys. Which brought the paranoia of getting close. I'd changed and didn't like it any more than they did. "What's wrong? I been pretty tough on you guys?"

"Naw," he said. Which meant yes. "You know, we all liked him."

I felt my throat get tight. "Okay," I grunted.

I'd lost my temper last time Lieutenant Jaimeson flew in. He wanted to put me in for a medal for staying behind with Dan. He said nothing about an award for Dan. My suggestion that he put Dan in posthumously for the Congressional Medal of Honor drew a blank look. I could see he had no perspective on what happened that day. I gritted my teeth and tried to remind myself he "fought" this war from a desk. When he tried to play a father figure to me about Dan's death, I blew up. Later I regretted it, but the road to Hell is probably paved as much with regret as with good intentions. At the time, I wondered if he'd get me transferred if I seemed to take it too hard.

"Think he's gonna want to see me?"

Tony smiled. "The way you tore into him last time was awesome. But yeah, he's gonna want to see you."

"Guess I shouldn't have done that. He's the best supply sergeant we've ever had."

Tony laughed. "Jaimeson keeps us stocked with a lot of things, especially booze."

The faint wopp, wopp-wopp of chopper blades announced his immanent arrival.

"Sergeant Kennelley back yet?"

"No. Want me to send him to The Well if he gets here in time?"

"Yeah. And bring the lieutenant to The Well. I'll serve him some of the Scotch he brought for us last time." I hoped he wouldn't keep asking me if I felt "really all right" this time.

"Hi, Doug," Lieutenant Jaimeson said as he ducked through the door of our impromptu bar. I'd just set two glasses on the ammo-crate table.

"How ya doin' lieutenant?" I asked. "Two fingers?" He wasn't much of a drinking man, but a little good Scotch relaxed him. He believed that the trip here was fraught with danger.

The infrequency of his visits kept my impatience from spilling over. Taking it slow and easy proved to be the way to get him to agree with anything—and to stay out of our way.

"Yeah, two fingers." He took a sip. "That the last stuff I got for you?"

I nodded. "Really smooth. What's up?"

"I'll get right to the point."

That would be refreshing, I thought. Then he frowned, scrutinizing me like he couldn't decide if I would expire at any moment. "How are you feeling?" he asked.

I sat up straight, raised an eyebrow, and glared at him. "Goddam good enough to bite the head off a rat. A *big* fuckin' rat."

"Uh-h-h, you look good," he added hastily. "Much better than the...last time." He took another sip—a big one. Then pulled out a map. There's a group of NVA active in this sector, terrorizing the locals who had been helping us before. Now, if they're seen talking to us, they risk being tortured and killed, along with their families, and their villages burned. You know what they do."

Yes, I thought, I know better than you do. You've only heard about it. "So you want us to find and eliminate them."

"Yes." He tossed a bundle of papers on top of the map. "Supplies are on the way. Tomorrow." He got up and looked out the door. "Well," he said, "it's getting late. Not a lot of sunlight left."

I looked at my watch. Sure enough, only five or six hours.

"Let me know if you need anything else." He scurried out the door and up the stairs. I listened as the wopp-wopp-wopp of his chopper carried him away. I could still hear the sound when Kennelley came down the steps.

"So what's gonna happen?" he asked.

"I shouldn't tell you. I bet you stayed outside the wire until you saw him leave."

Mike laughed. "No, but I'll remember that for next time."

"I almost told him to look carefully for snipers in the tree line before he popped out of the staircase. He's afraid to come to our digs, convinced it's very dangerous."

Mike laughed. "I should have popped off a few rounds when he came up."

"He's afraid of helicopters, too. Poor guy. I feel sorry for him. Anyway— we'll be gone for several days. It's a 'spy-and-die' mission."

"A what?" Mike asked. He'd caught on to so much in the time he'd been with us, he seemed like an old-timer. Sometimes I didn't realize he hadn't been here long enough to learn it all.

"Since we can't tell the difference between the South Vietnamese, the Viet Cong, and the NVA, unless they're in uniform, we might get information that would lead us into an ambush or a booby-trap. If the locals are afraid of us, they might give us bad information. We can beat any enemy we can find. But sometimes we don't know who to fight—who the bad guys are."

"So—spy and die?"

"Willie's name for this kind of shit. Not real clever, but the name stuck."

"I think I'll go through my gear," he said. "I'll be in my digs."

I nursed the Scotch for a while, poured another. Sergeant Kennelley and I got along so well my resolve not to get close to anyone was fading. We spent a lot of time talking about everything from our missions to our C rations. And women. If we can talk about women, I decided, then I could talk to him about how I was changing. I walked across to his digs and knocked on the door. "Got a minute?" I asked him.

"Sure. Come in."

I sat on a section of a tree trunk. "Ammo cases getting hard to get?"

"Nah, tree trunks are just sturdier."

I didn't know how to start. I wondered if I was losing it, going down a path of no return.

"I'm kind'a worried," I said.

"You got a feeling you're gonna find your golden BB?" It was another way of asking if I had a premonition I was going to be wounded or killed.

"No, it's not that. I guess I don't like what I think I've turned into."

"I don't understand," Mike said. "You've been here long enough to know how to stay alive. Hell, everyone depends on you. Gotta be something else."

I didn't want to say what I was thinking, but the words seemed to have a will of their own. "Before, I never even wanted to hurt anyone..." I looked between my knees at the floor.

"So is that what's changed?" he asked.

"Yeah. Big time." I took a deep breath. "I told you about when Dan bought it. You know, he and I grew up together." I stopped until the frog in my throat went away. "I got really mad about that. Mad at God that He'd let Dan die. In a crazy way, I was mad at Dan that he left me. Kind of hurt that he did. I know that doesn't make sense. Then I blamed Charlie, so I started...uh...kind of getting even. Every time I killed one of the little bastards it felt good. Getting revenge. Looking for another kill as fast as I could find it. I realized I'd started to like the killing. But I don't want to. I've lost the person I was in my small home town. I'm afraid I'll never get him back."

Mike rubbed the back of his neck, the way he did when he had taken something in, and didn't quite know what to say about it.

"I'm not sure what to tell you, Doug. I was raised in a small town, too. We won't ever be the same." He got up from his tree-trunk chair and leaned on the doorway, looking out at nothing in particular.

"I've been wondering about that, too," he said, still staring into the trees. "I dream about it sometimes. Wake up with a start. But it doesn't bother me that much. I don't particularly *like* doing it, though." He turned and looked at me. "Maybe it'll go away when you go back to the World."

"Yeah," I said, meeting his eyes. "It probably will." He didn't believe it. I didn't either. But having advanced a theory about it, I felt better. Voicing my fears made them seem smaller. I knew neither of us would be the same, I just hoped I hadn't totally killed off the gentleness I used to have.

"Sometime I'd like to go home," I said. But to what? Dan wouldn't be there. There was no one in my high school class I wanted to see. My parents were upset with me. I felt like a displaced person.

"How old are you, Doug?" asked Mike.

"Eighteen. Last December."

Mike raised his eyebrows. "You joined up at seventeen?"

"Yeah," I said. "My dad didn't like it."

"I was eighteen. My parents didn't like it either."

The next morning, when the supply chopper landed, three FNGs got out. Jaimeson hadn't told us they were coming. Everyone uttered a collective groan. Once again we were going on a mission, dangerous in itself, and having three FNG's made it worse. We'd probably loose one or two of them, I thought. It reminded me of my first few missions with Dan.

I got the unloading and sorting of our new materiel started, then ambled over where some of the guys had a crap game going in the shade of a tarp. I didn't play, but I liked to watch. The dice stopped just short of the toes of a pair of spit-shined new boots, topped by neatly bloused BDU's. Gotta be an FNG, I thought, and looked up. It took a moment to recognize him. Then my jaw fell open.

"Hullo, Sergeant. Long time no see," the FNG said.

"Jeezus, Frank, is it really you?" I asked. "How's the family?" I knew Frank from high school. I had visited him and his Navajo family where they lived on the Navajo Reservation. The Res.

I assigned two of the crap shooters to look out for the other FNGs. I told Frank to stick with me. "The jungle's a long way from the Res," I said.

"Ah-h, you *biligaanas*," he said. "I'll be okay." Biligaana, a Navajo word, generally meant non-Navajos, particularly whites. It was not usually a term of endearment.

At 0300 hrs. the next morning, we climbed into two trucks and lurched off. In the thin pre-dawn light, I watched JR's flag make a valiant effort to unfurl in the still air. The sight of it always gave me a sense of home. Or home away from home. Somewhere to come back to. JR brought it along when we moved from the old digs.

Although the area had been declared secure, we drove without headlights. The night belonged to Charlie. The heat and humidity belonged to all of us, as did the variety of insects, which never went away, and would take Vietnamese or American blood without prejudice. Maybe the bugs had a day shift and a night shift, I thought. That must be how they keep up the constant attack. I slapped absently at some flying thing.

Frank sat next to me. He hadn't yet learned how to sleep almost anywhere. I watched him doze off, then as the truck swerved, start to fall forward off the bench, jerking himself awake.

"Brace yourself against the side of the truck and lean against the man next to you," I told him. His face wrinkled up. "Yeah, I know, they're sweaty, smelly, and dirty. You are too."

"I'm ready for a nap just about anywhere. It would help if we could get some *real* food and get away from the damn bugs," he said.

"Don't worry, it'll get worse. We get back, you can make us some fry bread."

"Sure. Get me some honey and powdered sugar for it and I will."

When I looked back again, Frank's head had fallen forward. He leaned against the man next to him, oblivious to the odor, dreaming his own dreams.

I studied Frank's face. Although his father was white, Frank had the typical high cheekbones of the Navajo. Under six feet by a few inches, but slim, Frank seemed taller. I remembered the high school girls, both Indian and white, moonstruck by his good looks.

After we bounced and tossed back and forth for a small eternity, the truck stopped. The tailgate dropped with a bang, and I made a mental note to chew someone's ass for making so much noise. We piled out. Most of us were skinny, and the hard wooden benches chafed our bony butts. I could hear the standard bitching about the mission, the truck, the army, the weather, and a variety of other things. Normal. We spread out along the sides of the road. Mike and I assigned point and flank. We formed up and moved out into the jungle, following a trail. Several miles later, it led us to a small clearing, about a hundred-fifty yards wide, where we took a break. I wondered what the grass, which grew hip-high clear to the other side, might be hiding. We'd go around.

The heat and humidity had shot up as the day wore on. More thirsty than usual, I'd emptied one of my canteens. I thought I'd save the other for the march back. My mouth felt like I'd been sucking on a big wad of cotton. Frank sat with his back against a tree, helmet on the ground beside him, M-16 across his lap. He had been raised a hunter, and kept his rifle at hand. An opportunity to bag game could come at any time. And here, we, too, were game.

"Frank. Put your pot on," I said. "I know you're hard headed—do it anyway."

We started around the clearing. I knew something had gone wrong when one of the men did a quick left-face, and fell with a yelp. I never heard the shot. All of us hit the ground. Then we heard the unmistakable bark of an AK-47 on full-auto.

I looked for Frank. He was crouched down a couple of yards away from me. "Frank! Get down, dammit!" I yelled. He didn't move. I lunged for him through the grass, grabbed his legs, and yanked as hard as I could. He lit on his side and looked surprised.

"Come on!" I said, motioning to him.

As we crawled through the trees, full-auto fire raked the area where the team had been just seconds before. I heard more AK-47 fire, then our M-16s answering. We had crossed a gap between the trees that had very little cover. We had to get back.

"Run for it when I do!" I told him. I could see two of our men behind the trees. "Let's go!" I yelled. We made the last ten or twelve feet in about two strides and dove behind the trees. More fire came from both sides, but we could see nothing to shoot at. Frank looked alert and scared. Good, I thought, scared is cautious. Not scared is stupid. Eventually, stupid gets you killed.

Our radio man, Corporal Miculevicz, motioned to me from the right. I could see Mike next to him, looking at his map, compass in hand.

"Stay here, Frank!" I said over my shoulder as I crawled to Miculevicz.

"Whatta you think about moving around the perimeter to the left," Mike said.

"Where are they?" I asked.

"Dunno, maybe in those trees." He pointed to a thicker stand of trees across the perimeter of the clearing.

"Sounds good," I said. I crawled back to Frank, told him what we were going to do. He nodded and we moved out. Except for the clearing, we had no more than twenty yards visibility in any direction. We dashed from tree to tree, stopped to look and listen, hoped we wouldn't stumble into a whole squad of NVA circling toward us.

Frank heard them first, held up a hand. We ducked back behind the trees. I saw Frank move past me to a small bank that offered a some concealment. Just then two of them popped up at the edge of the circle. I centered the torso of the closest one in my sights, and decided I'd wait until he came two steps closer. Frank would probably aim for the same man, I decided, and swung my rifle to the second NVA.. My stomach churned with fear and with the feeling of turmoil that comes with the knowing that I was about to kill someone.

In a firefight, time becomes plastic. It can flow gently or stop entirely, but usually goes slower than normal. Then, after it's over, it seems everything that happened took place in a split second.

In slow motion Charlie took two more steps toward us. I squeezed the trigger, and when I looked again, he was on the ground. I aimed and squeezed the trigger again. I expected to hear Frank firing at the other one, and looked toward him, but before I could make out more than his shape in the depression, I started taking fire.

I flattened out behind the tree, turned on my back, and flipped the selector switch on my M-16 to full-auto. I turned and quickly located the position from where I thought the enemy fire came from, and squeezed off a burst. I still didn't hear Frank fire at all, and wondered if he had been hit. Two more NVA suddenly appeared, and I squeezed off another quick burst, fairly sure that I had missed. I'd emptied my rifle. I still heard nothing from Frank.

"Frank! Shoot, goddamit!" I yelled. "Are you okay?" He looked back at me, still crouched over his rifle, frozen with fear. I needed him *now.* "Help me, goddamit!" I yelled as I fumbled to load another magazine. I looked up at Frank as I shoved it into the magazine well. The lip caught and pushed the first cartridge part of the way out of the magazine. As I slammed it into place, the round popped free, turning backwards in the magazine well. My rifle was now jammed, and Charlie would overrun my position in a few seconds.

Fear worked at cross-purpose to my hands as I tried frantically to free the magazine. My fingers were uncoordinated. I yanked the magazine out and flung it away, then worked the bolt several times to clear the action. I could see Charlie starting to move, and realized that I would never be able to get another magazine into the rifle in time. I reached for my 1911A1 pistol. Before I could get it out of the holster, I heard Frank fire two rounds, taking Charlie out. I heard more full-auto fire from behind us, the sharp snap of M-16s instead of AK-47s. Then a deafening silence fell around the clearing.

My heart had wound up to about a thousand beats a minute, my breathing almost as fast. I had to make myself calm down. I looked over at Frank. He hadn't moved from his cover behind the bank, and didn't look like he'd been wounded.

"You okay?" I yelled.

He nodded.

We checked to make sure the bodies were not going to suddenly come back to life. One of them was still alive.

"Hey, we got us a POW," I said, looking back at Frank. He hadn't moved from the depression. He sat there with his head on his knees. "You all right?" I asked, already knowing the answer.

When he looked up, I saw the stricken look in his eyes. We now had something else in common. He had just killed for the first time. He would relive it again and again, probably for the rest of his life, or build walls around it where it would break free from time to time. I pulled out my canteen and handed it

99

to him. He tipped it back, then made a face and spit out a mouthful.

"Where'd you get that? Out of the truck's radiator?"

I couldn't help but laugh. "You don't like our water with all those halazone tablets and dead microbes in it?" I asked. "Don't worry. Sometimes we drink it straight out of the swamp."

Tentatively he tried another sip, spit it out, and tossed my canteen back.

"This is the second time you've scorned my offer of water," I said. "Remember the spring water we drank that time we hiked up to the cliff dwellings on the Res?"

When I'd visited Frank, he took me to a cliff dwelling that had survived almost intact. The only water we'd found on that hike had a vile sulphur taste from bubbling through a coal seam. Frank knelt down and started to drink it. I told him I still had some water, and tossed him my water bottle. He tossed it back.

"Remember what you told me?"

"Yeah. I said you'd better keep your water, you'd need it. I called you a *biligaana*," he said with a smile.

"Kind of like I was a fuckin' new guy?" I asked.

He laughed. "Yeah, I guess so."

Unlike my visit to Frank's, there would be no fry bread, no mutton stew tonight. We would feast on our standard fare—C-rats. And no fond memories of the events of the day.

Our search the next day netted us some of Charlie's training materials and a cache of small arms and rice. We took samples of the propaganda and blew up everything else. The brass considered our mission successful, making the pronouncement like religious leaders blessing the collection plate. We thought we had only one casualty, the soldier who got wounded in the clearing firefight. He would probably heal up okay, and after all, we told ourselves, he had his ticket home.

I didn't realize we had another casualty that day, one who never saw a medic and would never see home again.

For two days we slept the sleep of the exhausted, feeling that we had earned a good rest. I hadn't seen Frank since we returned. He had moved in with Mack. I found him sitting on his cot, leaning against the log wall. He had his feet up, head and arms on his knees. I stuck my head inside and pretended I didn't see him. "Frank? You there?" No answer. "Can I come in?"

He looked up. "Yeah."

"Where's Mac?" I asked, jerking a thumb at the other cot.

"Dunno."

We sat for a few minutes in silence. I knew he needed to talk, first about anything, then about the firefight. I had brought a fifth of Singleton's twelve year old single malt scotch, almost worth its weight in three-day passes. I could think of only one possible explanation of how it survived being broken or stolen before it got to me. Divine intervention. I'd had it a week or so—another miracle—waiting for a good time to open it. I cracked the seal, took a pull on the bottle. It slid down easy, giving new meaning to smooth. Another pull and I could feel it clear to my toes. I offered it to Frank.

"Naw," he said, waiving it away. "You know how us Indians are."

"What? You're not telling me you won't drink with a *biligaana* are you?" I asked with mock astonishment and a touch of indignation. I held out the bottle again. "You never had problems with it in high school."

"Ah-h-h-h, must've been my white blood. I'm just a half-breed, you know." Frank took a sip and handed it back.

"Hey, you have any idea what that is? It's twelve-year-old single-malt Scotch. I can't think of anything better. Except maybe fifteen-year-old. You pissed off at me or something?"

"Well...it's pretty smooth," he said, taking a significant swig from the bottle this time. "Waa-a-a-a! It's smooth, but..." He blew out his breath. "Jeez!"

We passed the bottle back and forth. By the time half of it had disappeared, we both had relaxed.

"Remember that old bull? Your family all thought the bull had gotten sick and was going to die? How many times did you shoot that thing before he ran off?" I asked.

"Yeah, I remember that" Frank said. "They decided I was the one who should shoot it. We had a .38 Special. I faced the bull, aimed carefully at his forehead, and squeezed the trigger. The bullet bounced off. I shot him four more times, and just gave him a headache. Goddam hard-headed bull!" He looked at me like he knew what I was trying to do.

"That story must have gone around the whole reservation. People started calling me Dead-eye. 'Hey, Dead-eye, what's the hardest part of a bull's head?' they'd ask, and then they'd laugh. I never knew a .38 wouldn't penetrate the front of a bull's skull. But I sure scared the bull. He got well. We had him around for years after that, called him Stripe because the hair grew back white where those .38s ricocheted off."

We laughed. Loud and long.

"I'm glad he survived," Frank said. Except for hunting, I'd never done any killing. Until the other day." Frank looked up. "Did you...feel that way too?"

"What did you feel?" I asked.

He looked down. "I guess the worst part of it. It felt good." He looked up, then back down. "I liked it," he said.

I didn't expect him to say that. Until now, I thought he and Hoagie were having the same problem. Frank's went a lot deeper.

"Felt like getting even with...someone."

"I felt that way." I didn't want to tell him I liked it, too.

"This is gonna be like that final in high school. But I'm not gonna make a C on it when it's over."

In one of our high school classes, Frank and I were in the top of the class, along with another kid. We all accumulated the same number of points by the end of the semester. I got an A, along with the other kid. Frank got a C. The teacher didn't like Mexicans or Indians.

Frank stared at me. I felt better, thinking that he meant he'd get an A on this one.

"It's a strange thing," I said, "seeing a man that close, knowing he will kill you if he can. It's terrifying. It's almost a shock when he fires at you. I think that's when the anger comes in, with the realization that he, or you, or the universe, has changed this weird balance of things. If you don't kill him, he kills you." Frank sat up straight, his eyes large and focused on mine.

"Feel familiar?" I asked.

He nodded. "Yeah, for a while I almost couldn't figure out why they were shooting at us. Then I understood that they were going to kill us, and I froze up. I had to realize that they would kill you, too, before I got mad enough to do something. A huge rage came over me. I don't think I've ever been that mad. It felt so strong, I would have killed them with my bare hands. I couldn't have done anything else but kill them. I liked it. Liked the power. But I'm not sure I like...liking it."

I wondered if both of us were unbalanced in some way. It didn't seem anyone could feel this way without being a little crazy. Maybe it was a question of degree. Was it possible to get over it, I wondered.

Frank made it through his first two weeks. He had become, as one of the corporals put it, "One gung-ho sum-bitch." He became our point man, which made him popular with everyone, not only because they didn't have to do it, but because he had become very good at it. He felt his heritage gave him the ability to move quietly and unseen. He honed his skills so he could live up to the reputation he'd acquired. Often he would scout out Charlie, then return like a shadow to report on numbers and location. He never got caught.

Sometimes I got a twist in my guts watching him. He reminded me of Dan.

On one of our patrols Frank disappeared for an inordinate amount of time. We heard the stutter of AK-47 full-auto fire. Everyone froze, and it came again, this time a mix of AK-47 and M-16. Then silence.

Mike and I double-timed it in the direction of the sound. "Hey," I hissed. We're moving too fast to keep out of an ambush. If they set one up, they'll get us both. Tony will end up leading the team."

"Tony can get 'em back if he needs to," Kennelley whispered. We began to hear short bursts from an AK, single shots from an M16.

"Okay, we'll double-time it." What could have gone wrong, I wondered.

We found a dead NVA in a shallow foxhole not far away, his throat slit, and another up ahead, dispatched the same way.

"Looks like Frank found the sentries they posted," Mike said.

A hundred yards ahead we found Frank's body leaning against a tree next to the bodies of two NVA.

"Look, there's a blood trail. There were at least two others." Mike knelt next to Frank. "He's gone," he said. "Charlie must have thought there were a bunch of us, not just one guy." Frank had accounted for himself quite well. But he'd paid a terrible price for it.

"You know most Navajos don't believe in a hereafter?" I said. "I wonder what Frank believed."

I knelt and unfastened his web belt with its canteens, grenades and ammo, and lifted him up over my shoulders. Mike took his belt and rifle and we started back. By the time we got back to the team, the exertion had burned off most of the anger I felt. Sorrow and a vague feeling of failure burned in my belly.

CHAPTER ELEVEN

A Leg Up

Mike's tour had ended about a month before mine. Both of us decided to stay on. Most of the outfit thought we were crazy. We had a notion that we could make a difference. Among other things, we could teach the "youngsters" in our team, no more than a year or two our junior, how to stay alive.

We'd been given a temporary assignment as "advisers" to a South Vietnamese outfit. Training ARVN soldiers to defend their country seemed a logical step in stemming the tide of communism. Everyone knew the commies were trying to take over the world. Countries would fall like dominoes if not for the USA. We couldn't quit now.

Our supply chopper arrived with Lieutenant Jaimeson aboard. He was securely strapped in, and the doors were closed. He didn't like heights.

Jaimeson handed us a batch of re-enlistment papers. Then he started one of his long-winded spiels about what a tremendous job we'd done, and how he knew we wouldn't disappoint him or the outfit. I looked at Mike. He rolled his eyes. Oblivious, Jaimeson got more wrapped up in his sales pitch.

"I thought I'd re-up, but if I gotta listen to all your bullshit, you can forget it." Mike said. He handed back the papers.

"Same here," I said. The lieutenant looked stunned. "Look, we've already decided to re-up. You don't need to sell us on it."

Looking crestfallen that he couldn't finish his spiel, Jaimeson held out a pen, and Mike signed with a flourish.

I held the pen poised above the dotted line, my heart pounding. I couldn't see anything but the forms and the lieutenant's pen, waving back and forth like a windshield wiper. My mind fluttered. Sign it—no, don't—do it –don't. Prickles of sweat dotted my forehead.

"Well, you gonna sign the goddam thing or not?" asked Lieutenant Jaimeson.

"You tryin' to help me decide, Lieutenant?"

I glanced at Mike. Hell, we're a team, I thought. I signed.

The first mission of my second tour turned out to be the first step of my departure from 'Nam. We were on one of the tributaries of the Ho Chi Minh Trail that fed materiel from Laos into 'Nam. We had two wounded to carry back to the Vietnam border. We followed a trail hacked out of the thick jungle, so we didn't have to carry the litters cross-country. Our government's official position that we had no military personnel in Laos or Cambodia hadn't changed. That meant we couldn't get a dust-off for another two or three hours' march, until we crossed the border into 'Nam. No military in Laos, no wounded, no chopper, no dustoff.

We plodded along in total exhaustion with that practiced stare that sees nothing, yet is programmed to react to anything out of place. Trip wires. Footprints from retreads, as we called the sandals Charlie cut out of tires. Any other sign or movement that was out of the ordinary.

Mike suddenly raised his hand and everyone melted into the foliage. Further ahead, Jones, our Montagnard point man, had spotted something. He signaled Mike, then disappeared. Jones could become invisible and move so quietly that no one could hear or see him, not even the other Yards.

I'd been working drag, bringing up the rear, making sure we didn't get surprised. I scanned the trail behind us, then moved up to see what was going on. Exhausted, I didn't watch where I stepped. My foot kept going down when it should have stopped on solid ground. Too late, I flung myself sideways. I'd stepped into a small pit, covered by a woven mat and leaves. One of the filthy bamboo stakes sliced up through my skin, deep into my leg. The pain made everything in my peripheral vision go dark. I fell to the ground and rocked back and forth, fear keeping me from crying out. Up close and personal with a punji stake.

As I lay there, I saw an old man on the trail, coming my way. He watched me squirm, trying to move into the brush. Then pulled a wicked looking knife from a scabbard tied around his waist. Most of the Yards carried one like it, about eighteen inches long, and sharp enough to shave with.

Where the hell is everyone? I thought as he approached. Then Jones, who had appeared behind him, touched the barrel of his M-1 Carbine to the base of his skull. The old geezer froze. Jones whispered in his ear, almost like a lover, and he dropped his knife.

My leg felt like I'd stuck it in hot coals. Two of our Yards crept up, still wary of the stranger. They rolled me over and slit my fatigues to the knee. The old man said something to Jones. "He friend. Help us," Jones said. "No VC. Help American sojers."

My leg hurt so much I didn't care who he might be. "Where are you, Mack, goddammit?" I moaned. The pain kept moving up my leg, burning so bad it surprised me to see there were no blisters on my skin. Mack came at a run. He pulled back my pants leg, then looked into the shallow pit.

"Oh, Gawd," he said, shaking his head. He dug a syrette of morphine out of his medical pack.

Mike appeared from somewhere. He stared at the pit, and grimaced. "Je-ezus Christ, can't you watch where you're going?" he asked. "Goddam ground-pounder."

My leg hurt so much I couldn't think of anything cute to say back. Mike shrugged off his pack and reached inside for the flask he always carried. He knelt next to me, easing it to my lips. "Some guys will do anything to get into my private supply."

I swallowed a mouthful, almost choked as he kept pouring the fiery liquid down my throat. It dulled the burning in my leg and put a glow into my belly. So this is what it's like to be helpless, I thought.

Mack put on his medic's face. It felt strange to see him look at me the way I'd seen him look at other wounded. "You rammed that thing about four or five inches up into your leg. I wish to hell I had some penicillin."

Jones walked up, followed by the old man. We called him Jones because no one could pronounce his real name. He looked worried. The old man pushed his way past Jones until he could see what happened to me. One of our Yards decided he'd gotten too close and grabbed him. The old man looked at me and started chattering gleefully.

"What the hell's he saying, Jones?" Mike asked.

"He say, you step on punji stake, you die," Jones answered encouragingly.

The old man evidently could speak a few words of English, two of which were "you" and "die." He nodded his head vigorously. "Yoo diee-e-e! Yoo diee-e-e! Yoo diee-e-e!" he said over and over, laughing, rubbing his hands together. For a moment it looked like Mike was about to inflict the same forecast on the old man.

"Hey," I said, "We're all bunched up here, making noise. Charlie could take the whole team out with one grenade." I needed to salvage some of my authority. I wondered if the morphine thickness I felt in my tongue slurred my words.

I swam off into a soft, murky world. Everything I knew about punji stakes passed through my mind. Made of bamboo, sharpened to a razor edge, then fire-hardened. Charlie mixed feces and urine with things like rotten fish heads and other garbage, let it brew, then smeared it on the sharpened ends. Fuckin' great.

"This is gonna hurt," I heard Mack say. He grabbed my leg and squeezed. I didn't feel anything. Must have been the drugs. "I'm tryin' to squeeze out anything I can get out," he explained, but his voice sounded like he didn't think it helped much.

Our Yards made a litter out of branches and ponchos. I wanted to walk out, but felt too dizzy to get up. The booze, the drugs, and now the jouncing litter sickened me. I wondered if I would puke or pass out first.

The next thing I knew, Mike shook me awake.

"We're gonna ask for a dustoff," he said.

"We back in 'Nam already?" I asked, still groggy.

"No, but we're gonna get one anyway.

I slipped into oblivion.

Once again, someone shook me out of a good sleep.

"Wake up, ground-pounder, it's pill time!" I looked up, about to tell some orderly he could go to hell. Mike stood there, his grin large as the pain in my leg. The sun shone through a window with real glass in it. A real building. Then I remembered. We'd gotten a dustoff from the wrong side of the "line," the faint red line on our map that indicated the border. We got another lift out of the field hospital. Mack had kept me doped up, so I didn't remember much of it.

"Hey, good to see you! Really good!" I said, feeling relieved, almost ecstatic. I tried to sit up, but it took three tries before I could make it. "I could almost get used to being here except I miss the filth and the insect bites!" I frowned, trying unsuccessfully to figure out how long I'd been here.

"Well, I knew you'd miss the fine things in life we enjoy in the field, so I brought this," Mike said. With great ceremony, he produced from behind his back a package of C rations.

"Ah, get that shit away," I told him. "But what if I could get us some ice cream? Remember ice cream?"

"I haven't had ice cream for..." He shrugged.

The hospital had all sorts of delicacies. "Hey, Julie!" I yelled. A short, plump nurse looked up from the other end of the ward.

"Are you going to give me more trouble, Sergeant?"

"Never. Not you. Especially if you get us two ice creams."

"Two?" she asked. "Now you know I can't get anything for anyone but patients."

"Yes, ma'am," I said, "But I'm truly hungry. I could eat two."

A few minutes later she reappeared with two containers of vanilla ice cream and two spoons. "Eat fast so I don't get caught," she said and walked away. Since the nurses were officers, that made it an order.

"Man, it's been a long time since I even thought about ice cream," Mike said, scraping the bottom of the cardboard carton for the last drop. "Hey, if you're just going to let that melt, I'll eat it!"

"Bullshit!" I said. "I was just thinking about when we re-upped. How long had we been in the field before then? Six weeks? And then two weeks before I stepped on that damn punji stake. We've been away from civilization long enough to forget about the small joys it brings. I slept on the ground for so long, the first night here I almost got down on the floor to get comfortable."

He looked at my leg, discolored and swollen to half again its normal size, tied up in a sling contraption. "So, when's that gonna heal up?"

"They haven't told me anything," I said. "I haven't talked to a doctor. My fever's been kind'a high. They keep me pumped full of antibiotics and painkillers. I didn't know a damned infection could hurt so much."

"What do you mean, you haven't talked to a doctor? You nuts or something?"

I told Mike how the doctor refused to take the time to talk to me. "I think he's more interested which of the nurses he's going to sleep with after rounds than talking to his patients."

I caught Mike's eye. "But look at this. It's what I'm worried about." I pulled back the sheet to show him the dark streak that looked like a bruise running up the inside of my thigh. He frowned, then launched into the standard bullshit about getting well that no one believes but it makes you feel better anyway.

"Anyhow, you gotta get your ass back. I took your Winchester out and shot it. Couldn't keep my shots on a five gallon gas can at two hundred yards. I tried shooting at beer cans at a hundred. Even after I figured out how to adjust your scope, I only hit about one out of three. If we need to reach out and cap someone, we be screwed without you."

"Whatta you mean, you couldn't keep your shots on a *five gallon gas can*? That's gotta be a foot and a half wide and two feet tall! I can hit *quarters*—as in twenty-five cent pieces—at two hundred yards!" I wondered if Mike would know how to give the rifle its necessary tender loving care. I rattled off a list of instructions for care and cleaning.

"Sure. I'll take care of it," Mike said. How'd you learn to shoot like that, anyway?"

I told Mike about Dan and the thousands of rounds we'd shot in the Arizona woods. "Never had anyone teach me how to shoot. I just did it. I had a .22. I wanted to hunt deer with Dan, but I didn't have a deer rifle."

"So did you get one?" Mike asked, stacking the ice cream containers.

"Yes. From my mom. Still got it. A Winchester Model 94 with a long, octagonal barrel and a full buckhorn sight. It's a 30-30. My father told me she paid for it. Spent her money for something she didn't think I should have."

"Why would she do that?" Mike asked.

"I don't know. War terrified her. To her, guns were tools of war. Maybe she was afraid I'd be somewhere like 'Nam, and wanted me to be as good as possible so I could protect myself."

"Her fears came true," Mike said.

They sure did, I thought. And now I was in the hospital, weak with an infection, wondering if it would heal.

Mike rambled on about the team, but after a while we both fell silent. He stood up, ready to go, not wanting to, but knowing he could do nothing more for me. I could tell he didn't like leaving me in a bad situation. Our outfit didn't operate that way.

"I'll be okay," I said, forcing a smile.

"Yeah, I know. Just in case, there's a pharmacist's assistant here, Lance Corporal Thomas Riley. Short, stocky, red hair. Not a bad guy for a jarhead. One of Mack's buddies suggested I talk to him. You need anything, let him know. He'll contact me if he can't get it for you. I gave him some souvenirs, promised him more. When you get out, you'll owe me big time."

I was sure Mike knew that by arranging a connection to our team I wouldn't feel so alone. He looked down the ward at what seemed like a mile of injured men in hospital beds. "Keep your socks dry," he said.

After he'd gone, I thought about my parents. I regretted that the parting with them had been so difficult. I hadn't seen them since I joined up, almost two years ago. I missed them.

I wrote home only once, when Dan was killed. About three weeks later, I got a package in the mail. The return address had mom's name at the top, the same street, but a different street number. Must be the neighbor's. Inside were two tablets and a letter. They were in a drawer next to my bed. I maneuvered around until I could reach them and read the letter again.

Dear Doug,
I have enclosed a kind of log I've kept about what has been going
on here. Nothing earth-shattering, just day-to-day stuff. When

we didn't hear from you for so long, we were frantic, and a little upset that you didn't write sooner. I'm not trying to make you feel guilty, but please write more often. It has been particularly hard on your dad, who blames himself that you haven't called or written.

For a long time we both wondered if we would ever see you again. One day after I finished the dishes, I stood in front of the sink, staring out the window. Something told me you were alive and okay. Since then, I've relied on that feeling for comfort. I try to tell your dad you are okay, but he doesn't understand. Maybe it's something only a mother can know for certain about her son.

I've been teaching school. First grade. I have put money in your account every month. Don't worry, I can afford it. Right now, I don't think there's anything else I can do to make things better, or to hasten your return. So I feel like I'm doing something. If you need air fare to get home, or if you have to have money for expenses, it's there. Or call.

I hope you can find it in your heart to forgive your father. He has suffered a lot since you've been gone.

I love you.

Mom

P.S. Please don't say anything about this letter. The return address is JoAnn's.

I decided to write to mom, in care of JoAnn Hudson, her neighbor.

The days passed slowly. I'd been in the hospital for about ten days. I gained strength. No one came to see me, and I wondered what had happened. I knew they might be out in the field. If so, a short mission could take a week or more. I started to go stir crazy. I thought my mind would snap if I had to stay in bed for another day, so I asked Nurse Julie for a wheelchair.

She stopped and looked at my leg. "I'll ask the doctor on duty," she said. A short time later she returned—without the wheelchair. "The doctor said no," she told me. "You're to stay in bed."

"Did he say why?" I asked. "My doctor always hurries through our ward and never tells me anything. He barely glances at my chart."

"He said that you had an abnormally high temperature. Just rest and keep that leg elevated."

I wondered if the infection had gotten worse. I'd had my tonsils out at the tender age of twelve. Hadn't been in a hospital since then. Everyone knew that more people died in military hospitals, or left mutilated, than went home whole.

Julie must have sensed my fear. Her patience seemed boundless. Between bathing me and helping with bodily functions, she got to know me well. But the doctor's orders had to be obeyed.

"What's the doctor's name?" I asked.

"Dr. Samuels. Now, are you going to give me a hard time about it?" she asked, frowning.

"No. Sorry. Would you tell him I want to talk to him?"

"Sure," she said, eyes softening. "I just wouldn't expect too much."

CT, a black nurse on night shift, had become my favorite. Tall and slender, she had high cheekbones and beautiful dark eyes. Often she would give me a massage with some kind of fragrant oil. She turned me over on my stomach, my leg propped up on pillows. It hurt like hell to move, but the benefits made it worthwhile. Usually I fell asleep before she finished. She let me sleep until the end of her rounds, then came back and turned me over.

One night when she returned, her usual tough exterior had vanished and she looked as if she had been crying. "Hey, CT, you okay?" I asked.

"Oh sure," she said, and rubbed a hand across her eyes.

"What's going on?" I asked.

She stopped fussing with the sling that held my leg. "President Kennedy's been assassinated," she said in flat voice.

For a moment I couldn't comprehend it. It sounded like a terrible lie. "You mean he's dead?" I blurted out.

CT nodded. "I just found out. Yesterday. In Texas. Some guy with a rifle in a building on the parade route shot him in the head."

I felt my breath go out with a whoosh, as if something had knocked me down. I knew what it looked like when someone got shot in the head. I didn't want to think about it right now.

"He got shot while he was waving to the crowd from his car," CT said. "His convertible. A goddamned convertible."

One of the wounded in a bed near me managed to get a radio, and all the ambulatory patients in the ward gathered at the foot of his bed, late into the night, listening to the news. President Kennedy had favored the military. Who knew what Johnson, the new president, would do? Men who never batted an eyelash over their wounds wept quietly into their pillows. We listened to the aftermath in a state of shock, then horror, as Jack Ruby killed Lee Harvey Oswald.

I got a second shunt in my leg. Both drained fluid into a bottle at the side of my bed. Gooey-looking thick puss. Sometimes darkish, like the ooze coming out of a dead body. My temperature hovered around a hundred degrees. I couldn't get more than a few words out of Dr. Samuels when he made his rounds. He said the antibiotics didn't seem to be working, waved off my questions, and went on down the ward.

I began to have senseless dreams. My mom in a desperate hurry, riding a bicycle. Dan, ahead of me in the woods and beckoning to me, waving his arm. President Kennedy at his inaugural address.

Once again, I asked for Dr. Samuels to stop and talk to me. He didn't. The SOB.

Toward the end of the week, a different doctor made the rounds. Short, dark complected, his frizzy hair made him look harried. He wore round glasses with thick lenses. When he smiled, I knew immediately I would like him.

"Hi, I'm Dr. Rabinowicz."

"Hi, Doc. Where's Samuels?"

"He's off today," he said, frowning and looking from my leg to my chart. He poked my leg. It hurt.

"Ow! Take it easy! That's tender!"

He looked surprised. "You have feeling there? That's good!"

"I sure do! " Without thinking I blurted out the question my fears hadn't let me ask. "Am I gonna lose my leg?"

"Well, son, if that infection spreads, it could kill you." A professionally non-committal answer. Rabinowicz frowned again as if he expected my leg itself to cause problems. He pressed the skin below my knee again, raised his eyebrows as I flinched. Taking the cap off the syringe he held, he jabbed it into the IV line plugged into my arm. "Yes," he said. "I think there is a good possibility we'll have to take that leg off. We have a few more days. If it improves..."

I didn't hear the rest. He sounded as impersonal as a florist discussing a wilting plant. I tried to imagine myself with one leg, not able to do any of the things I'd been trained to do. No more five mile runs. Or patrols. Long marches. I wouldn't be in the army. I wouldn't even be able to walk. I wanted to scream, it's *my* life, *my* leg—I'm *not* a some kind of wilted houseplant!

I drifted off into a feverish sleep, filled with more dreams, this time about missing legs. Some amputated halfway up the shin, some at the knee or at the hip. One had a flap of greasy skin with yellow fat inside it. It turned out to be mine. I kept trying to fold the flap over the stump.

I woke up sometime after dark. An orderly was making his rounds, giving out pills. When he got to my bed I braced for the usual dose of bad humor. "Look-e-e what we got tonight," he said, peering down into the small paper cup. "Vitamins and minerals to keep you strong! And the red one's dehydrated roast beef! Just add water!"

"Where the hell have you been?" I snapped. I rinsed down the pills with shaky hands.

"Tough day?" he asked.

"Yeah. Sorry. I just thought Uncle Sam had forgotten me."

"Nah," he said. "The guy who does this ward went on sick call. I'm just behind. You know, the usual hurry-up-and-wait." He looked at my leg. "Maybe you got yourself a million-dollar wound. Your ticket home!"

His intention of cheering me up kept me from grabbing him and hitting him in the mouth. I didn't want to go home. I couldn't just watch as my country fell apart from the top man down. Kennedy's head exploded. Jackie crawled out onto the trunk, they said. I wanted to fight back. At the same time, a fleeting thought planted some doubt that I *could* go home after what

I'd become. Who am I? I thought. What have I become? How would I act if I went home? Right now I attacked first, then looked to see who or what I'd attacked. Attack is what I'd become. Get them before they got me. Whoever "they" were. I'd almost hit the orderly in the mouth. I tried to remember when I'd changed, but couldn't. I didn't know myself anymore, and that was the most frightening of all. "Yeah, maybe it's a ticket home," I said to the orderly.

I started to feel drowsy. In the back of my mind a voice told me that losing my leg would release me from a lot of horrors. I could go home, be pampered, and have a disability income. I even wondered for a moment if this might not be so bad. I'd become bone-weary of the bugs, disease, lousy food, and guerilla warfare. No one in my outfit would hold it against me if I went home because I lost a leg. A part of me wanted release from this hell. I could just let it happen.

Then anger burst over me, fragmenting the drowsy, drugged oblivion I'd slipped into, putting my "poor me" attitude to shame. What the *hell* could I be thinking? I refuse to be some goddamn candy-ass quitter! Cut off my leg? While I still have life in my body, *no one is* going to take it off.

I felt like a patchwork quilt with a lot of unfinished squares. Then the uneasy, drug induced sleep returned.

CHAPTER TWELVE

A Clear Understanding

I'd been in the hospital for three weeks and Dr. Samuels still wouldn't talk to me. I watched the steady stream of patients making their way through the ward, in wheelchairs or on crutches, missing arms, legs, or both. It provided a constant reminder of what was about to happen to me. My spirits plummeted, following my attitude into a black hole.

The next evening CT showed up with a wheelchair. "C'mon," she said. "We're goin' for a ride."

I just lay there, staring at the ceiling.

"I thought you wanted to get out of that bed," she said, challenging me, pushing the chair closer.

"If I don't?" I sulked.

"You don't got a choice. Get yo' white ass up and out of that bed. You goin' on a ride."

She pushed my wheelchair with her on rounds that night, wheeling me past beds that held men missing legs and arms and eyes. Some had been so covered with bandages I had to search for the human being underneath. Most of them smiled at CT and kidded with her. By the time she helped me back into my bed, what was left of my self-pity had been almost shamed out of existence.

"Learn anything?" she asked.

"Yeah."

She sat down in the wheelchair, next to my bed. "In the World, I worked in a burn unit," she said. "Some of the patients we had showed more courage than you could imagine." She paused for a few minutes. "Except for some of the guys here." She stared out the window.

"You want to save that leg of yours?"

"Of course! But what can *I* do?"

"Only everything that counts." She leaned her chin on her hands and sat there silently, staring through me.

"One of my patients was a little girl. Eleven years old. Her mama got drunk and passed out, smoking a cigarette. Their cracker-box house went up in flames. One of the firemen carried her out. She had burns over sixty-five percent of her body. The doctors didn't think she'd live, but each day she improved. She went through the baths and the debriding, scraping off the dead skin, then the skin grafts. When she could talk again, she started telling us all about what she would do when she got out of the hospital. Her grafts took, almost every one of them—very unusual—and she had minimal scarring. Before her discharge I asked her how she did it.

" 'It's simple,' she said. 'I close my eyes real tight and see in my mind that my skin is healing, and will soon be whole. Then I watch it. I make it heal. I see it happen.' "

I was skeptical that what worked for an eleven-year-old girl would work for me. I knew I had nothing to lose, and nothing else to try. "So how would I do something like that?" I asked her. "Anyhow, I don't have any burns."

CT said nothing.

"Would you help?" I pleaded, overwhelmed by the effort it took to ask.

"Yes. I will," she said.

CT made some suggestions on how to "see" my leg healing and tried to help me imagine the antibiotics eating up the bacteria. Even though I felt foolish, I closed my eyes, imagined healthy tissue and saw antibiotics eating the 'bad-guy' bacteria. They looked a little like Jell-O, like the movie about The Blob, but beneficial blobs, eating scowling, wormlike germs. Slant-eyed, Charlie germs. It turned out to be a great fantasy. I began an Antibiotic Army, and every time I got an injection, I had Antibiotic Recon Patrols chasing and ambushing Charlie Bacteria.

I had the same feeling about playing this game as I did when we went with our gut feelings—our hunches, intuition—in the field. Not a logical process, not something that could be explained. It always paid off. Maybe this would work the same way.

Two days later, the black mark up the inside of my thigh had almost disappeared. By the end of the week, my temperature had dropped to one-half degree above normal. I woke up one morning with a certainty that my leg would heal.

Later that day I saw Dr. Samuels. Tall, slender, movie-star handsome, and well aware of it, he had his entourage of attractive nurses in tow. His surgical team. He stopped at my bed, an attractive scrub nurse at each side. Maybe he has talent as a surgeon, not just as a womanizer, I thought. But I don't want to find out.

He gave me a smile full of perfect white teeth. "Hope you're feeling better this morning, soldier," he said, the sentiment phony as the smile. He turned to his team, started describing the surgery they would perform to remove my leg.

"Ah, pardon me, but what the *hell* are you talking about?" I asked.

The doctor turned, clearly irritated that I had interrupted his litany. "Yes?"

"Would you mind telling me what you think you're going to do to me?"

"No one's told you? Your leg has to come off before you get a bad case of gangrene. We've been putting you off because we've had more urgent cases, but now you're on the schedule." He consulted the clipboard "Surgery in four days." He smiled, as though I should appreciate him for sharing his plans to separate me from my leg.

"Doctor, please, look at my leg," I begged, flipping back the sheet. "It's getting better!"

Dr. Samuels slapped the clipboard closed. Without acknowledging that I'd even spoken, he dropped it into the holder at the end of the bed. As if other supremely important tasks demanded his time, he strode down the ward, his team in tow.

"Hey, Doc! I want you to look at my leg!" I called out. "Doctor! Come back, please..."

Samuels led his team out of the ward.

Numb from his bombshell, I began to think of alternatives. I had to get out of the hospital. But even if I could, I couldn't check into another one. The army had a monopoly on military hospitals. I hadn't healed up enough to be on my own. Then I remembered that Mike told me to get in touch with a corporal if I needed anything. I couldn't remember his name. A pharmacist's mate, Mike said. The next time Nurse Julie came through the ward, I would ask her to help. Hours passed. An orderly sauntered by. I asked him if he would find her. He didn't know her. I described her. "She's off," he said over his shoulder as he left. The seeming emptiness of the hospital closed in on me. Usually all the bustle and poking and prodding made me wish everyone would go away. Now I felt deserted. Then a nurse I'd never seen before walked into the ward.

"Please!" I yelled. "I need some help." I must have sounded panicked, for she stopped and spun around, eyebrows raised. "I need to get in touch with someone. It's very important."

"Well now." She came up to my bed. "Just who is it you need to see, and why do you need to see them?" Heavyset with grey hair, she stood with her feet shoulder-wide, hands on hips. She looked harried and tired. Almost as worn out as her patients.

"I...I need..." In desperation, I blurted out the truth. "I'm gonna lose my leg. They're gonna cut it off. I want to see a friend of mine first." Compassion replaced the stern look on her face. I felt vaguely ashamed. She certainly would not approve if she knew the thoughts running through my mind.

"Who do you want to talk to?" she asked.

"I can't remember his name, but he's a pharmacist's assistant, a lance corporal. He knows how to get in touch with my buddy. He's short, stocky—a redhead."

"All right. I'll see what I can find out for you."

"Can you do it now?" I pleaded. She looked back over her shoulder as she disappeared through the swinging doors at the end of the ward.

I must have looked at the clock a thousand times in the next hour. Finally she came back through the swinging doors, followed by a lance corporal. "Is this who you're looking for?" she asked.

"I'm Tom Riley," said the Marine.

"Yes, and thanks a lot," I said to the nurse.

When I told him why it was urgent, Riley said it should be no problem to get a hold of Mike. Unless he had gone off on a mission.

"I understand. How soon can you try? I don't have much time. Just tell Mike I need the things the Saigon cobbler fixed for me."

"The things the cobbler fixed for you?"

"The Saigon cobbler. He'll know what I mean. Tell him I need them in three days or it's too late."

He looked around to see if anyone could hear. "I could use some goodies. Souvenirs, Charlie's stuff," he whispered.

"Name it," I told him. "I'll get it for you. Whatever you want."

"You must want to get in touch pretty bad."

I nodded. "You want a goddam tank? I'll get it for you. Want your own chopper? I'll get it for you."

"I'll find him," he said, and ambled out.

Now came the hard part, the waiting. Afternoon turned into evening, then night. I hadn't heard from Riley. I stroked my leg, told it not to worry. When CT came on, I told her what happened, and asked her for something that would help me sleep. She brought me a pill. I tossed and turned anyway, waking up feeling like I hadn't slept. Breakfast came, then lunchtime ground laboriously into mid-afternoon, and still no word from Riley. Nurse Julie brought me my handful of pills and an injection.

"Your leg is better, and your temperature is down. But something's bothering you."

"Yeah," I said. "There is. I need to talk to Dr. Samuels. He doesn't seem to think I'm getting better. He just ignores me. Can you ask him to talk to me? I've *got* to talk to him. This is healing, and he wants to..."

She looked at my leg, then frowned. "I'll leave a message in his box. He'll get it in the morning." She hesitated. "Did he talk to you the last time you asked?"

"No. I want to ask him about..."

"I know," she said with a sad smile, and smoothed my sheet.

"I also need to talk to a pharmacist's mate..." At that moment Riley walked through the swinging doors at the end of the ward.

"I delivered your message," the lance corporal said. "He said to tell you he's en route with your golf club. Don't know how you're gonna play golf in bed."

I stifled a war-hoop of relief. "Maybe I'll just do some putting," I said.

By noon the next day my anxiety had returned. I decided that I needed an alternate plan and the ability to move around. I buzzed for Nurse Julie.

"I want to get up. Would you bring me some crutches?" I asked.

"You know it's against Dr. Samuels' orders."

"I'm getting up. If I have to try it without crutches, I'll do it." I sat up and lifted my leg out of the sling that kept it elevated. I started to swing my legs over the side of the bed, feeling faint from the exertion.

Nurse Julie grabbed my arm. "Okay, okay," she said. "Just hang on. I'll get you some crutches. But stay in bed until I get back. Okay?"

I nodded, and she hastened off through the those swinging doors that represented the gateway to freedom. She returned a few minutes later, followed by Dr. Rabinowicz.

"You again," he said, smiling. "Where'd you get hurt, anyway?"

"Laos, sir."

He raised his eyebrows. "An operation that never happened?"

"Yes, sir."

He asked me some questions while he looked over my chart and my leg. "I spent some time running a field hospital in the Delta. I think you might do well to get some exercise."

"They're gonna amputate my leg tomorrow," I told him.

He looked surprised. "Lie back," he ordered, and started pulling at the dressings on my leg. It hurt, and I winced. "Hmmm, you have feeling there?"

"Yes, sir. Just like last time."

"And there?"

"Ow! Yes."

"Who made the decision to amputate? Doctor Samuels?"

Nurse Julie looked at my chart. "That's right," she said.

"He's the senior surgeon," he said, as he prodded my leg. He frowned, then, he said, "I think you have a good chance of keeping this leg. It looks a lot better than the last time I saw you."

My spirits soared.

"The problem is Dr. Samuels doesn't."

My spirits plummeted. "How can he have any idea if it's better or not? He won't even look at it!"

"I'll see what I can do," he said.

"Please, Doc, I don't want to lose my leg. Samuels won't talk to me, and it's healing..." If Mike didn't make it, maybe Dr. Rabinowicz could do something. I might still have hope. That was a lot of maybes.

"I asked my nurses twice to leave Dr. Samuels a message to talk to me. I haven't seen him."

Nurse Julie nodded. "I know he got the last message," she said.

"I'll see if I can find him. And I'll ask him to talk to you," Dr. Rabinowicz said.

I felt clumsy with the crutches at first. I banged my leg into a chair and would have fallen if Nurse Julie hadn't caught me. After that, she followed behind me, pushing a wheelchair in case I collapsed. The slightest bump on my leg hurt, but it felt so good to get out of bed I didn't want to quit. No more bedpans, I decided.

I spent that evening visualizing a healthy leg, commanding the patrols of the Antibiotic Army as they made their sweeps and blew away Charlie-germs. I thought about the five mile runs we used to take before breakfast every day. If anyone had told me I would miss them, I would have laughed.

I wobbled up and down the ward one more time on crutches. The exercise exhausted me. I got back in bed and Nurse Julie strapped my leg back into its harness. I fell asleep and dreamed about waking up with nothing below my left knee, trying to tuck a flap of skin over it to hide the stump. I woke up yelling. CT gave me another pill, which worked just enough to make me groggy.

I'd still heard nothing from Mike. I felt frantic. Several times my breath came so fast I was panting. My heart raced wildly. I'd talk myself down, then go soaring back into fear and anger again. That fuck. That *fuck* Samuels.

Samuels had ordered me prepped for surgery the next morning, so I got only liquids for dinner. I'd heard nothing from Rabinowicz. By sundown, panic had lodged in my throat like a vampire bat. Then I heard the swinging doors at the end of the ward give a long, drawn-out squeak. I looked up just as Mike stepped into the room.

"Jeezus, am I glad to see you!" I said.

He put his finger to his lips. "There's a nurse in there." He pointed at the doors he had just stepped through.

"A black nurse? Real pretty?"

"Yeah."

"She's okay. God, I thought you'd never get here. Did you bring it?"

"Here's your golf club."

Months ago, Mike asked for help shooting his .45 cal. Government Model pistol. I bought a bucket of old golf balls from the officer's golf course, and we used them for targets. He didn't believe anyone could hit such a small target. I taught him how to hit the small targets, and hit them fast with his .45. During one of our training sessions he held up his pistol and said, "Some golf club, huh?"

He held out a canvas bundle, tied with a cord. Inside, my own commercial-made .45 cal. Government Model was holstered. There were two magazine pouches, four loaded magazines, and a box of Uncle Sam's finest ball ammo. I worked the slide, dry-fired it a few times to make sure it still worked, then slid a loaded magazine into the magazine well, leaving the chamber empty. I stuck the pistol under my pillow and breathed a sigh of relief.

"Thanks," I said, handing the rest back to Mike. "All I need is the pistol."

"So what's up?" Mike asked.

"They were gonna try to cut off my leg tomorrow morning. But now it won't happen."

Mike looked worried. "They want to take off your leg? Shit, it looks a lot better!"

"It is," I said. "I've been up on crutches. But the damn doctor won't even talk to me. He's too interested in 'his schedules,' but mostly in his adoring entourage."

"I'll check with you tomorrow. I'll look for bloodstains and bullet holes."

"You're a sicko," I said. "But that may be what you find. If I'm still alive, I'll have both legs."

He patted my good leg and disappeared through the double doors.

Sleep and I played tag that night. I'd doze off, only to wake with a start. I must have reached up under my pillow for my .45 a hundred times. I had no firm plan for my showdown tomorrow. How did I get into this mess, I wondered. I thought I wore the white hat. But I couldn't let them cut off my leg when it was healing. What would John Wayne do?

I'd been awake long before they came the next morning. Dr. Samuels had several good-looking nurses with him, as usual, as well as some of his operating team. I blessed his habit of seeing his patients before surgery, even if it was only an opportunity to flirt with his staff. I went over what I would say and tried to calm my breathing. Dr. Samuels, as usual, acted like a guru surrounded by devotees. The group moved leisurely down the aisle from patient to patient, chattering and laughing. Finally they got to my bed and stopped.

Samuels pulled my chart out of the holder at the end of the bed and looked up. Oozing gravity, he moved around to the left side of my bed. As if he had a checklist, he consulted the chart, frowned, looked at my leg, then shook his head. "No change," he said.

"Hey, Doc," I said. "You have to listen to me! My leg is healing! I've been up on crutches. I can walk. It doesn't hurt hardly at all."

He glanced at his now silent entourage and nodded somberly. "Don't worry, son. We're going to take good care of you."

"No, Doc, you're not taking good care of me," I said. "You didn't hear a word I said!" He paid no attention to me, and, frowning, continued to read my chart.

"Hey, Doc! This is the first time you've looked at my leg! How can you tell it isn't better? Doctor Samuels! Please! Listen to me!"

He continued reading my chart, shaking his head sympathetically. And still not paying the least bit of attention.

"Why don't you want to admit my leg is healing up? Are you afraid to admit you're wrong?"

He closed the chart and looked up as though to rebuke a child for a temper tantrum.

"Goddam it, you fucking quack butcher, you're gonna talk to me whether you want to or not!" I yelled. I pulled the pistol out from under my pillow.

I stuck it in his face. With my left hand, I pulled the slide fully to the rear, and released it. The sound as it slammed forward, chambering a round, was as loud as the breech slamming shut on a 155mm howitzer. At last I had the doctor's attention.

Pop-eyed, he stepped back, dropped the clipboard. His entourage drew together into a tight knot at the end of my bed and let out a collective gasp. Samuels, ash-white, stared directly into the big, black hole in the muzzle of my .45.

"Get down on your knees, you sleazy butcher," I commanded. "Get down on your knees, right now! You hear me, goddammit? Or I'll blow your head off!"

"Doh-doh doh," he stammered. Slowly he knelt, never taking his eyes off the hole in the end of the barrel. He held up his hands, palms out, mesmerized.

"*Look at me*, you sonofabitch!" He looked up, no longer the cocky surgeon blithely discussing my dismemberment. His eyes looked like polished glass, his jaw trembled like jungle foliage in the rain.

"You want to live, asshole?" I thundered.

His lips moved, but no sound came out. Faintly, he nodded his head.

"Then hear me real good. You take my leg off, *I'll kill you,* even if I have to hunt you down for the rest of my life. I'll make it my *mission in life* to find you and kill you!"

I leaned forward and thrust the pistol closer. *"Do you understand that?"* I bellowed.

Dr. Samuels froze in place. His devotees all leaned back as if blown by a hard wind.

I heard a noise to my right, on the other side of my bed. Out of the corner of my eye I saw an orderly push one of the beds away from the wall. He thought he could sneak up on me. When he crawled over the bed next to mine, I pushed up on the pistol's safety with my thumb. If someone tried to grab the .45 from behind me, the safety should be on. Whether he was a butcher or not, I didn't want to kill Dr. Samuels. Not unless he cut off my leg. Not right now.

Before the orderly could grab the pistol, I turned and handed it to him. "Here. You can have this," I said. "But be careful, it's loaded."

My unexpected move startled him, and he almost dropped it. He backed up against the next bed, holding the .45 like a hot potato. I heard footsteps running down the hallway. Two military policemen burst through the doors, an orderly behind them. For a fleeting moment I considered pointing to the orderly who stood there holding my pistol and yelling, "Look out, he has a gun!" Instead, good judgment overcame my strong, inspired urge, ruing the loss of a great stunt. I was in trouble up to my ears. But now I would face it two-legged.

"What the hell's goin' on here?" one of the MPs hollered.

Dr. Samuels, looking pale and embarrassed, answered with a moan, closed his eyes tight, then jumped to his feet and raced down the aisle. I thought I could see a wet stain down one leg of his scrubs.

The drugs I'd been taking would stock a pharmacy, and my fevered nerves had been on edge. I turned and banged my leg against the support that held it up. That hurt. I sucked in my breath, and everything started to go black. As the ward came back into focus, I heard a babble of voices. Dr. Samuels' devotees all talked at once to the MPs. "No, he isn't shot! No one shot him!" the orderly chimed in, pointing down the hallway where Samuels had disappeared. An MP held my .45, and waved it around as he asked questions.

"Hey, buddy," I said, "That .45 is loaded." He looked blank. "You're pointing it right at us. Why don't you unload it? Or let me unload it?"

"Oh, yeah," he muttered and looked at the pistol. He started to hand it to me.

"What the hell...?" His partner snatched the pistol away, swinging it toward the foot of the bed, where a dark hand grabbed it. CT's hand.

"I don't know what you people think you're doing, yelling and hollering in *my ward*, but *I want it stopped*! *NOW!*" She bit out the words in a low voice that carried an unquestionable authority. "*Get out of here! All of you!*"

Surprised, everyone stared at her, like the kid game where the players freeze when the music stops.

"*OUT! NOW!*" She pointed to the door.

"This man's under arrest!" ventured one of the MP's. "You can't..."

"Don't tell *me* 'can't,' buster, not on *my* ward. You're not taking one of *my* patients. *He's* not going anywhere. He's not *able* to go anywhere! Now you get out of here or I'll call Lieutenant Colonel Meyerson and tell him you're causing a major disturbance in *his* hospital. Now *GO!*"

Reluctantly, Dr. Samuels' entourage left with the MP's. "We'll be back for him," one of them said.

"He'll be here. And you better have real big roll of red tape," CT said. She turned to me and glared. "*You* I'll talk to later." She picked up the aluminum clipboard. Holding it over my .45, she flounced out the door at the other end of the ward.

A few heads raised up from pillows to see if CT and the MP's had gone. I felt everyone's eyes on me.

"Way to go, man," said a scarecrow with a bandaged chest, in a bed across the aisle.

"Should 'a shot that bastard," someone said.

"Yeah," said another voice. "Shoot Samuels, give us back Kennedy.

It looked like I'd saved my leg. At what cost, I wondered.

CHAPTER THIRTEEN

Almost Leavenworth

I hadn't slept much the last few nights, wondering what would happen to me now. At least I still had both legs. Midway through a delicious dream about Sara that involved a sleeping bag and a cold six-pack of beer, the feeling of someone watching me kicked in. With a start, I came half awake, fumbling through the blankets for my M-16.

"Good afternoon." Dr. Rabinowicz stood at the end of my bed. "I just wondered how I could tell you I'm your doctor now, without getting shot." He looked serious.

"Ah, it's pretty easy now. I have a limit of scaring the hell out of one doctor per hospital stay. You're safe. Anyhow, The MP's took my artillery with them," I lied. C. T. had given my .45 to Lance Corporal Riley, who promised to return it to Mike.

"Well in that case, I guess I better concentrate on getting that leg of yours healed up. If that's okay with you?"

"You bet it is. Sweetest words in the world."

"You're not out of the woods yet. It could still have to come off. We have to get rid of that infection. I'll do my best for you though—if you'll do your part."

"Anything," I said, and meant it.

The next morning I woke up once more with the feeling that someone was watching me. When I opened my eyes I saw a short, bird-chested U.S.

Army captain. He looked half lost under his hat, which he'd pushed back on his head. Peering out from behind thick glasses, he held a briefcase almost half his size. He bent over and squinted at the clipboard on the end of my bed, straightened up and adjusted his uniform. He started when he realized I was awake and watching him.

"Sergeant, I'm Captain Henry Langswell Morton. From the J-A-G's office," he said.

"Jay-ay-gee? What the hell's that?" I asked.

The look on his face told me I had just committed heresy. Captain Henry Langswell Morton drew himself up to his full height of five feet, six and one-half inches, and stuck his narrow chest out as far as it would go. "J-A-G," he said, "Is an acronym. It stands for Judge Advocate General." In a tone of voice designed to convey the weight of his burden, he said, "I have been appointed as your attorney."

I felt panic—this diminutive, near-sighted ninety-eight pound captain could end up the only thing standing between me and Leavenworth.

He pulled a chair up to my bed, took a legal pad out of his briefcase, then produced four brand new pencils from his inside pocket, all sharpened to needle-sharp points.

"Let's get to work," he said, leaning back in the chair. "First, I want to tell you that Captain Fowles, who will be prosecuting you, has offered to allow you to take a Section Eight discharge. It seems you have a rather irregular military record. As a matter of fact, there are periods of time that your MOS, your Military Occupational Status, that is, and your assignments are nonexistent. I have to ask you to consider the Section Eight, or face some litigation. The possibility of prison time is real, but remote. Remote, that is, as long as I am your attorney."

I stared at this little guy, who I could squash like a bug with one hand, probably even from my hospital bed. Yet he had just taken me out with his words. I felt short of breath. I never imagined anyone would ever try to kick me out of the army. A Section Eight, unsuited to military service, left a mark almost as bad as a dishonorable discharge.

"No way," I said. "I won't agree to that."

He nodded and carefully wrote on the pad. "I'm not surprised. I expected that. Okay. You better start by telling me what happened to your service record. Why are you unaccounted for at times?"

"I guess you don't know much about Special Forces. We do a lot of clandestine..."

His eyes lit up as if I'd spoken magic words. He sat up straight. "You mean, you're...SF?" he asked, reverently.

"Yeah, that's how I got this." I pointed to my leg. "Happened in Laos. One reason it's this bad is, we couldn't get a dustoff until we almost crossed over into 'Nam. About a three hour hike."

"You've been in Laos?" he asked, his eyebrows making tents over his coke-bottle-bottom glasses. "Really?"

"In Laos, Cambodia, and a few other places. Thailand is where we're based. But don't think you can go find out anything."

He nodded. "What happened to your leg?" he asked. He set down the legal pad, carefully placed the pencils on it, and stood up. Holding his hands behind his back, he inspected my leg, frowning as if someone had to do the unpleasant task, and he was the one.

"I stepped on a punji stake."

"A what?"

I told him the story. He looked spellbound, almost in a trance. Oh great, I thought, now I've got a mediocre paper pusher who's a wannabe SF and thrills to war stories. What I need is a good lawyer. A great lawyer.

CT poked her head through the doors and looked at us. I motioned for her to come closer, but she disappeared. A few minutes later the doors opened again, and Mike walked in.

"Are you busy?" he asked.

"Naw. Just swapping war stories with my lawyer here." Mike looked puzzled. "Sergeant Kennelley, I want you to meet Captain...uhh..."

"Captain Henry Langswell Morton," piped up the little man, looking boldly at Mike as though he might be another renegade who needed taming.

"He's from the Jay-Ay-Gee's office. Cap'n Hank for short, meet Sarge, or Mike, for short." I thought Cap'n Hank fit in the mouth easier than Captain

Henry Langswell Morton.

Cap'n Hank stared at Mike. "Are you SF, too?" Mike nodded. Cap'n Hank smiled and took his hand and solemnly pumped it up and down.

"My client received his wounds," he said conspiratorially, "in Laos."

Mike looked down at Cap'n Hank. "I know. I helped carry him back. We thought about just dumping his ass and saving ourselves a lot of trouble, but we got him a dustoff after we lugged him across the 'line.' Well, almost across."

Cap'n Hank looked at Mike, uncertain whether his new found loyalty to me called for him to defend me from Mike.

"What's the 'line'?" he asked.

"The border. On the map, it's a line," I said. "The choppers won't set down on the wrong side of it. Not supposed to, anyway."

Mike pulled up another chair. We talked about our A-Team and told more war stories, some of them slightly embellished. Cap'n Hank drank in every word. He stood taller, puffed out his chest. Suddenly he looked at his watch, and, with an exclamation, jumped up.

"I'm late for a meeting!" he said. "I'll be back tomorrow!" He grabbed his briefcase, and looking much like a sparrow trying to take off with half of someone's sandwich, he trotted to the doors. He stopped and looked back. "Thanks, sergeants. Thanks for talking to me."

"I found out something about Captain Henry Langswell Morton," Mike said. "On the way in, I saw Lance Corporal Riley. 'Your buddy lucked out,' he said. I asked him what he meant.

"He said you got a real good attorney. The other prosecutors gave your little Captain the nickname of Horrible Henry. He graduated second in his class at Harvard, then studied military law. After that, he joined up. Riley said he's good. *Very* good. Wins almost all of his cases."

Finally, I thought, some good news.

"Looks like you've got a break with this little guy. You owe some goodies, though. So far, I've paid for you in the coin of Charlie's tools of war. But I'm out of goodies, so you're gonna have to rejoin the war—pardon me, rejoin your station as advisor—and capture some more of the enemy's good shit.

And you know something else?" Mike looked over his shoulder to see if we could be overheard. "You know who gave me back your golf club? CT. You owe that nurse big time."

"I almost forgot," I said. "She gave me a message for you. Said she forgot to tell you that you're really dumb."

"Does she know I'm the one who brought you that package?"

"I guess that's what she meant."

Cap'n Hank came every day for three or four hours, always with a clutch of sharp pencils in his inside pocket. He asked me questions, wore the pencil points down writing notes on his pad, and kept me updated on how he would handle my defense. He always asked me if my leg had healed up any more. The inflamation had subsided, and I'd been walking around the ward on crutches, thrilled with the improvement.

"I want you to walk into the courtroom without crutches if you possibly can," he said. "That will be worth more than a dozen witnesses and a hundred pages of testimony."

I made it my goal.

After our sessions on defense strategy, Cap'n Hank always wanted to know more about what our outfit did. I obliged, telling him about some of our missions and assignments and some of the training schools we'd attended. As I got to know him, I realized he had a genuine passion to do what we did. If he only knew, I thought, he wouldn't be so crazy about it. But even though I knew exactly how difficult it could be, I still couldn't wait to get back to my outfit and endure more of the same. How could I call him crazy for wanting what I myself wanted to return to so desperately?

One night after we'd worked late he became so quiet I asked what was bothering him.

"I'll never get to do what you're doing," he told me. "At birth, I had an imperfectly formed valve in my heart. They didn't know how to operate on things like that back then. When I turned fifteen, they did operate, and it's a lot better. But I still can't run more than a hundred yards or so."

"How'd you get in the army?"

"My family is what you would call influential. But having influence isn't as important as good health. Or choosing what you want to do. Or a lot of things."

As the trial date drew closer, I'd almost run out of war stories for Cap'n Hank. My leg had just about healed, and I knew it would only be a matter of time before I would go back to my team—or off to serious prison time. Two days before the trial, Mike brought visitors.

"I want you to meet my new friends. This is How," he said. A bright-eyed Vietnamese stepped forward. "And this is Low." The other Vietnamese stepped forward. "How is a barber. Low is a tailor. They're the How Low Brothers."

"That's really bad, Mike."

He shrugged. "No joke. That's their real names."

Whatever their names, they did great work. How gave me the best haircut I'd ever had and shaved me with a straight razor without so much as a nick. Low took my measurements and had me try on a new uniform, standard issue, baggy everywhere but in the shoulders.

"We'll be back day after tomorrow," Mike promised.

Cap'n Hank spent the day with me, going over the way I would testify. The realization that these next two days might be the last of my freedom for a long time gave me a tightness in my chest that made it hard to breathe.

The following morning the four of them arrived together. Nurse Julie agreed to stand guard while we sneaked into the nurse's lounge, which had the only full-length mirror in the hospital. I shaved and tried on my uniform, which fit beautifully. Low even produced a pair of spit-shined issue shoes. The image that looked back at me, though gaunt and pale, looked like a professional soldier.

"What's with the decorations?" I asked Mike.

"Cap'n Hank's orders. He picked your Combat Infantryman's Badge, your SF patch, and your purple hearts. Nothing else, he said."

"I hope to hell he knows what he's doing." I looked at the purple hearts. "Goddamn purple hearts. Take a look around this ward. I don't want to wear them. I never got hurt bad enough to deserve them. These guys here are the ones who deserve them," I said, gesturing down the ward."

"I'd wear them if Cap'n Hank wants you to. I did a little more checking on him. He's lost only two cases in the last two years."

"Let's hope I'm not number three."

My anxiety that night reminded me of some of the more dangerous missions we'd gone on. I couldn't sleep, so I tried to remember what happened and made notes for Cap'n Hank, who still had an insatiable appetite for our stories. I dozed off at last and dreamed I wandered through an enormous old hotel. I put my foot through the rotten floorboards in an endless hallway and fell, then got trapped in a dusty cupboard.

Cap'n Hank, Mike, How, and Low woke me at 0600 hours. The court martial would begin at 0800. How shaved me and Low fussed over my uniform, pressing out a few last wrinkles. The orderly left me a breakfast tray which Mike, How and Low ate. It was too much like a last meal for me to eat it. My stomach kept trying to swim into my chest. As How buttoned up my shirt, Dr. Rabinowicz and Nurse Julie arrived.

"You look like a former patient of mine," the doctor said. "Except he didn't look so healthy. I've got some medication for you. Sitting with your leg bent at that table all day will cause some swelling. It probably will be painful, too. If you want to last the day, you'll have to pay attention." He pointed to the tray Nurse Julie carried, which had four small paper containers. "I've labeled the cups. Keep them on the table in front of you and use them as you need them. Captain Morton agrees that will actually reinforce the psychological impact of your case. I, of course, being only a lowly doctor, had nothing to do with that part."

Dr. Rabinowicz's contribution of little white pill cups comforted me. And having some pain medication available was a good idea. We left the ward to murmured wishes for good luck. I heard a wolf whistle. Someone yelled, "Hey, pretty boy!" The others chimed in. "You can do it!" and "Lady luck's sittin' in your corner!" Too bad the men in these beds couldn't be the ones who judged my case.

We entered the courtroom at 0755 hours and sat at the table in front of the rail. As I had been coached, I leaned my single crutch, which I still needed, upright against my end of the table, drawing everyone's attention, in case they forgot I had been wounded in the service of my country.

"Even these officers have feelings," Cap'n Hank whispered, as he lined up the little pill cups and a glass of water. "Maybe not much, but some." He opened his briefcase and took out a slim manila folder, and placed it squarely on the table in front of him. The pill cups stood out on the polished expanse of empty table.

"We're lucky. We have two officers on the panel who have commanded combat units. And one who came up through the ranks."

"Panel?" I asked.

"Jury, to use the civilian term. Except these are all officers."

The idea of being judged by officers gave me a headache, and my stomach rumbled like a distant bombing raid. We rose when the judge and the panel of officers entered the room. After we'd been seated, the judge called me to stand and hear the charges against me read. As I reached for my crutch, I knocked it onto the floor. Cap'n Hank stood, walked around behind me to my right side, and handed it to me. He smiled and winked. The first coup of the trial.

Dr. Samuels testified, along with two others from his entourage, about the events of that morning. Cap'n Hank had an objection now and then, and some questions for Samuels, but for the most part, he just listened to the testimony.

The prosecution called its witnesses. Remarkably, not a single patient in the ward had seen a pistol or heard me threaten Dr. Samuels. I took a pain pill, washed it down with water. The panel watched me, as we knew they would.

Cap'n Hank questioned one of the MP's at length. He hammered the point that the MP had never seen me with a pistol, that the pistol alleged to be at the scene was, supposedly, in the hands of an orderly. He berated him with the fact that no pistol had been taken for evidence. "Are you sure it ever existed at all?" he asked. Before the MP could answer, Cap'n Hank said, "That's all. No further questions."

He called Dr. Rabinowicz. Cap'n Hank had a list of a dozen or so of Dr. Samuel's cases that he asked various questions about, which the court ruled as pertinent over the objections of Captain Fowles, the prosecutor. Then he went back through the list, asking Dr. Rabinowicz if he agreed with the diagnosis. Reluctantly, one by one, Dr. Rabinowicz told the court that he did not agree with any of Dr. Samuels' diagnoses.

"Do you believe Dr. Samuels to be a competent physician?" Cap'n Hank asked.

Dr. Rabinowicz frowned and fidgeted. Finally he said, "I have been asked to cooperate in an investigation of Dr. Samuels by the hospital. I think my answer to the question might prejudice that investigation."

Captain Fowles looked as though he had no knowledge of an investigation of his client. He gave Dr. Samuels an incredulous stare.

Evidently Cap'n Hank expected this answer. "Thank you, doctor. Since that's the case, I have nothing further."

Cap'n Hank called Dr. Miller, one of the hospital's surgeons, as our next witness. I took another pain killer.

After establishing that Dr. Miller did not know me and had never talked to me, Cap'n Hank elicited, with some difficulty, Dr. Miller's opinion that Dr. Samuels' diagnosis and treatment was unnecessarily drastic. "Had I been Sergeant Walker's doctor, his treatment would have been very different," he said.

"Is it correct that you found other diagnoses made by Dr. Samuels to be too severe."

"That is correct," Dr. Miller said.

"Thank you."

Cap'n Hank turned and looked at me. "Defense calls Sergeant First Class Douglas Walker.

My turn had come. I felt like I'd swallowed a rock. I was grateful for the incessant coaching Cap'n Hank had put me through. I would tell the truth, just phrased a bit differently than I would have phrased it myself. My testimony, he said, would make or break me. This time I didn't drop my crutch, but as I made my way to the witness stand, I felt everyone in the room follow my steps, aware that I walked on my own two legs.

Cap'n Hank asked me for a brief explanation of how I received my wound. After a condensed version of the incident, he asked, "Do you expect to regain the use of your leg?"

"Dr. Rabinowicz told me I can expect one-hundred percent recovery," I said. "I will be back with my unit in two or three weeks." An optimistic diagnosis, but possible.

"Dr. Rabinowicz has conferred with you about your recovery?" he asked.

"Yes. In detail."

"He has no plans to amputate your leg?"

"No, sir. None."

"Tell the court about your relationship with Dr. Samuels," Cap'n Hank said.

"I had none," I answered.

"What do you mean? Wasn't he your doctor?"

I recalled our rehearsed answers to the letter. "He refused to talk to me. When I asked him questions, he wouldn't answer them. He kept saying I shouldn't worry, 'they' would take care of me."

"Why did you believe your leg would heal and not need to be amputated?"

I frowned and looked thoughtful. "It's kind of like getting over a bad cold. One day you wake up, and you know you're a lot better and will be well shortly. My leg felt better and better each day. When I could walk on it with crutches, I knew it would heal. Dr. Rabinowicz agreed with me."

"Let me see if I understand. Your doctor would not take the time to talk to you. Your leg had been healing. You were walking on it, and you felt that it would continue to heal. Dr. Rabinowicz told you he expected a complete recovery. You expect to be back with your outfit shortly. Now, you're only using one crutch to get around on that leg? And Dr. Samuels wanted to cut it off it. Is that correct?"

"Yes, sir."

"You told me you would rather spend time in Leavenworth with two legs than spend the rest of your life as a cripple with one leg. Is that correct?"

"Yes. It still is."

Cap'n Hank paused.

"No further questions," he finally said.

The prosecutor's turn came next. After the routine questions to establish where I had been on the day in question, he cut to the chase.

"Did you threaten Dr. Samuels' life?" he asked.

"Not necessarily," I said.

"What do you mean, 'Not necessarily'?" he asked. "Did you, or did you not, tell Dr. Samuels, 'You take my leg off and I'll kill you. I'll kill you if I have to hunt you down for the rest of my life. I'll make it my mission in life to find and kill you if you do.' Did you say that to Dr. Samuels?"

I knew he had done exactly what Cap'n Hank wanted him to do.

"Only if he cut my leg off, which wasn't necessary," I blurted out before he could object.

"Do you think you are better qualified to judge that than a United States Army doctor?" he asked, leaning over the podium and glaring.

As we had rehearsed in the unlikely possibility I would be asked this question, I put my left ankle on my right knee. The pain was so intense I thought I might black out. I managed a weak smile, and the courtroom came back into focus. I had to concentrate on my answers. I wondered how my voice sounded.

"Dr. Rabinowicz thought so. So did I," I said, rubbing my aching leg. My answer took the wind out of his sails. He asked a few more questions, then sat down.

The Court recessed for the panel to deliberate. Then, several hours after lunch, for which I'd had no appetite, we were called back into the courtroom. We watched as the panel filed back in.

"If they're looking down, expect a decision we may not like," Cap'n Hank said. "If they look at you, it should be favorable." They looked at me, and they were frowning. I started to sweat. My leg hurt like hell, and I grabbed another painkiller from the cup on the table. I had just taken two an hour earlier and had that warm, fuzzy feeling, everything muted and soft. Now the courtroom grew dimmer and farther away. I knew someone was talking, but I couldn't be sure who. Even though it seemed important for me to listen, my endurance had been stretched to the limit. The courtroom faded as I slipped into oblivion.

I woke up feeling deliciously numb and pain free. The bed, rather than elevated at the shoulders with the leg-sling, was flat as a Midwest prairie, and I lay on my stomach. I had begun to think I'd never again sleep in that position. CT sat by my bed, reading a magazine.

"Is that all you nurses do around here, read magazines?" I asked.

She smiled. "How'd you like me to palpate your leg?" she asked, smiling maliciously.

"At least I still have it."

"That you do. And you're a free man. But you're a free sergeant, not a free sergeant first-class."

"I guess I passed out. What happened?"

"Yes, you passed out. They announced their verdict and busted you to sergeant. And docked you three month's pay. You must have startled them when they pronounced the verdict and you fell out of your chair into a pile on the floor."

I looked at her sitting there next to my bed. She had a lot of things she could be doing besides sitting here waiting for me to wake up. A lump formed in my throat.

"You have helped me so much," I said. You've given me more..."

"Oh, come on now," she said, self-consciously. "I'm glad you think it helped. Just pass it along to someone else."

I held her eyes for a moment and smiled.

The double doors opened and Cap'n Hank walked in. He looked displeased.

"They dropped the charges?" I asked, my heart in my throat.

"No, they found you not guilty..."

"Yeee-e haw!" I yelled. "Damn, you did it!"

"Not so fast. They found you not guilty of attempted murder and assault on an officer. But they found you guilty of endangerment."

"That's fine with me," I said.

"You've been reduced two grades in rank and will forfeit three month's pay." He frowned apologetically. "I regret that."

"Hey, that's fine, a slap on the wrist. I can live with that."

"Well, if you can, I guess I can. I expected to win this one hands down."

"Hey, Cap, I think you did a really great job. As far as I'm concerned, you won it big time. I thought for sure I'd see prison time and a dishonorable discharge."

"Not with me as your lawyer."

About that time Mike came in. "Jeezus, are you still lyin' around?" he asked. "Lieutenant Jaimeson wants to know when you're coming back."

"Did you tell him about the verdict?"

Mike smiled. "Yeah, I did. And he got really *pissed*. Swore good as a sergeant."

"Oh, great. That's all I need. What's he gonna do, put me on some kind of supply detail?"

Mike looked blank for a few seconds, then laughed. "No, you don't understand! He didn't think you should have been busted. You've already been promoted. You got one stripe back already. He said in three months you'll be back to your old rank, if he has anything to say about it. And he will."

Under the covers I gave my leg a squeeze. A gentle one.

CHAPTER FOURTEEN

Color Guard

Mike had been gone for several days. The brass had determined that if we could find NVA and VC forces in our sector, it would verify the sorry performance of the ARVN. So our team went out looking for Charlie.

Thanks to Dr. Rabinowicz's latest diagnosis of my injury, Lieutenant Colonel Meyerson himself determined my hospital stay would be extended. Cap'n Hank wrangled his way through an incredible stack of paperwork on my behalf, then announced that I would not be reassigned somewhere else. I could imagine where Captain Fowles would have assigned me—file clerking in some recruiting center, or guarding a missile silo in Nebraska.

Dr. Rabinowicz pronounced me healed, and that I would be returned to my unit in two weeks. He allowed me to leave the hospital the next day, but only for the afternoon. I breathed a sigh of relief.

A few of the dens of iniquity adjacent to the base were decent enough to visit and have a drink. Fully intending to disregard the two-beer limit the doc gave me, I set out with three other ambulatory patients I'd met in the hospital.

We were a sorry looking bunch, bandaged and scabby. I wore a bag taped to my leg that still drained my wound. Bob had his left arm in a sling. I met Chris, with a big gauze bandage from the knee down, and an orthopedic shoe. He knew Hal, who had a belly full of some kind of parasites we don't have in the States. Hal couldn't wander too far from a men's room. We told him some beer would be good for him. He agreed. Enthusiastically.

We still needed more medical attention than could be provided in the field. We were all skinny, and had patches of skin raw from infections, insects, and various general abrasions. We had gooey places on our bodies from a variety of ointments. None of us could walk very far, long, or fast. For comfort I wore my faded, patched fatigues. I looked more military than my companions, whose uniforms consisted of mix-and-match pieces of cammo, utilities and khakis, some new, some ragged. Hal wore a blue T-shirt.

We desperately needed to have some fun after all the doctors and needles. Rest and relaxation, the doc's Rx, didn't sound as good as I & I—intoxication and intercourse. The kind of shape we were in, intoxication probably wouldn't take much more than the two-beer limit, and I doubted if any of us had the strength for more than verbal intercourse. We intended to find out.

The shortcut through the parade grounds made it easier for us to get off the base. We saw the color guard, practicing on the wide expanse of grass. We thought that after they went by, we could hobble across without interrupting their routine.

"These guys are good," I said. "They look like a cross between a crack marching unit and a drill team." The men appeared to have been selected by similar height and build. They wore dress greens, and we knew from their campaign ribbons and decorations that they had seen combat.

Hal nodded approvingly. "Jeezus, they move like they're wired together."

Their huge American flag, made of some material that shone like silk in the sun, looked spectacular. The color guard marched up our side of the field. We waited to cross, standing in front of the reviewing stand, where the brass and the VIPs would sit. As the color guard approached, they did an "eyes right." The captain's silver star, an award for bravery in action, gleamed brightly from its bronze background. The division and brigade flags dipped, and, with Old Glory held high, they passed the reviewing stand. Although a bit wobbly, we stood at attention and snapped our right hands up to our brows, saluting the colors. Once past the reviewing stand, the division and brigade flags snapped back into place.

By the time we shambled across to the other side of the field, the color guard had done an about face, and was marching back again. Proud and precise. The American flag gleamed in the sun. I kept trying to swallow the lump in my throat.

Again, we stood at attention as they approached. Our salute was more crisply executed this time. Again, the flags, except Old Glory, dipped at the command of the captain of the guard. He halted, performed an abrupt right face, and stared directly into the eyes of each of us, as if acknowledging that we had been honorably marked by the battlefield. Then, ramrod straight, he returned our salute. After a snappy left face, he marched on. We stood for a few moments, then turned and quietly walked away.

When we got to Woo's Place, Bob helped me negotiate the steps in front of the veranda while Hal hobbled up with Chris's help. Woo wasn't his real name. It must have been too difficult to pronounce, and like the Montagnard we called Jones, he ended up being called Woo. He served as bartender and bouncer. His welcoming smile revealed a wide gap from a missing front tooth. He lost it one night in a fist-fight with Strider. We had further sullied our reputation at this establishment when a fight started with some fly-boys. They fell down a lot and broke some tables and chairs. It took a substantial amount of U. S. currency to restore our welcome.

We sat and drank quietly that afternoon, our thoughts filled with the impromptu honor from the color guard. When the time came to leave, Chris stood and held out his beer bottle. We silently toasted with the plain, brown-glass containers, sealing the experience of the day like a secret handshake.

CHAPTER FIFTEEN

Cap'n Hank's Purple Heart

Finally, Doctor Rabinowicz discharged me from the hospital, and I went back to our digs. Rabinowicz said to knock off the alcohol while I took the last of my meds. I figured that meant that some booze would be good for me, so I headed for The Well.

Kennelley sat at the ammo-case table, writing a report.

I felt the glow of relaxation from two stiff shots of good single-malt Scotch. "Damn," I said, "It's good to be back here. If it hadn't been for Cap'n Hank, I'd be headed for Leavenworth. Mike, you think of any way I could pay him back some?"

Mike pursed his lips. "What's he want more than anything in the world?"

"He wants to be Special Forces. He wants to do the stuff we do. If he only knew."

"Got an idea," Mike said. "We could take him on a 'patrol.' We could use the trails around here to conduct a pseudo-hunt for Charlie. It's relatively safe, but to the uninitiated, it would have the feel of being in mucho peril."

"Stroke of genius! Let's go walk some trails, figure out which ones to use. And make sure there's no sign of Charlie."

We set out the next morning and walked several miles of trails. Nothing but some old sign from re-treads. I hadn't regained my strength, and when we got back, I shucked off my gear and collapsed onto an ammo-case chair. My leg hurt, but not too much, and I was so glad to be back, I didn't care.

"Taking Cap'n Hank on a recon of that little valley is a stroke of genius," I said. "We got any more beer?"

"Yeah," Mike said. He handed me a cold beer.

"Jeezus, this is Coors! Since when did we get some real beer?"

"You ain't the only one who has talents in the trading department," Mike said.

"We do this right, Cap'n Hank is gonna believe he's been on an authentic reconnaissance mission," I said, tipping the can back. "We got any more Coors?"

"Jeezus, you crippled or what? Can't get up and get your own?" Mike asked, throwing me a can of Coors hard enough to make it spew out when I opened it.

Two days later Cap'n Hank arrived on the supply chopper. He was scared, and sat in the center of the cargo bay. But at least the chopper jockeys didn't have to close the doors like they did for Lieutenant Jaimeson.

He jumped out, looking relieved to be on terra firma.

"Hey, Cap!," I hollered. "We got a mission that came up. Five of us are going. We could use a sixth man."

His eyes got big and round. "Oh-h-h, you mean I g-get to come with you?"

"It could be dangerous. You might not want to go," Mike said.

"Oh no! I'm not worried about that!" Cap'n Hank blurted out, desperate not to be left behind. "I want to go!"

"C'mon, then!" Mike said. "Get into your gear. We gotta hurry! Pilot's gonna drop us at the insertion point. Chopper jockeys would do almost anything for a fifth or two of good Scotch.

We got Cap'n Hank outfitted with an M-16, unloaded, an issue Government Model 1911A1 pistol, also unloaded, leather holster on a web belt, magazine pouch, two magazines, two canteens and a canteen cover. Inside the cover were four grenades we had deactivated.

Somewhere Mike had found a Vietnamese Army tiger-stripe camouflage outfit. The diminutive size fit Cap perfectly. We gave him a "war paint" kit,

146

camouflage grease paint in green, black and brown. We all smeared the stuff on each other's faces and hands for the concocted mission.

"Well, Cap, you look damn mean with those tiger-stripes and all that war paint," Mike told him.

"Just keep your head down and your eyes open," Mack said.

We stalked the ghost of Charlie, taking each curve in the trail with an exaggerated concern for what might lurk there. Cap'n Hank managed to do a good job of mimicking our movements and the way we held our M-16s. His eyes were wide and darted from side to side, looking for threats. We took a break half-way through the loop. Cap'n Hank dined on C-rats as though he'd been served a fine delicacy.

Earlier that morning we stashed an AK-47 with a full cotton ammunition belt, complete with oval-shaped Chinese buttons, just off the trail. With some help, he "discovered" it as part of a weapons cache.

On the way back, we did a live-fire drill with M-16s. Cap'n Hank was delighted when he hit two beer cans full of water. The hydrostatic shock ruptured the cans, like minor explosions.

I wondered if we'd pushed it too far when we seated Cap next to the open cargo door for the return to our digs. Cap had been scared to the point of freezing up. By the end of the flight, clinging to a cargo tie-down strap, head out the door, he peered at the green canopy below. He had earned a large measure of respect from the team. He would never fit into an outfit like ours, but as our guys put it, he "had heart." High fucking praise.

Cap'n Hank had spotted JR's American flag flying above our digs on the way back. He sat up straight and pushed out his skinny chest. "Look at that! If that's not a sight for sore eyes," he said. "Even if it is against regs."

Everyone stared. We had become used to the flag that JR had taken the responsibility to raise and retire every day. Cap's comments reminded us how beautiful it was, and what it meant. By now it had some rips and holes from bullets and ordnance, but we wouldn't have traded it for anything. As I watched it unfurl on the breeze, I realized how glad I was to see it.

Cap'n Hank's adrenalin hadn't burned off even after we got back to our digs. He on sat on a case of grenades, holding the AK-47, prepared and ready for more. Cap had the ammo belt draped over one knee. He smiled at Mike. "I sure liked shooting that M-16!"

"He's learned to swear like a sergeant major," said Parkhurst, as our pseudo-mission was celebrated with some beers.

"You mean him?" I asked, watching Cap'n Hank do the blister-foot limp as he returned from the latrine.

"Sergeant, gimme a goddamn can of suds," he growled at Mike.

"Yeah, I see what you mean, Parkhurst," I said, stifling a laugh at Kennelley.

Mike looked at Cap'n Hank for a split second as if he might separate his head from his torso, then smiled, grabbed a beer out of the cooler. "Here you go, Cap," he said.

Mike heard the high-pitched whine first. He dropped his half-full beer and yelled, "Incoming! Jeezus, we got incoming!"

Everyone hit the dirt except Cap'n Hank. Then the first round hit. Mike yanked Cap off the crate where he sat, frozen in owl-eyed fear just as two more rounds whistled in. We scuttled to the doorway of the digs and dove inside. Mike threw Cap'n Hank down the log steps and leaped in after him. One of our Browning .50's drowned out the pop of small-arms fire. As we disentangled ourselves I could see that Cap's Cheshire-cat grin had faded. Pain contorted his face. Gingerly he reached behind him, then extended his hand, red with blood.

"Holy shit! Mack, get over here!" yelled Parkhurst. "Cap's been hit!"

"Oh, no! Lemme see," I said. There were three bright red stains on Cap's back, one high on the right shoulder, one on the left shoulder blade, and one almost in the center of the small of his back. Parkhurst had pushed him back down on the floor, where he lay in the middle of all his equipment. How he managed to hang on to it when Mike tossed him down the steps, I couldn't guess.

"You okay, Cap?" I asked idiotically.

"Give me a little room," Mack said. "Can you move your legs?" he asked. Cap wagged both feet. "Let's take a look." Mack, pulled out his knife with one hand, Cap's shirt tail with the other.

"No!" Cap yelled, "Don't cut my shirt!"

Mack's blade stopped as it touched the tail of Cap's tiger-stripped cammo shirt.

"*What?*" Mack asked.

"Don't you dare cut up my shirt!" Cap ordered. It broke the tension and everyone laughed.

"That's sure as hell a first," Mack said. "Can you move enough to get your arms out of it?" Cap started to unbutton his shirt. As he moved his arm back, he winced and his face went white.

Mack pulled his shirt to the side. Someone slid the sleeve from Cap's other arm and carefully folded the bloodstained shirt. Mack examined the wound at the small of his back. He probed delicately with a small tool from his kit. Cap'n Hank winced but didn't make a sound.

"Sorry...oh, shit! I gotta see where this...oh, good!" he said.

"Jeezus, make up your mind! Is it oh shit, or oh good?" I asked.

Mack looked relieved. "It didn't touch the spine," he said. "Now let's see the others. He's gonna need X-rays to be sure."

Cap's shoulder blade had stopped the second small fragment, the third burying itself in the muscle above his right shoulder blade. Mack reached into his kit for a syringe, plunged it into Cap's arm.

"What's that?" Cap asked.

"Morphine. A good, solid dose. You'll be out until after they remove these fragments. They're gonna start hurting pretty quick. You might not know it, but you're in shock right now."

"I'll miss my chopper ride!" he said.

It got so quiet I could hear everyone breathe.

"Promise me something," Cap'n Hank said, his voice growing softer as the morphine took effect. "Don't let them tear up my tiger stripes. And I want those fragments. This may be the only time in my life... Promise me..."

"You got it, buddy," I said, but he didn't hear me.

Mike and I arrived at the hospital the following afternoon. I'd spent most of the night drinking to ward off a major guilt trip. I only intended to give Cap'n Hank a taste of the real thing, not to end up visiting *him* in the hospital. One thing for sure, I wouldn't let Dr. Samuels practice his hack and chop medicine on my attorney.

Cap'n Hank lay on his stomach. The head of his bed had been slightly elevated, bringing him to eye level when I sat down. Somehow he had talked the nurses into getting him a pair of pajama-type pants. He had two white bandages on his bare back. A splotch of iodine and half a dozen ugly stitches marked the spot on his shoulder blade where the third piece of shrapnel hit. Cap'n Hank's tiger-stripe cammies were hung carefully on wire hangers on an IV rack next to the bed, the back of the shirt facing out so everyone could see the blood stains.

"They got upset when I told them I wanted my .45 here with my cammies," he said.

"I'll bet they did," I said. Might have something to do with a previous incident."

"But look at this!" He held out three jagged pieces of shrapnel. "I'm gonna have three scars!"

"What did the sawbones tell you?" I asked.

"Aw, he said I'd heal up real fast, I'd be right back with my outfit." He looked around to see if anyone could hear. "I didn't tell him I'm with the JAG, so don't let on, okay?"

I glanced at Mike. "Sure, Cap, no problem. You were not with JAG when you were wounded. You were on a Special Forces recon patrol. That's the truth of the matter. "

He looked relieved.

"Ah-h, who is your doc?" I asked with a wicked grin. "Samuels?"

Cap'n Hank made a face. God, no, it's Jacobs. Samuels is on administrative leave. Lieutenant Colonel Meyerson's orders."

"Great. Maybe he'll have time to work on bladder control," I said.

I saw Dr. Rabinowicz several beds down the aisle. When he looked up, he put his hands on his hips and frowned. "If that's what you do to your lawyer after he *wins* your case, it's a good thing for me you're walking okay. You *are* walking okay?"

I laughed. "Yeah, doc, you did a great job. It's still sore, and I overdid it the other day on the mission where Cap, here, saved our asses. But thank God, the leg's still there—and almost healed." I poked a thumb in Cap's direction. "When are you going to kick him outta here?"

Rabinowicz looked at his chart. "Tomorrow, according to Dr. Jacobs."

"Would a little liquid refreshment be in order for him then?"

"I don't know why not." He looked at Cap's stitches. "He's got to watch for infection. Otherwise, it looks good. He's been telling everyone on the ward about your little adventure. People are walking clear around the building so they don't have to come through here."

"Aw, I haven't been that bad," Cap'n Hank said.

Rabinowicz shook his head in mock seriousness. "You guys come back here about two o'clock tomorrow. You can have him."

By three o'clock we were all at Woo's place with Woo behind the bar as usual. Sometimes I wondered why we went to dumps like this, then realized they were all dumps.

"I'm buying," I said, sliding into a booth next to a window long ago painted shut. "What'll it be, Cap?"

"One of everything!"

We proceeded to marinate Cap in mixed drinks, Mike and I having at least three to his one. By the time the rest of the team showed up, we'd almost gotten too drunk for the presentation we planned, Cap almost too drunk to receive it. Regardless, and with great fanfare, we commandeered the band's raised platform. With a flourish and many slurred words, we tried to present Cap with his official adoption certificate. Parkhurst finally took it away from us and read it aloud.

Yea, Verily and Forsooth,
Know Ye All Men By These Presents
(As well as by those of us who may be absent.)
That
Captain Henry Langswell Morton,
Having bled for his country, in the line of duty, and above the call of duty,
Having taken a substantial part in saving the
ass of one of the members of this Team,
And having blown the suds off the top of a quantity

of beers with said group, is Hereby inducted Into
Special Forces A-Team,
India Company (a.k.a. India Ink)
As
Honorary Commander-In-Chief, Legal Affairs
YOU ARE NOW HONORARY S. F.
ACT LIKE IT.
DO NOT EVER FORGET.

Everyone who had gone on the bogus-turned-real mission had signed it first, then the rest of the team signed. Cap didn't know what to say, but before he could get misty-eyed, we voted unanimously that he should buy a round.

We took him back to the bachelor officer's quarters about twelve hours later. Having been drunk, sick, sober, and drunk again, he had started to sober up once more. He got out of the jeep, stumbled, and frowned like he'd forgotten something.

"Hey! I didn't tell you! I'm gonna get a purple heart! I'll bet no one in the whole goddamn JAG's got a purple heart!" He stepped back from the jeep, pulled himself up sort of straight, and saluted.

We returned his salute with all the respect we could muster.

CHAPTER SIXTEEN

Marksmanship

"The POWs still alive?" I asked Thu, one of the Vietnamese Rangers we were teamed up with.

"One has died. The other, having watched *how* he died, has told us much."

"So he's earned a painless death?"

Thu's almost deadpan look conveyed annoyance at what he believed to be interference. He shrugged. "All things are relative," he said.

"And the one I shot in the ass? You are keeping him in good enough shape to travel?"

Thu smiled. "He believes we are keeping him alive so he may see how we interrogate prisoners. The wound to his buttocks is not serious. Tomorrow he should be well enough to find his way back."

We'd captured three NVA after a minor firefight. We tied their hands and marched them back to our camp. The ARVNs missed no opportunity to torture them. They stuck slivers of sharpened and fire hardened bamboo under their skin and into the face of my butt-shot prisoner. Like cuts from a razor, each one drew blood. I wondered if the prisoners would lose so much blood they couldn't walk.

We got back just before dark on the second day. Sleep came in patches that night, unusual, since I could sleep soundly almost anytime. I felt uneasy about what was to come.

Working with these Rangers produced a mix of admiration and disgust. They fought fearlessly and ferociously. But the way they interrogated prisoners had to be the most appalling thing I'd ever witnessed. It made me queasy. They could keep a prisoner alive for days. Usually the second day of non-stop screaming made the prisoner so hoarse his vocal cords could no longer produce sounds.

I saw the corpse from the interrogation they had just finished. All his fingernails and toenails were gone. Large patches of skin had been peeled off until his body looked like it had been skinned. It had blisters on it, and some charred flesh. Obviously, death came as a merciful escape. I shivered at the memory, despite the heat of the day.

We cleaned our arsenal and re-stocked our rucks. That afternoon Thu brought us some rice with vegetables and tiny pieces of meat. I handed Mike a bowlful.

"I don't have much stomach for the way they torture prisoners," I said.

"Yeah," he said, holding a piece of meat between two chop sticks. "I can think of a half-dozen places these little pieces of meat could have come from. This looks a little like skin, doesn't it?"

My stomach churned. "Great. Thanks, Kennelley. Now I can't eat this. We got any C-rats?"

"Let me check our stock of gourmet food," he said. He pulled out two boxes of C-rats. "Aha! Simulated meat!" He looked at the other... "And— simulated meat!"

I opened the can and took a bite. "I never thought anything could make this stuff taste good. Marginally, anyway." When we finished our feast, I mashed the cans flat and tossed them aside.

"You ready to go talk to the Charlie you ass-shot?" Mike asked.

"Talk, or scare the shit out of him?"

"Yes. Let's go find Thu."

Thu was cleaning his rifle. After he reassembled it, he loaded it and chambered a round. I handed him the rice and meat. He shoveled it into his mouth with his fingers.

"You want to talk to him now?" he asked, between mouth-fulls.

I nodded. While I waited for Thu to bring him to us, I wondered how the one NVA that had gotten away reported the deaths of their comrades. They undoubtedly told their superiors we were a full company, not just a small patrol.

Two days ago we located them by the smoke from their cooking fire. Stryder, who was on point, gave us hand signals indicating there were eight of them. Mike flanked them on the right, I took the left. I could hear one of them coming toward me, not making any attempt to be quiet. Nice going, I thought. Thanks for the warning. I stood behind a tree and watched as a sloppy-looking NVA soldier stepped into view. He leaned his rifle against a branch and unbuttoned his pants. Not twelve feet away, facing me, he proceeded to relieve himself. I had him covered with my rifle, and wondered if he would see me.

"Harumph," I said, a moment later. His eyes, unfocused with the pleasure of relieving himself, darted left and right, then straight into the muzzle of my M-16. Realizing he'd left his AK-47 behind him made his eyebrows spell out an 'oh shit' look. As he let go of himself, his stream, which had been aimed on the ground, made a wet mark on his ragged pants. When he reached for the AK-47, I pulled the trigger.

As if on cue, I heard M-16s to my right. Cautiously I advanced, hoping I hadn't gotten in their line of fire. I could hear branches and leaves rustle in front of me. I got a glimpse of another NVA, running down into the valley below the trail. I almost had him in my sights when something yanked my foot and I fell on my face. I'd tripped on a root. By the time I got up and found him again, he had cleared the little stream we'd been following. I watched as he hot-footed it up the far bank. Too far away, I said to myself. Then I decided, why not take a shot at him anyway? Just before he left the clearing, he turned to the right. I added Kentucky windage to my front sight and squeezed the trigger. He fell ass over teakettle. Stryder took off after him, running like he was running a foot race with the devil. The wounded NVA had stopped and crawled a good fifty yards into the brush by the time Stryder caught up with him.

"This one almost got away. Pretty good shot you made!" Stryder said, as he dragged him back. "Want to hand him over to the ARVNs?"

"Naw. Not yet, anyway. They got the other two."

"What'd you have in mind?" Mike asked.

"We'll let him heal up a little, then send him back. I'll tell him I shot him in the ass on purpose, and that all of us shoot that well. He can tell that to his outfit. Stryder, that was a good catch. Never seen anyone run like you do."

For two days we'd fed my prisoner more than he usually ate in a week. His wound had healed enough for him to take a message to his NVA buddies. Nguen, in charge of the so-called interrogation of prisoners, dragged him in front of us and threw him in the dirt at our feet. He looked like a skinny kid—one who would shoot us without hesitation. He lay on his face, hands tied behind his back. He probably expected a bullet in the back of the head. I flipped him over with the toe of my boot.

"Stand up!" I yelled at him. Nguen repeated my words, with equal volume, in Vietnamese. He struggled to his feet.

"You will eat and drink, then return to your unit!" Mike yelled, echoed by Nguen.

I pointed to his hands, and Thu cut his bonds.

"Sit!" I yelled, pointing at the ground in front of me.

Nguen brought him rice and water.

"Eat! I yelled, and when he didn't move, I stepped closer. Stabbing at him with a finger, I shouted, "Eat! You will eat NOW so you will have the strength to give your fucking comrades a message from us!" Nguen repeated what I'd said.

Then Mike stepped up to him so fast he involuntarily moved back. "You want to hurt us? You hurt *one* of us, we'll hurt a *hundred* of you! You hit us with a stick, we'll hit you with a goddamn club!"

Nguen translated.

"You kill *one* of us, we'll kill a *thousand* of you!" I hollered so hard my throat hurt. I picked up my M-16 and walked toward him. Fear contorted his face. "I shot you in the ass and I did it *on purpose*! Tell your comrades *all* of us shoot that well! You come close, we will *kill* you!"

I waited for the translation.

"Now go! Get out of here before I change my mind and kill you!" I motioned for him to move, then poked him with my rifle barrel. He stood, took a few

halting steps, looked over his shoulder. I fired a burst over his head, and in spite of the bullet holes in his ass, he ran like a rabbit. Thu and Nguen joined in, shooting over his head.

"Run you sonofabitch, run!" I said. I hoped Thu and Nguen wouldn't hit him.

We laughed as we watched him run for dear life, first one hand holding his ass, then the other. He got to the tree line and disappeared

"Shot him in the ass on purpose," Kennelley said. "Wow. You walk on water?"

"No, but I don't sink past my ankles."

CHAPTER SEVENTEEN

The Ahn Che Army

One of our searches for Charlie's caches turned up a large amount of medical supplies—basic stuff like bandages, compresses, antiseptics, and a variety of injectable drugs labeled in Vietnamese and in Chinese. We tossed everything into a pile and started to burn it when Mack intervened.

"That's a lot of medical supplies," he said. "It seems a shame to just burn them."

"We can't leave them here," Mike said. "Charlie will just carry them off."

"True." Mack said. "Suppose we take them with us?"

"What are we going to do with them?" I asked.

"Well, if we ever run out of something..." Mack shrugged. "It just seems too bad to destroy all this stuff."

We ended up carrying the medical supplies back with us. I told the team to jettison the meds at the first sign of trouble. No sense trying to carry the weight of something we might never need and getting hurt because of it.

Back at our digs, we stored the supplies in water-tight steel containers and forgot about them. Not for long, though.

The monsoon season blew in with a fury that left everything wet or damp. We still did our routine patrols to make sure Charlie wouldn't use the weather to sneak up on us. Otherwise, we wouldn't have shot at the two Nuns.

The rain was pounding down, limiting our visibility at times to just a few yards. I had lost myself in the misery of our wet, cold patrol. I wasn't paying attention when Tony stopped, held up his hand, pointing up with two fingers. I snapped into danger mode, held up a fist. Everyone melted off the trail.

"What you got?" I whispered.

"Two gooks, about thirty yards, right side," Tony said.

"Still see 'em?"

"Yeah," he said. "Wanna move closer?"

I took a few steps forward. I saw two dark silhouettes move off the trail to my left. I fired a burst from my M-16 into the air. Tony followed suite. The dark shapes dropped to the ground. Tony started to move forward, rifle at the ready.

"Tony! Wait a minute!" He stopped, looked left and right, as if there might be others. "I've seen a lot of 'em drop after being shot. Something's wrong about these two. Make sure they aren't going to roll over with an AK."

Cautiously, we advanced. I prodded one of the soggy, mud-spattered forms with the barrel of my M-16.

"Ayieee!" it screamed. The other one looked up at me as if she'd just seen the devil incarnate.

"Don't shoot!" I yelled, wondering if the only reason I hadn't shot them both was because I had been so startled, or because they didn't appear to have guns. It didn't feel like they were a threat.

We got them on their feet, hands behind their heads, and realized they both wore uniforms. Black uniforms like long dresses with a white kind of a head cover.

"Get Thu up here!" I yelled. "I think we almost killed a couple 'a nuns."

Thu acted as if mortally insulted when we asked him to translate for us. Talking to women, we knew, he found insulting. Talking to two nuns would have been utterly beneath his station in life. Mike took him off to the side and whispered in his ear. When he brought him back, he chattered in Vietnamese with them.

They were nuns from the orphanage at Ahn Che. Two of their sisters had been hurt when a wall collapsed on them. Against orders, they had gone for help.

"Maybe we've found a use for Charlie's meds," Mack said. "I'll go back with them..."

"No way!" I said. "Anything happens to you, we're screwed."

We took the nuns back with us and showed them what we'd taken from Charlie. They cackled excitedly, putting aside various vials and supplies.

"I guess we could load this into a couple of rucksacks," I said.

"Good idea," Mike said.

He returned later, laughing to himself. "With their treasures all loaded, the rucksacks fit them like a full-size coat fits a ten year old. When we took the frames out, the pack by itself barely fit well enough they could carry them."

I knew as we watched them go out past the wire that our curiosity would get the best of us. "You know this isn't the end of it," I told Mike.

"I know. We're gonna have to check on Ahn Che. But how?"

Two days later, we climbed aboard a chopper that happened to make a slight detour en route to our next mission. Eventually we transported all of Charlie's medical supplies to the nuns. Several times Charlie raided the orphanage, once just hours before we arrived.

A Navy Lieutenant was on board our chopper. I raised my eyebrows at Mike. Shorthand for "how the hell did he get here?" Mike shrugged.

"Meet Lieutenant Scott Allerton," said the chopper jockey. This pilot had ferried other medical supplies and materiel we'd traded for to Ahn Che. His vow of secrecy was sealed by good scotch, which was replenished on every trip. "All those souvenirs you been selling to the REMFs?" he said. "Talk to Scott. I'll bet he'd pay a lot more."

We got a three-day pass from Lieutenant Jaimeson and put out the word we needed a ride to Saigon. The next day a chopper landed and we loaded our goodies. A light truck and two ARVN MPs met us when we landed. They unloaded the big canvas bundles we brought into the truck. The chopper's engine started to rev, and I hollered at the pilot to wait, and pulled out two fifths of Chivas Regal from the bundle, holding one behind my back.

"Hey, Allerton," I said to the pilot. "You still drink Chivas Regal?" His eyes got big and his smile got wide.

"I sure do!" he said. I handed him the bottle.

Saunders, his co-pilot, leaned over the collective, head almost stuck clear out the pilot's door. His expression of hopeful optimism could have won an Oscar.

"Saunders, Allison told me you don't drink!"

"You tell him that?" he asked Allerton. "That's bullshit!"

"Oh, then this other bottle must be for you!" Saunders gave the bottle a reverent look.

"You know, Walker, you and Kennelley are a couple of real troublemakers!" Allerton said. "But thanks! Call us if you need a ride!"

"In three days," I hollered. Allison nodded as the chopper took off.

That night we were supposed to meet Lieutenant (jg) Wiedel Fuller, USN, at one of the downtown bars. Either we were early, or he was late. We both had a good buzz on by the time he came through the door.

"Sorry I'm late," he said. He looked like Cary Grant. He must have been six feet, three inches tall, broad shouldered, and had thick, wavy black hair. Several women followed him with their eyes as he came into the room.

"She'd better be good lookin' for you to have kept us waiting so long," Mike said.

He laughed. "Let's go look at the goodies. So I can go get a drink."

We'd parked the truck in the alley next to the building. I walked carefully on the slimy surface, not wanting to fall and find out what made it slick. The ARVN MPs, both carrying M-16s, stepped out of the darkness. At a gesture from Mike, they opened the tailgate. The thick rolls of white canvass almost glowed in the dim light.

"Untie it, please, Huan," Mike said.

Wiedel stared at the assortment of Charlie's tools of war. A dozen AK-47s, four SKSs, a light belt-fed Chinese machine gun and some personal effects lay on the canvas. He shined a small pocket flashlight on them. The other bundle contained more AK-47s.

"Damn, these look good. I bought a couple of AKs a while back that were so rough they must've been here since the French."

"Could have been," I said.

"Pistols?" he asked.

"In the box. One with a holster only. One with holster, belt and ammo pouches. Two more, pistols only. A bunch of ammo belts for the rifles."

"Where the hell did you get this stuff?" Wiedel asked.

"We've been collecting it for a quite a while. Got a project our outfit's working on. Got a problem with any of this stuff?"

"No," he said. He picked up a wallet from the pile of personal effects. A letter written in Vietnamese had been carefully folded and placed in the wallet. I had the odd feeling that it had belonged to some hapless NVA soldier who probably kept it to read over and over until one of our 5.56 mm bullets found its way into his vitals. Wiedel tossed it back in the box.

"I thought about offering you less, but this is good stuff. I'll pay your price."

"And throw in dinner," Kennelley said. "And drinks."

Wiedel smiled. "Sure. Why not? We eat and drink in this place a lot. Food's good as the drinks."

"You want this stuff delivered somewhere?" I asked.

Wiedel turned, gave Huan and Jocko a visual evaluation. "They okay?" he asked, pointing a thumb in their direction. Mike and I bristled.

"They're two of the best ARVN soldiers we've ever found. Lieutenant Jaimeson fought a regular paperwork campaign to have them attached to our group," Mike said.

"You think we'd have them with us if they weren't one hundred per-cent dependable? We'll guarantee delivery," I said, icily.

"Hey, sorry. I just didn't know. Can I send dinner out here for them?"

Our MP's were almost drooling. "That would be nice," Mike said. Wiedel had redeemed himself.

Inside, Wiedel spoke to the maitre 'd and we were whisked off to a booth in a corner where the noise still hammered our eardrums, but a few decibels lower. The American top forty with a Vietnamese accent. After Wiedel bought several rounds of drinks, we ordered dinner.

As the waiter left, Wiedel put his napkin in his lap, pulled a package out of his jacket. Holding it below the table, he wrapped it with his napkin. He laid the bundle on the table and lifted the edge. I could see a fat, thick envelope. Mike slipped it into his shirt and buttoned it up.

"That's what you asked for the goodies. You guys better be careful." He lowered his voice to a whisper. "You got more there than most gooks make in fifty years. So what's this project you're doing?"

"You ever hear of Ahn Che orphanage?" I asked. He shook his head. "It's an orphanage run by Belgian nuns. They take in kids. There's a hospital, too."

"You're kidding!" he said. "You guys are supporting an *orphanage*?"

"Yeah, we are. Partly," Mike said. "That's where most of the money will go."

He gave us a knowing look. "Yeah. Sure. So *most* of it will go there."

"Look, dammit, we pay Huan and Jocko, grease a palm or two for the truck. The rest *all* goes to the nuns. They're always short of something, and Charlie keeps coming and taking their food and medical supplies. They get about ninety per cent of the money. Got it?"

"Shit, I didn't realize you were serious. I just thought you were greedy." He finished his drink, waved at the waiter. "You know, in a way you guys could be supplying Charlie. Or this fucking regime here in the south. Ever think about that? Charlie steals all the stuff they bought for the orphanage with your money, and takes anything else they have. Usually rape a few nuns, kill some of them maybe. Why don't you do something about that?"

"In case you haven't heard, we can't go do anything we want. The army thinks there's a good reason for us to go where they tell us and only if they tell us. We can't decide to be based out of an orphanage," I said. "Anyway, what else could we do?"

"Actually, a lot. You guys get a fair amount of time between missions, right?"

"Sometimes," I said.

"Why don't you take the next batch of AK's and show the nuns how to protect themselves?"

The idea of a bunch of armed nuns running Charlie off made me smile. Mike laughed. "Christ, can you see Sister Claudette marching into the fray with an AK-47 under one arm?"

"That's not all I've got in mind. You wouldn't want to get caught doing this." Wiedel looked around, then leaned over the table. "You ever see the tax collectors make their rounds?"

"I didn't know they had tax collectors," Kennelley said.

"Ever seen those old APCs with an escort? Usually full platoon strength, all of 'em ARVN? The ones that are totally impressed with what bad-asses they are?"

"Yeah, I've seen them," I said. "I didn't know what they were."

"Those guys collect a lot of money. Some currency—Chinese, not much Republic of Vietnam bills, they're too worthless. American. Gold, jewelry, precious stones—anything of value." He looked back and forth from me to Mike.

"You're suggesting we knock off the tax collector?" I said. "You gotta be kidding."

"I wouldn't suggest any such thing. All I'm saying is that these guys would probably run off if attacked. Especially by someone well armed, well trained. After all, who are they going to call for help? And who would believe them if they said the U.S. Army did it?"

We were silent for so long Wiedel must have thought we didn't like the idea. "Well," he said, "I just thought you might..."

I looked at Mike. I knew what he thought by the look on his face. "Hey, knocking off the Vietnamese IRS is... "

"Is the next goddamn thing we ought to do," Mike said. "Hell, yes!" He laughed. In our advanced stage of inebriation, it seemed funny. Hysterically funny. I laughed. Wiedel laughed. Mike slopped his drink all over the table trying to raise the glass for a toast. "Here's to tax collectors. We'll give those kids Christmas and Happy Buddha day...all at once!"

I looked at Wiedel, whose laughter seemed strained, as though he just realized the company he kept had gone mad. "Uh, if you don't mind me asking, how are you going to get away with it?" he asked when we stopped to catch our breaths.

We discussed several plots, all of which had obvious flaws. We decided the best way to accomplish the task was the same way the bad guys in a western movie held up the stage. There would be a few minor differences, though. It would be the good guys who, in the spirit of Robin Hood, relieved the bad guys of their loot. Instead of a stagecoach, it would be an armored personnel carrier. And replace the Sherwood Forest with jungle.

"There's one other thing you might think about," Wiedel said. "If those nuns don't have some way to hang on to what you give them, Charlie or the ARVNs are gonna just take it. Now if you spent some time training a dozen guys to be their security..."

"I am either so drunk I didn't understand you, or you're so drunk you don't realize that's crazier than anything we've talked about yet," I said. "With ARVN conscripting all the men, even teenagers, where would we find 'nuff men for a bodyguard? An orphanage-guard?" My tongue tried hard to make words.

Wiedel shook his head. "I thought you ground-pounders were a little smart. Guess 'snot true." Wiedel's tongue seemed to be deserting him, too.

"So you goddam chipper skippers are so smart, where are they?" Mike had taken exception to Wiedel's comment.

"All over. How many times you seen men, or boys still in their teens, that have been wounded, lost an arm or leg, or an eye, begging on the street? An' they're not as bad as the ones with both legs off, or both legs and eyes. They don't get as much money begging as the really bad off ones do. People don't feel as sorry for them." Wiedel looked like he was about to pass out.

"Hey," I hollered, waving my hand at the waiter. "Coffee. Three cups!"

Wiedel's head had dropped down on his chest. I took a cup of hot, black coffee and waved it under his nose. One eye partly opened. "Ah-h man! I gotta get up. What time is it?" He sipped the coffee, looked around. "Shit. I never been to bed yet."

"C'mon, Wiedel. What the hell good are a bunch of crippled ex-ARVN beggars?" Mike asked.

A light came on, and I understood what Wiedel meant. "You're saying these guys may be disabled, but can still handle an AK-47, or throw a grenade."

"Yes. And not just ARVNs, almost anyone who was a wounded—civilians who were hit with artillery, rockets, small arms fire—whatever. I think a lot of them would be loyal to anyone who would take them in, feed them, give them a place to stay. Provide medical care."

"That sounds pretty simple," I said. "Maybe too simple."

"Jeezus, the Ahn Che Army! You gotta be kidding!" Mike said.

No one spoke for several minutes. Mike and I were thinking about orphanage security, manpower and training. Wiedel broke the silence.

"You might find this strange," he said. "I think I would be interested in a piece of the action at Ahn Che."

"What would make you want to do that?" Mike asked.

"Just between us?"

We nodded.

Wiedel sat up and took a sip of his drink. "I got married once. Don't know if you knew that." He paused long enough for us to shake our heads. "We lived together for two years before I joined the navy. She wanted to get pregnant, and we were having sex all the time. Kitchen table. In the shower. On the couch. Even in bed sometimes. I thought it had been great sex, but when she didn't get pregnant...she laid the blame on me. I went to a doctor, and found out I'll never have kids of my own. But, ha-ha, never told her that. And you two are never going to tell anyone about that, right?"

We both nodded affirmatively.

"I tried to talk her into adoption, but she wouldn't have any part of it. I even did a lot of research into how to do it, where the kids come from, how long it takes. I'd gotten sold on the idea. I wanted kids, too. Didn't appeal to her, though. When I came home on my first leave she told me she was pregnant and wanted a divorce. Some other navy guy. Could'a been worse. Could'a been an army guy. Sorry. Jeezus, I don't believe I'm telling you this."

He twirled his empty glass around in the water ring on the table. We waited until he looked up before saying anything.

"So how do you want to help?" Mike asked.

Wiedel's face broke out in a wicked grin. "You know, I always wanted to be a damn ground-pounder like you guys. Uh, no disrespect. I joined the navy because I couldn't do long hikes. Always wanted to see things close up."

Oh Christ, I thought, another Cap'n Hank, just a bigger version.

"How about a large infusion of cash?" Wiedel said. "Think that'd move things along?"

He stood suddenly, and with only a hint of wobble in his gait, marched out the door.

"What the hell?" Mike said.

"I don't know. But I don't think we've seen the last of him."

CHAPTER EIGHTEEN

The Old Man

Our team had been involved, unsuccessfully, in an effort to train a South Vietnamese Army Unit to do things the U. S. Army way. That had been the plan in 1964—to train their army and to relocate their people to a safe area. The theory was that perhaps we could leave some day. We didn't buy it. The people did not want to be relocated, and the South Vietnamese army did not want to fight. We found the task hopeless. Mike and I asked Lieutenant Jaimeson for another assignment, which prompted him to visit.

"Look, sir, the whole goddamn South Vietnamese Army, especially this captain and his officers, are badly inflating their reports of contact with Charlie. Their body counts always end up way higher than the actual number of kills, and they always report enough captured weapons to arm a regiment. They don't do shit compared to what they report."

He held up a hand. "Look, I know that's happening. It's common knowledge."

Mike and I looked at each other, baffled. "What do you mean it's common knowledge?" Mike asked.

Lieutenant Jaimeson frowned, looked at his boots, then back at Mike. "You're not going to like this," he said. "You know the favoritism the Vietnamese government shows to some of its army units?" We both nodded. "Well, these so-called reports determine how U.S. military aid is passed out. The ones that list the fewest South Vietnamese casualties, the highest body counts and captured weapons, get the most. Of everything. Best report writer wins."

I thought about some of the ARVN officers and the luxuries they had—staff cars, liquor, cigarettes—even hand-tailored uniforms and women to admire them. I wondered how much of the materiel from the U. S. they diverted to the black market.

"Yeah. Maybe we just didn't want our suspicions confirmed. Get us out of this," I said.

"I'll see what I can do," Jaimeson promised.

That afternoon we watched his chopper lift off. "Great," Mike said. "He can just fly off. He must be a damn sight smarter than we are."

"Can't be. He's an officer," Parkhurst quipped.

"Arright, until Jaimeson gets us out of this, we got a job to do. Let's do it," I said. We walked back from the LZ with our morale at an all-time low and our enthusiasm even lower.

The unit we had been stuck with had an ARVN captain for a commander. Parkhurst had nicknamed him 'Roo,' because he looked like the baby kangaroo in the Pooh stories. Captain Roo shouted a lot. Maybe he thought it would increase his physical stature. At the moment we found Roo shouting at a toothless old man, who squatted on the ground in front of him, a helpless pile of skin, bones and ragged clothes. I saw a wet stain spread in the crotch of the old man's pants, then puddle on the ground.

"This doesn't look good," Mike said.

"Ask the Captain what the problem seems to be," I told our ARVN translator. Roo answered in a long and emphatic burst of Vietnamese.

"Captain say old man is Viet Cong. He knows location of stash—weapons and food," our translator said.

I couldn't understand the words, but the old man pled with Roo, then with us. "No VC, no VC," he shrieked again and again. He shook his head and looked alternately from us to Roo, who suddenly cuffed him hard on the ear.

The blow knocked the old man on his side. He dragged his legs up through the mud of his urine into a fetal position and whimpered. Roo yelled again, then kicked him in the ribs. When the kick produced no results, he grabbed the old man by the front of his shirt and hauled him to his feet. When he let him go, the old man quit wailing and slumped into a kneeling position. Roo unleashed a torrent of angry words. The old man didn't move.

I wondered what Roo had told him, why he'd become so quiet. Before I could ask, Roo drew his American made 1911 service pistol. He worked the slide and pressed the muzzle against the old man's head.

Mike and I yelled for him to stop. I reached forward to grab the pistol. Everything skidded into slow motion. I could see my hand move forward as if, intent on its own course of action, it had severed diplomatic relations with my brain. I had made a bad mistake.

Roo looked up, meeting my challenge with all his pride and authority on the line in front of his troops. He glared contemptuously. He raised the muzzle of his American-made pistol. For a moment I thought he would point it at me.

The details of the pistol stood out with amazing clarity. I could see the machining marks on the slide and the front sight. I wondered if, in a split second, I would see it lined up between me and Roo's dark, angry eyes. The parkerized finish had worn away from the muzzle and the trigger guard. Roo's fingers, wrapped around the grip, were the size of a child's. I could see the split fingernail on his trigger finger, which was touching the trigger. My arm returned to my side like a wayward child come home.

He seemed to weigh his options and pointed the pistol back at the old man. Then abruptly, he holstered it. Through our translator I started to remind him about the agreement our governments made about the treatment of civilians, and the correct method of questioning suspected Viet Cong—none of which meant much to Roo. He stood there, feet planted wide, hands on his hips, and gave me and Sergeant Kennelley the most contemptuous look I had seen since basic training.

"You Americans are fools," he yelled. "You know *nothing* about my country, or how these people must be treated! Your methods of interrogation are *useless!* You know nothing about how to *fight!*" His face was turning a deeper shade of red by the word. "You are all *fools!* "

I thought the confrontation had ended with his tirade. Suddenly, as if words could not express his frustration, Roo drew his pistol again, placed it against the old man's head, and pulled the trigger. He stood over the body and glared at us, the .45 huge in his small hand. His men stood behind him, Mike and the rest of the team behind me. I knew that if anyone made a quick move we would have a firefight with the South Vietnamese Army.

Slowly Captain Roo holstered the pistol. He made a crisp, military about-face, and standing erect, his small chest pushed out, strutted off to his car. His lieutenant barked out an order and the ARVNs moved off in the direction of the car. For a few seconds we stood around the old man's body.

"Well, where do we go from here?" Parkhurst asked.

Back in our hooch, we looked to each other for answers. There seemed to be none.

"What the hell are we doing here?" Mike asked. He hurled his helmet against the wall. I caught it on the bounce.

"Lieutenant Jaimeson better be bringing new orders for us," I said. "The whole damn south Vietnamese army has a big incentive not to fight." How the hell, I wondered, when we leave, could they stem the tide of communism that pocked the face of the globe like cancer.

"Maybe we'll go back with the Yards," I said.

That night I dreamed about going home.

CHAPTER NINETEEN

Compassion

True to his word, Lieutenant Jaimeson convinced the brass that we were too valuable to be stuck training soldiers that didn't want to be trained. We were back at our old digs, and had done two recon patrols in the last week.

The good lieutenant sent word he would fly in to meet with us. When his chopper landed, we could see fresh holes where it had taken small arms fire. He jumped out of the cargo bay, stumbled and sank to his knees. I started toward him, but Mike grabbed my shirt sleeve.

"He's scared. Give him a minute to pull himself together."

Medics with two rolled-up stretchers came running. With practiced efficiency they lifted a soldier from the chopper, then the co-pilot. Mack was waiting, and would patch them up before they were flown off to a field hospital.

One good thing about Jaimeson. He didn't pretend to be a front-line officer. He listened to us, then usually stayed home and let us do things our way. As a consequence, he didn't add to our burden in the field, and we got results with very few casualties.

Still kneeling next to the chopper, his chest rose and fell as if he'd been chased. In a way he had—by the phantoms of the chopper ride. He stood, knees wobbly, as we approached. He tried to talk, but couldn't. We each took an arm to steer him off to our jeep.

"Hey, this is his stuff," someone yelled. I turned just in time to see the gunner toss out a duffel bag, then pick up a big cardboard box. Suddenly Jaimeson came to life. He whirled around and strode back to the chopper.

"You drop that box, you'll lose those stripes!" he yelled.

"Arright, arright, Lootennant," the gunner said, gingerly setting the box down. "Just tryin' to help." He turned away.

Jaimeson inspected the contents of the box. "The co-pilot a friend of yours?" he asked. "Yeah," the gunner said. He looked at the toe of his boot. "We been together a long time. 'Bout eight months." He scowled. "What's it to you, anyway?"

"I got something for you." The lieutenant pulled a fifth of Chevis Regal out of the box. "He drink Scotch?"

The gunner nodded, eyes fixed on the bottle. "Will you give him this?" Jaimeson asked, holding it out.

"Yes, sir, I sure will." He took the bottle with the same care as if he'd been handed the Holy Grail.

"You and the pilot can share this one," Jaimeson said, handing up another fifth.

"Wow. Thanks, lieutenant. That's really nice. Sir."

Mike and I looked at each other. If we hadn't seen it, we wouldn't have believed Jaimeson could have that much understanding and compassion. He rose a dozen notches in our estimation.

The next day Jaimeson briefed us, and the morning after that we left our digs on another recon patrol. We reached our objective after three exhausting days, climbing and descending steep, foliage-choked ridges, to a series of digs Charlie built. We verified they were abandoned.

On the way back, I got that uneasy feeling in the pit of my stomach. There were no workers in the paddies from the village ahead. I looked back at Mike and brushed my hand up the back of my neck, a signal that meant my guts, or my intuition, told me something had gone awry—danger lurked ahead. He nodded, repeated the signal for the rest of the team and pointed off the trail.

I overcame my disgust of the stagnant, leech-infested water, and waded across to the trees. From there we had a clear view of the squalid collection of thatched huts that made up the village we had just skirted.

Peering over a fallen tree trunk, I saw North Vietnamese Army soldiers.

Well-equipped professionals. Around forty of them. I knew if they saw us, we'd be fighting for our lives.

Even though I didn't understand the words, I strained to hear their voices. I guessed it was a village meeting, attendance mandatory. The loudest voice seemed to be speaking the most often. No doubt it belonged to the political officer, giving orders, telling the people what they could and could not do. The voice became louder, and I saw a group of soldiers appear around the side of one of the huts, dragging an old man and a young woman.

We watched the old man, probably the head man of the village, fall to his knees. He bent his head forward, clasping his hands as if in prayer. The officer who had been haranguing the villagers drew his pistol and shot him in the back of the head.

Terrified, the woman cried and struggled with her captors. One of the soldiers grabbed her by the hair, pushed her head back, and forced her to her knees. He slapped her face and yelled at her. When she did not respond, he jerked her to her feet, ripped her blouse open, and yanked it off. The C-rats I'd forced down earlier on the trail started to move upward as he stripped her naked and unbuttoned his pants. His fellow soldiers cheered his raw, brutish acts.

I gripped the stock of my M-16 so tightly my hands ached. As soon as the first soldier finished, another soldier slapped the woman, who kicked and struggled to get to her feet, and he, too, raped her. I watched her fight again, earning several more cuffs about her face. Then she lay still. The rest of them followed suit, laughing, kicking and punching her when they finished. Slowly I turned my head. I could see the frown on Kennelley's face. We'd been trapped into witnessing this.

Their surge of lust satisfied, one by one the soldiers left. The woman curled up on the ground and drew up her knees. Wrapping them with her arms, she rocked slowly back and forth.

One of the soldiers had hung back from the others. Now that his comrades had left, I expected him, too, to violate her. He rose from where he squatted against the wall and walked toward her. Her face twisted into a grimace of terror at his approach. He drew a pistol from his belt, and stood holding it at his side. He threw it down and walked away.

As she began to crawl toward it, I had to fight the urge to run and stop her. I could feel the tension from the team, and I said a silent prayer that none of them would try to help, announcing our presence. When she reached the pistol she knelt in the dirt of the village, beaten and bloody. She put the muzzle up to her temple.

I looked away. I heard the shot.

We made our way back to our digs. Everyone was subdued, and no one made the usual small talk.

Lieutenant Jaimeson debriefed us, typed up his report and told us how pleased the brass would be. He neither mentioned the incident with the woman, nor did he notice his praise fell on deaf ears. The three-day passes he gave us we accepted without comment.

After he left, I found Mike, slumped into a chair. He gave me a blank look, then frowned. "You thinkin' what I'm thinkin'?"

"Yeah, I probably am," I said. "What?"

"This last mission was bullshit."

Mike poured us each a slug of Scotch from Jaimeson's cache, tossed his down, and choked. Then I did the same. "God, that stuff's got a bite," I said.

He grinned and poured two more. "Wouldn't be any damn good if it didn't."

"I don't understand what's happening," I said. "These people don't seem to have any sense of purpose. There's no...ah...patriotism. How could it get so bad they'd let that happen to the head man and the girl?"

"Why should they do anything? We didn't want to tangle with those NVAs either.

"Well, hell no. Of course not. There were too many of them. But how'd the whole village get like that?"

Mike shrugged. "Everything is all screwed up," he said. "They tell us to find out what keeps ARVN from extending the boundary of their 'controlled' area. But they know ARVN doesn't control shit, the 'safe' boundaries don't exist. So they're telling us to find out what's keeping imaginary boundaries from being extended when they already know why—they know it's the Viet Cong and the NVA. They sent us on a political mission. A goddam fool's mission. And they *used* us so someone could have a damn report to show some fat-ass colonel. What would have happened if one of us bought it or got shot up? And for absolutely nothing."

"Like that goddam doc who wanted to cut off my leg. Shit, I thought I'd bought a ticket to Leavenworth. I just don't know anymore. This is not the way it's supposed to be. We're supposed to be..." I couldn't find a word for what we were supposed to be. "Important? Valuable? Assets? But no. We're expendable. Just a goddamn commodity. Think we should talk to Jaimeson?"

"What's he know? Nothing. What could he do, anyway?"

"Nothing," I said. "And neither can we. And you know what? The bastards'll do it again. Just wait and see."

"Let's go get drunk. Really drunk."

We got a chopper jockey to take us to Saigon. Mike and I took Lieutenant Jaimeson's case of premium Scotch and made some deliveries to contacts we'd cultivated for materiel at times when Jaimeson's sources failed, then set out to do some serious drinking.

We stopped at Woo's place. I made note of the scars the spinning tires had worn into the steps the night I drove the jeep inside. The dimly lit, cavernous room felt subdued. The platform where we gave Cap'n Hank his award held no trace of hilarity. The place stank. "Plumbing's stopped up again," Mike said.

"Damn green and yellowy paint. Hey, he's painted some of it white," I said. "Woo!" I yelled. "What's with the white paint?" Trahn, one of Woo's sons, came out from behind the bar, wiping his hands on the nondescript gray bar towel he used for just about everything.

"Ah, not painted. Washed," he said, flashing his gap-tooth grin.

"Why washed?" Mike asked.

"French sojer. He bre-e-e-ed on wall. Squirt brudd on wall."

"Okay. Where's Woo?" I asked.

"He not here," Trahn said.

"Well, that explains everything," I said.

We settled into one of the booths and ordered drinks. After a few mixed drinks, I asked for Scotch. It tasted like diesel fuel.

"Trahn!" I yelled, "Don't you have anything better than this rot-gut?"

Trahn apologized profusely. "You pay?"

"Hell, yes. You know damn good and well we pay."

From beneath the bar he produced a bottle of Jim Beam. "That's not scotch, but it's more like it," I said. "Slightly more."

"I know I've had enough to drink to make a jarhead pass out," Mike said, "but I'm not feeling it very much."

"Me neither. Want to go?"

He nodded.

We walked the streets in silence, passing the Jim Beam back and forth.

CHAPTER TWENTY

Taxes Not Exempt

I watched the supply chopper land. We were short of a lot of things. Almost out of ammo. We still had enough of Lieutenant Jaimeson from his last visit.

The pilot came around the side of the chopper with a map. "Hey, you guys know where this is?" He pointed to a place on the map. "Ahn Che. Some sort of hospital."

"Orphanage," Mike said. "It's an orphanage. What the hell do you have for Ahn Che?"

He shrugged. "A couple of crates. Heavy. Looks like ammo. Funny thing, they're for some navy puke. Lieutenant Wiedel Fuller, USN. How'd the navy get way up there?"

"I don't know," I said. I did have a general idea, though. "Wait a few minutes, I think we can take you there."

Mike and I started everyone drawing on the ammo that just came in. "Don't take more than you're supposed to. Be sure you got two hundred rounds over what it takes to fill your magazines," Mike said. We always had to be prepared to leave at a moment's notice.

"Now that's done, do we call the lieutenant?" I asked.

Mike nodded. "I guess it would be truthful, sort of, to say we know of ammo being moved into the area. Probably should check it out."

"Just don't tell him it's one of our choppers its coming in on."

Mike laughed. "That would really confuse him."

A few minutes later he returned. "Lieutenant Jaimeson thinks we better go see what's going on. I told him it might take several days."

"I'll go tell that chopper jockey we're going. Personal delivery for his boxes."

The flight to Ahn Che took about an hour. Parkhurst and Willie accompanied me and Mike. We left Tony in charge.

"We haven't heard from Wiedel for a while. I wonder what he's up to," I said.

The chopper circled Ahn Che, giving us a look at the huts that had sprung up around the old building that housed the kids.

"What the hell?" Mike yelled over the noise of the chopper. "There are armed guards!"

As we considered our options, a figure ran out of the building, waving and motioning us to land. "That look like Wiedel?" I yelled.

Mike nodded and motioned to the pilot to land.

When we got down, Wiedel ran over and pumped our hands up and down. It took four of us to unload each crate. "Ammo?" I asked.

"You want to know?" Wiedel asked. I shook my head. "I hoped I'd see you guys. Didn't know where to find you."

"This has turned into a long, dry flight," I said. "Got something that would wet a parched throat?" I motioned to Willie and Parkhurst to stay with the chopper. Wiedel ushered us into the building. The ancient structure had thick walls and high ceilings. Wiedel's office, spacious as most Vietnamese homes, looked odd with nothing but his cheap metal desk set in the middle of the big room. Wiedel produced a bottle and some glasses. There was about four fingers left.

"How about sending this out to the guys with the chopper?" I asked.

Wiedel stuck his head out the door, then handed out the bottle. "On its way," he said.

"How about telling us what you're doing here?" asked Mike.

"Remember last time we talked? I thought I could find some men who could and would protect this place rather than beg on the streets. I couldn't have been more right. And so far, they've been fiercely loyal. Who wouldn't

178

be if they were taken off the street, given a place to stay, and three squares? We need ammo for training, and to keep Charlie from walking in here and taking anything they want."

"Aren't you afraid of becoming high profile? Won't the NVA send a bigger force than you can handle?" I asked. "And what will happen if the navy finds out?"

"I won't be in the navy for long. And sure, we could be wiped out. But they've made it so far, just a bunch of nuns. Shortly we should have some operating capital. We can buy whatever we need. In 'Nam, everything is for sale."

I thought I knew the source of this capital. "You know, you can only get away with knocking off the tax collector once or twice."

"Oh really?" he said, smiling at me like he knew something I didn't. "To change the subject, I've got a treasure trove of human resources." He pulled back the curtain. "All these guys out here have specialties of some sort. The big guy with his leg off at the knee? Expert at explosives. Got shot in the knee. The little guy? Took a bullet in the chest. They did a crude job of removing his left lung, but his specialty—stealth—doesn't require moving fast. The guy cleaning the rifle? Sharpshooter. And so on. I found a one-armed mechanic who can fix armored personnel carriers. I even found some ex-soldiers who have all their parts. Deserters probably. I don't care. As long as they're loyal." He surveyed the scene like a commanding officer reviewing his troops.

"I'm not sure where this is going. But it's going to take a lot to hurt this place from now on," he said, looking like he was about to burst with pride.

Someone knocked on the door. "Come!" he yelled.

The door opened and an olive-skinned soldier stepped into the room. "Wiedel," he said, "I wanted to remind you we have another load of cargo coming in. If they see the U. S. chopper, they won't land."

I thought I could detect a slight French accent. And I wondered who else would be bringing them ammo. Had to be the ARVNs.

"Maurice, meet Dan and Mike," Wiedel said. "We don't use last names here. Maurice is my second in command. He could run this operation as well as I do. Probably better. Maurice, these two are friends. Friends of the orphanage and personal friends."

Maurice's icy blue eyes cut through everything about me and looked into the core of my being. He gave Mike the same visual assessment, and only then, having decided he approved of us, did he smile. He shook my hand, grabbing it in a vise-like grip. I looked at his hand. He had only three fingers.

"I guess we better get going," I said. "We don't want to interfere with your shipment."

Wiedel walked out to our chopper with us. We made no small talk, no mention of times past. I had no idea how he would separate from the Navy or what he would be doing to finance the orphanage. I didn't want to know. And I certainly couldn't condemn him. He could help a lot of Vietnamese if he survived. I chose not to think what the U.S. Navy would do to him if they found out.

We found our pilot in the kitchen, eating a big stack of pancakes, bacon and eggs. "Guess what?" I told him. "I forgot to bring something for you. There's a bottle of Chivas Regal with your name on it in my digs. Can you take us back now?"

After lift-off we didn't say much. I couldn't decide if I liked what Wiedel was doing. An hour later, we flared out and touched down at our digs. The Chivas Regal we gave the pilot produced the usual wide smile, and the chopper rose into the sky.

That night Mike and I shared the opinion that one way or another, disaster would catch up with Wiedel. If no one knew we had even been there, it would be best. I called Willie and Parkhurst to our digs.

"I think there's going to be trouble for Lieutenant Fuller, maybe for Ahn Che too," I told them. "It would be a good idea not to talk to anyone, not even the rest of the team about it."

"Maybe no one else will find out about it. Maybe there won't be any reason to talk to us," Mike said.

We were wrong. The following week, Lieutenant Jaimeson flew in with two serious looking navy captains who were even more scared of coming here than Jaimeson.

We were in my digs cleaning M-16s and .45 Government Models.

"Wanna bet who they want to talk to, and what about?" Mike asked.

"Nope," I said. "That would be a good way to lose money."

Lieutenant Jaimeson stuck his head in the doorway. "Can I come in?"

"Sure," I told him. "Pull up an ammo crate and sit down."

He looked at my ammo case table with a poncho for a tablecloth, covered with rifle and pistol parts.

"I never got very good at that," he said. "I could get them apart, but never seemed to get them back together."

Easy to believe, I thought. "Ah, nothin' to it after you've done it a million times."

"I, uh, wanted to tell you what's going on, even though I'm not supposed to." He reached into his pocket for his bottle of antacids.

"You ought to get those in rolls, Lieutenant. Pills in a bottle can rattle, giving away your position," I said without thinking.

Lieutenant Jaimeson looked blank. "Huh?" he said.

"Nothing. It's not important," I said. Silly me, I thought. When is he ever going to be out in the field?

"Those captains," he said, "Are from NIS—Naval Investigative Service, or something like that. I've got orders to assist them in any way possible. When you went to Ahn Che to look for any unusual shipments of ammo, your report indicated there were none. That is correct?"

"None that we knew of," Mike said. "Do they know Willie and Parkhurst were with us?"

"I don't think so," the lieutenant said. "And if they don't ask, I'm not going to tell them."

Good idea, I thought. "There's got to be more," I said. "Those two REMFs wouldn't come all this way just for that."

Jaimeson paused for a minute, then got up and looked out the door. "There is more. A lot more. Somehow a Lieutenant Wiedel, a naval officer, had something to do with the Ahn Che orphanage. Three days ago, on a tip from an informant, they found his body about thirty miles south of Ahn Che, dressed in fatigues with no insignia. He had three gunshot wounds to the chest. If not for his dog tags, they couldn't have identified the body."

There's still more, I thought. About tax collectors.

"My throat's a little dry," Jaimeson said. "You don't have...uh...anything, do you?"

Mike got his flask out of his ruck and filled one of the tiny shot glasses. Jaimeson tossed it down, then coughed. Mike refilled the glass.

"Here's the clincher. They found Fuller's body next to a shot-up armored personnel carrier. It belonged to the Vietnamese government's tax collectors. The bodies of almost a full platoon of ARVNs who were escorting the APC were scattered around next to it. The APC had been emptied of everything they collected. "I want you two to tell me if you had anything to do with this, or if you knew about it." He looked back and forth from me to Mike. "I want to know the truth," he said.

Mike spoke first. "Lieutenant, we had no knowledge of this incident. We had drinks with Wiedel before we went on our last bullshit mission, looking for Charlie's old digs so some fat-ass major... well, anyway, it was before then. Wiedel kept telling us *we* should knock off the tax collector."

"And that's the truth," I said.

Jaimeson locked eyes with us both. "Okay, I believe you. I'd better get back. I'm supposed to be looking into some bad ammo. Captain Stevens told me not to talk to you two. Don't let me down."

Lieutenant Jaimeson peeked out of our door, then beat a hasty retreat.

"So it's not okay to lie *to* him, but if necessary, it's okay to lie *for* him," Mike said.

"Sure. He's an officer. So what's so hard to understand about that?" I asked.

Mike poured another small shot and downed it. He handed me the flask and I took a hefty pull on it. We had just started to reassemble our artillery when Jaimeson returned with the two navy captains in tow.

"May we come in?" he asked.

"Door's not locked. Oh—ha-ha, there is no door." Mike said.

The first captain to step into our modest abode banged his head on a low support beam. The second crouched and stepped in. Five men in my tiny room put us about one over capacity. Or considering who they were, about three over capacity.

"Not much of anywhere to sit," I said. "If you'll wait a couple of minutes, we'll have the artillery put back together." We continued to re-assemble our M-16s and 45s. When assembled, we loaded a fresh magazine into each, chambered a round, checked to make sure the safeties were engaged on everything. The 45s, as usual, we stuck in our waistbands.

Our anchor-clanker captain visitors seemed a bit uncomfortable with the idea of hot hand and shoulder artillery. Both seemed to think our M-16s, which were leaning up against the wall, might suddenly go berserk and spray bullets around the room. Their looks also told us that carrying a .45 in the waistband would not be tolerated on their turf. Our looks told them that our turf was a lot more dangerous, and we didn't give a damn about their prissy turf rules.

"Never know when we might need those in a hurry," Mike said. "There's people out there want to kill us." Both captains involuntarily turned toward the door.

We pulled the poncho off the table, which was made of stacked ammo case chairs. We unstacked them and everyone sat. Genius, I thought. Our captains didn't look impressed.

The most irritating of the two began to question us.

"What do you know about the robbery of the tax collector and the shooting of his personnel that occurred about ten days ago?" he asked.

I liked him less and less. "Would you repeat that?" I asked.

He repeated the question word for word, more tersely and emphatically.

"You know, if I understand correctly, Lieutenant Jaimeson agreed to help you with your investigation, and Mike and I agreed voluntarily to help as well. If that's the way you're going to phrase your questions, I think I'll wait until I have a lawyer to answer them. Captain Henry Langswell Morton is our attorney. He works out of the JAG's office." They looked at each other, wondering, I guessed, why two sergeants would be represented by Captain Morton of the JAG.

"All right," Captain Number One said. "Did you know Captain Wiedel Fuller, USN?"

"What do you mean? Is he a..."

"I mean what I said. Quit being evasive."

"Oh, okay. No, I didn't know him. I never had sex with him."

Number one turned quite red.

"Oh-h, so you didn't mean 'know' him the same way the bible means 'to know'? You said you meant what you said."

Before Captain Number One could say anything, Number Two, evidently the senior officer, spoke up. "If we could, let's all take a deep breath. And by the way, I'm Captain Ames, this is Captain Donovan. What we're trying to find out," he said, "is what happened to Lieutenant Wiedel Fuller, and if he had anything to do with robbing the tax collector. You two are not under suspicion. Having told you that, I can't use anything you might say against you, even if I wanted to. Mind if we start over?"

"I don't." I looked at Mike. He shook his head.

"Captain Ames, Captain Donovan, I'm Sergeant Douglas Walker. I pointed to Mike. "This is Sergeant Mike Kennelley." If we were going to get downright chummy, I could play along.

"I think we can ask what we want to real quick, then get out of your hair," Captain Ames said. I liked him more and more.

"Did either of you know anything about the robbery of the tax collector?" He looked at me. I looked him in the eye. "No, sir. I did not."

"Sergeant Kennelley?"

Mike gave him a direct look. "No, sir, I did not."

Since Ames decided to be straight with us, I thought we should tell him about Wiedel's suggestion. I looked at Mike, who nodded almost imperceptibly.

"Sir, there is one more incident I think you should know about. It's the only other direct knowledge we have concerning your tax heist."

"I would appreciate that," Captain Ames said.

"We met Lieutenant Fuller in a bar in Saigon. The three of us tied one on. We mentioned to Lieutenant Fuller that we have given money to the orphanage at Ahn Che. He told us about the tax collector and his APC. He said we should rob it. He'd gotten pretty drunk, and it sounded like complete nonsense. Like why not rob Fort Knox? Is that about all, Mike?"

"It's all I can think of," Mike said. "About Lieutenant Fuller—it sounds like he could have been kidnaped. I don't want to besmirch his reputation, but I haven't seen many men drink as much as he did that night."

Yeah, I thought. Not many. But you're one of them and I'm another.

"I guess that's about it," Ames said. "Captain Donovan, anything further?"

"What bar were you in?" asked Donovan.

"Wow," Mike said. "There's a million bars in Saigon and we've been in about half of them. We usually go to a dozen or so in the course of a night."

Donovan nodded. "Okay. Thank you both."

"Watch your heads on the way out," I said.

"Thanks for your cooperation," Ames said. He shook hands with both of us. Evidently Donovan didn't find a handshake appropriate for someone of his importance.

They ducked through the doorway. A few minutes later I heard their chopper spin up and take off.

"I think we should retire from the souvenir business," Mike said.

"Well, for a while, anyway."

CHAPTER TWENTY ONE

Anne With An "E"

I stepped off the airliner in San Diego. People crowded past, some staring at my uniform as I walked by. The comfort of being home on leave, back in the good ol' U. S. of A., bolstered my near-depleted reserves. I could carry on long enough to do what I had to do, now that I didn't need to worry about someone shooting at me. Herded like cattle, my fellow passengers and I waited for the luggage carousel to cough out our bags. I grabbed mine, then hurried off to find an information booth.

American girls looked like dessert after more than two years in 'Nam. The only Caucasian women we saw there were a few nurses and an occasional reporter. And the uniforms they wore were nothing at all like the clothes the girls in the airport were wearing. On my right I saw a young woman heading for the information booth at the center of the terminal. Her uniform with its short skirt and close fitting blouse proclaimed voluptuous femininity. Her long, fire-red hair cascaded in waves, shimmered over her shoulders, fell halfway to a tiny waist. Below that were dancer's legs. She looked drop-dead gorgeous. She opened the gate at the back of the booth as I stepped up to the front.

When she turned and looked at me, I couldn't move. I had started to lower my bag to the floor before her presence froze me into immobility. The weight strained my arm and broke into my thoughts about how Irish she looked. How beautifully Irish. To my astonishment I realized she looked me up and down much the same way I looked her over. I recovered first.

"Hello," I said, lowering my bag the rest of the way. "I need to find the cargo department." When she didn't say anything, I asked, "Do I pass inspection?" and did a small pirouette. Flustered, she put her papers on the side counter and her creamy Irish skin turned strawberry.

"I'm sorry," she said. "I just... just..."

"It's okay. I'm flattered." I'd been burned brown by the tropical sun, all hard muscles, my weight trimmed down to less than it had been when I graduated from high school. I hoped this redhead liked what she saw.

"How can I help you?" she said without a hint of an Irish accent. That disappointed me a little. Very little.

"I need to find the cargo office." Remembering the purpose of my visit dampened my spirits. "I want to find out when my buddy arrives."

Her brow wrinkled. "He's coming in on a cargo plane?"

"Uh-h, yes. In a coffin. It should arrive soon, if it hasn't already. I want to make sure it's shipped on time and coordinate my flight to Phoenix with it. Her face paled and her forehead wrinkled. I didn't want any phony sympathy. But I didn't want to close my feelings off completely, to be defensive and brusk.

"Did he die in..."

"'Nam," I said. It seemed to take a few moments for her to realize where that was.

"Let me see if I can help you." She asked me some questions, then picked up the phone. No luck. She dialed again, asked more questions. The third time her voice became more emphatic, as though running out of patience. She dropped the phone onto the hook with a small crash, reached up and took an earring from her right ear lobe. Gold with a small ruby. As I took in every detail of her neck and dainty ear, I knew I had something to give to her.

She made one more call, turned and asked, "What's your name?"

"Walker. Sergeant Walker."

"Sergeant Walker," she repeated into the phone, then looking at me out of the corner of her eye, she said, "He's good looking, Sandy. Just take care of him." She hung up the phone, reached for a map of the airport, and put it on the counter. A common focal point, a distraction from our unspoken observations of each other.

"Your friend's remains should have arrived at about nine this morning," she said, showing me how to get to the cargo area. She looked right at me as she spoke—open, friendly. And beautiful.

"Thanks," I said, and bent to pick up my bag.

"I get off at noon," she said. "You could leave your bag here if you want."

I recovered my surprise with a smile. "You know my name, but I don't know yours."

"Anne. With an 'e.'"

"I'll be here, Anne with an 'e .'"

I found the building she showed me on the map. Its location, off the end of one of the runways, was immersed in a jet-fuel smell and the howl of engines. A yellow sign with black letters that said "OFFICE" hung over the door. Alice in Wonderland, I thought, looking at the tiny-looking door set in an acre of metal siding. For all I knew, the door might have been growing as I approached. Or could I be shrinking? My mind switched to Irish Anne, casually pushing back her red hair with a dainty hand, her short, manicured nails, the creamy skin of her neck and throat, a small ear with a gold and ruby earring.

I collided with the door, which broke the spell. I looked down at the knob. Just above it a sign said, "PULL." I rubbed my forehead, hoping it wouldn't turn into a big red lump by noon.

"Is Sandy here?" I asked the man behind the desk.

"She just left. You Sergeant Walker?" I nodded and handed him my papers. "So you're going to accompany the casket to Sky Harbor Airport?" he asked. I wanted to tell him no, I would accompany the body to the V. A. Cemetery. I nodded, feeling a little tight in the throat.

"Let's go see," he said.

He led me out the back door of the office, and I stopped dead in my tracks. "My God—," I choked out. A row of gleaming aluminum coffins stacked two and three deep lined the back of the cavernous building.

"These are all...?" I almost asked if they were all servicemen killed in action, even though I knew they were. My escort, not realizing I'd stopped, had gone on half-way down the stack of metal boxes, which seemed to stretch on forever. I tried to keep my mind from picturing the contents. I turned and

188

walked back to the office and dropped into a chair. I leaned my head in my hands. A few minutes later the clerk reappeared with my papers.

"Oh, there you are," he said. "Your flight is a charter. There are only two... ah...remains. Arrival time is 3:00 this afternoon. Umm....480-376, that's the last six numbers, is yours." He held the sheaf of papers out to me, pointing at a long number. "Someone you knew?" he asked.

"Yeah. Something like that," I said. It took a second or two for the world to stabilize when I got to my feet. "Thanks."

When I returned to the concourse, I stopped at a bar and asked for a shot. Almost ten hundred hours, I had two hours to kill. I didn't want to be drunk when I met Anne, but I needed something to wash away the gleaming, silver caskets. I ordered another shot. The barmaid smiled at me as she poured. I tossed it down, then walked around the airport. What did I think could come of it, meeting Anne for lunch? A beautiful woman. Someone like that had to have a boyfriend. Or a husband. Maybe I felt attracted to her because I hadn't talked with an American woman since Sarah and I split up. Maybe just because of her beauty.

I thought about the ring. It was for Sarah, or so I thought when I bought it from a jeweler in Saigon, an old man and his wife who looked older than Methuselah's parents. Tiny Chinese dragons encircled the gold ring. The intricate detail captivated me. As they chased themselves around and around, their ruby eyes sparkled. Then I got the Dear John letter. The ring hadn't been for Sarah after all. Maybe it was for Anne.

At ten minutes before noon, I sauntered over to the lobby and sat where I could see Anne's information booth. I watched her as she gave directions to a young couple, then wrote something on a clipboard. When she put it down, she looked around the lobby until she saw me. She waved. When a girl dressed in a the same kind of uniform arrived, I headed for the booth.

"Hi," I said, bringing a flush to Anne's face. She opened the gate and stepped out. "My bag?" I asked. She dragged it out from under the counter.

I followed her across the lobby, not having any idea of our destination. A number of fast food places appeared. I hoped she had something better in mind. She walked past them, turned toward a sign that said "Smuggler's Inn."

The decor matched the name—dimly lit, and the high backs of the booths provided privacy.

The hostess led us to a booth. Anne scooted all the way across, then smiled. I took the cue and slipped in next to her. She picked up a menu, turned a page and set it down.

"I don't usually do this. Actually, I don't ever do this." She said the words as though she simply stated a fact.

"I don't want to make you uncomfortable," I said. We don't have to..."

"No," she said, looking at me with clear eyes, "I don't feel uncomfortable. Do you?"

I laughed. "Yes and no. I usually have three feet and four thumbs when I'm around a beautiful woman. Other than that, I'm not uncomfortable."

"Tell me then, before the cocktail waitress shows up. How are we going to handle this?" she asked.

"I'll be flying out in three hours. I haven't been home for almost two years." I leaned forward and looked closely at her. She wore very little makeup, and, like her hair, her long eyelashes had a reddish tinge. No mascara. "I would consider it an honor if I you would allow me to buy your lunch."

She looked back at me, a hint of a smile.

"If you do, no salesman will call and I won't ask for your address, so you won't even get junk mail from me." I hoped I sounded clever.

She smiled, her teeth even and white. Her eyes lost their contemplative look, replaced by that home-town, cover girl beauty. If only I didn't have to go back.

She made a mock salute. "Very well, Sergeant Walker. I would be pleased to allow you to buy my lunch. Does that mean drinks, too? Because I warn you, I have fully inherited that trait of my ancestors." She smiled. "I can drink most men under the table."

"I just got paid, several months worth. Lots of hazardous duty pay. Soak it up if you want, but I'd feel bad if you tried to drive home and..." I shrugged.

"Don't worry. I don't always try to drink my dates under the table. Just one other thing. Do I have to call you Sergeant Walker?"

I laughed. "Please don't. How about Doug, for Douglas? Anne with an 'e' and Doug for Douglas."

The cocktail waitress stopped at our booth. "Drinks?" she asked with a smile.

Anne ordered a margarita, I asked for Singleton's, which they had. "Neat, please."

"Can I see your IDs?" Damn, I thought, feeling my face turn red. I handed her my military ID, thinking she'd forget to look at my date of birth. She frowned and handed it back.

Anne looked shocked. "You're not twenty-one?" she whispered. I shook my head. "I'd like to change my mind," she told the cocktail waitress. "Bring me a Singleton's with a beer chaser."

The waitress looked doubtful. "Well..." she said. "Okay. It's slow." Then she smiled. "I guess if you're old enough to be in the army, you're old enough to drink." She leaned closer. "Just don't let me get caught."

We made small talk through the first round. We ordered lunch and another round. I looked at my watch. Thirty-five minutes of my three hours had gone. I enjoyed Anne's company immensely. It felt so good to be next to a clean, soft, beautiful woman, it almost hurt. It had only been a couple of years by the calender, but seemed like decades by what I'd been through.

When our steaks came, she ate with a hearty appetite, so I felt free to assuage my own. When the dishes had been removed, I winked. She ordered another round of drinks.

After a trip to the ladies' room, Anne slipped closer to me where I had put my arm on the back of the booth.

"I wanted to ask you more about your trip," she said, "But there's a kind of a guard you put up when you told me about it. Would you rather I didn't ask?"

Her words dissolved the armor I had carefully built around my feelings. I looked away. The thought that tomorrow I would have to tell Shirley how JR died put a lump the size of Texas in my throat. I gulped half my drink. "I...no. Please. I don't want to talk about it right now."

"I'm sorry," she said. She took my hand. Her fingers were warm, her grip firm. "Something hurts. I can tell." She looked at me with such concern I felt self-conscious.

I told her about some of our activities, what we were doing, where we'd been. I talked about the beauty of the country, the monsoon, the food. "But that's enough of that," I said. "How about you? You must have a boyfriend or..."

"A husband?"

I shrugged.

"No, neither one. My boyfriend told me I was 'too strong' for him—whatever that means."

I thought I understood. She was not a wilting violet. I found that attractive, along with many other things about her, enough to set off my hurry-up-and-detach alarm. The woman I loved left me. Friends got killed. My heart beat fast, and I wondered if she noticed.

"I guess I'm not submissive enough. Somehow I threaten men," she said, staring blankly. She pulled her hand away and reached for her drink. When she didn't return it to mine, I reached for it.

"I don't find you too strong. He must have been a wimp. So...is there someone in your life now?"

"Not any more." She looked up. "There must be someone special to you, though."

"Same situation. Know what a Dear John letter is? I'm not even going to see her before I go back to Nam. We were going to be married."

She nodded. "I was married. I'd just turned sixteen. Then he decided he liked to hit me. I got divorced when I turned seventeen."

I frowned, imagining ugly bruises on her magnificent skin. I took her hand in both of mine. "I'm sorry," I said.

"I didn't stay with him. I was pregnant. When I got a divorce, my mother and father disowned me, kicked me out. I got my aunt to let me stay with her. Got a job, a GED, and I'm putting myself through college. Accounting and office management. It's slow, but I'll make it."

The determination in her voice touched me. "You know, you're someone who is really brave. And there won't be anyone to give you a citation or a medal. But I think you're going to be a great success," I said. "You've got what it takes." I squeezed her hand. She squeezed back.

"Don't they ever want to see their grandchild?"

She looked strained. "I...had an abortion." She sat still, watching me closely. Watching for disapproval, I thought.

I shrugged. "That decision, rightfully, was yours to make."

"You must not be a Catholic. My parents are. More Catholic than the Pope."

"I'm not sure what I am. I'm learning to be less judgmental, I hope."

"Good," she said, sounding surprised. "You have a gentleness about you. It's easier to see the side of you that's a fighter. That part scares me a little."

I looked away, uncomfortable having someone see through my shield. I glanced at my watch. My time had gone. I wanted to stay, to take her in my arms, to be held by her. Since I would be leaving, I could admit that much to myself, let my guard down a little.

She looked at her watch. "I'll show you a short-cut through the airport," she said. I left enough to cover our bill and leave a twenty dollar tip. After all, the waitress had put her job on the line for us.

In every major airport in the world, there are plain, unmarked doors, usually with a keypad above the knob. Their anonymity always incited my curiosity. We stopped at one of them, and Anne punched numbers into the keypad. The door swung open. We descended into a room so long I couldn't see the other end. A labyrinth of conveyor belts moved an infinite variety of bags and parcels. Out of chaos came ranks and columns as luggage carts delivered new recruits of marching luggage.

"Wow," I said, wondering who dreamed up this nightmare.

"I'd go nuts working here," she said.

We followed a well-defined, painted walkway across the restricted area she'd told me to avoid earlier. A small train of baggage cars whizzed by. She caught my hand and pulled me back. The Irish beauty saved the warrior.

We stood under the sign outside the office. As I dropped my bag, she stood on her tip-toes, put her arms around my neck. Our lips met and she held herself tight against me. I pulled her close and kissed her again, until we had to come up for air. We held each other, filling needs we didn't realize were there as other feelings came out of hiding and made demands.

I felt her pull away suddenly. "Ouch!" she cried, bending down, rubbing her leg. "I got a cramp!"

"Sit on my bag," I said, and knelt next to her. I intended to rub the cramp, then realized more touching would tantalize both of us with something we couldn't have.

"Let's get you on the plane," she said. "I'll be okay."

The woman behind the desk took my papers. She raised her eyebrows. "We had you paged, Sergeant Walker, but you never answered. The flight with your...ah...the body...has been postponed until ten tomorrow morning. They contract for this kind of cargo and as long as they get it there..."

I stared at her, not thinking about the flight. Uh, that's okay," I told her. "I'll be back tomorrow."

When I turned back, Anne looked pale.

"I didn't know," I said.

She nodded.

"I'll find a hotel tonight."

"No!" she said, then opened her purse. Producing a small compact she dabbed at her face. "I'll drive you. I want to," she said, as I started to protest. Snapping the compact closed, she led us back on the path between the yellow lines, moving so quickly I almost had to run to keep up with her.

When we pulled onto the interstate, she drove aggressively.

"We're quite a ways from the airport," I said after a while. "Is there a hotel in this direction?"

Her foot eased off the accelerator and her grip on the wheel relaxed. "No. Not that I know of." She glanced at me, then back at the road. "Would you stay with me tonight?" she asked.

I nodded. "Yes." I cleared my throat. "I'd like that very much."

We parked the car in a covered, numbered space at her apartment complex. "What will your neighbors think if a guy hauls his luggage into your apartment and leaves in the morning?" I asked.

"They'll probably think I slept with him," she said with a smile.

The sparsely furnished apartment almost felt too clean. I wiped my feet conscientiously before stepping onto the off-white rug. "Put your bag down anywhere. I'll be right back." She flitted into the kitchen like a bird, then popped back out. "Do you like lasagna? It's homemade."

"Actually, yes, I do, but we had a big lunch."

"I'll put it out to thaw. It's almost 4:30, you know." I hadn't been watching the time.

"Wonderful," I said. She smiled and I listened to kitchen sounds. I heard the clink of glasses and the pop of a cork. She reappeared long enough to kick off her shoes and run like a leggy colt down the hallway. "Be right back."

I sat on one of the two stuffed chairs that constituted the major furnishings of the living room, and unlaced my boots. A pile of pillows surrounded a gas fireplace. In the kitchen, a small table and two chairs sat alone in the breakfast nook. I could imagine her sitting opposite the empty chair. Homemade lasagna for one.

"It's not much, but it's all mine," she said. I turned around and gasped at the contrast the emerald-colored robe made with her hair and skin. My reaction pleased her. She had expected it, and posing provocatively against the doorway, she enjoyed it. Not nearly as much as I did.

"I'll give you the rest of the tour." She took my hand and led me down the hallway. "This is the bathroom." The big, fluffy towels that women like were hanging from the racks with accompanying hand towels and face cloths. "And...this is the bedroom."

She stood with her back to the wall. I turned and moved toward her. I could see her uncertainty. I held out my hand.

"Let's go talk about things," I said. I led her out into the living room. "We can sit in front of the fireplace."

She laughed and reached for the switch. "It's electric. There's no heat, just a light that flickers. You don't need a fireplace in San Diego. Oh, I forgot the wine. Be right back."

I tossed half a dozen pillows in front of the fireplace. She handed me the bottle, which I scrutinized as if I had any idea what we were about to drink. "A good year," I said, filling our glasses. "We'll pretend it's snowing outside."

"Tell me about other women you've been with," she said.

Of all the things she might want, I didn't expect that at all. My entire sexual experience had been with Sarah and a couple of other one-night stands. "You are far more beautiful than any of them." I put my hand against her cheek and kissed her lips.

She stared at me for a moment. "You really mean that, don't you?" Two tears rolled down her cheeks. Fearless before the fangs of battle, a woman's tears turned me to Jell-O. And worse, I could see that she realized it.

"Oh, it's okay! That just sounded so—so sweet!" she said, as two more tears rolled down the same path. She put her hands on the sides of my face and kissed me gently, then harder. She pulled back, then fell into my arms. Holding my arms around her, feeling her snuggle inside my embrace felt more comforting than anything I could remember. We sat there for hours, months, years, or at least until she had to move.

"My foot's gone to sleep," she said.

This time I gently massaged her foot and her leg, not worried about fueling the flames of passion. Even if it poured gasoline on them.

"You have dainty feet," I told her, eliciting a giggle.

We settled back on the pillows, curled up facing each other.

"Why are you coming home with your friend's body?" she asked. "Was he special to you?"

I took a deep breath. "Yes. He was special."

"You don't have to tell me," she said.

"It's hard for most people to understand how a group of soldiers can be so close they will do anything for each other, even if it means they could get killed doing it. Sometimes guys will promise they will do something without hesitation if it is meaningful to a comrade." I sat up straight, took her in my arms.

"JR was a good soldier. And he had one quality in particular that endeared him to everyone. He reminded us of home. There were a thousand things he did and said that brought home—the USA—to our minds, and even to our physical setting. When he got up in the morning, he would hold the photo of his wife, and smile. He had an unshakable optimism that we would be okay. His positive attitude sometimes was irritating, but over time, it was welcome. He never got hardened to what we did, somehow maintaining his better nature. And that rubbed off on us all.

"He got a big American flag—JR's flag, we called it—and raised it every morning and retired it every evening. That meant a lot to even the most cynical guys in our outfit.

"One night JR came looking for me. I always knew when a man had something on his mind and wanted to talk about it. After a few shots of scotch, JR got quiet.

"'Sarge,' he said, 'I want you to do something for me.' I told him I'd do anything he asked. He sat for a while, trying to swallow the lump in his throat. 'Something's gonna happen,' he said. I knew he meant he would be killed or wounded. A lot of guys had premonitions. 'I'd rest a lot easier if you promised me you'd take me home. Talk to Shirley.' She was his wife.

"You got it," I said. "I'll get some leave—"

"'I'd like Shirley to have our flag,' he interrupted. 'Will you do that?'

"I told him I would move heaven and earth if necessary to bring him and the flag home. Two days later he was killed."

"I'm sorry," she said. "I shouldn't have asked."

"It's okay," I said. "I've got to talk to his wife. This kind of helps me get my thoughts collected." The electric fireplace must have been smoking. My eyes were watering.

"You asked me about other women," I said, trying to change the subject.

She looked at the electric fire. "I don't really know what men like women to do."

"I know what some men like, but men like different things. So do women."

"What do you like?" she asked. She moved over next to me and pushed me back on the cushions. Her tongue probed my mouth. I could feel her smooth, even teeth, her firmness through her robe. I had become hard as granite, my need all the more urgent because of her willingness. A fleeting panic raced through me. It had been a long time.

I sat up, gathered her into my arms, and carried her into the bedroom.

When I slipped between the sheets with her, she held out her arms. I pulled her close, took one breast in my hand, kissed her neck. The passion went out of her. She started to cry. Icy shafts of fear shot through my insides. I found myself going soft, wondering how I could have caused this. I turned on my back. She turned on her side, facing away, still crying. I lay next to her, wishing I could find some way of comforting her. I turned and started to rub her back. "It's okay," I said. She flinched and pulled away. I needed to be held, comforted, so badly myself, I had little left to give. After a while I slept.

Still half asleep, I smelled the scent of her hair, her soap, felt her breath on my chest. I realized we were in each other's arms. This time she didn't cry. The silk of her hair and skin, pressed full against my body, gave me the first escape I'd had in months. For a few hours, the war, my grim reality with JR, vanished like a bad dream.

In the dark before morning, I pushed myself up on one elbow and watched her as she slept. Her soft hair with all its curls had been tossed around her head, over her face, as she slept. Perhaps she felt my gaze, for she blinked, then opened her eyes. Her eyelashes were just as long, just as red as in the airport. No mascara.

She pushed her hair from her face, rubbed her eyes with her fists, like a child.

"Good morning," she said, then yawned and stretched. The curves and peaks of her silky nightie were delicious reminders of what it concealed. I marveled at her first-thing-in-the-morning freshness, gentle and delicately feminine.

"Don't go away," she said, and with her hair bouncing over her shoulders, she ran into the bathroom and back.

Slowly, as if suddenly timid, she made her way across the bed. She laid her head on my chest and put her arm around me. We made love for a long time, slowly, gently, touching backs and legs, buttocks and breasts, graduating to the most sensitive places, until quivering, she drew me into her. Satiated, we slept again.

I awakened before the alarm went off. Anne raised her head and smiled, gave me a kiss.

She cooked breakfast and we sat at the kitchen table, making bacon and eggs disappear.

"We need to go soon," she said.

Then I remembered the ring. "I have something for you." I rummaged through my bag. "I bought this for you, I just didn't know at the time it was for you." I handed her the box.

"For me?" She opened it, and the warmth of her smile filled me. "It's beautiful," she said, turning it around and around. "There's so much detail and the dragons are tiny, perfect. It will go with my ruby earrings." She slipped it on the ring finger of her left hand and smiled. "It fits."

"I watched you sweep back your hair yesterday, then you took off one of your earrings. That's when I felt certain the ring belonged to you. It's very old. The dragons represent continuity. But I need a favor in return."

"Oh," she said, suddenly looking serious, "What is it you want?"

"Say a little prayer for me...once in a while."

The cargo liner looked just like a passenger jet from the outside, but inside there were no seats, just bulkheads and cargo nets, boxes, and two gleaming caskets.

"Now that you know he's aboard, you'd better get to your flight or he's going to get there without you," Anne said. She had pulled some strings, got me on a passenger flight for Phoenix.

"Wait here," she said, and talked to the flight attendants at the gate. "You're going to be the first one on," she said when she came back.

"What did you tell them?"

"I said you were bringing a soldier's body home for burial. Your friend. And you'd been wounded. So you're first on."

We stood at the gate, just another couple holding hands, looking longingly at each other. They called my name. I walked down the ramp to the plane without looking back.

CHAPTER TWENTY TWO

JR's Flag

Shirley Johnson could not have been over five feet tall, one of those tiny, well-proportioned women. With her short and curly blond hair, she looked like Sandra Dee. She stood at the gate, looking at the other servicemen, trying to recognize me from a photo. I recognized her from the picture JR carried in his wallet. I waved and she walked toward me.

"Sergeant Walker?" she asked.

"Yes. Mrs. Johnson?"

"No," she said, smiling, "Mrs. Johnson is JR's mother. I'm Shirley."

I smiled back. "Hi. I'm Doug." I felt awkward as we stood looking at each other.

I picked up my bag and we began a round of questions with airport personnel, trying to find where the plane carrying JR's coffin would land. We found out that arrangements had been made with one of the local mortuaries to pick up the casket and take it to the VA Cemetery.

"I made reservations for you at the Airport Hilton," she said. "I hope you don't mind. The house is so crowded with JR's parents and mine and the kids."

"No, that's fine. Actually, I'm exhausted. I didn't get much rest last night," I said, relishing the remembrance. "I'll sleep until it's time to go."

Shirley drove in silence, the bench seat as far forward as it would go so she could reach the pedals. My knees were jammed into the glove compartment.

When we pulled into the Hilton, she parked in the lot, rather than pulling up to the door. She got out of the car and followed me to the registration desk. "Would you like to meet me in the lounge for a drink?" I asked.

She looked through the door of the lounge and made a little nervous gesture with her hand. "Oh, you know how noisy those places can be," she said.

"Uh, well...I should get cleaned up a little," I said, starting up the stairs. Shirley followed me into my room and stood looking out the window. I got out a cotton shirt and jeans, put them on the counter in the bathroom.

"I'll be right out." When I came back she hadn't moved. Her eyes were red, her face blotched.

"I didn't want to break down and cry in the lounge."

"I'm sorry. That's my fault. I should have realized...I'm not too good at these things." Jeezus, I thought, Walker, you got solid bone between your ears.

She reached up and patted my shoulder. "You're doing fine. I'm so glad you're here."

I pulled out one of the chairs for her and sat down across the small table.

"I'd like a drink. You?" She nodded.

I called room service, asked for some of the little bottles that almost made one drink.

"Would you like to hear some stories about JR? About the things we've done?"

She nodded.

I wondered where to start.

"JR had a lot of qualities that made him a great soldier. He had an extra dose of bravery. We knew we could count on him, and he always went the extra mile. We went on missions that took us away, almost out of contact, for weeks sometimes. We had to watch out for each other to survive. JR seemed to know what everyone went through, and how to help them. He would have made a fine sergeant."

This isn't going well, I thought. She looked bereft, and tears still spilled down her cheeks. My mind raced to find a lighter story. "One time we let the Montagnards serve JR dog meat. We ate it all the time when we were with them. The Yards, as we called them, considered dog to be a delicacy. But JR wouldn't touch it. One night we let him think they'd cooked a small goat. He said it tasted good. The next day we told him what he'd eaten. He got sick and threw up. He stayed mad for a long time. Then someone told one of our chopper jockeys about it. Everyone laughed, even JR, and we knew he'd gotten over it."

Her tears, unabated, rolled down her face, threatening to soak her tissue. I went into the bathroom, yanked the top off of the tissue dispenser and set the box on the table. Her grief unnerved me. I thought maybe if I kept on talking, she wouldn't cry so much. Maybe she felt that if she could keep on listening, she would feel better. I was out of my element. Way out.

"He always shared the goodies you sent him. The whole team knows what a good cook you are. He could have sold those cookies for twenty dollars apiece. They were something from home. And they were delicious. Those care packages meant a lot. To all of us."

She sighed. "I'm glad you enjoyed them. Sometimes I almost went crazy without him. When I baked cookies, I knew I was touching something he would touch. I felt better doing it."

"JR was a good man," I said. "God, I'll miss him."

We sat there, lost in our thoughts.

"The VA said I couldn't use his flag to drape the coffin," she said. "They told me it might not be the right size, and they stressed the importance of having a crisp, clean flag."

I felt shocked and suddenly very angry, insulted, and a few other things. "I want to meet the guy who told you that. I'll give him some advice that he *will* listen to."

"I told them I'd go to the newspapers and TV stations if they wouldn't let me do it. Then they decided size and clean crisp-ness might not be so important."

I opened my bag and took out JR's flag. It had been properly folded and wrapped in a piece of a poncho, tied with parachute cord.

"This is JR's flag," I said. Gently I untied the cord. "It flew over our digs. It got stained and torn from..." I shrugged. "From bullets and shrapnel I guess. Before I left, we washed it as best we could." I handed it to her.

"JR raised that flag every morning," I said, "then retired and folded it every evening. He loved that flag, and it boosted our morale unbelievably, especially when we came home and saw it above our digs, unfurled on the breeze. One time a mortar round knocked the flagpole down. JR took off out of the safety of our digs at a dead run. Bullets and shrapnel came down thick as rain around him. He grabbed the flag, pole and all, and dragged it back to the stairway. Still half exposed to enemy fire, he unhooked the flag, and stumbled inside with it, unscathed."

Shirley reached for a tissue and wiped her eyes. "I want another one," she said, as she twisted the lid off of a second small bottle of Jim Beam. I would have paid a hundred dollars for a shot of good single-malt, but I settled for the same. I tossed it back, and it reminded me why I was partial to good Scotch.

"A few days later we put up a new pole. JR had just returned, and the first thing he did was to raise the colors. They'd been in a firefight, and his shirt had a big rip on one sleeve. His uniform was mud-encrusted from toes to chest. Even the two bandoliers of ammo he still wore were caked with mud.

"After he raised the flag, he stood back and looked up. He shoved his helmet back, chin strap dangling, and watched the flag unfurl. He put his hands on his hips and started laughing, dancing that little jig he always did when he felt pleased with himself. Then, turning to the tree line, he made a one-finger salute, and yelled, 'Fuck you, Charlie!' We all laughed."

My throat felt dry. The Jim Beam still looked like the best of the selection. I poured one more into my glass. I needed more fortification to be able to tell her how it happened.

"Anyway, we were at new digs on a ridge that overlooked the trail—the Ho Chi Minh Trail— when it happened. We weren't really well situated, and we relied heavily on one of the firebases for artillery support. That afternoon Charlie tried to breach our perimeter. We opened up on them with the 50s and M-60s."

"Fifties and sixties?" she asked.

"Machine guns," I explained. "They tried two or three times to get through. We held them back, but we took a lot of mortar rounds, and they managed to knock out one of our 50s."

I looked over at Shirley, as she sat on the edge of one of the chairs, holding the flag against her breast. She took a breath. "Were you there when it happened...did you see?"

I nodded, eyes on my boots.

"How...?"

I took a deep breath, swallowed the lump in my throat. I reached for one of the tissues as I felt my eyes sting, then overflow.

"It was crazy. After all the stuff we did—being shot at, booby traps, the diseases, all the mortars, rockets—neither of us had been badly hurt. Several times other guys got shot up, or picked up shrapnel. I'd let my shield down and allowed JR to become my friend. It's so hard to get close to someone and then..."

I wiped my eyes again. My voice wasn't working very well.

"We went out the day after we put up the new flagpole, a one-day recon, looking for the outfit that shelled us, checking traffic on the trail. We were actually in pretty good spirits when we got back. Some of the Montagnard women had cooked something with rice—we usually didn't ask about the source of the meat. Afterwards we collapsed for a couple of hours and it started raining. We had a bottle of good Scotch and were about to settle down to a poker game. JR hadn't shown up yet, so I went to get him. I climbed up the stairwell and poked my head out. Through the rain, I saw JR coming across the compound, about thirty yards away. I started to say something cute, like maybe he wanted me to have his share of the booze."

I gulped the last of my drink. "Charlie launched a single mortar round at us. No one heard it coming in, because of the rain, I guess. JR had a smile on his face and raised one hand with some letters. From you, as it turned out. He read your letters until they fell apart at the folds. Out of nowhere, there came a bright flash and a big bang. It threw him about twenty feet. It blew me back down the stairwell. I ran out into the compound where he fell. When I got to him...I knew he was gone."

She stared out the window. I looked at the floor for a while.

"How did you know?" she asked.

I could see JR's mutilated body now as clearly as the day it happened.

"I knelt beside him and felt his neck for a pulse. He had gone on." So much for not lying, I thought, but she should never know how badly it mutilated him.

"I just can't... It just doesn't seem..." She picked up JR's flag and held it to her. More tears slid down her cheeks and dripped onto the flag. JR shed his blood for that flag. The tears of this innocent would now anoint it with love for her fallen warrior.

"I can't believe I'll never see him again." She held JR's flag tighter, touched ter cheek to it, as if she could feel him there. An anguished moan rose up from inside her, sounding much like a wounded soldier. But her wound would take a long time to heal, if it ever did. As much as I wanted to, I couldn't ease her grief, except to be there. I, too, had lost someone I loved. JR died, and I came through almost three years alive and whole. In some crazy way it seemed unfair.

I took her hand, and she squeezed so hard it hurt my fingers. She became still, her breathing slowed. When I stood up, she opened her eyes. I looked down at her, makeup streaked, eyes red. The wife of my dead friend.

"He wrote a lot about you," she said. "He liked you, liked the way you ran the team."

I tried to smile. I knew my voice would fail.

"He wrote me that they weren't sending enough men and supplies. Is that true?"

"We thought the war would be over a lot sooner if they sent more person-nel and materiel. Once they didn't send us the magazines we ordered for our M-16s. They said they didn't have any, and we ran out."

She looked puzzled. "I know the M-16 is a rifle. Magazines?"

"A magazine holds the ammo, the bullets. It goes in the bottom of the rifle and..."

"Oh, you stick it up inside and slap the bottom? Like in the movies?"

I laughed. "Yes. Not much in the movies is real, but that is. Sometimes the magazines would get lost or damaged. We traded, sight unseen, for a 'box' of them. A 'big box,' the supply sergeant told us. It turned out to be a connex box, a huge steel shipping container, with some 5,000 magazines."

"That must have kept you for a while." She looked thoughtful, then frowned. "You ran out of them? How can they send you there without giving you what you need?" she asked, incredulous. "Damn them to hell!" This brought on a fresh round of tears, as though pinch-penny supply had something to do with JR's death.

Abruptly her tears stopped. "I need to freshen up," she said, and still holding JR's flag, went into the bathroom. A few minutes later the door opened. Her face still had some red blotches, but she looked more composed.

"Can I unfold this?" she asked, holding out JR's flag. "I'd like to see it."

"Sure," I said. "I'll help you."

Carefully she spread out the flag on the bed, tugged the edges until it lay flat. "It's all wrinkled," she said. "I'll iron it. And mend it. I want his flag on his casket. I've already told them that. They aren't too happy about it but I don't give a *damn* what they want. JR would like it."

I looked down at the flag and thought about what this particular flag meant to me. I would never forget the sight of those stars and stripes flying above our digs as we came back to our place of relative safety. The rips and tears it endured from shrapnel and bullets. How it had always been the embodiment of what we fought for, and for each other. I knew JR felt the same as I did. Undoubtedly he would want the flag, this particular flag, to grace his coffin.

I showed her how to fold the flag. She wrapped it in the piece of poncho and tied it with the parachute cord. She set her purse on the bed by the flag and faced me. "I thought my tears were already cried out. Talking to you has brought me a...kind of understanding." She stood on her tiptoes, and I bent down to receive her embrace. I sensed her fragility. At the same time, her strength. She was a survivor.

The next day I rose early and ate at the coffee shop in the hotel. I didn't fit into this "normal" life. No one acted scared and I didn't see a single person carrying a rifle. Could I ever fit back into my old life, I wondered. I finished my breakfast and went back to my room. I tried to iron my uniform with the travel iron I'd bought.

Too often the same thoughts plagued me. Why did JR have to die? Why did some guys come home without arms and legs? Did it make any sense at all?

I ironed a wrinkle out in the leg, only to find out I'd ironed one in on the other side. Then I made a double crease trying to iron that out. Frustrated, I flung the iron across the room, making a dent in the window sill. I spit-shined my dress shoes and donned my uniform. The shoes, when I laced them up, felt foreign to feet that had worn nothing but boots for over two years. Finally I stood back and looked at the finished product in the mirror. I decided I looked good. Maybe a little wild-eyed, but good nevertheless.

I went to the bar, ordered a double shot on the rocks. No one asked me for ID. The ice cubes were the ones that had the holes through them. I fished one out and crushed it between my thumb and forefinger. Smashing something felt good. Crushing the second one sent pieces of ice down the bar. A middle-aged business type turned and frowned at me. I stared back, hard. He looked away, drained his glass, and left.

The bartender with his white towel wiped his way to my end of the bar. "You havin' kind of a hard time, man," he said, scrubbing studiously, not looking at me. I bristled. He filled my glass with the light amber-colored scotch whiskey. "On me. Compliments to the uniform." Only then did he look at me. I didn't know whether to punch him for his sympathy or shake his hand. He was just trying to be nice, I realized. Maybe he's a vet. Why did I always have to attack?

"Thanks," I said. "Sorry. I'm kind of edgy. I came home with the body of a friend."

"Someone you fought with?" he asked, still watching the white towel making circles on the bar.

"Yeah," I said.

The motion of the towel ceased, and he looked up at me. "I'm really sorry, man," he said, and went back to wiping the bar.

I tossed back half the shot, and the familiar glow soothed me. I began to relax. I was about to order another when someone called my name. I grabbed my bag, waved at the bartender. Then on second thought, I turned and faced him, executed my best, crisp salute. "Thank you," I said.

The drive to the cemetery didn't take long. We pulled through ornamental iron gates painted white. The headstones were at ground level, stitching the manicured grass with neat rows of white squares. It struck me as incongruous, this treeless oasis, the white headstones set in artificial green turf, surrounded by brown.

The driver pulled up where a casket rested, poised over a hole. Spread over the casket I saw JR's flag, mended and ironed. I sat on one of the folding chairs under the awning. It would be hot, probably over one hundred degrees. With the humidity so much lower than 'Nam, I felt comfortable.

The honor guard arrived and took their stations. A few minutes later the small parade of dark sedans with shaded windows converged on the canopy. The driver assisted Shirley from the limo. She wore a black veil. Somberly, the family formed under the canopy. Shirley saw me sitting in the back row and motioned to me to sit next to her. She held out her black-gloved hand and clasped mine, tightly.

A man wearing a cleric's collar stepped forward. "This is Sergeant Walker, Father Harding," she said. I stood and smiled stiffly at the stranger who stared at my uniform. "He was with JR when...at the end," she said.

Father Harding seemed to be at a loss for words, which seemed odd for someone in his line of work.

Shirley introduced me to her in-laws. "Doug, this is JR's mom and dad." The Johnsons didn't look at all like JR. His father didn't have JR's height. His mom, also short, had coarse features. Mr. Johnson looked me up and down while Mrs. Johnson stared.

"Your son was a fine soldier and a good friend. I'll miss him," I said, holding out my hand. Immediately Mrs. Johnson burst into tears. "I'm sorry, very sorry," I added hastily.

Mr. Johnson led her to a chair. The look of loss on his face hurt so much I had to tun away.

Shirley introduced the other couple, who were quietly watching. "Doug, this is John and Elsie Sommers, JR's aunt and uncle. Elsie is Mrs. Johnson's sister. They named JR for John." They both stared, and I found myself at a loss for words.

Then John offered his hand. "Nice to meet you," he said. I made the landing at Normandy." A wordless understanding passed between us. "You home now?" he asked.

I shook my head. "No, sir. I have to go back."

"May God watch over you," he said.

"Thank you." I liked the man.

Father Harding's message about life and death seemed so foreign to me that I quit listening. Shirley shifted her weight several times, giving me the impression that she, too, found it lacking. I stared at the coffin, closed tightly, locking in the horror that it contained so little of JR's body—all we could find. I'd been told they put sand in a casket to make up the missing weight when not much of the body could be found. It must be different than the sand in this desert burial ground, I thought, absently.

Each time the honor guard fired, Shirley flinched. The last volley faded and the bugler rose to play Taps. The honor guard moved to the casket and lifted JR's flag. As they folded it, there seemed to be an unusual air of concern that this simple ceremony be performed perfectly, beyond its usual precision. Silence followed that last, drawn out note, poignant, beautiful, as it faded to a terrible finality. The Sergeant of the Honor Guard presented the flag to Shirley.

As the gleaming box bearing the remains of JR was lowered into the ground, the tightness in my throat grew. Shirley moved forward and picked up a handful of the sandy soil. Holding her hand over the coffin, she opened her fingers. A small, metallic sound echoed up from the grave as it dropped on the coffin. I watched her square her shoulders and stand straight, then sobs shook her.

I rose from my chair and went to her. As her knees buckled I caught her and held her as she cried.

The small crowd dispersed. Some of them expressed their condolences. Some knew their words were futile, and some, relieved that their obligation had ended, left quickly. JR's dad led his wife to the car. She was still weeping.

"I would like it if you'd come to the house," Shirley said, lifting her veil. She took my hands. "Please."

I squeezed her hands and closed my eyes. I thought of Sarah, who had found someone else, of Anne, who I'd probably never see again, of Dan, gone with JR, both to a better place. Loneliness crashed in on me, all the nights wrapped in a poncho trying to keep out the rain, trying to keep warm, or lying on top of it, hoping it would be at least a little deterrent to the insect kingdom below. Struggling with the final loss of JR. Trying to make sense of it all.

Right now my resolve to return, to serve my country and finish the job I couldn't define, was wearing thin. I was no quitter, but I had to find myself.

" I can't, Shirley, I just can't. I'm sorry. I'll miss him." I gestured at the open grave. "Write to me sometime. There's never enough letters."

CHAPTER TWENTY THREE

You Did Ask

The old Mercedes limousine rolled to a stop on a nondescript back street somewhere in Saigon. Its headlights cast shadows through barred gates set in thick walls. They swung inward. Our car pulled into the walled courtyard, and I heard the gates close with a clang. If anything happens, no one will know where to look for us, I thought.

An Oriental with a chest like a steel drum joined the driver to escort me and Mike from the courtyard and through a heavy door. I noted the bulge of muscles under his coat as he stopped at the end of a dimly lit hallway, and stood aside. Blinded for a moment by the lights, I stepped into a room with a low, semi-circular couch on one side. Throw pillows lay in a heap on a Persian rug in front of it, and beyond, the sheen of the hardwood floor ended at the folds of a blood-red, velvet curtain. A delicate incense tinged the air. Mike, squinting, stood next to me.

"There are drinks on the table, please help yourselves," said the Oriental muscle-man. Neither of us moved. "Be seated. Please," he said, his voice carrying little accent. As I sat, I pressed my arm against the .45 Colt Government Model tucked into my waistband. I'd need an equalizer if I had to disagree with him.

"Mike, I don't like this. We don't know who's back there. Let's just get the hell out of here."

"They haven't frisked us," Mike said. "That's a good sign."

"True. Wonder how they knew who we are."

Mike shrugged. "You can buy anything..."

"Yeah, yeah, I know—in 'Nam."

After enough time had passed to show us the importance of our unknown host, he made a center-stage entrance through the curtain.

Moving to the end of the couch, he seated himself. From a tray on the table he selected a tiny cup and poured tea from a diminutive pot. "Thank you for waiting. I will show you the merchandise now," he said. As he turned back to the curtain, a young girl emerged. She stood about five-feet tall and wore the traditional *aodai* and sandals. She walked toward us, hands clasped, eyes on the floor. She sat gracefully on a cushion, her legs tucked up under her. What appeared to be her carbon copy followed her into the room, and sat on a cushion next to her.

Our host handed one of the girls a newspaper and she began to read in Vietnamese.

"French," he said. She spoke rapidly, and although I couldn't speak French, she sounded fluent. "English," he said, after a few paragraphs. She did not speak English as fluently, but she would be able to function in an English-speaking environment. He waved his hand at the other, who also read in Vietnamese, French, then English. The old man motioned with his hand and they moved to the couch and sat next to us. Both had almond-shaped, dark eyes and black hair with blue highlights that sparked like electric current. The girls' complexions were flawless, lighter than my own sun-browned skin. The effort they made to sit very straight, looking down at their hands, enhanced their exquisite femininity. Both looked fragile and bore a frightened look, like maidens in a fairy tale who had been left as a sacrifice to monsters.

American soldier monsters. Us.

Mike looked at our host, who smiled condescendingly.

"You may have them for four thousand American dollars," he said.

I rounded a curve in the trail, and there was Charlie. He had an old French 9mm submachine gun and raised it up to fire a burst. I heard Mike's cut-down 12-gauge go off behind me, and as I dropped flat on the trail, he fired it again.

I took stock of my body, which seemed to be functional and complete. Charlie lay on his face. Mike still held the shotgun on him, in case he came back to life. I reached down to turn him over. The full loads of #4 buck had caught him from an angle, one in the belly, the other at the base of the ribs. The broken ribs, stark white and spattered with blood, stuck out at an angle. As I turned him over, most of the contents of his body cavity slid out on the ground with a slosh.

Just for a moment I saw an image I'd seen through my rifle scope on one of our missions, a red cloud of exploding head. This one also had white fragments of bone, washed in red. The image from my memory, along with the smell of fresh blood and entrails, turned my stomach. I lurched to one side and puked until I got the dry heaves.

I tried to get down a few swallows of water, which brought the heaves back and the water up. I crouched there, miserable, helmet on the ground, holding my head between my knees. I could feel something happening to me, and when I looked up, the leaves, branches, trickles of water on the trail, all stood out strangely, like images from a 3-d movie. The colors were deep, bright, phosphorescent. Everything appeared distant and far away, like looking through the wrong end of a telescope. Unsure what had happened, I reached out and touched a vine. My fingers unexpectedly reached it and closed around it, although it looked yards away. I closed my eyes, and when I opened them again, everything looked normal.

"You okay?" Mike asked.

"Yeah. I think I'm just tired. Maybe hallucinating." I frowned.

"What?" Mike asked.

"I don't know. Premonition. Something happening."

We had been busy that season with a number of missions. We roped down from helicopters, usually at night. We did two low-altitude, low-opening jumps, LALOs, barely able to get our 'chutes open before we hit the ground. We set up ambushes, chased Charlie up hill and down dale, and booby-trapped his trails. Sometimes we got chased. So far, we'd always won the game. But lately we'd had too many close calls.

"Y'know, we've gotten sloppy," Mike said. "Maybe we need to tighten it up."

"That's what I'm saying. We're burned out, exhausted, and we've become careless."

I pointed to Charlie's gutted carcass. "Case in point," I said.

"That's what I mean," Mike said. "That was too close."

"We could take some of our accumulated leave. We must have six weeks."

We asked Lieutenant Jaimeson for a week off. In the maze of Saigon back streets, we'd found and frequented a few small bars. One of them had dancers who were well endowed and reasonably attractive. Tonight, the only dancer was old for someone in her line of work. Sixteen-going-on-fifty. She started to do a strip-tease, dancing, if it could be called that, on a low platform. She gyrated and shook her hips, thrusting out her small breasts, making eyes at the customers.

"Some turn on," I said.

"Yeah, like a bucket of cold water," Mike said.

A well-dressed Vietnamese army officer saw Mike watching as she removed her top. "Hey, sojer," he said, "You wan' fuckee-fuckee? She num-bah one fuck, stay all night, ten dolla!"

Mike dismissed him with a cool stare and turned away. "Let's get the hell outta here," he said, downing the rest of his beer. "We might as well get our own girls."

"Yeah, right. Wouldn't that be great," I said. I tipped up my half-full bottle and chugged the rest of it.

Mike and I had never engaged the services of a prostitute, though some of the high-class Vietnamese call girls were stunning. In training, we had seen the standard films showing the results of different venereal diseases and had been given the standard warnings, with the standard results—neither of us were impressed. It was the horror stories we heard from other soldiers that left us with no desire to slake our male-hormone thirst. And Mack, our medic, scared us with vivid tales of debilitating diseases, like the "black sif" that did not respond to penicillin.

We had been invited to a party thrown by some of the chopper jockeys. They'd hired some prostitutes, and when they tried to get Mike to take his turn, he gave them a disparaging look. "Hot, sweaty meat flapping together isn't enough," he said. "There's gotta be more to it than that."

On past occasions I'd been rather vocal about my own distaste for using prostitutes. No one suggested that I take my turn, nor did anyone question my reasons.

Mike had gotten a Dear John letter about a month ago from Lynne, his fiancee. It came as no surprise. He was relieved, he said. I didn't buy it. When Sarah broke up with me, I felt like I'd been ripped out by the roots.

We left the party early and walked along the streets, headed for Sergeant Mays' house, where we could crash.

"No sense being in a hurry," I said. "There won't be anyone to greet us, no one to hold, no one to care."

"Yeah. Bummer," Mike said.

The next morning we relaxed in Sergeant Mays' hot tub. Mays, our wizard of a supply sergeant, got materiel for us that no one else could find. We traded him for equally unavailable hard liquor that Lieutenant Jaimeson miraculously managed to send from our base in Thailand.

Still tired, I lay down for a nap. I tossed and turned, unable to fall asleep. Mike's disdain last night for the emptiness of "hot, sweaty meat" made me think about the depth of the feelings I had for Sarah the summer after our junior year. Feelings I thought she also had for me.

I'd bought a huge Navajo turquoise ring the day before school started, and gave it to her to wear on a chain around her neck. She accepted. We were officially going steady.

"I love you, and I love this ring," she said, admiring the stone. We had been dating for eight months, almost a record for high-school relationships, and we could still talk and kiss for hours.

"My parents are gone this week," she said, setting me off on an instant sexual fantasy. We hadn't "gone all the way," although our back seat petting included almost everything else. Sarah always let me know we would not "go all the way."

After the Saturday night dance, Dan and Marty dropped me and Sarah at her parents' house. "I'll be right back," she said, as soon as we were inside. A fire had been laid in the fireplace and a round box of long matches lay on the hearth. I took one and lit the fire, grabbed some cushions and sat on the floor.

A few minutes later Sara returned and sat on the floor next to me. When I took her in my arms, I realized she had taken off her bra.

We sat on the pillows and kissed. She relaxed into my arms, and I felt content—for the moment—just to hold her.

After we stared into the flames for a while, Sarah got up, took my hand in hers, and led me to her bedroom. She unbuttoned my shirt and tossed it on a chair, pulled my T-shirt over my head and put her arms around my waist. She sat on the bed and kissed my belly as she rubbed her hands up and down my back. "I like touching your bare skin," she said, as she unbuttoned my jeans.

The feel of her firm breasts and smooth skin felt sensual beyond anything I'd known. I pulled back, wanting to see her, then felt her take my erection in both hands. Skyrockets.

She closed her eyes, moved my hand between her legs and let out a little sigh as I touched her. When I eased myself on top of her, she moved her hips against me, then guided me inside and I pushed myself down, as deep as I could. Exquisite fire. Initiation. Satisfaction and heartache. Opening of a door that would never close.

Less than a year after I left for Nam, I got a letter from Sarah, telling me she'd found someone else.

Mike and I were making the rounds the night after the offer of the pimp in uniform. We watched the same skinny dancer try to persuade the patrons they should use her body. I felt completely bored, and wondered why we had taken more than a weekend pass. About that time an Americanized Vietnamese came through the door, looked around, and walked directly toward us. He stood over six feet tall. Muscular. Dark hair close cropped, wearing slacks, a shirt open at the neck. Loafers with the little leather window with a coin. A bright penny.

"Good evening Sergeant Kennelley and Sergeant Walker." He flashed us a smile full of ivories. "I am Chou Myet," he said. "May I sit down?" He answered his own question by pulling out a chair and joining us.

"Do we know you?" Mike asked, a sharp edge in his voice.

The Vietnamese smiled. "I am here to offer you what you asked for last night," he replied.

Mike and I looked at each other. "We didn't ask for anything," Mike said.

"And that doesn't answer the question. Who the hell *are* you?" I added.

Touching his fingertips together, Chou leaned forward. "Ah, but you did ask for something. You," he looked at Mike, "You expressed a desire for your own girls."

"I hardly meant that I wanted a whore," Mike said. He frowned and looked at me out of the corner of his eyes.

"And you, Sergeant Walker, expressed the opinion that it would be great." He frowned. "I understand what you wish to purchase. I have two excellent young girls."

"Wait a minute. Do I understand what you're saying?" I asked. "You think we want to *buy* two girls, and somehow you have two girls that you can *sell* to us?"

"Exactly. Except it is my employer who has the girls. It is he who is willing to sell them to you."

We looked at each other. I almost laughed, but to my surprise Mike looked interested. I could feel my stomach tighten up. I wouldn't buy a girl, not under any circumstances, I told myself.

"So who is this employer of yours?" Mike asked. "Where is he?"

"He thought you might wish to speak to him. He is waiting outside." He stood. "Would you follow me, please?"

Mike shot me a look that said, "Why not?" He started out the door.

Reluctantly, I followed. I wouldn't let him go alone. Outside, parked at the curb, an old Mercedes limousine reflected the night lights. Made in the forties, it looked like it had just been driven off the showroom floor. Leaning against the rear of the car stood a bodyguard built like a wedge. Next to the driver's door, another slab of muscle. Chou rapped on the glass and the back door opened. He stepped back and motioned for us to enter the vehicle. At the same time, the two giants got into the front seat.

I looked at Mike and frowned. He shrugged and stepped into the car, sat on one of the jump seats that reminded me of a Chicago taxi. I hesitated for a moment, then stepped in behind him. The door slammed, and the car pulled smoothly into the street. We were committed, at least to inspect the merchandise. I turned in the narrow seat, bringing my pistol into a more accessible position.

"Good evening, gentlemen," said a voice with a crisp British accent. The other occupant of the back seat, an old Vietnamese, was dressed in what I guessed to be a traditional Mandarin costume. Both hands were perched on the carved ivory head of a black ebony cane.

"I believe you are interested in making a purchase?" he asked.

"Maybe," Mike said.

"Maybe not," I said, hoping Mike would back off.

"Do you like my car?" he asked. "It belonged to my father." He caressed the soft leather seat with a wrinkled hand. "I will tell you about the girls. They are twins, sixteen years old. Unplucked flowers, sheltered from the realities of life. They know nothing of the way of the streets. Not yet."

I shook my head, thinking of the dancer at the bar and rolled my eyes at Mike. The old man saw my gesture. His eyes burned through me, smoldering. "It is well known that my word is good," he said, emphatically, "about anything for which it is given."

The scent of incense filled the room. I wondered what was behind the red velvet curtain. The old man sipped his tea, pleased with the impression the girls had made on us. He watched me eye them, as if he knew I wanted to caress their smooth skin, explore the hidden curves under the *aodais*. Perhaps the callousness we had taken on to survive made the idea of buying two human beings seem less preposterous. But this is the twentieth century, I thought. It's not possible to just *buy* someone. Not even in 'Nam.

"I have some questions," I said.

"I will be happy to answer them," the old man said.

"Why do you want to sell them?" I asked. "I mean, to us, for this price?"

He skirted the issue, talked about several different things, eventually telling us we would lose the war. "I am in the process of liquidating certain assets that I do not feel I can take with me to the North," he finally told us. "They will win. Those who are well established in the North will have—shall we say, certain advantages? And those who would come North afterwards will not be as welcome." He laughed at our discomfort. "Do not worry. You will fight for a number of years and lose many lives first."

We both bristled, and the old man shrugged. "Do not misunderstand. I do not say it is good or bad. Just inevitable." He smiled.

"So the girls are some of the 'assets' you are liquidating?" I asked, not mollified. The old man nodded.

"Where are their families? What's their background? Where did they learn to read, and why are you so anxious to get rid of them? Why can't you take them North?" Mike asked.

We were used to briefings that gave us the big picture, all the facts, point blank. The Oriental way took twice the patience of Job. With many allusions and tangential forays, he told us the girls had become a political liability.

"They are half Vietnamese, half French," he said. "You have heard about how political adversaries from time to time disappear or are found murdered? It is not uncommon. Their parents suffered the same fate almost six years ago. There is no family that will take them in—except as prostitutes or slaves. No one to come looking for them. Though they had Catholic parents, they have been raised Buddhist, but not strictly. As you have seen, they have been taught to read and write. This makes them still less than desirable for most of my customers. And there is the question of their ages. If they were younger, their minds could be molded, or they could learn the ways of the street." He paused and looked at both of us. "They can still be sold into prostitution. If so, they will not live very long. To survive, a prostitute must be tough, worldly wise. These two have lived protected lives like the fragile flowers they are." He shrugged. "There are not many like them, but unfortunately their usefulness is—limited," he said, waving his hand as if to dismiss the consequences of selling them.

I found it unthinkable that these girls should end up with the hard features of the dancer in the bar, the barely-hidden wrinkles, and after a few miserable years, suffering the ravages of venereal diseases, die untreated in a Saigon back alley. I looked one more time at the two girls. A voice inside my head, or my heart, had started a persuasive argument that they needed us to protect them.

CHAPTER TWENTY FOUR

Our Girls

"How much did you say?" I heard Mike ask.

"You may purchase both girls for four thousand American dollars. That is my price for these two perfect pearls," our host said.

Shocked back to reality, I picked up my drink, gulped it down, and said politely, "Thank you. I'm sorry we can't do business. Will you take us back now?" I stood. To my consternation, Mike sat there, looking at the girl sitting on the low couch next to him. He looked like a high-school kid with a case of puppy love. I groaned.

"Hey, buddy, let's talk," I said.

"I will return shortly," our host said. "If you wish to further examine the merchandise..."

I grabbed Mike's arm and pulled him up from the couch, stepping over the pillows toward the curtain where I hoped our whispers would not be overheard.

"What are you going to do if you buy a girl?" I asked. "Where are you going to keep her? Jeezus, we're not talkin' about a house pet, Mike. These are girls...human beings!"

"Well, Sergeant Mays wants to sell the house," he said. "We could buy it. It has three bedrooms, a big kitchen—and the hot tub in the back yard. When he goes home, he'll lose it anyway, so we can get it cheap. Bet we could get it for a thousand." I glanced back at the beauty who had been sitting beside me.

She quickly looked down. I thought I caught a glimpse of hope, as though we might be their last chance. Or maybe that was what I wanted to see.

"What would *I* do with a girl?" I said. "Not just a girl, like a girlfriend—but someone who thought I owned her! We could get in a world of hurt from the army, too. They have all sorts of rules about indigenous women. This is deep shit."

"When have we ever worried about rules and regs all that much?" Mike asked. I looked back at the girls, sitting perfectly still on the couch, heads bent as if meditating. Neither one would ever give us any flack about anything.

"Look at them," Mike said. "They look so innocent. If he makes prostitutes out of them, they'll be lucky to look as good as the one in that bar in a few months. We could keep them from being miserable and dying young."

"Well...that would be their fate, all right." I felt something inside me caving in. "How much do you think he'd want for the house? A thousand?" I heard myself leading the conversation the opposite way I thought it should go. It was absurd. Illegal as hell...maybe. I mentally calculated the contents of my safe-deposit box at the Hotel Saigon. I had about five hundred dollars in cash in my wallet. Mike probably had about the same. If we could buy Sergeant May's house, and get our host to come down on the price for the girls, my share would take less than a fourth of my capital. What the hell, I thought, the money's just sitting there.

"You know it'll cost a fortune to have someone look after them while we're gone?"

"We'll pay them off in souvenirs," Mike said with a smile.

We negotiated with the old man at length. He would accept no less than two thousand American dollars for each girl, the equivalent of about fifty years' wages for most South Vietnamese.

"Okay," I said. "Let's do it."

Body Guard Number One appeared from behind the curtain, and we gave him a thousand American dollars as a deposit.

"You are trusting us for the rest of the money?" I asked.

Our host sat quietly for several minutes, staring so hard at me I wondered if his flinty, black eyes could strike sparks. Then he smiled. I got chills.

"You have been here for over two years," he said. "You will be back. One way or another, I will see you again." I had no doubt that anyone who tried to cheat him would regret it dearly.

The old man said he would deliver the girls the next day. After we had them examined by a doctor and found they were as he represented them, we would pay the balance.

"I guess the first thing we ought to do is tell Mays we want his house," I said.

Mike nodded. "We need to stop at our safety deposit boxes before we visit the good sergeant."

"Yeah. And then we better find some REMFs and sell some souvenirs. We're gonna need more cash. Still think they're worth it?" I asked.

He raised one eyebrow and smiled.

When we stopped at Sergeant Mays' warehouse his clerk jumped up as we came through the door. "Hey, they've been lookin' all over for you guys! Your leave has been canceled and you've got another assignment." He looked at his watch. "And you got less than an hour!"

For a moment I thought I would pass out. Mike looked at me like would I please tell him we hadn't heard what we had just heard. I shook my head.

"Shit. Now what do we do?"

"We go," Mike said, looking red-eyed with fury. "We don't have a god-damn choice."

I felt like an extra in an old-fashioned movie where everyone moved in jerky, fast motion. We retrieved our gear from the weapons locker, double-timed it back to our hooch, and changed into fatigues. As I shouldered my field pack, Mike sank down on his bunk.

"I can't believe this is happening," he said, running his hands through his hair. "What's so damn important that we gotta go right now? They lose a general and want us to find him? That old man will show up with the girls tomorrow, and we won't be there. We'll never see them again. *And* we'll lose our money."

I, too, was afraid we would lose our girls. *Our* girls? I thought. How could some-one I didn't know, who had never been mine, suddenly be so important to me?

"Hey, I think I know what we can do," I said, looking at my watch. "I'll bet Mays would meet the old man and tell him what happened. You want to find the team, tell them not to leave without me, and I'll go find Mays?"

"Think he'd do that?"

"He's gotta want some souvenirs to take home," I said. "Guess I better tell him we want the house, too."

"Okay, hurry up. We got about fifteen minutes."

We shot out of our hooch on the double, with all our gear. Finally, I thought, a reason to be glad for five-mile runs. I careened around the corner of a building, almost colliding with a second lieutenant and a non-com. In spite of his indignant order to get my ass back there, I kept going as fast as I could. When I burst through the door to Mays' office, the clerk looked up, wide-eyed.

"We under attack or somethin'?" he asked.

"Where's Sergeant Mays?" I gasped.

"He ain't here."

"Look, I gotta get in touch with him. Where'd he go?"

"I dunno. I got things to do," he said, turning back to his typewriter.

"I got an emergency," I said. "I gotta talk to him in the next five minutes. You must have *some* idea where he is. If you find him for me, it's worth a fifth of Scotch."

Magic words. In a few minutes I had Mays on the phone. I told him where to meet with the old man. "Just tell him we still want the merchandise," I said. "And we want your house. We'll talk money after we get back." Mays agreed. I dropped the phone back onto the desk and ran. "Hey, don't forget my booze!" yelled his clerk.

I found our team, threw myself into the waiting chopper, and we lifted off. Eventually we touched down on a tributary somewhere in the Mekong Delta and scrambled aboard a waiting gunboat. On board was a spook, who seemed to know our destination. I took him for one, with the typical odd camouflage-pattern fatigues. He looked about five feet ten and wiry. He had a blond beard. Then I saw his eyes. Blue—ice blue—flat, emotionless eyes that showed nothing, but had the look of command, one who expected others to do as he ordered. A .45 Government Model rode in a holster on his belt, and he held a Belgian assault rifle across his lap. His worn and faded uniform bore no insignia of rank, name, or outfit.

"Another bunch of spooks," I whispered. "We're seeing more spooks than regulars."

Mike smiled. "Don't forget, there are some who might put us in the same category."

I laughed. "I guess it's a question of degree.

"Anyway, I found out we're looking for a pilot and his passenger. They bailed out of their aircraft because of mechanical problems," Mike said. "I asked if they were Air Force pukes or South Vietnamese, but Jaimeson didn't say."

Mike paused, and we looked to see if our newcomer would fill us in, but he remained silent.

"I got told to take the team and go find 'em," Mike went on. "So..." He gestured to the man with the glacial eyes, "Sergeant Hollings here knows where they're supposed to be and will brief us on the rescue operation."

Hollings pulled a map from a tubular case. He unrolled it, pointed to a red circle. "This," he said, "is where the plane, a small Cessna, went down at an extreme rate of descent. Mechanical malfunction of some sort. We expect our people to be about here." He tapped the map with his finger.

Hollings briefed us on the terrain, showing us on the map the few hills and drainages. "I'll be going in with you. We'll split up into three teams. Each one searches a third of the area. We don't expect to find Charlie around here. However, that could change at any time. Just to be safe, assume that Charlie may find us."

I raised my eyebrows and looked at Mike. Neither of us had been prepared to let someone take over our team, much less some complete mystery man. I saw Mike shake his head almost imperceptibly. I wondered if he knew something I didn't.

"We're about fifteen minutes from our LZ," Hollings said. "Any questions?"

The team looked at Mike, instead of Hollings. I grinned. Commandeered by an outsider, we were still a team.

"I don't think we have any questions, Sergeant," Mike said, and turned back to the team. "All right, do a last minute check of your gear. You left in a hurry. Make sure you didn't forget something." Mike caught my eye and looked toward the stern of the boat and its two unmanned fifty caliber machine guns. I stood and made my way to the stern.

"What the hell is going on?" I asked, when out of earshot. "Are we going to let this guy take over?"

Mike frowned. "That's what we're supposed to do. Lieutenant Jaimeson introduced me to some captain, who briefed me while you were hunting down Mays. Then Jaimeson told me we're at Sergeant Hollings' disposal. Do whatever he wanted."

"Who *are* these guys?" I asked. "Why are they so important they're sending *us* out, instead of the usual search and rescue team?"

Mike shrugged. "Beats hell out of me."

We watched the river flow by, both of us lost in our thoughts.

"I take it you got a hold of Mays?" he asked.

"Yeah. He said he'd meet the old man for us, but I wonder if he'll talk to Mays."

"Maybe we blew it."

"About two minutes," Sergeant Hollings said. We both jumped, neither of us having heard him approach.

The boat nosed into the almost vertical bank, which was several feet higher than the bow. After we disembarked, I watched as the crew turned the gunboat downstream.

Hollings split the search area into three sectors. Mike and I split up our team. He took the first sector and I took the second. Hollings took the third, but not until we had set some parameters. Mike called out the names of those who would go with Hollings.

"Tony, you are liaison with the team and Sergeant Hollings. Whatever needs to be done, he will tell you, and you will give the orders. Everyone understand that?" Our guys nodded.

"Sergeant Hollings?" I asked.

"That's fine," he said. "I applaud your unit integrity. I can work with that."

We spent the afternoon slogging our way through mud and stagnant water.

Before sunset we regrouped, not having found any sign of the missing men—or anyone else. We strung hammocks between the trees, rubbed insect repellant all over each other, and climbed under mosquito netting.

Early the next morning we left to comb the north-eastern part of the search area. At mid-day we stopped to chew on some dehydrated rations.

"You know, this new shit makes C rats taste good," whispered Corporal Pike. "And I never thought anything could do that."

The radio clicked three times. "They found one of 'em," I said. About five seconds later, it repeated the clicks.

"Well, well, the secret code. Got your code book?" Pike said. "I don't know why these guys gotta be so different. No insignia, no names—it's like a bunch of kids with secret decoder rings. Who the hell are they?"

I laughed and shouldered my pack. "The clandestine of the clandestine," I said. "We can pack it in now. That's all I care about. Let's head for our rendezvous point."

We arrived before the others, and although we'd seen no sign of Charlie, I decided we would take cover behind the trees and wait. They returned in the late afternoon, carrying the two missing men on makeshift stretchers improvised from their parachutes.

"You find them or did Hollings?" I asked Kennelley as we munched dried carrots and washed them down with iodized water.

"Hollings. They were about three hundred yards apart. One's still alive. He's dehydrated and has a concussion, but he should be okay."

I walked over where Hollings sat on a tree trunk, eating C-rat peaches. "Where'd you get that?" I asked.

He grinned. "You eatin' the new dehydrated stuff?

"Yeah," I said, making a face.

"It's not really that bad if you use a lot of water."

"Maybe not, but our water always has so much iodine in it, anything it's mixed with tastes like unadulterated shit." I looked at the parachutes, which had a camouflage pattern. "That must make them hard to spot from the air," I said.

226

Hollings drank the syrup from his peaches and looked up. "Also makes them hard to spot from the ground. They crossed a line on a map. We couldn't send the cavalry in for them. That's why you're here." He shrugged. "They're lucky we came this far."

He set the can on the ground and mashed it flat, then reached in his pack. "Here," he said, tossing me a bottle of tiny pills. "Halazone. That's what I use. Try it in your water instead of iodine. It doesn't taste as bad."

"Thanks," I said. I motioned to the 'chute pulled up over the body. "What happened?"

"He broke his neck. Slammed into a tree maybe. Neck's got an odd twist. Take a look. Tell me what you think."

Gingerly, I pulled the fabric away from the body, exposing the man's face and chest. Not even the way his head was twisted to one side, or the unreal pallor of death that lightened his dark complexion, could keep me from instantly recognizing the man. His black hair, still braided in strands that reached a few inches below his ears, merged with his beard and the matted pelt on his chest. His shirt, sleeves cut off, unbuttoned almost to the waist, frayed and dirty, looked like the same one he wore when I saw him last.

On the left strap of his load-bearing harness, the Fairbairn-Sykes knife remained secured in its upside-down sheath. I pulled it out, checked the edge against my thumbnail, verifying its sharpness. I fingered the point of the blade, once again feeling his knife prick my skin in the place he was showing me to plunge it into a man's kidney, causing pain so excruciating the victim could not cry out.

Replacing the knife, I pulled the leather thong across the hilt so it wouldn't be lost. I leaned over him. He once stood a head taller than me. I became filled with a sense of frailty and loss, much the same way I'd felt before Dan's death. I walked across the clearing and sat with my back against a tree, trying to keep my mind still.

Eventually Mike came to check on me. He sat and leaned against the other side of the tree. "Someone you knew?" he asked.

"Yeah. His outfit came through our digs about the time you showed up," I said. "He showed me how to use a Fairbairn-Sykes." I stood and shouldered my pack, pointing to my own Fairbairn-Sykes, rigged like his. "It's getting dark," I said.

"Did you know him very well?" asked Mike.

"Hardly knew him. He seemed powerful, so big, yet quiet—deadly. He just seemed...invincible."

Mike's look was a mix of fear and annoyance. "I hope you're not gonna tell me you're having some kind of premonition."

"Okay. I won't say shit."

When we got home, we stopped at Sergeant Mays' warehouse. Mays ushered us into what he called his office, a steel cargo container set against the building with a door cut through both walls for access. "What the hell did you get me into?" he asked in a low voice. "Those guys are nasty characters."

"What do you mean? Where are the girls?" Mike asked.

"They made me go with them. They didn't have the girls, but they still expected me to pay for them. When I told them I didn't have the money and tried to explain that you were called out on a mission, they asked me to come with them so I could explain it to their honcho. I said no, but if he came here, I'd explain it. This one big guy—Chinese, I think—grabbed me by the seat of the pants and the collar of my shirt and carried me out the door like a rag doll. Then ..."

"Did you see the girls?" Mike interrupted.

"Then they stuffed me in the back of an old Mercedes limo. Looked brand new. I wouldn't mind having that car. It would be..."

"So where'd they take you?" I asked. I felt like I'd already had the patience of Job, and it had worn thin.

"I have no idea," Mays said. "We drove somewhere in the city, stopped at some automatic gate. They escorted me inside, and after a while this old guy in a fancy-schmancy costume came in and sat down."

"He's a Mandarin," I said.

"Mandarin? Like those little oranges?"

I wished I'd kept quiet. "Yeah. So what happened?"

"He asked about the weather, the war, commented on the traffic. Even asked me how I liked his car. Then someone brought a teapot and some of those itty-bitty cups. I started to think he might not be the ramrod of the outfit when all of a sudden he told me you had been called out on a mission. That surprised me some, so I told him you hadn't expected it. He said he knew that. How the hell do you suppose he knew?"

"So did you tell him we still wanted the girls?" asked Mike.

"Yeah, I told him you wanted to meet with him as soon as you got back. He said, 'Very well.' Nothing else. Just 'Very well.' Then he got up and left. His henchmen brought me back to the bar. When we got there, the big barrel-chested guy got out and held the door for me. Then without saying a word, he got back in the car and drove off."

"Oh great. Just fuckin' great," Mike said. "They didn't tell you where to meet them?"

"They wouldn't talk to me. The orange guy just got up and left, and they took me back. They didn't say goodby or go to hell or meet us at high noon. They just left."

Sergeant Mays looked from me to Mike and back. "Hey, I did my best. They scared the hell out of me."

"Yeah, I know you did your best. And we appreciate it a lot. I've got an NVA officer's pistol with holster and belt in the weapons locker." Mays' eyes went wide at the mention of such a desirable souvenir. "Call it a down payment? Treat us right on the price of the house, and we'll find some other rare and wonderful stuff." I hoped we'd still need the house.

"The house!" he said. "I almost forgot." He stood, fished around in his pocket, pulled out a small key ring. "Here. It's yours. We'll work something out," he said, tossing the keys to Mike. "Call me tomorrow."

The next day we took the money for the girls from our safe-deposit boxes, then went to the bar where we hoped the Mandarin would show up. We spent the afternoon nursing drinks. By sunset we wondered if our luck had run out. I had sunk into such a foul mood I didn't hear the voice until Mike turned around.

"Sergeant Kennelley, Sergeant Walker," someone said. I recognized him mostly by his penny loafers. "Would you come this way, please?"

Damn right we'll come this way, I thought.

He ushered us out to the old limousine, and we drove off into the maze of the city. We reached the remote-controlled gates, and again they swung noiselessly into the courtyard, then clanged as the locking mechanism engaged. Penny Loafer and the Chinese guy escorted us into the same room where we first saw the girls and waited with us for our host. As before, the old man made small talk until I thought Mike would lose his patience entirely.

"I believe we have some unfinished business," the old man finally said.

From behind the heavy curtain, our girls appeared, clinging to each other, clearly apprehensive of their fates with their new masters.

I reached into my shirt for the money we owed him. The bodyguard frowned, and with one smooth movement, pushed back his coat and pulled a pistol part way out of his waistband.

"Money," I said. Slowly I brought out the envelope. "I have the money." The pistol disappeared, the frown with it, the face went blank again. I handed it over to the old man with a shaking hand. "We want to pay you now. We have decided that the girls are as you have represented them. Later, we will have them examined for their own benefit."

He took the envelope and handed it to Penny Loafer. "It has been a pleasure doing business with you, gentlemen," he said. My car is at your disposal. Where do you wish to go?"

I looked at Mike. "Mays' place? Or should I say, our place?"

Mike nodded. "Yeah. *Our* place." He held out his hand to the young beauty who had sat on the couch next to him only a few days ago. She regarded him with a mixture of fear and curiosity.

"Our place," he repeated. "We've got a home now."

His bodyguard put the girls' luggage—two small bags—into the limo, and delivered us to our house. The four of us stood on the sidewalk and watched them disappear.

"I can't believe they're ours. We *own* them," Mike said, as if he needed convincing.

"Yeah. But why do I have a swarm of bees in my belly? There's an angle somewhere. The old man will show up with the MP's and we'll end up in the stockade. Or the girls will run away. Or someone'll show up and claim to be family. The furthest thought from my mind right now is spending the night with a Vietnamese beauty."

So far, I avoided thinking about the extent of our endeavor. I felt like I'd walked into a tunnel as it caved in. "Shit, you know how many rules we're breaking? We could spend the rest of the war in Leavenworth. And then some."

"Yeah. But I've got a good feeling about it," Mike said. He looked dreamy-eyed and smiled. "A real good feeling."

"Let's go set up housekeeping," I said.

Built during the French occupation of Vietnam, our house had big windows and a wrap-around porch, giving it an air of cool openness. When I opened the door, it looked shabby, sadly in need of paint and a general cleaning. When we brought the girls inside, the furniture looked worn. The dirty floor looked bare without a rug.

The threshold seemed to mark a forbidding boundary beset with unknowns. The four of us stepped inside the door and looked around the living room.

"We gonna stand here all day?" Mike asked, making me jump.

Mike and I had the small bags that held the girls' worldly possessions. We stood in the middle of the living room in a cluster, as though in a hostile environment, without knowing what should be done next. The girls ended the quandary with a simple response from their training.

"Tea?" they said, almost in unison.

"Would you like tea?" said the one who had sat next to me. She had a deeper voice than her sister, her expression more decisive. When she spoke I saw even, white teeth through her sensuous lips. I wondered what it would be like to kiss her, to explore the curves under her *aodai*. "Please," I said. "Tea would be great."

She skittered across the floor to the kitchen door like a small creature trying not to call attention to itself. Tentatively she looked in, then jerked back, eyes wide, and spoke to her sister in Vietnamese, her tone conveying her amazement. Together they peeked around the door jamb at the pile of dirty pots, pans and dishes mounded up in the sink. More Vietnamese followed until it seemed they had agreed on the tactics required to conquer the mess. The two miniature warriors moved out into the kitchen.

Mike and I took their places at the door jamb and watched as they found the few cleaning supplies and went to work. "I feel like a fifth wheel," I said.

"Yeah. And somehow this place doesn't look as good as it used to."

"You gotta admit the kitchen is groaty. Let's sit before we get drafted." I plopped down in an easy chair and Mike fell onto the couch. Neither of us could ignore the tinkle of dishes being washed or the brisk sound of the scrub brush on the floor's patina.

"I could go for a beer," I said.

"Yeah."

I stood and walked cautiously to the door. The 'fridge sat across the wet floor, a distinct two-tone of before and after. I motioned to Mike. "These two are workin' away like crazy!" I said. One of the girls knelt with a scrub brush. The other had started to dry a stack of clean dishes. As soon as she heard us, she called to her sister, who hopped up from her bucket. Both of them ran across the room, and placing their hands palm to palm, bowed to us.

"What the hell...?" Mike said.

"Uh, girls...I just wanted to get a beer..." I said, which set them off, one to the 'fridge, the other to the sink for a church key. With much bowing, they presented us both with beers. From the doorway we watched, perplexed at the automation of their performance.

"What else may we get for you?" asked the more assertive of the two. I already loved her voice.

"Ah...nothing. Right now. Thanks anyway." My words brought another round of bowing, so we retreated to the living room. The clink of dishes and the scratch of the brush took up again

"Think maybe we should find out what their names are?" I asked. "We're not old enough to vote and we *buy* two girls, for God's sake. And we don't even know their names. Are we screwed up, or what?" I looked around the room. "And this place is a dump."

"It's not that bad. It just needs to be cleaned up."

"Yeah. With a fire hose."

"So now what?" Mike asked, after we sat in silence for several minutes. "It sounds like they're through in there."

Almost soundlessly the girls reappeared from the kitchen. The one with the sexy voice carried a tray I didn't know we had. In the center, proudly clean and gleaming, sat a coffee pot, accompanied by two mugs. She set the tray on the table in front of the couch, and they knelt on the other side of it.

"We have made tea for you," she said, pouring from the coffee pot into coffee mugs.

"Great," Mike said. "I always liked hot tea with my cold beer."

The girls, kneeling at our feet, watched us expectantly.

"What is this? Teahouse of the August Moon?" I picked up a mug. "Cheers," I said. Mike raised his mug, sipped his tea, then chased it with a swig of beer. The girls looked pleased.

"Somehow I don't think this is getting off to a very good start. Any ideas how we're going to handle bedtime?" Mike asked.

"They seem to know what needs to be done in the kitchen. I wonder if they've been trained as well..." I said.

"Trained in bed? Our unplucked flowers?"

The girls spoke rapidly in Vietnamese. The one with the sexy voice looked at us expectantly. She put her arm around her sister, who was more timid.

"I don't exactly feel like the conquering hero," I said. "Let's show them the rest of the house. Maybe they'll catch on." We stood, the girls stood—and bowed.

"We're going to show you the house," Mike told them. They bowed again.

We entered the short hallway single-file. Mike led, I brought up the rear. My mind had a field day with the ridiculosity factor, heightened by the effort not to admit that neither of us had any idea how in hell we ended up playing house in Southeast Asia. We first stopped at the bathroom. The girls peered in, then wrinkled their noses, and, speaking in Vietnamese, pointed solemnly from the sink to the toilet, tub and shower. The mirror hung askew on a squeaky hinge, dirty and cracked.

"I guess this isn't exactly antiseptic either," Mike said.

I looked at the black mold on the shower tiles. "You got that right. Perceptive. Let's get it over with. Show them the bedrooms."

We marched into the first bedroom, seeing the unmade bed as if for the first time. The other bedroom looked even worse. The girls had pointed to the beds, glanced at each other, solemn, wide-eyed. Mike and I looked at each other in perturbed silence.

"We will clean for you," I heard from the one with the sexy voice. Names, I thought. We really should know their names.

"Fine," Mike said.

"First..." I said, but too late. With Mike's approval, they were off to the kitchen, then back in a flash with bucket, mop, soap and rags.

"Our beer's getting warm. And our tea's getting cold," I said. We burst out in nervous laughter.

The girls cleaned the bathroom, then showered and presented themselves for further instructions. I knew when I saw their raw hands that as a rule, they didn't do heavy housework.

"Let me see your hands," I told them. "Look at this, Mike," I said. "They're red and bleeding!"

Mike frowned and sat up. "You're right. I wonder what they were using to clean."

"Don't we have some of that stuff we use for chafed skin?" I asked. "That lanolin and cortisone stuff."

"Sure. That'll help." He jumped up and headed for his bedroom. The girls looked frightened, kept looking at their hands, at me, at each other.

"Sit on the couch," he told them when he came back. When they hesitated, Mike said, "Don't worry. It won't hurt."

"I don't think they're worried about the cream. They don't want to sit while we're standing," I said. We both sat on the coffee table. "Please. Sit on the couch and hold out your hands."

As carefully as possible we rubbed the cream onto their hands, gently massaging it into their skin. At first they seemed uncomfortable with this new experience, but as it soothed, they relaxed and giggled, stealing quick glances at us through their bangs. I gazed in fascination at their tiny, delicate hands. Like children's. As healthy young males, the presence of two beautiful, sexy young women had not been lost on us. Nor had their fear, their extreme insecurity in this new life.

"Names," I said. "This is a good time to find out names."

There was an exchange of Vietnamese. The more timid one said "Rose," but she was talking to her sister. More Vietnamese followed, the other sister shaking her head and pointing to herself as she said what sounded like Lee. Having settled the issue between themselves, they faced us.

"My sister wishes to be called Rose," said the less timid one. "I do not wish to change my name. I am Li."

We sat on the couch after dinner, the girls at our feet, awaiting our every whim. But we'd run out of whims, and didn't have much of an idea how to get everyone to bed.

"Okay, Rose and Li. It's bedtime," Mike said.

"At least we now know who we're going to be sleeping with," I said.

They disappeared into our bedrooms. They returned, wearing long silk garments which buttoned up to the neck. Mike and I slept in T-shirts and shorts. For now, we had no idea of having anything more than a chaste night. When both girls fell asleep on the couch it solved the problem. "I like Li's voice," I said. "I think it's sexy." I felt a twinge of guilt treating a real person this way. It was like picking a puppy out of a litter.

"She's the dominant one," Mike said. "If either of them can be called dominant. After Lynne, I'm ready for a woman who absolutely isn't." He bent down and picked up the other twin. He stood there for a moment, holding her in his arms, and smiled. "Rose. Round and firm and fully packed."

"You're sick," I said, and bent to pick up my sleeping beauty. I had that feeling in my belly like going over a dip.

Several hours later I woke up to find myself alone. I swung my feet off the bed and onto something soft and warm. When I realized what I had my feet on, I yanked my legs back up on the bed.

"What are you doing down there?" I asked, eliciting a confused look from Li. She rubbed the sleep from her eyes, fear taking its place.

"Come and sit with me," I said, and led her into the living room to the couch. She sat stiffly on the edge, looking afraid.

"Come over here with me, please." I settled back on the couch and held out an arm. Reluctantly, she moved back against the couch, half turned toward me. "I don't want you to be afraid of me," I said. She regarded me intently with her lovely dark eyes.

"I am not afraid," she said. "But I don't know what to do."

"Would you like to put your head on my shoulder?" I asked. Timidly, she moved against me, a small, fragile creature, and laid her head on my shoulder. Her black hair shimmered with electric blue flashes. "Why were you sleeping down there on the floor?" I asked.

"I did not sleep," she replied, after a pause. "I do not sleep on a floor. You moved over. I got out of bed to prevent crowding you."

As I searched my mind for something comforting to say, I felt her body relax. She snuggled closer, letting out her breath in a sigh. Maybe she felt safe enough to fall asleep. I wrapped my arms around her, and we dozed on the couch the rest of the night. Several times I came half awake, realizing who rested in my arms and where we were.

I was in way, way over my head.

One morning about a week later I managed to ease off of the bed without waking Li. I found Mike in the kitchen, drinking beer.

"A bit early for beer, isn't it?" I asked

"I had to have a beer," he said.

"You had to?"

"Yeah. We're out of scotch." He did the usual thing he did when he was upset, sticking his finger in the bottle and wagging it back and forth.

"Okay, so what's wrong?" I asked.

He watched the beer bottle pendulum for a few swings. "I feel so goddam horny sometimes. Rose curls up against me and I get so hard I have to turn over or get up. If I don't, I think I might lose it and rip off her nightie-thing and rape her. It's about to drive me nuts."

I thought about what he'd said, and the possible aftermath. "It sounds like we're having the same problem. There's only one thing that's kept me from doing something I'd regret."

"What's that?" he asked.

"To begin with, these two have no idea what it can be like if it's good.

Being forced for the first time would destroy that." I took a deep breath. "And I'm having feelings for Li I swore I'd never have for another woman. If I can possibly hold out, then—well, I'm not sure. I think they could really love us. For who we are—for *what* we are. And that would be better than anything."

I got up and opened the liquor cabinet. "Damn. You're right. No scotch." I got a beer out of the 'fridge.

"I hope you're right," Mike said. "I'd like a relationship without all the goddam fear and mistrust."

We each had four more beers.

CHAPTER TWENTY FIVE

Getting To Know You

The story of our purchase received a nod and a wink. Fortunately no one asked what our long-range plans were, for we hadn't thought past setting up housekeeping in Mays' house.

"We gotta get them physicals," Mike said. We called in some favors, and after all the poking, prodding and testing the U. S. Army could think of, the girls were pronounced healthy.

We spent another week getting to know each other, settling into a routine. Li would cater to my every wish. I had to be careful not to think out loud or she would be up to fetch whatever I had mentioned. We took Li and Rose on shopping trips and bought all sorts of dishes, pots, pans, food, and a thousand little things. We bought them more clothes than they could possibly wear.

They bathed and massaged us, soothing knotted muscles with the surprising strength of their little hands. Li washed me in the shower and led me to the hot tub—the Vietnamese idea of bathing. Or perhaps the French idea. I sank into the steaming water, relaxed and fell asleep. Later, Li shook me awake, dried me, and led me to a low pallet. I lay on my stomach as she massaged the knots out of my back and legs. Her touch felt soothing, but not relaxing enough to quell my desire for her. I opened my eyes as she moved from one side of the pallette to the other. Her cotton halter, still wet, clung to her breasts. When she bent down, it fell forward, giving me a full glimpse of one shapely breast.

"Please, turn on your back," she said. My desire boiled over—I wanted her now. I pulled her down next to me, and took her breast in my hand. She closed her eyes and I felt her stiffen. She would serve me with her body, but I knew she didn't want to. I reached for my towel, draping it over my middle. "Please go ahead with the massage," I said. I had tightened up, she had become hesitant. "It's okay," I said, catching her hand and giving it a squeeze. I tried to relax. "Would you bring me a beer?" I looked at her body as she scurried to the kitchen. The skimpy, wet outfit showed all her curves. What the hell am I saying, I thought. It's *not* okay.

When Mike and I got home the next day, Li and Rose met us at the door and bowed.

"Please, sit," Li said, and nudged me toward the couch. "I will bring you a beer." She untied my boots and pulled them off. Rose followed suit with Mike.

"We've got to break some of these habits," I told Mike.

He propped his feet on the table, wriggled his toes. "Yeah...some of it's kinda nice, though."

"Oh sure. Like standing and bowing whenever we come into the room, I suppose. I came in from the back yard yesterday. They ran to the door, bowed, then got me a beer. I came back two minutes later and they got me another beer. I hadn't finished the first one."

"I know what you mean," he said. "I found myself sneaking in, trying not to make enough noise for them to hear. But they did, and came on the run, awaiting my command."

Li and Rose came back with our beers.

"Please sit down," I said. They looked at each other, and sank to the floor.

"I don't believe this," Mike said. "Okay, you two. Please get up."

They both stood and bowed.

"Rose, Li, would you sit on the couch?" I asked.

I sat on the coffee table, facing them, and Mike pulled up a chair.

How do I begin, I thought. "There are some things we don't want you to do." Li gave Rose a troubled glance, which she returned.

"Do we not please you?" Li asked.

"No," I said.

Mistake number two. Both of them clasped their hands in their laps and lowered their heads, as if in prayer.

"I mean..."

"Nice going," Mike said.

My brain burned in overdrive. "What I mean is, there are some things we wish you would not do. Just as when I came here, I had to learn some of the ways of your country."

Rose looked up. "You want us to leave?" she asked, beginning to cry.

"Gotta hand it to you. Real smooth," Mike said.

I turned back to the girls. "Look at me, please," I said. They raised their heads an inch or so and peered up at me. I knelt in front of them. Unaccustomed to looking down at me, I had their attention.

"You know that we are soldiers."

They nodded.

"We are very important and very different soldiers."

They nodded again.

"We have extra special skills. We go into the mountains and the jungle for long times. For this, we are paid much money."

Both pairs of eyes opened wide.

"You belong to us. And since we are very important soldiers, that makes *you* very important, too." I paused to let my words soak in. Li and Rose leaned forward slightly.

"So you cannot act like peasants," I said, forcefully.

They looked at each other and sat up straighter.

"You must act like you are important. Next week when we are gone, you must run the house. You will have money to spend, and what you do is for us. And we are *important* warriors. Do you understand?"

Both girls nodded enthusiastically.

"How do you wish us to be different?" asked Li.

"No more bowing," I said. "You may meet us at the door, but no bowing."

A rapid exchange in Vietnamese followed with some head shaking. Then they reached an agreement.

"Okay," Rose said. "We will no longer bow to you when we are alone."

"No," Mike cut in. "No bowing to us or to anyone, wherever we are. Ever."

Another exchange in Vietnamese followed. They shrugged their shoulders.

"Yes," Rose said. "We will not bow."

"You must not stand and watch us eat," Mike said. "It is poor manners in our country to stare at someone when they are eating. You must sit and eat with us. You may serve us first, but then you must sit at the table and eat with us. Understand?"

The girls looked at each other and spoke in French.

Rose turned back to Mike. "Is this what the woman of an important American soldier would do?" she asked.

"Yes," said Mike. "Hopefully," he added, with a raised eyebrow and a sardonic smile.

They looked at each other and nodded. "Very well then. We will serve you, then we will eat with you."

"These things will please us," Mike said. "Will you fix dinner now?"

They stood and scurried, giggling, into the kitchen.

On the days we could sleep in, Mike and I got used to breakfast in bed. Sometimes we had no idea what we were eating. It usually had rice mixed with meat or seafood. It always tasted good. We moved out on the sleeping porch, a kind of a big, screened in room, with beds at opposite ends. Ceiling fans stirred the air. A heavy curtain down the middle of the room didn't do much for noises, but provided some privacy. Rose and Li, in keeping with our request that they eat with us, would bring us each a tray, draw aside the curtain, and return to the kitchen for their own trays. Usually they sat on the bed, cross-legged, balancing the trays in their laps without spilling a grain of rice or a drop of tea. We were slobs by comparison.

One morning when we were half-awake, waiting in bed for breakfast, we heard the crash of glass. Then a cry of pain. We shot out of bed. Mike grabbed his M-16, I snatched my .45 Government Model from the night stand. We ran into the kitchen. Rose, curled in a ball against the kitchen cabinets, cried out in pain and held her foot. Li hunched over her, a bloody dishtowel in her hand. Our abrupt appearance like wild men, wearing only shorts and carrying guns, frightened them both. But there seemed another element of their fear, which I couldn't place. Realizing we were not being attacked, we set our weapons on the kitchen table.

"What is it?" I asked Mike, as he bent over Rose.

"She's cut her foot. I think that's all." He pressed a dish towel against the wound and Rose cried out. Very gently he lifted her and carried her down the hallway to the sleeping porch, speaking softly as if to a child, telling her everything was all right.

Li had been crouched behind a kitchen chair like a frightened animal. I took her hand and gently raised her up, explaining softly that if she could sit on the bed and hold Rose's hand, it would help. I went to my duffel bag and dug out our medical kit. We always carried minor surgical equipment like forceps and sutures.

Mike probed the cut and Rose cried out. He reached back and squeezed her hand. "You're gonna be just fine, babe, but I gotta get that piece of glass out. Okay?" She nodded, and wiped the tears from her eyes.

"Do you see it?" I asked Mike.

"Yeah, it's a small piece," he said. It's deep, and it's gonna hurt to probe it. Got any morphine?"

I took a morphine ampule and showed it to Rose. I explained that it would deaden the pain, but might hurt a little bit at first. She flinched as I plunged the needle into her soft flesh.

"I'm sorry," I said. "You'll feel better now. Maybe even sleepy." A few minutes later the drug took effect. She fell asleep, and Mike removed the glass from her foot.

"Li, can you find a sheet to tear up for bandages?" I asked. "That would help." She jumped off the bed and came back with a sheet. I showed her how to tear strips of bandage. We put a compress over Rose's wound and wrapped her foot.

"This is gonna need stitches," Mike said. "And a tetanus shot, maybe some antibiotics. I think I got all the glass, but an X-ray wouldn't hurt. Let's get her to the hospital."

Li came in as I hurriedly dressed. She grabbed my hand, holding as tight as she could.

"I want to go, too! Please? Can I go with you?" she looked up with fear in her eyes, tears running down her cheeks.

I squatted down and held her hands, wondering why she seemed so terrified that we might leave her alone. "Sure you can go," I said. "I'm not about to leave you here."

We jumped into our stolen jeep, Li up front with me, Mike holding Rose in the narrow back seat. I made record time to the hospital, where it took four stitches to close the cut.

The next day all three of us waited on Rose. She kept trying to get up to cook or do menial things until Mike threatened to tie her to the bed.

Li kept watching me, looking away quickly when I noticed, like a child who expected some hidden transgression to be discovered.

"What's wrong?" I asked.

"Will you beat Rose?" she asked in a timid voice. My jaw dropped. It sounded more like she wanted to know if they both would be beaten.

I sat her down on the couch and put my arms around her. "Why in the world would we beat Rose?" I asked her.

"Rose broke a bowl. And caused much trouble when she stepped on it." She looked up at me, afraid of what my answer might be. "And...I helped her."

"I think we need to have a family meeting," I said.

We sat on the bed with Rose. Mike and I had some experience with the ARVNs dealing with cultural differences—such as the importance of people, compared to material things, the difference between accidents and deliberate neglect. The girls seemed to accept our version when we explained. But when we said we did not believe in beating women, it caused raised eyebrows and many questions.

"Did you get a beating for something like breaking a bowl?" I asked Li.

"Of course," she replied, with such matter-of-fact-ness it stopped my clock.

"If you don't beat your women, how do you get them to do what you want?"

Mike smiled maliciously.

"Don't go there," I said.

They had some difficulty understanding that women were treated as first class citizens in our society, yet not always equally. That reminded me how hard it had been for us to accept that here, women were considered slightly more important than livestock. Sometimes less. As we tried to tell them how we felt about them, we surprised ourselves, finding we had come to care for them far more than we realized. An unnerving discovery.

The way we handled the incident of the broken bowl made a major impression on Li and Rose. Having been raised with the belief that they were inferior, their purpose to be subordinate to men, it would take time for them to change. Finding the changes to be safe, they ventured out onto this new ground little by little, which in turn, encouraged them to reveal some of their desires and fears.

"Jeezus," Mike said, "I'd go break the whole damn set of dishes if I thought it would help!"

"Somehow I don't think it's a lesson that can be pounded in. They're going to learn by example. We better be on our toes," I said.

That night Li climbed into bed without the fear that had been in her eyes over the bowl. Instead of turning her back to me, she snuggled against me. Timidly she put an arm around me, like clinging to a big brother for protection. Citing patience as a virtue, I settled down to endure my tortured celibacy for another night.

We had five or six days of leave left. Rose's foot had almost healed, so we decided to go on a shopping foray for shrimp. Like tourists, the four of us drove around the bustling city. We stopped under the trees at a park which had a fountain. On one of the benches a couple desperately groped each other, kissing long and passionately. The man wore a uniform I guessed to be French. The woman, evidently a photojournalist, had carelessly left her camera bag on the ground, an invitation to a snatch-and-run thief. Several times they came up for air, stood and held hands. He would consult his watch. Again, he would sink to the bench and embrace the woman, kissing her desperately. With a many tears on her part, they said their goodbys, and went in opposite directions.

Mike and I watched as the couple, oblivious of their audience, punctuated their parting with glances over the shoulder, waving, and blowing kisses. We grinned at each other. Li and Rose bubbled over in French, shaking their heads and shrugging.

We bought a mountain of shrimp and on the way home we picked up several bottles of wine. The dinner production turned out to be a gala affair, with Mike in the kitchen, cooking more shrimp than we could possibly eat. The three of us set the table. Li and Rose were scandalized that I would participate in so menial a task, much less that Mike would cook.

I set out four wine glasses. Perfectly cooked, the shrimp and the wine complimented each other. After Li and Rose had a glass or two of wine, we realized that they were not used to alcohol. Li pushed back her plate, then her chair, and came over to sit in my lap. Mike stashed the leftovers in the fridge, and disappeared with Rose.

Li looked preoccupied.

"Can we talk?" she asked timidly as I carried her to the living room.

"Anytime you want," I said. "About anything." We sat on the couch.

"I want to tell you about the way we lived," she said. "We were raised at first by nuns. They were very strict, and we owned nothing. They were supposed to be the brides of Christ, but we never saw a man in our quarters. Once in a while we went to the country, always in a closed car. We never saw how the city looked. Then someone took us away. They said our parents died."

Li told me that from then on she and Rose received lessons in Buddhism and never saw the nuns again. They were still kept inside, away from the street and other people. Their teachers insisted they understand how important it is for them to learn to make men happy.

"One of the women who taught English got big in her belly." she said. "One day she told us she would have a baby in two months. We spent lesson times talking about babies. Before, we had no knowledge of this.

"When we saw men by themselves, they were friendly to us. But when the men were with women, they acted superior to all women. The Sisters taught us that is right. But the soldier and the girl in the park—they acted differently."

"How so?"

"She—ah, looked important to him. And they kissed?"

"Yes."

"Why did he kiss her?" she asked.

"You've never been kissed?" I asked. She shook her head.

She could speak three languages but didn't know why people kissed. "Well, kissing is something a man and woman do when they feel attracted to each other." Now that I thought about it, I didn't know if I could explain it.

"Are you attracted to me?" she asked. "Do you want to kiss me?"

Li was incapable of guile. She asked a straightforward question and deserved a straightforward answer.

"Yes, Li, I am very attracted to you. And I want to kiss you."

She climbed up in my lap and put her arms around me, like the woman in the park.

"Teach me," she said.

Her breasts rose gently with her breath. Her lips parted. I wanted a lot more than a kiss. My lips met hers. A smoother softness I'd never known, yielding and willing. I kissed her lightly, and again, then more forcefully. She kissed me back, her arms tightening around me. I kissed her throat, gently bit her ears and her neck. She squirmed, and I relaxed my arms so that she could pull away. She clung to me. I carried her into the bedroom and we sat on the bed.

I found the buttons on her *aodai*, unfastened them, and slipped it off. She pulled back, but only to release her undergarment. I pulled off my T-shirt, leaned back and took her in my arms. She bent to kiss me. Her breasts brushed against my bare skin, her nipples hard, setting me on fire. The world went away and reformed between my legs. I stroked her lightly from her breasts to her hips and she opened herself to me. Her breathing quickened as I felt her wetness.

I leaned forward and started to enter her, whispered that it might hurt. Although her inexperience aroused me beyond anything I'd known, her innocence slowed and gentled my passion. With a moan, she pulled me forward. I felt her tense, squeezing her thighs against me, whimpering, then tugging fiercely. Raising her hips against mine, she locked her arms and legs around me. We rose and fell in an ancient rhythm, until I felt a barrage of five-hundred pound bombs go off inside.

For a long time the next morning we lay in bed, content just to touch, to hold each other.

"I like that kissing," Li said.

"Me, too."

Tears filled her eyes. "There are so many things I am feeling that I do not understand." I pulled her closer. "I liked what we did. I want to do it more. Is that something that is permitted to do? To talk about?" she asked.

I searched carefully for the right words. "Yes. It is permitted to do it. What most people want is someone who won't do it with others. A lot of men do it with more than one woman."

She looked thoughtful, then asked, "Do you want do it with other women?"

I still feared she might not want me. "Yes," I said. "Sometimes." I thought about some of the nurses and correspondents I'd lusted after. A gong rang so loud in my head it hurt. I knew I only wanted her. And I'd be a fool not to give her my loyalty. "But more than that I want to have just one woman. You."

"Do all soldiers have just one woman? Or not do it unless they have their own woman?"

"No," I said. "Many soldiers go to a prostitute." She looked blank. "A lady of the night."

"Oh-h," she said. "So this is what ladies of the night do with men." She laughed, hiding her mouth behind her hand. "It must be a wonderful way for them to live."

My face contorted into a grimace.

"It is not so?" she asked, genuinely surprised.

"No," I said. "It's a hard way to live. Some men are rough—and there are diseases. Some are fatal." The look on her face told me she did not expect that it could be life threatening or dangerous.

"When we do it, can it be talked about?" she asked.

"You can talk about it with me. Or Rose."

She thought for a moment. "Will you talk to others about doing it with me?"

"No. Not even to Mike."

"Then I won't either," she said. "Except for Rose." She laughed, and drew close to me.

We lay together, feeling each other's presence, drifting in and out of sleep. We awoke when Mike knocked next to our room divider. Li pulled the sheet up over us.

"Yeah," I hollered, not wanting to be bothered, yet knowing we had to get up.

"You two gonna stay in bed all day?" he asked. "Want some breakfast?"

"Sure," I said. "We'll be out in a few minutes."

When we came out, we held hands. Li pulled her chair against mine. All through breakfast she leaned against me, or we held hands, touching each other as if breaking physical contact would cause us discomfort.

"Where's Rose?" I asked, realizing only the three of us were at the table.

Li froze. Her eyes widened with fear. "Is she all right?" she asked.

"Oh, yeah," Mike said. "She's still asleep."

Li started to leave, then looked up at me. I nodded.

"Looks like things are going well for you two," Mike said, wistfully.

"Yeah," I said. Oddly, I found myself thinking of Sarah, the things other guys insinuated, the fights I'd had. I'd never told anyone anything about Sarah. Except Dan. I wanted to tell Mike more, but found it hard to talk about it.

"Something happened last night that brought us together. It feels really good."

"Good," he said, smiling. "Maybe it will for me and Rose, too."

"Give it some time, Mike," I said.

Off and on during the day Li and Rose shared conspiratorial confidences, speaking in French and Vietnamese, punctuated with glances at us, ending with multiple major cases of giggles. Mike and I played the ignorance game. It couldn't be more evident what Mike hoped they were talking about, and from Li's blushes, and Rose's incredulous looks, I doubted it could be anything else.

We had two days before we left. Our mission, a recon patrol, would keep us in the field ten days or so. But suddenly, ten days seemed a long time. For the first time since we'd been FNGs, I didn't want to go.

The more Li and I made love, the more I wanted. I found the smell of her, the curves and crevices of her body, her slender arms around my neck, something I craved all the time. I felt more disturbed by this new need than by our next mission.

Mike suggested we leave the girls home that night and head to our old haunts for liquid reinforcement. Booze had become the proven substance for calming the fears we denied we had.

Mike climbed up on a barstool at Trahn's Place and sat there like a dark cloud on a mountain. After Trahn waited on us, he moved to the far end of the bar in response to Mike's mood. Thankfully, the dancer had left the platform. The silence sounded almost unnatural.

I tried to sort out my own feelings, wondering how to bridge the gap between what we had to do in the field and assuming the responsibility I now had for someone soft and innocent. I feared that somehow I'd lose my new, gentle world, surrounded with so much coarseness and violence. Li cared for me, but did she have a choice? Would she change her mind?

"Goddam!" Mike said suddenly, banging his beer bottle on the bar. "It just doesn't pay to get close to someone. I feel so fucked up right now I don't know if I'm comin' or goin.' And I don't even know for sure how she feels." He motioned for another beer.

I felt sure Li had been coaching Rose, and it would help. But sometimes when Mike and Rose were together, he got uptight and withdrew. No one could change that but Mike. I wondered how much hurt he carried from his teenage bride who'd sent him the Dear John letter.

"Things have changed for me, too," I said. "In more ways than one. And I can't figure out if I like it or not. Never been scared before going on a mission—well, you know what I mean, not this bad."

"Yeah," he whispered. "It's one thing to get scared when the shootin' starts. But being afraid even before we leave?" He looked around to see if anyone heard.

"The only thing I can figure is that when we leave on this patrol, we gotta switch back the way we were, just like changing frequencies on the radio. Actually, we've gotta be better than we've been for a while. Both of us were getting sloppy."

Mike sat quietly for a while, swirling his beer around inside the bottle, watching it intently, as if it would produce an oracle.

"You know," he said, "It's almost like I quit caring. Got careless." He turned and faced me. "Maybe I needed...maybe we both needed...to have a reason to tighten it up? A reason to care whether or not we came back?" He chugged the rest of his beer. "Jeezus, I hate to even think it, but it's almost like we were trying to get ourselves killed."

The words struck like hammer blows. All of a sudden I could remember taking chances. Small things, like knowing I hadn't been watching for trip-wires, or standing up before checking to make sure Charlie wasn't there. I did it even though I knew the eventual outcome would be fatal.

"Rose is still afraid of me," Mike said. "I think I've been expecting her to start trying control trips and guilt trips. That's what Mary Lynne did. But that's nuts. Rose is different. It's like waiting for the softness to wear off. And she feels it. I gotta quit doing that."

"Yeah, you have to," I told him, looking him in the eye. "You're the biggest part of the problem."

He looked non-plussed, then laughed, stuck his finger in his beer bottle and wagged it back and forth like a pendulum on green weenies.

"Why didn't you tell me?" he asked.

"You might kick my ass if I did."

He frowned, stared at the beer-bottle pendulum. "Can we switch back and forth? Come back between missions, gentle-up, get the strokes we need? Then go out again and make it back?"

"Yeah, we can. I'm not ready to go home in a box."

He looked startled. "Neither am I."

I chugged the rest of my beer. "Let's get out of this dump. Go to some of the high-class joints," I said.

CHAPTER TWENTY SIX

Young Gee

We stumbled home after a bout of sampling the wares at some of the better bars in Saigon. Rose and Li were waiting up and fluttered around us like butterflies when we came in. After they determined that a good night's sleep would cure us, they led us off to bed.

The next morning we drank potfuls of coffee and started going through our gear. We would have to leave mid-morning the next day. I heard a vehicle and looked out the window to see an American military truck pull up outside the house. Mike joined me at the window.

A corporal got out of the driver's side, then opened the passenger door. A Vietnamese civilian with a pair of crutches got out. His left leg had been amputated at mid-thigh.

"It's Tully," Mike said. "Sergeant Mays' corporal. Someone's with him. Looks like Mays' houseboy."

I went to the front door to let them in, Li and Rose on my heels. "Girls, we need to talk army stuff," I told them.

As they vanished into the kitchen Rose asked, "Beer?"

"Yes," I said, "Please."

Corporal Tully's eyes opened wide when he saw the armament spread over the dining room table. I had been reassembling my M-16 as Mike re-packed grenades in the canteen covers we used to carry them. "Shee-it, you guys keep that stuff with you?" he asked.

"All the more reason to, now that we have some precious cargo to protect," I quipped.

As soon as Tully and the Vietnamese were seated, Rose and Li brought four bottles of beer. Li looked at the Vietnamese, then at me. I nodded, and he took the beer.

"Tully, who's your friend?" I asked. "Does he speak English?"

"This is Young Gee," he said. "Gee is Sergeant Mays' houseboy. He's worked for him for almost two years now." Tully looked at him and said, "He claims he doesn't speak English. But I think he understands a lot of it. Anyway, Mays said you might be able to use him."

I nodded at Li and she said something to Gee in Vietnamese. He smiled from ear to ear, showing white teeth with dark gaps top and bottom.

Tully whistled. "I'd heard you two got yourselves some real lookers," he said. Mike and I involuntarily bristled, braced for the usual crude remarks.

Tully read our body language, threw up his hands and smiled. "You guys are just damn lucky," he said. "Do you know how Gee got hurt?"

We shook our heads. Everyone knew Sergeant Mays had a houseboy and knew of his legendary abilities in the kitchen. But we didn't know he had only one leg.

"Gee fought against the French," he said. "He stepped on a mine, but that don't keep him from being the best damn houseboy Mays ever had. It does keep him from something else. The mine not only took off his leg, but also his privates. So that's something you don't have to worry about. Do you want him for your houseboy?"

I looked at Mike. He nodded.

"Somehow we hadn't thought about leaving the girls home alone," I said, appalled.

"You bet we'll take him, if he wants to come to work for us," Mike said, looking at Young Gee. Evidently Mays had talked us up to Gee, for he sat there enthusiastically nodding his head. So he understands some English, I thought.

"I have another proposal you might be interested in. Actually, a couple of things I wanted to ask you about. I hear you guys are going to be gone for ten days or so. Master Sergeant Duane said to tell you he would be glad to sleep on your couch this first trip out."

Master Sergeant Duane—"Daddy" Duane, a gray-haired army lifer in his late fifties, happily married some thirty years to an army brat back in the States, had the reputation of being a one-woman man. Daddy Duane drank very little, but for what drinking he did, we provided him with the good Scotch whiskey he preferred. A respected army lifer, he could be a formidable opponent.

"I'd feel safer leaving the girls with him here, and Young Gee to back him up," Mike said.

I nodded. "Tell Duane we'd appreciate it. We've got something for him to take home." Mike had another Chinese pistol with belt and holster stashed away.

We'll fix up one of the bedrooms. Tully, we'll have something for you, too," I promised. "It might have to be liquid if we don't run across something on this patrol. Thank Duane for us, would you?"

Tully stood, snapped his fingers as if he just remembered something. "One more thing. We had some real pissed-off French motor-pool officers visit this morning. How about if I send some of our people for that truck someone parked in the middle of the street about three blocks from here? The Frenchies'd owe us a favor then, and it would get the truck out of your neighborhood."

"Truck?" I asked.

"Truck?" Mike echoed.

"Tie one on last night?" Tully said as he went out the door.

CHAPTER TWENTY SEVEN

Luck Gets Thin

We dropped into an area bordering the Iron Triangle looking for propaganda teams. In the first village we came to we found leaflets written in Vietnamese, but no sign of the outfit, probably NVA, that supplied them. In the next village we found three heads mounted on posts in the middle of the village.

"What the hell...?" Mike asked, wrinkling his nose against the stink.

"Heads," Chen offered cheerfully. The ARVNs loaned Chen to us for the mission. Half Chinese, half Vietnamese, he could speak both languages. And English.

"Ripe heads," he said.

"Whose?" I asked.

"Probably the local schoolteacher's and the headmaster's. They must have strayed from the People's Army approved curriculum."

The village looked deserted. The villagers knew that talking to us would earn them a death sentence if Charlie found out. We looked at the heads, which seemed to undulate as if they were still alive. Mike kicked one of the posts and a swarm of flies lifted off in a cloud like a dirty blanket. Before they landed again we could see the empty eye sockets oozing wetness like corrupted tears. Skin hung in shreds around their rictus grins. We took a step back as the flies returned to their feast.

Our orders were to bring back information and do everything possible not to be seen, not to engage the enemy. "Let's get out of here before they find us," I said.

We were too late. We'd already been spotted. An overanxious NVA soldier fired a single, premature shot, or we would have walked into their ambush. We scrambled off the trail and returned fire. The malevolent odor of the heads still clogged my nostrils, and with the crack of bullets overhead, my stomach cramped. I looked for Mike, gave him a hand signal that meant let's-get-the-hell-out-of-here.

We ran, staying ahead of Charlie for most of two days. Unlike the rest of us, Stryder, who usually took point, could keep up a pace that was part trot, part gallop, for hours. He was in his element. He forged ahead on point to make sure there wasn't another ambush ahead, then dropped back on drag to see if Charlie was catching up with us, covering the trail twice to our once.

We caught sleep in snatches. To keep going, we swallowed the big pills called green weenies. We chewed the dehydrated meat from our new rations, which tasted like jerky. Washed it down with our new halazone-treated water. Then it started to rain. We clung to a knoll we thought would be less wet, since it had running water instead of puddles. The trees and undergrowth were thick, and the raindrops were large. So large they slapped the leaves, making enough noise to deafen us to Charlie's approach. We had used or discarded most of our supplies. After a night of cold rain and another day of running with Charlie at our backs, exhaustion set in.

That night Mike and I huddled under a torn poncho trying to read a water-soaked map by a dying flashlight. We thought we were half a day's march from our secondary extraction point. We had just decided to radio for extraction when an AK-47 lit up the night with its muzzle-flash. We could see the silhouette of the rifleman not fifteen yards away, as he came out of the brush.

Instinctively, we both fired. At the same time, Corporal Lansky opened up with several bursts from his M-16. Charlie twirled part-way around and squeezed the trigger of his AK-47 as he fell. Bullets ricocheted off the ground, splashing us with mud. I felt something tug at my side. A fiery sting. Mike grunted and fell to one knee, his head bent forward, hands over his face.

"Holy Christ, Mike, you okay?" I yelled, my pain forgotten. I looked back and forth from where Charlie lay to Mike, not sure if Charlie had been totally wasted.

"Sarge, you hit?" Lansky's husky voice cried in a too-loud whisper.

"Kennelley's hit!" I called back. "Lansky, can you check out Charlie?" I looked back at Mike. "You okay?" The pain in my side stung like a hundred hornets, and I knew the warm, sticky feeling flowing down my leg meant blood. I fumbled in the mud for the flashlight, turned it on. Nothing. I smacked it against my palm. It gave off a feeble light. Mike had slumped over on his side in the mud. The red lens of the flashlight showed black all over his face, the color of blood under a red light.

"Oh, Christ," I mumbled, then yelled out, "Mack, get over here!" About that time Mike moaned and blinked his eyes.

"Shit, I can't see! I can't see!" he cried, and tried to sit up.

"Hold still, goddammit," I yelled. I pulled a compress out of my belt-pouch, tried to wipe his forehead.

"Ow, what the hell are you doin'!" he said, struggling into a sitting position in spite of my efforts to hold him down.

"Lansky! What's goin' on!"

"Charlie's wasted, Sarge. Want me to check the team?"

"Yeah, and for Christ's sake, get Mack over here," I hollered, just as Mack dropped to his knees in front of me. Mack took the compress, poured water on it, and wiped Mike's forehead. He probed what looked like a deep cut, then reached into his bag for another compress.

"Some gash you got. But it's not deep enough your brains are gonna ooze out, if you had any." He dripped something in Mike's eyes, which turned out to be water, while I held the poncho over him to keep the rain off his face. Mack looked at me like I was crazy.

"Your eyes are fine," he told Mike. "You just can't see when they're full of blood. Got a headache?"

Mike nodded. Mack reached into his bag again and shook two tablets out of a bottle. "I don't think you have a concussion, so this should chase it away. It's not as strong as morphine, which you can have if these don't work. But don't take any green weenies until I tell you it's okay."

"What's with the green weenies?" I asked.

"They're amphetamines," Mack said. "Didn't you know that?"

"Yeah," I said, "guess I'd forgotten. I sank down in the mud, feeling the left-over adrenalin and green-weeny-amphetamines make my heart trip. Everything had slowed down except the drumming in my chest. I could hear the rain again, smell the mud and decaying leaves we were wallowing in. Finally, my heartbeat slowed.

Lansky ran up, dropped down on his knees next to Mike. "He okay?"

"Yeah, lucky he's a damn hard-headed sergeant, or he mighta' bought it," Mack said.

"Everyone else okay?" I asked. "Was Charlie alone?"

"Yeah, looks like it. He just traipsed in among us. Shit, Sarge, you get hit too? You're all bloody!" His light showed a dark stain from my left side to the knee.

I stared at it. "Sum-bitch."

Mack cut away my shirt, then fingered the canteen case on my belt. "Take this off," he said. Carefully I unbuckled the belt, which also held my pistol. I didn't want it to fall in the mud.

"Look," he said. Inside the pouch we saw one of the grenades was broken open, and the extra magazine pouch I carried for the M-16 had been deeply grooved by one of the AK-47 rounds. "You woulda' had a bad gut shot if you hadn't been carrying all that scrap iron. Lucky it didn't set off that grenade. Goddamn, I never saw so much luck in one place. Let's see your side."

Mack poked me enough to make me wince. "I'll stitch this up, but you'll have to get it looked at when we get back. It's not deep enough to extend into the abdominal cavity," he said.

Mack's needle didn't really hurt, but when he drew the strands of suture through the holes, it felt like chalk-on-a-blackboard. I could feel it in my teeth. The horizon tilted, then stabilized.

"Let's get the hell out of here," I said to Mike. "If it doesn't quit raining, we're gonna have to make it clear to our primary for a dust-off. Or do you think we can chance it at the secondary?"

"Secondary," Mike said, one hand on his bandage. "It's closer."

"Secondary it is. If you can make it, we can get going whenever this meat-carver gets through with—ouch! Sweet Jesus, Mack."

"Why, I thought you were in a hurry," he said with his most innocent look. "Or do you want me to take the time to do this right?"

I rolled my eyes, tried not to fidget. Finally, he taped a compress over the row of neat stitches. The cut had quit bleeding. I was rewarded with two pills from the same bottle.

"This the same thing you gave him?" I asked. "Don't I get something better?"

"Shit, you guys start sleeping with young, beautiful women and all of a sudden you think you should get preferential treatment," Mack said with a smug look.

I looked at Mike. "There anyone who doesn't know?"

The next day we reached our extraction point and got a dustoff that flew us to the hospital in Saigon. They kept Mike long enough to look at his head and change his bandage. The doctor looked at my stitches and gave me the usual injection. Unknown to us, Mack had contacted Sergeant Mays' people, who told the girls we were back and in the hospital with minor wounds. They were on the point of hysteria when we drove up.

We were still filthy, carrying field packs and M-16s, wearing muddy fatigues encrusted with blood. Li and Rose were on us as soon as we came through the front door. Red-eyed but relieved that we were not badly hurt, they helped us change from our bloody uniforms.

"Is this a great way to come home, or what?" I asked Mike.

"Yeah. Maybe. We'll see," he said.

Daddy Duane looked at our bloodstained uniforms and raised a disdainful eyebrow. "You two don't slow down, you'll never make it to retirement." With a grin and a wave, he ducked out the door before we could say thanks.

The girls had Sergeant Mays' hot tub in the back yard ready and waiting. Mike and Rose took a shower together, Rose scouring him clean. When they finished and headed for the hot tub, Li led me into the shower. My energy level was on empty and I barely managed to keep my stitches dry. It felt so good to have Li take care of me, I didn't care about anything else. She finished scrubbing me and shampooed my hair with something that smelled like sandalwood. I almost fell asleep standing under the shower.

Mike and Rose were already in the big hot tub. Li led me out and sat me down on the edge with my feet in the water and ran back inside. She returned with a small step-stool, which she put on the ledge below the water's surface. It just fit, and I got wet from my hips down. Not satisfied, she arranged a stack of pillows behind me, covered them with a sheet of plastic. Then she poured the hot water over my chest and right side. I objected feebly until I realized how soothing it was. A few minutes later my eyelids were drooping.

The water in the tub came up to Mike's chin. He had fallen asleep, and Rose held on to him so he wouldn't slip under the water. I wanted to persuade her to let him slip under so we could watch him sputter. But I fell asleep before I could suggest it.

The next morning I awoke in my own bed, feeling stiff and sore, unable to remember how I got there. I moved slightly, and Li, curled up on my shoulder, raised her head and gave me a smile brighter than sunshine. I gathered her into my arms. The clinging silk outfit she wore with nothing on underneath made me forget my wounds and sore muscles. Still exhausted, I felt my eyelids close.

I awakened again in the dark. I'd slept all day. I smelled exotic, spicy food. The delectable aroma wafted its way from the kitchen, producing a hunger in me stronger than a team of horses. Or water buffalo. I slipped on the robe Li had insisted I buy for myself and followed my nose to the kitchen.

Li and Young Gee sat at the kitchen table. Li bounced up and hugged me tight—right over my stitches. When I winced, she realized what she had done. I could see the tears starting to form in her eyes, an apology on her lips, so I smiled, gritted my teeth, and whisked her off her feet into my arms. Laughing, she clung to me with all her strength, which reduced me to mere protoplasm. I had never known anyone so unassuming and innocent. I knew I loved her more than I'd ever loved anyone. I wondered what would ever become of her if something happened to me. It was too frightening to consider what would ever become of *me* if anything happened to *her*.

"I'm hungry as an old bear," I said, biting her ear, causing debilitating laughter.

"Dinner is ready for you now," she said. I put her down. She lifted the lid from a pot on the stove, and the aroma of spices filled the kitchen. It would have driven me crazy if she hadn't immediately dished me out a large portion. Young Gee set a bottle of some kind of sauce on the table, of which I became instantly suspicious. The Vietnamese poured concentrated fire on their food. Both of them stood there watching me, the suspense building, hoping I would like it. I took a fork-full of rice mixed with what looked like a variety of sea-food. I discovered the spices made it quite hot enough without the sauce. So hot my eyes began to water.

"Ambrosia and nectar!" I said, tears running down my cheeks. Both of them looked disappointed and puzzled.

"What is that?" Li asked.

"That means it is food fit for the gods," I said, thinking fast, hoping I hadn't upset them. "It's delicious. Very good. Now, please, sit down and eat with me. After you bring me some water."

"We have eaten, Li said. They remained standing next to the table, watching me eat.

"Where's Rose and Mike?" I asked. Li turned a deep shade of red and Gee did an about-face that would have been fast for a man with both legs. "Are they okay?"

Li looked at Young Gee, then said, "Oh, very much okay. Still in bed."

"Still in bed?" Then the realization sank in. "Oh. Okay. Then please, sit down. If you don't want to eat, get something to drink, but sit down, please. This is good. Very good. First, would you bring me a handkerchief?" I sniffed.

We were still at the table when Rose came in. She pulled her silk robe closer and glanced at Li. They smiled like a major conspirators. Rose filled two bowls with the rice concoction and fled back to the bedroom.

CHAPTER TWENTY EIGHT

Defending The Household

We had several more days to recuperate before we would go out again. We used them to address the question of security at the house. We were unsure of what might happen when we went on future missions. Charlie had been offering a bounty on some of the snipers and special-ops outfits ever since the French war. As far as we knew we hadn't become that important—or that well known. If they came looking for us at home and we were gone, we wanted the girls to be able to defend themselves. Mike worried that some of the service personnel who had stayed at the house in its crash pad days might not be aware it was ours now, and try to spend the night.

"Where are we going to get the girls something smaller than a .45?" Mike asked.

"I don't know. Sergeant Mays?"

The good sergeant, trying to liquidate his abundant and varied trading stock before he went back to the World, produced an extensive home-defense arsenal for us to choose from. We selected two Smith and Wesson Model 10 revolvers for the girls, a thirteen-round semi-auto Browning High-Power for Gee, and two pump shotguns. The revolvers, .38 Special caliber, fired a reasonably potent cartridge, were light and small enough to fit the girls' hands. The nominal fee we paid Mays included enough ammo to repel a major assault. He loaned us a light truck and directed us to the northern edge of the heliport where we'd landed the day before for target practice. I felt much better after the initial range session. Li showed better-than-average aptitude. Gee and Rose were afraid of the noise and recoil, but realized we wanted them to learn, so they did a credible job. At home, we stashed the loaded guns where it would be easy to grab them in a hurry.

Due to bad intelligence, our next mission was eventually cancelled. We set out to recon a propaganda group and got as far as touching down on the LZ that would be our pick-up point. Then we got orders to wait...and wait. The afternoon of the second day we were still there, and the mission was scrubbed. All of us suffered from sitting for most of two days on a hot, humid ridge with more biting, stinging insects than stars in the sky.

We flew back, stopping at the hospital. After they checked our bandages from the previous mission, we talked the nurses into lending us a locker for our gear. We tossed our fatigues into the staff's washer, then took a shower. In a little more than an hour we had cleaned up and hit the streets, looking for a bar.

Our choice turned out to be a bad one. We hadn't been there for more than twenty minutes when some of the hospital personnel arrived. Two of the technicians had seen Li and Rose when we had them examined. We bought their group drinks, they bought us a round. Then one loudmouth, still wearing scrubs, started asking about the girls.

"Damn fine lookin' women," Scrubs said in a loud voice.

His friend was wearing a black T-shirt and fatigues. "Yeah," he said, speaking loud enough to make sure we heard him across the tiny bar. "I wouldn't mind havin' a piece of that action myself!"

I could feel Mike tense up. "Let's go," I said. "It's not worth it." We chugged the rest of our beers and got down off of our bar stools, only to be met by Scrubs and Black Shirt.

"Hey, I know you guys are gone a lot. You could let us take care of those little slants while you're away," Scrubs said. I stepped between him and Mike.

"Yeah," Black Shirt said. "I'd like to get some a' that Asian poon-tang. Those little broads got boobs on 'em like no slants I ever seen." He leered down at me. A big boy, he stood about two inches taller and weighed a good twenty pounds more than either of us, but he looked fat and slovenly. My "it's-not-worth-it-Mike" mode was dissolving fast. I stared up at Black Shirt and took a step toward him. He backed up. I took another step, and another, backing him up, not taking my eyes from his. When he backed into a table, I hit him in the face as hard and as fast as I could. I heard one of the bones in my hand snap. The punch knocked him over the table and into a booth.

I turned and looked at Scrubs, then took a step in his direction. His eyes looked like an owl's. He let go of his drink in mid-air, turned tail, and was out the back door before the glass hit the floor. For a second, no one moved. I looked down at Black Shirt, who hadn't moved either. If he's still breathing, I thought, I'll wring his neck.

Suddenly I felt myself being dragged toward the front door. I looked to see whose hands were clamped around my arm, and discovered they belonged to Mike. "Not worth it, huh?" he said. "C'mon, let's get out of here!"

We ran down the street and hailed a taxi, one of the old French cars that looked like it had been built around two upside-down "U" shaped panels. We jammed ourselves into the back seat, and Mike gave him a number on one of the downtown streets. The first people the MP's would talk to would be the taxi drivers that hung out around the hospital. If this one told them he took us downtown, it wouldn't lead them to the house.

Saigon taxi drivers, as a matter of pride, drive as fast as their vehicle will possibly go. Off we went in a cloud of blue exhaust, in greater danger, I was sure, than the last two missions. Downtown we hailed another cab, and got out about ten blocks from home. We ran until we were a block away, slowed down, and looked to see if anything seemed out of place. We almost burst through the front door without knocking, then at the last moment remembered we'd armed our crew. We knocked, and Young Gee's voice called out, "Who is there?"

Mike and I looked at each other. "He does speak English," he said. "It's us! Open up!"

Gee opened the door and we piled in, slammed and locked it. My hand had begun to swell. I headed to the kitchen for ice, almost knocking Li down as I came through the door.

"Sorry," I said.

"Your hand!" she cried. "It is bleeding!"

"Yeah, I know. Some guy busted his teeth on it."

She looked horrified, then puzzled. "How did he do that?" she asked.

"I need some ice," I said, smiling in spite of the pain.

Mike came in just as I immersed my hand in a bowl of ice cubes. "I've gotta go for our stuff," he said. "I'll find out what happened."

I started to say I'd go with him, then realized I couldn't go near the hospital. Mike read my thoughts. "Yeah, you better stay here."

"Those goddam hospital pukes," I said. "Okay, go on. If you run into Black Shirt, give him my regards. Just not as hard." The pain and swelling in my hand began to subside from the ice.

"I'll be back," Mike said.

Li, solicitous, looked at me expectantly but never asked what happened.

Three hours later I'd worked myself into a sweat. What if I killed Black Shirt? What if the MP's had Mike and were beating the shit out of him, which they often did as part of their interrogation techniques. What if they came to arrest me?

I heard a truck pull up outside and peeked out the window. Mike and Tully got out. Mike looked battle-ready with his web belt, pistol, canteens, and all the other gear on it. My web belt, similarly equipped, he had draped over his shoulder. Two bandoliers of ammo were slung across his chest, both of our M-16s over the other shoulder, and one gear bag in each hand. He and Tully were laughing.

"This guy's the one?" asked Tully, once inside.

"In person," Mike replied. Again they erupted in laugher.

"He doesn't look that bad—yet. But then he never did look very good," Tully quipped. They laughed again.

"All right, what the hell is going on?"

"The guy you hit? You messed him up pretty bad. But he won't want to talk to the MP's," Mike said.

"How'd you manage that?"

"Well, I planned to sneak off with our stuff from the hospital. I figured they'd brought Black Shirt there. But we never got the keys to the locker. I went looking for the nurse. Found her in the lounge. She said I had a lot of nerve coming back. I told her I hoped we didn't get her in any trouble. She said we hadn't got her in trouble, not yet. But Richard, the guy with the black T-shirt, he's another story." Mike smiled. "She said you broke his jaw, knocked out some teeth, and gave him a concussion."

"No wonder my hand hurts," I said.

"I let her know, word for word, what Richard said to us about the Rose and Li. She didn't like that. I told her how we rescued the girls, bought Sergeant Mays' place, and that's when the lights came on. She had been around when we had the girls examined.

"She opened up the locker and clucked a little over the armament. As she left, she turned and said, 'Richard isn't very popular here. He's still in the emergency room. If he ever saw you with all that stuff, he'd think you'd hunt him down if he ever talked to an MP.'

"I found Richard and told him about how some soldiers go crazy for killing, especially revenge killing. And that you were a little twitchy anyway. Richard decided he didn't want to talk to the MPs. I said I'd tell you that. He seemed relieved. Immensely relieved. Said he'd never been hit so hard."

Mike started to laugh again. "I told Black Shirt he hadn't made you mad enough to hit him as hard as you could. So-o-o, your ass is off the hook. I think. You owe me big-time, more than you can ever pay. But buy me a beer, we'll call it even."

Rose jumped up to get him a beer and Li followed. Neither of us could understand what she said to Rose in French as they left the room. It was probably just as well.

The next day my hand had become so swollen I couldn't bend my fingers. At the hospital, the x-ray showed that I had broken a bone in my hand. I would have a cast for at least a month, the doc said. He told me to keep an ice pack on it and come back tomorrow. I'd get a genuine state-of-the-art plaster cast after the swelling went down. When he left the room, I slipped the x-rays under my shirt and got word to Mack.

"What the hell do you think I am, Jesus Christ, or just one of the disciples?" Mack said when I asked him if he could just wrap it up. He looked at the x-rays. "Let's see your hand," he said. "Is this where it hurts?" I flinched. "Here?" he asked, moving his fingers across the back of my hand. "Here?" he said, not waiting for an answer.

"Okay, we'll try wrapping it." He shook his head gave me a warning look. "You hit anyone before it heals up, you'll need a cast for sure. Probably surgery. Got that?"

I nodded. "Yeah. Thanks, Mack."

CHAPTER TWENTY NINE

Prejudice And Fear

We still had a month's leave left. Mack had put me on sick leave, so Mike took three weeks. That gave us a lot of time to do nothing. We took Li and Rose out every night to some of the finest restaurants in Saigon. We rubbed elbows with the press corps, businessmen of different nationalities, and members of diplomatic missions. These experiences had one common unpleasantness.

Mike and I dressed in slacks and shirts. Wearing a tie became more of a sacrifice than we could make in the name of being presentable. The girls wore traditional dress at first, then switched to American clothes, which they found in whatever colors and fabrics they wanted. It didn't matter what we wore, for nothing could keep us from looking like two American soldiers with two Vietnamese women. We were given tables in the rear of restaurants when we could see empty tables closer to the band and dance floor. "Ah, so sorry, those tables are reserved."

One night we watched a Caucasian couple who didn't like their table point to another one closer to the band. After palming a smiling maitre d' a bill, they were seated at the better table. I looked at Mike and he nodded. We picked up our drinks and moved to the table they had just left. As soon as we sat down, I saw a well-dressed Vietnamese man whisper to the maitre d', who scurried over to our table.

Mike glowered at him and muttered under his breath. "I'll tear the goddam building apart rather than settle for second rate. The bastards!" With much scraping and bowing the maitre d' said that, so sorry, the table is reserved. We were being shunned by Americans, Europeans and Vietnamese.

Mike smiled at him. "Tell the party you have reserved that table for them," he said, pointing at the table we had just left. He turned his back on the maitre d'.

"I am *sorry*, but I cannot do that," he said, more emphatically. Two well-dressed, stocky-looking characters, undoubtedly bouncers, came up behind the maitre d'. "Perhaps you do not understand. These tables are *reserved*," one of them said. I could see Mike's arm press against his waistband where he carried his .45 Auto. As I felt for my own, a fit of wisdom overcame me. If we started trouble here, we might be lucky and end up in the stockade instead of floating face down in the river. I stood up. "Hey, let's get outta here," I said. "My hand needs some ice." I said, trying to hint to Mike that I wouldn't be much good in a fight with only one hand. "I don't like this place anyway." I reached into my pocket and grabbed a fistful of change for our drinks, then threw it up in the air over the table. Coins tinkled loudly and bounced onto the dance floor, rolling everywhere.

"Keep the change," I said, smiling sweetly at the fuming maitre d'.

Once outside, we walked in silence. We had been to several bars in the previous two weeks that catered to servicemen. Raucous and bawdy, they made Li and Rose uncomfortable. Inevitably some of the guys made cracks about them, thinking they were prostitutes. A few carousers asked if they could have them when we were through. Then there were always the dregs who had to make a point of showing how gross they could be and asked in the vernacular if the girls were good lovers, or if they did specific things. That usually prompted one of us, feeling fully justified, to deliver the first blow. It looked like the so-called high-class joints were just as prejudiced and perhaps even more cruel with their barbs.

"*Damn*," Mike said. "No wonder the world's always having wars."

"Yeah," I said. "I remember my high school days in Arizona. The Mexicans who went out with Whites got the same type of treatment. You know, we haven't given much thought to our living arrangements violating army policy—and the damn government's, too," I said. "They're the worst for prejudice—the United States Army is particularly unforgiving to us enlisted peons."

Mike feigned surprise. "You, criticizing the army that feeds us? What's this war coming to? And last time we talked about breaking rules, who was it that said we shouldn't worry?"

Suddenly we heard footsteps behind us, coming at a run. Mike and I turned, almost drawing our sidearms. "Hey," hollered Corporal Bloom. "The Lootennant's looking for you guys! Mack says we got another mission, but not to say anything!"

I pulled Li tight against me. Again, my thoughts did not follow their usual pattern. Instead of wondering what the mission might be, making a mental checklist of my equipment, my mind filled with thoughts of Li's safety. I wondered when I'd get back to her. The realization something could happen to her before I got back hit me like a fist to the belly. Nothing Charlie had ever done scared me that much.

I had to make it back.

CHAPTER THIRTY

POW

We were assigned to an outpost just east of the Ho Chi Minh Trail in Cambodia. Officially we weren't there, but that didn't make it any less miserable.

"They say for half the year it rains here every day," Mike said.

"You're tellin' me. This is World War I with a reddish cast." The dirt we were dug into was red. "Sometimes I wonder what kind of a favor Jaimeson did us with this new assignment."

"Yeah. If I'd known we'd be away from the girls for such long periods of time, I would have wanted to stay with the ARVNs. Of course, we didn't know we'd have the girls then."

Water soaked into the denuded red soil of our hilltop, making a glutinous batter of mud. We had to pave the trenches connecting the bunkers with ammo crates and pieces of palette. Our digs were damp but sturdy, reinforced with logs and layers of sandbags. We were securely dug in.

I felt weary, body and soul. Over three years in-country, I had aged beyond calendar time. It had been months since I'd been home for JR's funeral, and I now saw a different face of this war. Maybe the answer to what I could do for my country had turned out to be more than I could manage. I would still do the best I could, honoring the oath I'd taken.

I sat down at the desk of ammo-cases in our office just as the blast of a mortar round shook our digs. Shrapnel whistled overhead. Tommy Hicks, my corporal, who had been with the team for almost a year, had gone to one of the villages with some of our Montagnard tribesmen. I came flying out of the subterranean room, my web belt and all its attached gear slung over one shoulder, helmet in one hand and M-16 in the other. I wondered if they had they been caught coming back.

Small arms fire punctuated the afternoon humidity. Over the berm, I could see Corporal Hicks running for the wire, carrying one of the Montagnards over his shoulder. Then he suddenly stopped running and reached behind him with one hand. He dropped to the muddy ground, the Yard still on top. Neither of them moved. Half way down the hill I could see the other three Yards who had gone with him, lying where they had been flung by the mortar blast.

"Goddammit, I tell 'em not to bunch up and what do they do?" I said, anger covering my fear that Tommy would go home in an aluminum box. I ducked as more bullets cracked overhead.

The pot-shots kept coming. We fired back into the trees, not knowing if we hit anything. By the end of the afternoon we had two more casualties, one American and one Yard. Just after sundown they landed a mortar round at the end of our digs, blowing up a rubber bladder-tank of fuel we had for the choppers. I could feel the heat on the back of my neck.

Flaming aviation gas sprayed one of the Yards, leaving him silhouetted against the flames, his flesh burning. His screams penetrated to the marrow. One of the other Yards, crouched low, ran him down and threw a tarp over him.

"Call the fire department?" someone cracked.

"Get your eyes back on the trees!" I yelled. We sat, watched, saw nothing. The gas had been contained and did not threaten our digs as it burned. Just as we planned, I thought. Wonder if the incinerated Yard feels better knowing that.

"Maybe it'll dry out the ground," someone offered.

"Shut up and watch the goddam trees," I said gruffly. Bad jokes helped us keep our sanity. And kept us from thinking about the men lying out there, knowing we couldn't help them.

It took until well after dark before our beacon of flames burned itself to oblivion. We went out after Tommy and the Yards. Our two infrared scopes were our eyes in the dark. We kept a continuous scan of the tree line. As long as we had no fog or heavy rain, we could see Charlie, but he couldn't see us. And if he shot from the trees, the muzzle-flash showed his position.

Under the cover of dark, we crawled out past the wire. When I reached Tommy, I thought I felt a faint pulse. Stifling the frantic urge to throw him over my shoulder and run to safety, I dragged him a few feet at a time through the muck to our digs. When I got him to Mack, both of us were covered with red mud.

"What do you think?" I urged him. He shook his head and uttered a non-committal grunt. He placed a finger against the side of Tommy's neck, lifted one eyelid. He turned away from him and put a hand on my shoulder.

"He's gone," he said.

We both flinched as another explosion boomed just beyond the wire. "Jeezus," Mack said. "Now what?" Then our infrared riflemen opened up and someone cut loose with the M-60 machine gun. I felt grateful I could leave Tommy's body for Mack to care for. I seemed to have discovered another chink in my armor.

"What the hell happened?" I asked one of the men who had a night scope mounted on his rifle.

"I don't know, Sarge. Something blew. Maybe they had the bodies booby trapped."

"I'm going back out," I said.

He looked back into the scope. "Wait a minute, they're coming in... They've got...looks like five casualties."

Five casualties? I thought. We'd already brought back Tommy and the man he had carried. There should be *four* at most. Were they bringing enemy bodies?

"Can't be. Lemme see," I said, taking his rifle with the big, clumsy night scope. "Damn!" I swore under my breath. The images were blurry, but I could make out silhouettes moving, crouched, one with a body over his shoulder, the others dragging what looked like smaller bodies. I couldn't tell who was alive, who had been wounded.

I met them as they came through the wire.

"Five, Sarge. The mortar got two of the Yards, wounded the third," one of them whispered in the dark.

"And?" I asked. By their silence, I knew they had something else. "Give," I whispered, as we pulled and carried the grisly burdens over the berm to Mack's makeshift hospital. Then I realized the other body was Corporal Salazar. "Sally," I said.

"He's bought it, Sarge," said one of the riflemen.

First Tommy. Now Sally. This is *my* team, goddammit, this is happening to *my* men. "Who the hell's the other one?" I asked, pointing the muzzle of my rifle at the unexpected small form.

"The one who got Sally. He had been booby trapping the bodies. Sally jumped him. The grenade he was using for a booby trap went off. Got them both."

"He still alive?" I started to shake, and my thumb found the selector lever on my M-16. It would just take a short burst. Payback. Goddamn slants. As I jabbed him with the muzzle of my rifle, I knew I couldn't do it.

Goddamn him anyway, I thought. "Get him to Mack, report back," I said, and headed for my digs. I had to find forms and write letters, the kind no one ever wants to write.

They brought the prisoner into my digs on a litter. A little guy, not over five feet tall. They stumbled coming in, tearing down the blanket from the doorway. The faint light shone out into the night.

"What are you guys trying to do, give them a nice, well-lit doorway to shoot at?" I growled and reached up over my desk to unscrew the single bulb, giving it a reprieve in its struggle to stave off the darkness.

They reattached the blanket, aided by curses barely audible. I screwed the bulb back in and looked down at the man who killed Sally. Someone had spread a field dressing on his belly, a big square gauze bandage, crusted with blood. He wore a North Vietnamese Army officer's uniform.

I grunted in disapproval as they set his stretcher in the corner. Our wounded would be tended to first, so it would be a while before they got to him. "Don't put any of the our wounded in here," I said. "They'll kill him."

I looked back to the letter I had started on the ruled tablet on my desk. I found it extremely difficult writing to Tommy's wife, telling her how he had died. How long ago had it been, I wondered, that they had celebrated their first anniversary? A month? Two?

Dear Mrs. Hicks:

It is with deep regret and great personal sorrow that I must inform you that your husband was killed in action today.

He was an exceptionally fine soldier, and I feel honored that he had been a member of my A-Team.

Your husband gave up his life saving one of his comrades in arms, and I have recommended him posthumously for the Silver Star for gallantry."

I had pinned some photos above my makeshift desk. Bordered in white, Tommy grinned down at me. Stripped to the waist, he had his hands on his hips, his skinny chest stuck out. Next to him, a figure with a cammo-painted face, draped with rifles, bandoliers, and a belt of .30 caliber ammo over his shoulders held a wooden mock-up of Tommy's corporal's stripes. The figure had a big wooden hammer and a ludicrously large spike, poised to nail the stripes onto Tommy's bare arm. An arrow pointed to this sinister character. Block letters next to it read, "SARGE." I took it down, set it next to my letter.

"Shit," I said. There would be no silver star. The Army could not decorate the dead or the living where there not supposed to be any American forces, thus no fighting, no bravery, no casualties. I would forward my recommendation to Lieutenant Jaimeson, who would chew my ass on his next visit. The matter would end there for the army, but for me and for Tommy's wife it would never end.

I sat and stared at the wall for a long time, not seeing sandbags and timbers but the faces of men who had gone back to the World—or somewhere beyond. I'd watched many of them die. Watched Dan fall face-down into a rice paddy. I'd gone home to bury JR. Shorty lost an arm from a booby trap. Andy had been blown to such small bits that we didn't find much of him. Tommy and Sally were gone. I could still see them, like a motion picture in terrible color projected from my memory onto the wall of our digs.

My mental movie was interrupted by the prisoner, who groaned and thrashed on his litter. I turned to see him struggling to sit up. I drew my .45 Auto and pointed it at him. "Lay down, you goddam gook," I snarled. He fell back on the litter. There's one language everyone understands, I thought. Forty-five auto.

"I ought to waste your fucking ass, help make up for the guys you shot up today." I didn't intend to, but it felt good to say it.

"You will make your intelligence people very unhappy if you do," he said in a thin voice with almost no accent. That confounded me. He closed his eyes as a spasm of pain passed through him, his hands gripping the side of the litter so hard his knuckles turned white. I holstered the pistol and looked at the door. Where the hell had the medics had gotten to? I wondered if anyone else knew he spoke English. He watched me, his dark eyes large in a pallid face.

"I also speak French and several dialects of Chinese. And Vietnamese, of course." He managed a condescending smile through the pain. "Do you find that hard to believe?"

I didn't want to admit that there could be anything admirable about him. The images of my reverie were too fresh, the ink still wet on the letter I had just written. It would be easier to see Charlie as illiterate, not as smart, definitely not smarter, or better educated, than me.

He closed his eyes and the muscles at the sides of his jaws knotted up. I picked up the field phone to check on our wounded, told the medics that this one is a live wire and apt to run off—or crawl off—if they didn't do something with him. I hoped someone would come and take him away or give him enough of some drug to knock him out.

I reached for my cigarettes, and his eyes followed my movements. "Cigarette?" I heard myself ask.

"Please," he replied.

Wary of getting too close to him, I lit two, squatted and extended my arm to hand him one. He closed his eyes and took a deep drag.

"Thank you," he said, smoke floating out of his mouth and nose. "Thank you very much."

"Where did you learn to speak English so well?" I asked.

"New York," he said. "I lived there for four years. Learned to speak French in Saigon, and Chinese in China–with Ho Chi Minh and General Giap." My eyes widened. He gave a weak smile. "No, I didn't know them. But I saw them, before the defeat of the French at Dien Bien Phu."

I took a closer look. His face looked smooth, except for a few wrinkles in his forehead and around the eyes. His hair had a touch of gray.

"How old are you, anyway?" I asked.

He grimaced. "Sometimes I can't even remember what year it is. I am fifty-five now. I have been a soldier for forty-seven years."

Blood dripped from the stretcher onto the dirt floor. Red soil mixed with red blood. I frowned, picked up the corner of the compress on his belly. "You're bleeding."

He nodded.

I could see how badly he'd been injured. "You were a soldier when you were eight?"

"Not much of one, I'm afraid, but a soldier nonetheless. I find it hard to believe myself. It is a very long time."

"Who were you fighting all those years?"

He took another drag and exhaled a blue cloud. His eyes seemed to focus on something inside the cloud. "You must know my country has been at war for hundreds of years." His face looked haggard, his eyes old. "Fighting has become a part of our heritage. Our way of life. Maybe war is in our genes."

I turned at the sound of footsteps. The medic slipped past the blanket and squatted next to the litter. He reached for the dressing, removed it with a yank. The blood, dried in places, stuck the dressing to the wound. The prisoner winced and bit his lip to keep from crying out.

"What will happen to him?" I asked.

The medic didn't look up. "They're giving him to the ARVNs. You hear that, asshole?" he asked. "Arvin! You know who that is?" The little man lay there as if he did not understand the medic. "The Army of the Ree-public of Viet-fuckin'-Nam, man," he said. "I bet those boys have some fun with you the way they go about getting their answers!" He smiled ominously at me, then looked back at his patient and glowered at him. "Goddam slant."

"What's with his wound?"

"The grenade he had went off. Sally got most of it. This guy got several chunks of it in the gut. Intestines are shredded, and probably his stomach.

He shouldn't be alive." He replaced the compress. "There's nothing I can do for him."

He broke open an ampule of morphine and stabbed it into the prisoner's thigh. As he rammed it home, he pointed to the cigarette. "Got any more of those?"

"Sure," I said, handing over the pack. "Keep 'em. He gonna last long enough for ARVN to come and get him?"

"Probably not."

He lit a cigarette and sat down against the wall, feet stretched out in front of him. "We got two wounded, and two of ours bought it. Two of the Yards bought it, plus one wounded and one French-fried." He jerked his thumb in the general direction of the litter. "He's the last one—a goddam fuckin' gook P.O.W." He drew out the sound of the letters. He glared at the prisoner, then wearily got to his feet. "Shit. I gotta get some sleep. They may be back tonight."

"You gonna leave him here?"

"There's nowhere else for him. Everyone else's got wounded."

"Wait a minute! If you leave him with me, what can I give him? If he wants water, or...you want to leave some morphine?"

"Jeezus," the medic said, looking from him to me. "What the hell do you care?" He started out.

I stood up. "Get your ass back in here! Now!" I didn't like him questioning me when I was the one who gave the orders.

"Look, I'll be here for the whole night, or what's left of it. I want some sleep, too. If he's out of his head with pain, or moaning for water, I want to be able to shut him up."

He gave me a half-dozen ampules. "Every two to four hours. Or all of them at once, and we won't have to worry about the little bastard. Water's okay. If he's bleeding internally, it won't matter. If not, and he dehydrates, he won't last. If ARVN gets him, he won't live. Thanks for the smokes." He lurched up the stairs and into the night.

I felt the POW's eyes on me. I looked down.

"Thank you."

I stared back. "You heard what the medic said."

"Yes."

"What will happen if ARVN gets you first?"

He looked away. "Very unpleasant things. I rather imagine they'll enjoy it, though."

I picked up the ampules. The devices themselves looked innocuous enough, a small amount of clear liquid, a short needle. It would be easy enough to inject him with all of them. And he might prefer to have it that way.

"Tell me," he said, interrupting my thoughts. "You've been here much longer than most—have you not?" He stifled a cough. Blood oozed out onto his lips.

"Yeah, a lot longer," I said. "Three times as long. I volunteered." Even as I spoke, I heard the voice inside my head asking why. I used to have answers.

He closed his eyes. "Sometimes it doesn't make sense," he whispered, as if he had read my mind. "After a while, you begin to wonder if there *is* any sense in it. You volunteered to be here, you say. My men are all volunteers. Dedicated. Well trained. We have volunteered for the duration of the war," he said proudly, "Even if that is ten or twenty years from now. You will never outlast us."

I thought about the Montagnard tribesmen who they forced to fight with them. They had to threaten to kill their families to get them to "volunteer." Still, I wondered...could it be possible for Charlie to outlast us?

I looked at the blanket hanging over the door. It shut out the world, except for a few cracks where flying insects were drawn inside, hypnotized, to beat themselves to death on the dim light bulb.

Outside, Mike's team pulled sentry duty, guarding the perimeter. I wouldn't have to make up a roster, so I could talk to this POW without interruption. I pulled the ammo-crate chair closer to his litter, took a new pack of cigarettes out of my pocket, lit two more.

"Why is it," I asked him, "That you don't want these people to have their own government? That's what we're here for, after all."

"Is it really?" he asked. "Have you ever asked yourself the same question?"

The confusion in my mind must have shown on my face. He smiled and went on.

"The Diem government is not supported by the people. Neither are the ARVNs. And they never will be," he said.

The light flickered and blinked. I couldn't imagine this bloody, mud-covered little man soldiering for more than twice my lifetime. His eyes stared and seemed fixed. I looked to see if he was still breathing.

"Before World War II," he said suddenly, "we fought the French. Then the Japanese. When World War II ended, the Chinese." A cough wracked him, his face turned grey. He screwed his eyes shut tight. Just as suddenly, he opened them again.

"You Americans see your country as the world's cradle of freedom. Yet you ignored our pleas for independence. You supported the French, who enslaved us. So after World War II, we fought the French again. Then China gave us aid." His breath, shallow, wheezed and gasped.

"Our soldiers travel the Ho Chi Minh Trail ten to twelve miles a day... carry fifty or sixty pounds. Weapons, ammunition, other materiel...the mortars used today. Fed, housed, by the people. Easier for us to support an army in the field than you."

I couldn't help but wonder how many of us would march ten miles a day, day after day, with a sixty-pound pack, committed to fight whether it meant five years, ten, or twenty. Or until we were killed. In the beginning I had that kind of commitment. Only for my own country, on my home soil, could I ever do it again.

"I'd always wondered why they help you. Feed you," I said. "Maybe sometimes the help doesn't happen spontaneously," I said, "like with the Yards. That would explain why you kill village headmen and teachers."

"The Viet Cong were called Viet Minh while the French were here," he went on without comment. "Your infamous puppet Ngo Dinh Diem...ah, pardon me. You see...I have also been a political officer."

The little man's voice rattled, like someone with a bad cold. He lay there with his eyes closed, and I studied his face. I could not help but admire his tenacity and idealism. No longer able to offer physical resistance, he engaged me with his idealism. A worthy adversary.

I remembered some of what I'd learned about Diem, the President of South Vietnam. Many Vietnamese hated him, longed for the return of the Viet Minh. Diem's attempt to insult the Viet Minh, calling them communists—Viet Cong. Instead, it became a rallying cry, a badge of honor.

Why, I wondered, were we supporting his government?

The prisoner's eyes opened again. "The people will never support you," he said, as though he hadn't stopped. "Like the French, if you bomb and shell their villages from a distance...burn them because they help us, or the Viet Cong...you become an imperialist aggressor, here to conquer...not liberate."

His words stung. "But can't you see that your country will be swallowed up by the communist tide?"

"The people don't even know what communism is. They support us because we oppose the man your country backs...the oppressor, who took their land. This is why the people of Vietnam support us, not the ARVN." The anger in his eyes had not weakened. "As a political officer..."

The prisoner winced and his fingers tightened on the litter. He moaned and began to cough, covering his mouth with his hand, but the blood ran through his fingers. I unwrapped another field dressing and offered it to him to wipe up his blood.

"Are you ready for another?" I asked, holding up one of the ampules.

He shook his head. "I would like water." I reached for a canteen, found a tin can from a package of C-Rations, and held it to his lips. He coughed, his blood spattering my hand.

I realized I wanted to talk to him soldier-to-soldier, to find out how he dealt with the same heat, the same cold, bugs, disease, and all the hardships that we shared.

"I'll get the medic," I said. "Or more morphine."

"No! No, thank you. Please. I was trying to tell you..."

His words rushed out, and I wondered if he really wanted me to hear them or if talking kept his mind off the pain. Or both.

"Each of our units has a political officer, responsible for keeping morale high, reminding each soldier he is fighting for the liberty of his country, self government, freedom."

How could *he* feel that way? I wondered. Those were the things *I* fought to win for the South Vietnamese.

He coughed again, and I picked up the ampule and stabbed it into his thigh, squeezing the plunger. He's the prisoner. I'm in control.

He lay still for a few minutes as it started to take effect. "It is like your country's war for independence," he continued, as if he read my thoughts. "We are revolutionary war soldiers."

He stopped talking and I watched his knuckles go white again. He coughed and gagged. I knelt and lifted his head so he could spit blood into a field dressing. After a few moments he relaxed.

"More water?" I asked.

"Please."

I held the can to his lips and he drank. Then he lay so still I couldn't tell if he still lived. His eyes were closed, his face looked pinched and had a gray tinge. Finally I saw his chest rise and fall irregularly with his shallow breathing. I knew the end was close. His pain must be fierce, but it hadn't been long enough for another ampule. He would die soon anyway, I thought, and I stabbed another ampule into his thigh. I had started to get up when his eyes opened.

"Could I have another of your cigarettes?" he whispered.

I lit one and handed it to him. His hand shook as he took it, but after several drags, became steadier.

He pulled a dog-eared photo from his shirt pocket and handed it to me. I wiped his blood off the front and saw an old woman sitting in a chair. Three young men stood behind her. Kneeling in front were four children, two boys and two girls, who looked about eight or ten years old. He spoke again, slowly, with effort and urgency.

"My wife...my sons, grandchildren."

I nodded. "Nice looking family," I said, handing the photo back. He didn't take it.

"I don't want the ARVN to have it. They torture families...if they can find them. My family will never know what happened... Will you keep it...look at them from time to time?"

I looked at the photo again, put it in my wallet. So he had a family he loved. Would someone write to his family? Probably not.

My own mother and father, still hurt by my joining the army, hadn't written. How different from his family. They were proud of him.

"Why don't you go home?" he asked. His eyes were bright, feverish. Not just a question, he knew I felt tired and was ready to go home. I sighed. Right on the mark.

"Maybe I will."

"Yes," he said. "Please go home." He took a long drag on the cigarette. The smoke rose from his nostrils and wafted up to the bare light bulb where bugs flew insanely in circles.

When I looked down the cigarette had slipped from his fingers.

CHAPTER THIRTY ONE

The Light

We got a reprieve from the red mud to look for an NVA Colonel. It turned out to be so easy to find him, my superstitions kicked in, and I wondered *what* would go wrong, not *if* something would go wrong.

We climbed a knoll overlooking their camp well before sunrise. We were on the east side of their perimeter, so they would have the rising sun in their eyes. After what seemed hours, the camp came to life.

I saw my mark come out of his tent, stretch and yawn. For a few seconds he looked out at the camp. I took a deep breath and let out half of it. I centered the dot in the scope on his chest, and gently squeezed the trigger. The deafening explosion threw the jungle silence into chaos. Recoil slammed the rifle into my shoulder. As the muzzle rose, I worked the bolt, chambering a fresh round, just in case. I brought the rifle back down to find him through the scope, and verify the kill. The heavy bullet had knocked him to the ground.

Mike looked up from the small spotting scope he carried to tell me what I already knew. "The mark is down!" he said. "Let's get the hell outta here!"

We crawled backwards from the top of the knoll, trying not to be silhouetted against the sunrise. Suddenly bullets cracked above us. Damn, I thought, unable to pinpoint the source. Mike pointed at the top of the neighboring hill. It was higher than ours. They must have been using it as an observation post. The hair on my neck stood up. Overlooking something like that could get us killed. Mike signaled in the direction we had chosen for our alternate escape route. Our only chance would be a fast getaway. Abandoning any pretense of stealth, we ran down the slope, away from the enemy riflemen. The rest of our team, just below us on the hillside, had already moved out.

The first mortar shell exploded far enough away that none of us was hurt, and it lent wings to our feet. We weren't as lucky with the second. The blast picked Corporal Melvin Platt up off the ground and tossed him through the air. I heard him scream. When he hit the ground he didn't move.

Kennelley and Corporal Bloom got to him before I did. "What is it?" I asked, and looked down at Platt's leg to see the obvious. Blood darkened the cloth of his fatigues and below the knee it bent where it shouldn't. "Check out the shrapnel," Mike said, pointing to a sharp fragment stuck into Platt's chest. He lifted the unconscious man's arm across his shoulders and we ran.

Another mortar round landed further away and a third further still. "They're bracketing us, but they don't know where we are," I said.

We ran down to the creek and jumped behind the shallow bank for cover. "See anyone?" I asked. Everyone silently scanned the foliage over their rifle sights. "Cut some poles," I barked. "Double time."

We cut a slit in Platt's fatigues at each shoulder and slipped a sapling up each pant leg, through his belt, under the shirt and through the slit at the shoulder. The crude stretcher lacked any semblance of comfort and would probably rub off some skin, but we could get him out alive.

"How about his leg, Sarge?" asked Bloom.

"Tape it to the pole," I said. From the looks of it, Platt would go home without the leg. Fortunately, he hadn't regained consciousness.

Getting us all back from that mission renewed my belief in miracles. For some reason the NVA completely missed us. Or never pursued us. When we arrived at our pickup point, we checked it out. Charlie hadn't shown up to give us an unwelcome *bon voyage*.

We scrambled aboard our dust-off seconds after it hovered, the rotor wash beating down the grass. Mack was on board. The chopper rose and cut away, over the treetops. The cargo bay had become so slick with blood from Platt's wounds, I wondered if he'd bled out.

"Someone get the tourniquet back on that leg," Mack barked. He looked at Platt's chest and the protruding chunk of steel. Usually Mack wouldn't try to remove something like that because it would leave a hole that blood flowed out of. He grabbed Platt's wrist to take his pulse. With a worried look, he pulled up his eyelid. Shaking his head, he wrapped a blood-pressure cuff around Platt's arm.

I'd learned to keep quiet and let Mack work. At last he sat back and shook his head. "I don't think..." he started to say, then lifted Platt's eyelid again. He reached up and touched the eyeball with his finger.

"No reaction," he said, clinically.

"What's that mean?" I thought I knew but hoped I didn't.

He shook his head. "There's a faint heartbeat, but he's not going to make it."

Mack placed the stethoscope on Platt's chest. "He's gone," he said. When I started to ask Mack if he couldn't do something else, he cut me off. "He's gone, dammit!" he shouted, snatching off his stethoscope. "He's dead! I am not Jesus Christ!" Suddenly it seemed quiet in spite of the roar of the chopper. Everyone knew we'd lost him. The floor or the ceiling, a bootlace or a rifle sling, became objects of intense examination. Anything but the bloody body lying in the middle of us.

One of our own had been killed. It assaulted our collective belief that we were invincible.

An ambulance waited for us as we touched down. My eyes focused on the red cross on the side of the vehicle. Where were you guys when we needed you, I thought, irrationally seeking a target for my anger and fear.

Moving with speed and efficiency, they took Platt off the chopper and laid him on a stretcher. It was caked with dried blood. Must be been a busy day for them, I thought.

One of the corpsmen ran back to the chopper. "What meds has he had?" he asked Mack.

"What do you mean?" Mack asked, puzzled.

The corpsman looked confused. "I gotta know what you gave him, so when we medicate, we don't OD him!" he said.

"What the hell are you talking about?" asked Mack. "He's dead."

"No! He has a pulse!"

Mack and the corpsman ran to the ambulance and climbed in. The vehicle lumbered off, leaving the rest of us to stare.

The next day Mack reported that Platt survived the removal of the shrapnel, and would recover from the chest wound. But the war had ended for Platt. His leg had been amputated at the knee.

We got a three day pass for rest and relaxation—intoxication and intercourse, we called it. When we got back, we were sent on another mission. Almost a week passed before we came back. I kept wondering what happened to Platt. I caught a chopper ride to visit him.

I felt leery of all hospitals. My leg started twitching at the knee. I'd never been in this same hospital, but it looked and smelled too familiar for comfort. I peeked in, walked cautiously to the nurses' station. A nurse held a telephone to her ear, scribbling something furiously on a pad. She didn't look up as I approached. I hadn't seen a Caucasian female for a long time. I stopped and stared. I stepped forward, dazzled, and leaned on the high counter of the nurses' station. She looked like Miss USA to me, her fine, blonde hair soft like silk strands. It must smell like flowers, I thought. My eyes followed the outline of her blouse down to the hint of lace that attempted to hide the wonder of her breasts.

"What do you want, Sergeant?" she barked, still holding the phone against one ear with her shoulder.

"Uh, uhm, I'm sorry. Excuse me, Miss," I said, noticing that her left hand bore no rings. "Could you tell me..."

"It's Lieutenant, Sergeant!"

"Yes. Yes ma'am, Lieutenant. I'm looking for Corporal Melvin Platt."

She glanced at a clipboard. "C-17," she said, dismissing me by pointing in the direction of a set of double doors.

She didn't look up again. She wasn't Miss USA after all. Certainly not Miss Congeniality. I bet she's not a real blonde, I thought.

I walked between the long rows of hospital beds, looking at the numbers on their ends. These men had belonged to units that trained and fought together. After they were wounded, they were separated from their outfits and

286

became numbers in a hospital ward. I felt a drop of sweat trickle down my spine.

I stopped at C-17. At first I didn't recognize the face of the man asleep in the bed. Clean shaven, he looked younger than he did last time I saw him. The fear and tension were gone. A strand of brown hair fell across his forehead. With his eyes closed and his lips parted, he had a relaxed, boyish look. His arms were folded across his chest and one hand held a black book. *Holy Bible,* the gilt letters on the cover proclaimed.

I watched Platt's eyes flutter and open. He raised his head and smiled. He didn't seem startled, much less fearful, from his sudden awakening.

"Hey, Sarge," he said. "Nice to see you. Sit down."

"How you feeling?" I asked.

"Good," he replied. "Real good. I been up on crutches, and I'm going home in a few days. I'm glad I could see you first, though."

We made small talk about the welfare of the team, and I delivered messages from each of the men. One of the chopper jockeys took a Polaroid of all of us. We signed it on the back as a goodby present.

I felt awkward and our conversation lagged. "Are you going to be okay?" I blurted out, pointing to where his leg should have been.

"Oh, yeah. I'm okay. I'll be fine." His voice held none of the bravado, the false enthusiasm for the return to civilian life I'd heard so often. He sounded sincere, and it puzzled me.

"Well, I'm glad you feel like it's gonna work out," I told him as I stood. Then I remembered the nurse. "I just hope all your nurses aren't like that one at the nurse's station."

"Well, that's partly...I guess I'm a little responsible for that. She thinks I've flipped out."

"So how'd she get an attitude over that?"

"Well... Something happened."

"To her?"

"No. To me." He laid the Bible next to the bed and straightened the sheet.

"I tried to tell her, but she didn't believe me. I guess she thought I'd been hallucinating, and she called the shrink. I told the shrink I didn't know what she was talking about." He laughed half-heartedly. "Guess she got chewed out. I didn't want to talk about it with someone who might have the power to declare that I was nuts."

"What was it?"

He looked up, trying to decide if I'd understand. He must have thought I would. "You know, I 'died' on that chopper. My heart quit beating."

I nodded.

He took a deep breath. "Well, I have no idea where I went or how I got there. I had the warmest, coziest light you could ever imagine shining on me. I felt warm...and I had been cleansed, somehow. My soul. My very being. I had a feeling of relief, of being...unburdened, I guess. No words can come close to telling you how wonderful it felt."

He looked away, and his eyes filled.

"You know, you don't have to tell me about this."

"It's okay," he said. "It just felt so good. I had become...whole. Complete."

I involuntarily glanced down at his leg.

"No, I don't mean just in body. I never have been whole, even before that. I just never knew it."

I didn't understand, but I nodded.

"The pain in my leg went away. I kind of got...well, reconnected to something, like finding something I didn't know I'd lost. Something important. I wanted to stay in that light, but they were calling me. I knew I had to go."

"Who called you?" I asked.

"Friends," he said. "You know how you meet someone and feel you've known them for years? Or lifetimes? That's how I felt. They didn't call me by name, but by who I am." He stopped and frowned. "This is the hardest to explain. I could see my personality as a bunch of false notions about who I am—which isn't who I *really* am. Like little characters all squabbling over which one gets attention. So these—friends—they weren't calling that false part of me, but the real me. The part that loves my wife and my little girl, the part that's sometimes done things just to be nice, whether anyone knew it or not. The good and selfless parts—the only parts of me that are truly real.

"I had to go to them, those...entities that called me. Suddenly I *wanted* to go to them. It didn't scare me. I felt excited. They welcomed me—cheered for me. I felt healed."

He glanced up to see if I looked skeptical. I'd heard so many goldbricking excuses and stories I could tell when a man told the truth. I knew Platt believed everything he said. Believed it utterly. He pushed his pillows up and sat there for the longest time staring out the window before he continued.

"When I was in the light, everything was different. Some different kind of... of thinking. Or belief. Total acceptance. I had a chance to see kind of a review of my whole life. All the things I ever did became okay. No fault. Forgiven. I didn't like some of those things, and some were nicer than others. But all of them were part of a learning process. Sarge, I felt totally, completely loved and protected. Accepted. It was healing. To my spirit, I mean. I could see things so differently. Still do.

I nodded, uncomfortable, but fascinated with what he told me.

"I want to go back to that light," Platt said after a while. "That's where I found out what God is. God really is love so great we can't comprehend it. Not some old man we should fear who keeps track of things we do wrong."

We sat quietly for a while. Platt was talked out. This wasn't some sky-pilot philosophy teacher. This was Corporal Melvin Platt from our team, who'd been there, seen it, done it, died, and come back. Awesome, I thought. I was enthralled by what he had told me. It gave me a lot to think about. It stretched my belief system, but somehow it made sense.

I stood and started to say something, then realized there was nothing to say. His smile was full of understanding. When I held out my hand, he pulled me into a hug.

I got a ride back to Saigon and walked the streets for several hours trying to put Platt's puzzle together in my head. Finally, I quit thinking about it.

I couldn't explain it, but my heart understood.

CHAPTER THIRTY TWO

Carnage

We moved out. It was the eighth day without rest. Eight days of fire-fight tag with Charlie, of stealthy advance, running like hell away from or into his bullets. Eight nights of short snatches of sleep. We were cold and wet, worn down to the dregs of our energy. Then they disappeared. Vanished.

I jerked awake as my foot caught on a root and dumped me on my face. Startled, I realized I'd fallen asleep marching down the trail. This had gone beyond too much. We had to stop.

I signaled Mike, who had taken drag. Closing the back door. He nodded and everyone fell to the ground at the sides of the trail.

After I sat for a few minutes, I hobbled back to where Mike had propped himself against a tree, still watching our rear. I slumped down next to him.

"Christ, this has turned us into automatons. It's got to end," I whispered.

"You're tellin' me. I'm so tired..."

"Where are we?"

Mike consulted the map, then stabbed the plastic coating with a red grease pencil. It made an out-of-round spot, like a bright drop of blood.

"That's gotta be thirty miles from our insertion point," I said. The map didn't gauge our physical and mental state. If it had, the needle would have been on "E."

"Let's find some place that's half defendable and call a halt. We're low on ammunition and out of food."

Mike's face suddenly went on full alert. He held up a hand, cutting me off. He started breathing in and out, rapid, short bursts through his nose. "Smoke," he whispered. Nodded. "Yep. Smoke. Gotta be Charlie's."

Now I could smell it. A cooking fire? Great. We were in no condition to get into another fight with Charlie. Likely get our asses shot off. Using hand signals, I motioned to Mike that we should leave the trail, fade away quietly into the brush. I punctuated the message with raised eyebrows, making it a question. Mike frowned. He signaled that he wanted to find the source of the smoke, take them on.

This close to the DMZ it could be an NVA regular unit, a bad ass fighting machine. Fear tightened my belly. I didn't have the strength to think, but Mike seemed determined. Reluctantly, I nodded. He would take half the team, cutting around to the left of a small rise, the most likely source of the smoke. In two minutes I would lead the other half around to the right.

"We should get there a few seconds before you do," Mike whispered. "We'll take our cue from you."

I nodded. Trying to stay alert, I moved back up the trail in a crouch, tagging eight of our sixteen men, pointing at Kennelley. Silent as ghosts they gathered under Mike's tree. I couldn't hear his whispered instructions, just watched his lips move as he looked at each man. His eyes bulged, his lips curled back over his teeth. For a moment, a leer froze his face. A touch of insanity.

"Hey Sarge," someone whispered. "You want the rest of us over here with you?"

I frowned, put a finger to my lips, then nodded. I motioned to the others to join me. I prayed with all my thumping heart that Charlie hadn't spotted us, wouldn't wipe us out as we bunched up in groups. Quickly I explained, then told them we'd give Mike two minutes, then follow.

When I looked back at Mike, he held up two fingers, pointed to his watch. Still leering like a madman, he left the trail, as quiet as a shadow. When the two minutes passed, I motioned for our group to move out two by two. I took the lead. I moved from tree to tree watching for booby-traps and signs of the enemy. Then I froze. Voices. I signaled everyone to get down and tried to listen past the blood rushing in my ears. I couldn't hear the words but knew it wasn't English. I moved forward on my belly, pulling myself soundlessly an inch at a time. I pushed back my helmet, raised my head. I got a glimpse of a uniformed head and torso. I froze. Then realized the legs attached to it were busy carrying the torso away from me. The dryness in my mouth made me swallow all the more, loud enough I thought he would hear. I held my breath. He moved on.

I motioned to Stein to move up. Slow down, I thought, afraid he'd go too fast and make noise, then impatient for him to hurry up. I watched through the branches and leaves where the torso had disappeared. Nothing. We inched our way to the rise where Mike thought we'd find Charlie. Stein and I crawled forward another ten feet and looked. What we saw took our breath away. I counted about forty of them, uniformed NVA soldiers. Another twenty in black pajamas. Those were VC, half of them carrying AK-47s or SKSs. I felt my hair stand straight up. "Fuckin' four-to-one!" I muttered.

The clearing looked man-made, a depression dug out of the dirt, which was piled around it. A huge camouflage net covered most of it. I could see gas cans and wooden crates. Some of the crates looked like ammo cases. I felt sure the long, slender cases held rockets. Others, I guessed, mortar rounds. A stack of cardboard boxes looked oddly familiar. I hoped they contained rations of some sort. Shit, I thought. This is a group of VC getting re-supplied by the NVA. A bigger outfit than the one we'd been playing tag with. And better armed. Fed, rested, relaxed.

We inched our way back. I put my mouth next to Stein's ear. "You play baseball?" I asked in a hoarse whisper.

He turned his head and frowned. "What the fuck...?"

"Yes or no, goddamn it?"

"Yeah."

"Can you lob a chunk of C-4 onto that stack of boxes? Take another look."

A few minutes later he crawled back. "No. Too far," he grunted. "If I can get around there," he pointed to a spot further down the circular bank, "then yeah. I can."

"Okay. Go too far, you'll run into Kennelley. When it blows, we'll all start shooting. Anything happens before that, blow that shit any way you can. Then get your ass back here."

Stein smiled. His eyes looked sunken into his skull. He was ready to eat Charlie for lunch. Shrugging off his pack, Stein took a block of C-4. He pushed a detonator into the explosive. I wished he'd put it together somewhere else. An hour-long two minutes passed, and he crawled off.

I scanned the opposite bank. About ninety degrees to my left, I thought I saw a rifle barrel. Too straight for a branch. It hit me that we had seen no sentries. I started to shake, sure their sentries would open up on us any minute. Then some little runt in black pajamas spotted the rifle barrel. Must have been one of ours.

With much yelling, he fired a shot in that direction. Branches crashed behind me. At first I thought it was their sentries, then I realized my team had moved up. I caught movement in the corner of my eye. Stein ran forward with the block of C-4. I lost sight of him in the branches, but the C-4 appeared, arcing through the air, and landed between the rows of boxes. A perfect throw.

A uniformed soldier sprinted to the spot where the C-4 had disappeared. What if he threw it back at us, I wondered. As he bent over it, an ear-splitting ka-boom blew him into little pieces that rained down on the depression. Boxes and contents flew in all directions. AK-47s fired wildly, mixed with the sharper snap of M-16s.

I ran along the bank, yelling at everyone to watch out for Kennelley and the rest of the team. Two explosions rocked the ground, a third threw me off my feet. "Jeezus, what kind'a stuff they got in there?" I asked. Ruptured gas cans that had been hidden under a tarp started to burn. One exploded, driving me further down the bank. Total chaos.

Charlie would recover fast, though, and we needed to even the odds— or we'd have our own surprise. Right now, they were sitting ducks. Some, dazed, knocked down by the blast, tried to get up. I put my front sight on one of them, wearing a dirty-grey shirt and pants. For a split second I hesitated. Civilian, or soldier? I realized I didn't give a shit, and squeezed the trigger. He went down. I shot him again and he flinched. They ain't dead 'til they're dead, I muttered.

The fight moved faster than I could follow, yet certain things seemed cast in slow motion. I saw three more pajama clad figures fall, capped a fourth, then two uniformed soldiers. Another soldier ran directly at us. Holding his belly with his left hand, he had an old sub-machine gun in his right. He screamed incomprehensible words at the top of his lungs. "Get him, goddam it, get him!" I yelled as I yanked my M-16 clear of a branch. I reached over and kicked Kyster, lying next to me. Just as Charlie brought up the sub-machine gun, a burst from our left caught him. He spun around, blood spouting from his neck, and fell.

An NVA soldier spotted our position and fired at us from a prone position in the clearing. His first round hit Kyster, who screamed and doubled up. His other rounds went above us, climbing as recoil raised the muzzle of his AK-47. When I had my front sight on his face, I fired. Soupy-looking red blew out of the back of his head. He dropped the rifle, his hands going to his face. I shot him again. His head fell forward and he twitched.

"They ain't dead until they're dead." I felt power, exhilaration of control—and the kill. And anger. Rage that they'd made hits on some of us.

"Where's Mack!" I yelled, looking at Kyster, wondering if he'd bought it. Everything had gone to fast-forward. I could see movement on my left. Several uniformed NVA ran up a shallow wash toward Stein's position. "Where's Stein?" I yelled. "Oh, fuck! Murray, Cohen, follow me! They're closing in on Stein! Goddamn him anyway, I'd told him to get back here!"

The three of us ran, crouching, around the bank in a race for Stein. I couldn't see the NVA, and with the fire fight and Charlie's ordnance cooking off, couldn't hear them. Then several AK-47s, coming from Stein's position, all barked at once. My anger came out in a guttural roar as we raced toward him, heedless of limbs or anything else in our path. We burst through the branches, catching them unaware. One of them had stuck Stein with the bayonet on his SKS, and pulled frantically, trying to free it. Murray, firing from behind me, took out the other two. I pointed my M-16 at the one who tried to twist his bayonet out of Stein's body. When I pulled the trigger nothing happened.

I imagined that bayonet swinging around, piercing my guts. All of a sudden my machete appeared in my hand. I screamed so loud I tasted blood in my throat, yet I couldn't hear my voice. With all my strength I swung the blade and connected with Charlie's arm. His face contorted, and he screamed. I still couldn't hear. The rifle, Stein still impaled on its bayonet, fell to the ground, toppling his body forward. Charlie's severed hand still grasped the stock. The machete, as if commanding me, rose high over my head again, then down into the shoulder of Stein's impaler, cleaving him from front to back, into his chest cavity. Cohen, stepping around from behind me, leveled his rifle and emptied the rest of his magazine into him. When I bent over to pull the machete free, the stump of his arm doused me with blood from my waist to my shoulder. I swung again at the dead meat, splitting his skull like a coconut. "You-sonofabitch-you-killed-Stein-goddam-you!" I screamed as my machete scythed through his body.

"It's done, Sarge! He's dead!" Murray screamed.

His voice stopped me, just as a fountain of blood erupted from Charlie's mouth and nose. He choked and lay still.

"We're going up that wash where they came from and get us some pay-back," I said, motioning to Cohen and the others. I tried to pin-point the sound of Mike's M-16s from his position on the other side of the flames. I looked for a place to take cover inside the depression. In a matter of minutes they would regroup and come around on our flank. We had to act fast.

A small wash cut through the side of the bank, for drainage. "Into the wash," I hissed at Cohen. His face had gone ashen in spite of the heat, but he followed me without hesitation. We ran at a crouch, stopped at the edge of the clearing where the wash curved sharply. "When Murray gets everyone here, we'll have an open field of fire across the clearing without worrying about Kennelley being in our way. We might be able to waste the whole lot of them."

Cohen peeked around the bend in the wash, drew back suddenly. "A tun-nel!" he whispered loudly. "A goddamn tunnel!" Neither of us felt the exhaus-tion that had sapped us earlier. We wanted more kills.

I edged past Cohen, peeked around the bank at the tunnel. Just as I did, a head popped up. I pulled back. "There's one coming!" I said, grabbing my .45. "Get back, we'll let him go by, then waste him."

Footsteps pounded in the sand. A kid in an ill-fitting uniform raced around the bend. He was looking over his shoulder, across the clearing where the ordnance still burned.

"You fucking gook," I said aloud, thinking of Stein. He stopped, turned, and I shot him twice in the chest. "Finish him," I said, patting my knife. Cohen looked indecisive.

"Do it!"

Cohen drew his knife, flipped him on his face and shoved it in to the hilt, below the shoulder blade, next to the spine. The kid tensed, quivered, and lay still.

More footsteps pounded up the wash. We hugged the bank. They ran so fast they almost tripped on their comrade.

"He's dead," I said. Both whirled around. I started to shoot the closest soldier. Somehow I couldn't move my rifle. Cohen shot them both. This time he didn't have to be told.

"Look out!" someone yelled. Murray. He pointed his M-16 down the wash. Flame spit from the muzzle. I threw myself flat. He ran up and dropped to one knee. "You okay, Sarge?" I turned my head. Two more bodies lay in the wash. "They wised up. Would have gotten you if you'd stayed there."

"Yeah. Owe you a beer. Kyster alive?"

Murray nodded. "Stein?"

I shook my head. "Shit, it's quiet," I said. A few rounds still cooked off from Charlie's ordnance, accenting the silence. "Where the hell did everybody go?"

"Sh-h-h," Murray said, pointing downstream. We ducked.

"It's Kennelley! He's alone!" Mike had almost passed the entrance to the tunnel. "Hey, Peter Cottontail, there's a wolf's lair on your left," I yelled. Mike ran, zigzagging through the wash. A single shot rang out, hitting the dirt at his feet. He careened around the bend in the wash and almost landed on our pile of bodies.

"You hurt?" he asked.

"No," I said. I looked at the blood all over me. "That's Charlie's. I went kind of nuts back there."

"Well, your ass is in a sling now," he said, looking so serious I wondered what he meant.

"Bag limit is four. You got five," he said, pointing at the bodies with his thumb.

"Very fuckin' funny. Where the hell did they go?"

"Into the tunnel. The only place there's any cover. They disappeared faster than our fire could account for." He pointed down the wash. "That must be the back door. The good news is there's some gasoline that didn't blow. What do you s'pose would happen if we poured it down both doors and lit it? Maybe tossed some of Stein's stuff down after it?"

Everyone tensed at the mention of Stein. Of course, no one was superstitious about Stein's bad run of luck. The rubbing of rabbit's feet and other talismans was coincidental.

"Stein bought it?" Mike asked.

I nodded.

"Son-of-a-bitch," he said, pacing the word out like some kind of hellish curse. He scratched on the ground with a stick for a moment. "We need payback. Big time."

I looked around at the men, gaunt and filthy. Angry eyes. Hard faces.

We put out sentries. Two of them watched the entrances to the tunnel. We collected bodies, took personal effects and looked for any kind of papers or maps that would make our Military Intelligence weenies happy. We had twenty-six bodies, pieces of a couple of others. And no one to verify our kills.

Two fifty-five gallon drums of gasoline, placed along the far edge of the bank, had survived the explosions. One had a bullet hole in it about four inches from the top, but very little gas had leaked out. We rolled the drums to the entrances and let the gasoline pour out into the tunnels. It would have been a disaster if Charlie had decided to come out shooting at that moment, but he didn't.

When both drums emptied, we took four blocks of C-4, tied them in pairs, and gingerly set detonators into both. I carried one to the back door, Mike stood ready at the front. On the count of three, we pulled the pins, threw the lethal packages into the holes, and ran like hell. I leaped over the bank and waited. The earth shook from deep down below us and a fireball blew out the back door. I looked at Mike. "Yours didn't work," I said.

"That's bullshit, we set those detonators..."

Then the front blew, more spectacular than the back. We watched the column of smoke, making bad jokes about french fries and Gook fries, laughing too hard and too long. Everything became hideous and hilarious at once.

The laughter stopped short when Perez, one of our sentries, yelled something we couldn't understand, then fired several short bursts. Everyone froze. Mike signaled he would take the right side of Perez's position. I nodded. We circled.

Perez, sitting just below the bank, said he'd heard something . As we watched, a mat covered with leaves slid away, revealing another opening. A man's head appeared and he climbed out, an AK-47 slung over his shoulder. He reached down to help someone else who also carried an AK-47. Perez yelled at them to get down on their faces. The first man swung his rifle around, so Perez wasted them both. We should have waited before we moved forward, but our impatience drew us on.

We got to the tunnel just as two others crawled out, neither of them armed. They lay face down when we yelled. Their hair had been burned off, as well as most of their clothes. One had black, crusty skin over his back and legs. They were burned so badly that neither of them would live long. Allerton and Murray poked them with the muzzles of their rifles, made jokes about crispy critters.

I couldn't seem to focus on anything. I realized we stood in a close group around the tunnel opening. We had a long march out to our pickup point and almost no ammo. The familiar-looking cardboard boxes, filled with black-market C-rations lay all over the clearing. Some had been ruined. I should have told someone to scavenge. My mind wandered off, wondering how Charlie got U. S. Army C-rats.

I looked at Mike. Neither of us had the strength to figure out what to do.

"Can I waste 'em, Sarge?" asked Allerton, breaking into my reverie.

"I want one of 'em," Chase said.

"That's enough!" I yelled, my throat swollen and sore. "Fuller, Murray, go get Stein's body. We got a long way to go. Now MOVE!" No one moved. I stood there stupefied.

"We should draw straws to see who wastes them," someone said. "They're gonna die anyway, burned like that."

I walked over to Murray. "Listen to me, you simpering son-of-a-bitch! When I tell you to do something, you haul your ass off and do it because if you don't, I'll pull your fuckin' guts out through your nostrils so everyone can see you're a goddamn shit-bag! NOW—GO—GET—STEIN!"

Mike drew his .45 and walked to the middle of the group. He shot both of the bald, burned Charlies in the head once. When they quit quivering, he looked at Murray. He still held the pistol.

"You two shit-birds go get Stein," he said in a soft voice underlined with armor plate. Fuller and Murray looked at each other, then turned away. "The rest of you, grab enough C-rats to last for two days, then start off on the trail. Chase, you've got point." He holstered his pistol. Chase hadn't moved. Mike walked over to him, stuck his face so close they were nose to nose. "I said, *move out. You got point.*"

Chase stared at him for a moment. "Okay, Sarge." One by one the others followed.

I took drag, mostly so I could be alone. Or almost alone. I didn't want anyone to see the shakes I had. I knew what was wrong. Part of me, mind, or conscience, I didn't know which, could not accept that I enjoyed the whole firefight. It wasn't just that I did what I had to do to keep us alive. There was a line that I kept crossing, more frequently than ever, into rage, power, revenge. In some insane way it brought satisfaction. I wondered if there would be a time I wouldn't be able to cross back.

The POW officer I'd talked to weeks ago told me to go home. Maybe he was right. But regardless of his effort to seduce me into agreeing with his point of view, he and his men would kill me, kill all of us, without hesitation. And I would kill them if I could. That was the bottom line. Maybe I should go home. I looked over my shoulder at the wreckage of their camp and thought about the effort it took to bring all this materiel here. We had totally destroyed it.

In the background of my mind I saw a small-town kid with a .22 rifle. As we marched on, I could see other parts of my early teens. My first date with Barbara. A redhead. The painful silence as my dad drove us to the school dance. The unexpected pleasure of dancing close with her. An amateurish kiss in the hallway. Sitting with her at the drug store counter drinking cherry phosphates.

Now we had career oriented officers, ready to prosecute anyone for anything, if it helped them climb the ladder to promotion. The little guy, the grunt on the ground, in the heat of it all, seemed not to matter any longer. Expendable. No room for a home-town mentality.

I wondered if that kid in me would fade away. I said a prayer that he would not.

CHAPTER THIRTY THREE

All Good Things

No one opened the door when I knocked, which struck me as odd. Mike should have been there.

"Anyone home?" I hollered. I could see Li peeking through the curtains. She opened the door. She stood almost behind it until I got inside, then pushed it closed. Rather than her usual welcome, running up and jumping on me, she took my hand in both of hers. She had been crying.

I could see Mike slumped on the couch, Rose with her head against his shoulder.

"What's wrong?"

Mike looked hollow-eyed. "Good God, what happened?" Mike held up a page, one of a sheaf of papers that had fallen to the floor. "What is it?"

"It's our eviction notice," Mike said, without looking up, pulling Rose onto his lap.

I took the page he held out to me, picked up the rest from the floor. "What the hell do you mean?"

"Read it yourself. We're being ordered to live on base from now on."

"Where'd these papers come from? What's going on?"

Mike looked up and sighed. "It's a whole bunch of things. Someone from JAG brought them. It looks like Sergeant Mays is being investigated for dabbling in the black market. They started looking at us for the same reason, and somehow our little incident with Black Shirt, the time you drove the jeep into the bar, the connex box of magazines—and a few other things we've done have come to light. I guess finding out where we've been living turned out to be the last straw."

"Someone from JAG brought these? Who the hell brought them? Not Cap'n Hank!"

"JAG, yes. Cap'n Hank, no. But someone went to some trouble to get this stuff to us."

"Christ, it's been—what?—almost two years. They just *now* found out where we're living?" I sorted out the pages on the coffee table, scanning some of them, wondering if this would be our worst nightmare, or if we could do something about it. "Shit, we need to find Cap'n Hank or we're screwed."

Mike didn't look up. "I think we're screwed either way."

"I'm gonna try to find him," I said. "You okay with that?"

"Yeah. Do whatever you want."

"Christ, you sound like you've given up already," I said, with more edge to my voice than I intended. Mike looked so stricken I felt ashamed. And shocked. He *had* given up. He sounded hopeless and his perpetual spark of defiance wasn't there. That scared me.

Li had been standing next to me, quietly holding my hand. I felt something wet splash on my fingers, and realized she had been crying all this time. I picked her up and carried her into our bedroom. She sat cross-legged on the bed, so forlorn I felt torn between my desire to protect her from I knew not what, and not letting the lump in my own throat turn into tears.

Li got to her knees on the bed, put her arms around me and kissed me gently again and again. She pulled me down next to her on the bed, and we held each other. We felt comfort in our closeness. Then desire. Our love-making started with much caressing, ended with passion.

Mike and I met Cap'n Hank at a quiet bar not too far from the house. We'd had several drinks by the time Cap'n Hank showed up. He smiled big, but when he sat down his expression turned serious. "You guys have a tough situation here," he said, and signaled the waitress.

"Whiskey sour," he said. "You have Seagram's?" She nodded. We smiled, thinking of his initiation. He'd come a long way.

"I want to tell you what's happening and how you got dragged into it." He took a sip of his whiskey sour. "There has been some activity on the black market, by Army personnel, with Army materiel. They want to make some examples. Some deserve it. Some don't, some aren't even involved in the black market—like Sergeant Mays and you two."

"But we're gonna get screwed anyway," Mike said.

"No, I don't think so," Cap'n Hank said. "I've pulled a lot of strings. Called in some favors." He shook his head, looking from me to Mike and back. "You guys have been real lucky for a pair of mavericks. Jesus H. Christ on a crutch, you've been a whole goddam herd of mavericks! But you aren't going to be charged with anything. Neither is Sergeant Mays. What they did do is dig up the unorthodox stuff you've done, like hijacking that batch of M-16 magazines, some five *thousand* of them?"

He gave us an incredulous stare, back and forth. "Jeezus Christ, I can't believe some of the stuff you two have gotten away with. Stuff I never knew about!" He shook his head.

"This is probably the worst part. You're going to have to live on base. They've got a list of some other things, but nothing that amounts to much. You guys have made some poor decisions, but black marketeers you aren't."

"So we can keep the house, we'll just have to sleep on base, at least part of the time," I said, feeling relieved.

Cap'n Hank looked down at his drink. "I'm sorry," he said as he chased an ice cube around the glass with one finger. "I don't think they're going to let you do that, either." He looked up. "Or live with the girls. If you stay in Vietnam."

If I hadn't felt like I'd had the breath stomped out of me, I would have asked what he meant about staying in 'Nam.

Cap'n Hank looked frustrated. "I'm really sorry," he said. "I tried everything I could think of, but I couldn't pull it off. I've gone way out on a limb. This is supposed to be a confidential matter, and you aren't supposed to need counsel at this point. But I thought I could kind of do some things that would help."

"I'm sure you helped a lot already," I said, feeling a wave of appreciation for the lawyer with the soul of a warrior. "And we appreciate it. I guess it's time to marry the girls and take them home." I looked at Mike. Unlike me, he had a calmness about him that made me wonder if everything had soaked in. Then I realized he'd seen it coming. I was the one who had been blind.

After Cap'n Hank chased the remains of the ice cubes around his glass a few more times, he looked at me, then at Mike. "I wondered if you might want to do that, so I called a friend and asked what exceptions are being made."

"Exceptions?" I asked, my hopes sinking through the floor.

"I didn't have to ask what the policy is, I already knew. Right now servicemen can't marry indigenous women. Period. They are not allowed to go to the U. S. No exceptions." He thought about that for a moment. "Well, if you got a bird colonel, or a general to run interference, that might be different... "

"But for the likes of us, who don't know any brass, it isn't. Right?" I asked.

"I'm afraid so." He sighed. "I broached the subject with a couple of officers with enough rank to allow an exception. I still have bite marks on my ass. Goddamn assholes."

In spite of the circumstances, I smiled. This was a very different Cap'n Hank than the little guy who watched me while I lay asleep in my hospital bed. I was proud of him. He'd become a good friend, one with an uncommon quantity of intestinal fortitude.

"What would happen if I married Rose anyway?" asked Mike.

"The army wouldn't recognize the marriage, and you'd probably be disciplined. With the—well, with the record you guys have, it wouldn't go well." He looked at me. "And you've made an enemy. Remember Captain Fowles, who handled the prosecution at your court martial? He's now a major and out to make a name for himself. It would be payback for him. He could hurt you. It's likely you'd end up with some time in the stockade. Or worse. Even with me as your attorney."

"Oh great. Just fuckin' great," I said. "We chase Charlie all over hell's half-acre for damn near four years. We almost get killed a hundred times by him and the NVA, then the Army of the US of A tells me I can't marry the woman I love and have lived with for two years. What do the bastards expect us to do? Kiss them goodby and go back to the World?"

The look on Cap'n Hank's face became a mix of somber and sadness. He took a deep breath. "This is the worst of it," he said. "That is exactly what they expect. Except that when you go back to the world, your destination will be Leavenworth, if they can pull that off. Which is very likely, if you stay here during the investigations and the trials. I have arranged for you to be discharged—honorably, of course—and to return to the United States. You have five days."

He looked up, as if the answer to our dilemma was written on the ceiling. "You will never know how much your friendship has meant to me. I never thought my dreams would..."

He stopped, his voice hoarse, I guessed, from a lump in his throat the size of Saigon.

I put my hand on his shoulder. "Cap, it's been a two-way street. If not for you, I'd be sitting in a cell in Leavenworth already. I know you've tried to help us with this, probably to the detriment of your own career. As one warrior to another, you have my gratitude."

CHAPTER THIRTY FOUR

Legacy

I'd gone everywhere in the army bureaucracy I could think of. Now I was about to be thrown out of General Stinson's office. Admittedly, my clamoring for an audience with the general had been rather loud.

I knew I sounded desperate, maybe a little unbalanced. The captain at the desk was about to call the MPs when General Stinson's aide, Major Burris, came out of his office.

"What do you want to talk to him about, sergeant?" Major Burris stood over six feet tall, looked lean and trim. His tailored uniform perfectly fit his broad shoulders. The dark hair, gray at the temples, added distinction to his looks.

I snapped to attention, gave him my best salute. "I want to see the general. I want to get married." He looked thoughtfully at my sergeant first class stripes, as though he wondered if I wanted to get married badly enough to risk losing them. Then he asked me into his office.

"Sit down, Sergeant," he said, waving at a pair of easy chairs in the corner.

"I want to marry a Vietnamese girl," I said. "I've been all over the place, and it's going to take approval from someone like General Stinson. I've spent over three years in-country, and by God, the army owes me something. I'm going to..."

"Wait a minute, wait a minute, let me catch up with you. You've been in country for three years?" he asked.

"Three and one-half years. Mike and I are being ordered to live on base until we go back to the World, five days from now." I told him about some of our missions, that we were tired, worn out, and disillusioned. I explained how we'd found Li and Rose, that we'd lived with them for two years. That Mike and I wanted to marry the girls and take them home. "We've managed to fall in love with them," I said.

"I'm afraid I can't help you," he said, stiffly. "What you need to do is go to the legal boys at the JAG's office. Maybe one of their people can help you, but I doubt it."

"We already have. There's not much they could do—and we didn't have just some clerk helping us, either."

"Who did you talk to?" he asked.

"Captain Henry Rockwell Morton," I said. The name raised his eyebrows. He stared at me, then must have recognized my name. "Walker? So *you're* Sergeant Walker. I've read part of your file. And Sergeant Kennelley's." He leaned back in his chair. "You two are a couple of rogues. People like you are dangerous." I could feel my face turning red, but I bit my tongue. He held up his hand and went on. "But in your favor, you've had some damn difficult assignments. Interesting assignments. Your service in the field—a lot of it unofficial—has been invaluable. More than you'll ever know. And you have a powerful friend in Captain Morton. I don't know why he's gone to bat for you, but he's been on the verge of getting in trouble himself for sticking his nose where it doesn't belong." He looked at me as if I might be able to explain.

"Cap'n Hank's a good man," I said.

His eyebrows shot up again. "*Cap'n Hank*?" he asked. "*That's* what you call him?"

I nodded. "Did you know Cap'n Hank has a Purple Heart?"

He frowned. "Yes, I do. I thought he got it for tripping over a chair in a courtroom or something. He wears it all the time. What do you know about it?"

"He took shrapnel from a mortar, then saved the life of one of my men, taking a couple more chunks of shrapnel before he could get to cover. And he's an honorary member of our Special Forces A-Team. Ask him about it sometime." I didn't think it would hurt to give Cap'n Hank a bit bigger part in our adventure.

Major Burris shook his head. "I'll be damned. Look, if Captain Morton can't help you, I can't either. And the general certainly won't."

"It's not fair," I said. "If we leave, there's no telling what will happen to our girls. They're half Vietnamese and half French, and they'd probably get kidnapped and sold into prostitution..."

"Did you say they're half French?" he interrupted.

I nodded, wondering why their French parentage would matter.

"Where were they born?" he asked.

"Here in Saigon," I said, not really sure.

He looked wary, as if measuring the possibility that helping me could get him in a lot of trouble. "There might be another way. I could make a call for you... But what if I called Captain Morton to verify what you've told me?"

"Go ahead. I've talked to him twice today, and he should be in his office. I can give you his number."

Major Burris looked doubtful as he dialed the number. It took a few minutes to get through.

"Yes..." he said, followed by a series of uh-huh's, hmm's, and oh's, punctuated by nods of his head and several incredulous glances at me. Finally he said, "Thank you, Captain, you've been most...ah...enlightening. I'll do what I can. Unofficially, of course. And we never had this conversation." Evidently Cap'n Hank agreed, for Burris nodded. "Thank you," he said.

"Captain Morton told me he would consider it a personal favor if I'd help you." He picked up the phone, held it in mid-air for a moment. "Well...I guess if Captain Morton has been helping you..."

Much relieved, I watched him cradle the receiver between shoulder and ear. Hope springs eternal in the human breast, I thought, feeling cynical.

Whoever answered his call gave him another number. The second call also failed to connect him with whoever he wanted, and he hesitated, frowning at me when he hung up. I thought my luck had run out, but he picked up the phone again and dialed.

"Maurice!" he said. "Bill Burris. Yes. And you?" He leaned back in his desk chair. I thought the inane small talk would last forever. Finally he said, "I have one of our people here who has a...shall we say, a bit of a sticky wicket?

It's about two French Nationals. I wonder if you would talk to him if I sent him over? Wonderful. Sergeant Walker is his name. And, ahh... it would be something I'd know nothing about. Nothing at all. Yes. Thanks so much." He hung up the phone, wrote something on a piece of paper.

"I want you to understand." He stared at me. "It's my job to keep General Stinson's name out of anything that would unnecessarily take up his time or mar his record. The general *will not* help you marry this girl. He would try to keep you from it." He held my eyes. "Understand?" he asked.

I nodded. "Yes, sir. I appreciate it very much." He handed the paper across his desk.

"Go and see this man. Don't mention that you were here. Just tell him that you have two French citizens you want to get back to France. You can figure out how to get them home from there."

I smiled and took the paper. As I folded it and put in my wallet, he said, "They have papers, don't they?"

My hopes crashed.

"You *do* know how to get papers for them?" Before I could answer he went on. "One can buy anything in Vietnam. Especially in Saigon."

I nodded.

"One more thing. Captain Morton said he told you Captain Fowles is now Major Fowles. He wants to send you two up the river, all the way to Leavenworth. He's a dangerous man who will advance his career in any way possible, regardless who he has to destroy. That by itself would be a good reason to help you as far as I'm concerned. But I'm not. Right?"

"No sir, not at all."

"I usually have a drink about this time. Join me?" He pulled a bottle and two glasses from his desk drawer. It went down smooth and fiery. He asked me some questions about our missions, and we made small talk about the war. I felt uncomfortable talking to someone of his rank, but unlike so many high-ranking officers, he seemed to know how it felt to be in the line of fire. The man had "seen the elephant." Finally he stood. I followed his cue.

"There's another reason I'm...uh...not helping you," he said. Taking his metal cane from behind the desk he rapped it across his left shin. It clanked.

"'Nam?" I asked.

"Korea. I took great interest in the part of your file about your leg. Looks like you're walking okay."

"Yes, Sir. I am." I snapped to attention and saluted. "Thank you, sir. I'm sorry you couldn't help me." When he returned my salute, I did a crisp about-face and walked out the door.

I took a taxi to the address on the slip of paper. Located in the French quarter, the old mansion had been immaculately kept up. I asked the driver to wait, and, feeling entirely out of place, rang the bell. A butler answered the door. When I gave him my name and told him I had an appointment with Maurice, he showed me into a lavishly furnished room and asked me to wait. He took one long, sneering look down his nose at my uniform, and left. A few minutes later an attractive, dark complected woman showed me into an office. The wood floors were polished to such a luster I felt like I probably shouldn't walk on them. The paneling, along with the stuffed heads of some African big-game animals, gave the room the air of the British raj. I sat in a leather chair in front of an immense desk which did not have a single item on its polished top. A door behind the desk opened, admitting a short, dark-haired man. I rose.

"Ah, Sergeant Walker, sit down, sit down, please." He spoke with a sibilant French accent. He came around the desk, plopped his hand into mine. It felt damp and cold. "I am Maurice. I understand you would like to provide transportation for...?"

"Yes," I said. "I would like to arrange transportation to France for two girls—two young women—who are half French." We didn't have much time, so I decided I had no choice but to tell him what we wanted.

Maurice's smile vanished and a concerned look took its place. "Ah-h, I see. And these women have passports?" he asked.

"Unfortunately, no, they were born in Vietnam and have never applied." I hesitated, then told him what had happened to us. Perhaps he would sympathize with our plight. At least he would know we only had a matter of days left. His look of concern deepened.

"I presume there are no birth certificates."

I nodded.

"Well, that can be arranged. Passports, however, usually take more time than you have. And passports are expensive." I found his French accent to be strangely soothing.

"What would it cost for us to get Li and Rose on a plane to France?" I asked, wondering if we had enough money to pay for everything.

"Papers are the biggest expense. I would say, for birth certificates, one thousand dollars, American, for the two." He paused, pursed his lips, looked thoughtfully at the lion's head. "Passports for both, good ones, would be—shall we say, one thousand, five hundred dollars? Two thousand, five hundred dollars American for both of your French citizens."

I didn't want to seem too eager to agree. If he doubted we could pay too high a price, maybe it would be negotible. "And if I could raise that much money, this would guarantee they would both be flown to France, even if I had already left the country?"

"Another five hundred dollars, plus airfare—shall we say another three hundred dollars?—three thousand, three hundred American dollars. That would assure their arrival in France." Maurice raised an eyebrow. "As for guarantees, there never are any, you know. However, I am a businessman who has only his reputation. A good one. Remember who referred you to me."

"I can give you five hundred dollars now," I said. "Can I meet you tomorrow with the rest?" It looked like our only hope to get the girls out, and I had to risk it. I knew Mike would agree.

"Very well." He smiled. "You may come here tomorrow. Shall we say two o'clock? It should not take more than a day, perhaps two, to provide birth certificates."

I stood and he walked me to the door. I had mixed feelings about him, but as he said, the referral itself had been an endorsement.

When I got home, Mike and Rose were gone. Li said they had gone to eat at one of Rose's favorite restaurants and would be home early. She wanted to sit close to me, touch me, as if once she broke our physical contact, it would be gone forever. I wanted to let things sink in, so I didn't tell her what plans I'd made. I bounced between hope and uncertainty. Surely we can get them out. I hoped.

"Hey, I'm about to starve. How about something to eat?" I said.

She jumped down off the couch, headed for the kitchen. At the kitchen door she looked back, held out her hand. I joined her in the kitchen and sat at the table while she boiled a big pot of shrimp. I hadn't finished stuffing myself when Mike and Rose came home.

"Hey, sit down for a minute," I said. "I don't want to get everyone's hopes up, but I may have a solution." I looked at Mike. "I think we can get the girls to France."

"Great," he said, looking relieved and skeptical at the same time. "How?"

I told him about my meeting with Major Burris, then with Maurice. How he'd asked me to come back with the rest of the money tomorrow. We would have birth certificates for Li and Rose, then passports. "The only problem is that we would probably be gone by the time he could get the passports. We'll have to find someone we can trust to get them on a plane to France. We can figure out how to get them to the USA—hell, we can go to France and marry them, then bring them home." It began to seem real, even practical.

"How do we know this Maurice won't take our money and disappear?" Mike asked. I knew he wanted to believe it would work.

"We don't," I said. "But Major Burris recommended this guy. That's a pretty good recommendation. He might take our money and disappear, but it looks like it's the only hope we have. I'm willing to risk the money. How about you?"

"Sure," Mike said. "I don't think we should give it to him all at once. We can pay for the birth certificates now, and after he delivers, pay for the passports. Or do we need to have him get passports? Can't the girls get them with the birth certificates?"

"I guess they could," I said. "It's just having the time to go do it, knowing which palms to grease. You know how slow the government is. If we had time, Maurice could get real passports. He will probably get forgeries. If so, I sure hope they're good ones. But we don't have the time, and Li and Rose don't know how."

"We have five days. How much money do we have left?" Mike asked.

"I'm not sure, but we'll have a lot more than that. We haven't spent much on the house and the girls. We still have our pay bonuses. It's the souvenir sales that's been our jackpot. That's made us twice as much as everything else." We'd thought of the money as a good buffer in case we needed things we couldn't get through channels. We'd never imagined we might need a couple of passports.

"We need to get to our safe-deposit box," Mike said. "First thing tomorrow. Then we can take this Maurice guy the rest of his money for the birth certificates. I think we should tell him we'll pay for the passports after we see the birth certificates."

The next day both of us were at the big house promptly at two o'clock. We were shown into the same office and gave Maurice another five hundred dollars, explaining that we would like to see the birth certificates before paying for the passports. He seemed to have no problem and asked us to come back in two days.

On the second day Mike and I took a taxi to the house, only to find the gates closed and locked. We paid the taxi driver and skirted the grounds around the wrought-iron fence until we were out of sight of the road. We climbed the fence and stole through the foliage to the back of the house. It looked empty. I tried the back door. It swung open on well-oiled hinges. We went through the house, finding nothing, not even phones. The office where I met Maurice had been completely emptied.

"Damn!" I swore. "Looks like you were right about not giving him all the money."

"Someone's coming!" Mike whispered loudly, pointing through the window. "Holy shit, it's the ARVN! What are they doing here?" We raced for the back door, across the yard, and vaulted over the fence. We had no idea where we were, but the manicured grounds we'd landed in offered cover, and we disregarded the commands by our pursuers to halt. Then we heard shots. Whether they were firing into the air, or trying to hit us didn't matter at this point. We raced past a house, down a long driveway, and out into a street. Half a dozen blocks later we saw another ARVN patrol, and dodged into the bushes in front of someone's mansion.

"Well, we've found the Park Avenue of Saigon," said Mike.

That evening, after we regrouped at home, everyone wore long faces. We felt defeated. Suckered. We talked about visiting the French Embassy but didn't have much hope they would help.

That evening Mike and I attacked a bottle of Scotch and the girls drank mixed drinks. I had just started to pour another shot when someone pounded on the front door. Young Gee appeared and looked at us questioningly. I snatched up my .45 and stood just around the corner. Standing to one side, Young Gee opened the door, and a Vietnamese boy thrust an envelope at him and began to jabber at the top of his lungs. Young Gee got in a few questions, and the boy ran off into the night. Young Gee yelled at him to come back, but to no avail.

"What was that all about?" I asked.

Young Gee held out the envelope. "These are the birth certificates you paid for," he said.

We all went in the kitchen and spread them out on the table. The certificates were in French, and the girls read them, laughing over the discrepancies in the dates.

Gee interpreted the shouts from the delivery boy. The mansion had been raided by the South Vietnamese Government. Maurice got advance notice of the raid, so he emptied the house. The government troops found nothing, not so much as a paper clip, as we had discovered.

As I slipped the birth certificates back into the envelope I discovered a note. "Hey, look at this!"

> I think you will find the enclosed certificates satisfactory.
> I am sorry for the inconvenience, but I will not be able to
> assist you with passports.
>
> M.

The next day, a Friday, and we tried to find out where passports were issued and how to get them. We went from one office to another, waiting in lines in between, and learned nothing, except that about two o'clock the "Europeanized" offices closed for the weekend.

One of Young Gee's friends—for a price—swore he could get passports for the girls. We left money for him with Young Gee, strictly admonishing him not to give his friend more than half before he got the passports. "You tell him if he takes the money and there are no passports, I'll come back and kill him personally. Long and slow," I said, "like I've seen the ARVNs do."

"And I'll help him," Mike said.

Gee cringed and nodded.

The next night Mike and I visited one of our frequent haunts for a few drinks. It would be our last time at the place. Although we knew what was happening, it still didn't seem real.

"Four days and I'll be gone back to the World," Mike said.

"Yeah, I know. How the hell did I get the honor of spending another three weeks at our digs before I leave?" I asked. "We were supposed to go back to the World together. Want to trade?"

Mike looked somber. "I don't think I could stay there three weeks without seeing Rose again. I'll bet Cap'n Hank knew that and got me the earlier date."

"Yeah, but how did we end up with different dates?"

Mike shrugged. "Probably Captain Fowles. Anything make sense in this man's army?"

I shook my head. "Not any more."

We were quiet for a while, nursing our drinks. "Think it'll work?" he asked.

"Yes," I said, a little too quickly. "I have to think it'll work. I just couldn't do what I have to do if I thought it wouldn't."

"Ready to go?" he asked.

"Yeah. What a dump. Why'd we ever come here anyway?"

Cap'n Hank's predictions were correct, much to our dismay. Mike and I had been chewed out and ordered to live on base. The house would be declared off limits, confiscated and sold. But Major Fowles made the same mistake he had made at my court martial—he hadn't done his homework. Cap'n Hank had done the necessary paperwork to put the house in the names of Li and Rose. The army couldn't touch it now, it belonged to two Vietnamese, with birth certificates to prove their citizenship.

Our departure loomed large as Armageddon. Mike would go home the next day. I would leave for our digs. I had already decided that in the remaining time at our digs before I'd go back to the World, I would go nowhere and do nothing dangerous—regardless of orders. If I had to, I would sit in my digs and read, sleep, and drink. Most of the casualties we had were Fucking New Guys, or men who were short—due to go back to the World very soon. I wouldn't do anything risky. Lieutenant Jaimeson, if he ventured out, would be easy to manage, I thought, realizing how cynical I'd become.

Somehow Cap'n Hank arranged for us to get a pass on our last night with Li and Rose. We reserved a suite that night at a small place where it would be unlikely we'd run into anyone. We brought our own liquor, and ordered a lot of finger foods. We procured a case of Seagram's for Cap'n Hank. Young Gee found a record player and some old records. As a party, the evening was a dismal failure. Filled with despair and hopelessness, there was no cause for celebration. We danced with the girls to hits from twenty years past, all but forgetting Cap'n Hank and Young Gee. When the record player exhausted the stack of 78s, no one turned them over.

"We should discuss the arrangements we've made," Cap'n Hank said.

The arm of the record player made a faint scratching sound as it moved back and forth on the inside of the record, over and over. I almost commented on how our lives were going the same way when Cap'n Hank got up and turned it off. His look of anguish showed how much our plight had affected him. No one else, outside of our little circle, cared what happened to us.

"It's time, I guess. What have you got for us?" I asked.

Mike and I and the girls sat on the couch. Cap'n Hank pulled up a chair next to Young Gee. I felt my throat tighten up. This would be the last time we'd all be together.

"As far as I know, the existence of your safe-deposit boxes and the girls' bank account was our secret. As you agreed, I have closed them. But discretion is still of the utmost importance. You can imagine what Major Fowles would do if he found out.

"As you requested, I made a deposit of five thousand dollars from the money in your safe-deposit box to the girls' account. The balance now is over eight thousand dollars."

Cap'n Hank reached into his brief case. "Here are two envelopes. Each envelope has half the money left from your safe-deposit box. There is twelve thousand, two hundred fifty five dollars in each envelope." He handed one to me and the other to Mike.

"I had no idea we had that much," I said. I looked at Mike. "Did you?"

Mike shrugged his shoulders. "More or less."

Cap'n Hank took a third envelope from his briefcase and handed it to Mike. "This is the money from your private safe-deposit box," he said.

Mike nodded.

Cap'n Hank turned to the girls. "Li and Rose," he said, "the sergeants have given you the house, and the bank account with over eight thousand American dollars in it. They are now in your names. We are not optimistic that Young Gee's passport procurement will succeed. If you do get passports, you can use the money to get to France."

We had just given the girls the finances for a good future in Vietnam, if all else failed.

"I want you to have this," Mike said, as he handed me a thick stack of bills. "Five thousand. It's part of my divorce settlement. She sold the house. I got the money a long time ago and stashed it." I stared at the wad of American currency he'd slapped into my hand, like something he did every day.

"Why are you giving it to me?"

"Don't worry," he said. "Between what I'm giving you and the girls, I'll still have plenty to finance something back in the World."

"Mike, you should keep this," I said.

"Look. We've shared everything we've had for almost three years. God-dammit, just shut the fuck up and don't refuse to take the only thing I have left to give to you."

We usually covered our feelings with gruff banter, saying things to each other that would cause a fist fight coming from anyone else. This time I couldn't do it. I stuck out my hand, and when he took it, I held his in both of mine. "Thanks, Mike," I said, trying not to get all misty-eyed.

Li's eyes opened wide as she listened to Cap'n Hank explain how to get the money out of the bank as they needed it or how to make a transfer if they got their passports. She had become an adept manager of the household finances and could haggle in the marketplace like a pro.

Rose didn't seem to react much to the news that we were leaving each of them with the equivalent of about thirty years' income for the average Vietnamese. She had been withdrawn, clinging to Mike, content so long as they touched, the detached look in her eyes returning whenever he moved more than an arm's length away from her.

Cap'n Hank gave Li a card with his number on it. "If you have any problems, anything at all, even if you feel it is trivial, please call me. Or if you just want to talk. Do you understand?"

Li nodded. Cap'n Hank continued.

"Doug and Mike have made it possible for me to share something with them that is more important than anything I've ever had, or ever will have. I owe them a very big debt of gratitude. There can be nothing too trivial for you to seek my help about. If I don't hear from you every few days, I'll check on you."

Li nodded. "I will call you. Thank you," she said.

Cap'n Hank turned to Young Gee.

"The sergeants have given you a tenth part of the house. You will own it so long as you serve Li and Rose." Young Gee looked puzzled. "You will stay on with them as their houseboy so long as you please them with your service, living there as a part owner. And you will have a small salary every month, so long as there is interest from the money they have given Li and Rose. If the house is sold, you will receive a tenth of the profits. If Li and Rose leave the country, they will give you five hundred dollars if they feel your service has been worthy. However, if you no longer please them, they may dismiss you without a cent, and you will lose your interest in the house, your salary, and the five hundred dollars. Do you understand?"

I cringed at the thought that they might not leave Vietnam. I felt that with Cap'n Hank's help, it was possible for our luck to hold, and get them out.

Young Gee gave him a smile, showing the few teeth he had left and the gaps between. He turned to us, mumbling in Vietnamese. Placing his palms together he turned to the girls, making obeisant bows. I didn't know if Li understood what Young Gee's place would be.

"Young Gee can be helpful to you," I said to Li. "But you must remember that even though he is a man, you are above him. You are...his sergeant," I said, fumbling for an example. "You and Rose have been the women of mighty warriors and now you can never, ever, be slaves to any man." I looked intently into her eyes. "These are our wishes. Do you understand?"

Uncertainty changed to realization and sadness as she nodded slowly. A look of resolve replaced the uncertainty, then tears formed and she lunged for me, wrapping her arms around my neck. Finally, our parting had become a reality to her.

Cap'n Hank decided the time had come for him to leave with Young Gee. Not used to the drinks he'd had, Young Gee was wobbly on his feet.

"Don't worry, I'll take him home," Cap'n Hank said. "I'll be back tomorrow for the girls." We walked with them to the door. Cap'n Hank turned, looked up at us, and started to talk, took a couple of deep breaths first. "You two have changed my life. There is no way to repay you..."

As he stood tall and straight, I could see the difference in the kid from Harvard Law School with his needle-sharp pencils who quizzed me that first day in the hospital. Captain Henry Rockwell Morton, purple heart proudly displayed on his uniform shirt, had become a man all out of proportion to his diminutive size.

Mike stepped forward and shook his hand.

Cap'n Hank shook hands with me, stepped back, and for a moment I thought he would salute.

"God bless you," he said, hoarsely, and left with Young Gee in tow.

Now that we were alone, the final curtain had come down on our spirits. Mike fixed us a round of drinks, and we finished them in silence. I worried about him, lost as he seemed to be in a world shared only with Rose. The Dear John letter had been hard on Mike. I was sure this, ultimately, would be much worse. It seemed like the army he served so well had sent them a Dear John that told him they couldn't have each other. Damn the idiots that did this to us, I thought. With what we'd been through together, I couldn't help feeling a lot of heartache for them, almost enough to take my mind off my own. I could handle it. I didn't know about Mike.

Rose sat on his lap with her arms around his neck as he held her. Neither of them moved for so long I thought they'd fallen asleep. "Ready for bed?" I asked Li. Mike and Rose stirred and headed for their bedroom without saying a word. Li, attentive as ever, saw me frown. "You are worried about them," she said. I nodded.

Just before I closed our bedroom door, Mike went to the end table where he'd left his .45, picked up the big pistol, dropped the magazine, to make sure it was loaded. Replacing the magazine, he pulled the slide back just far enough to be sure there was a round in the chamber.

I'd seen him do that a thousand times, but tonight it gave me a chill.

Pistol in hand, he closed the bedroom door.

Li and I undressed silently in the glow of outside lights that shone through the curtains. Usually she put on a silk nightie, but not tonight. I watched her as she pulled back the covers, her shiny black hair falling over one shoulder, her smooth skin disappearing beneath the sheet. When she realized I drank in her every move, she smiled and pulled the sheet up over her breasts. I took her in my arms and we held each other for a long time.

I had dozed off when she pushed me over on my back. She usually fell asleep with one leg between mine, her chest against me, head on my shoulder. Usually that led to other things beside sleep, but tonight, feeling her naked against me only made me want to hold her. I could smell the scent of her hair like orchids blended with sandalwood. I pulled her up a little higher on my chest and gently kissed her neck. Neither of us moved for hours. My arm tingled when she raised her head and slid off of me.

"Are you asleep?" she asked. I shook my head. "You have shown much love in the wonderful things you have done for us. You have done so very much. We would have been sold..." She shuddered.

"As prostitutes?" I asked, wondering how she correctly came to this conclusion. I chalked it up to the fast pace of the Far East. Here women could be old at sixteen, men could be grandfathers in their twenties—dead or maimed much younger than that.

"I will never have another man!" she said with such force it surprised me.

"I want you to feel free to have..."

"No!" she said, loudly. "Do not speak to me of this!" she declared. She lay quietly for some time, then sat up and turned, facing me. "I have something to tell you. I hope it will please you."

"Okay," I said.

Her voice sounded small, pleading for acceptance. "I am going to have your child."

CHAPTER THIRTY FIVE

Butter Bars

Willie, Parkhurst and I stood in the bunker where Lieutenant Jaimeson sat at his portable field desk, reaching into a pile of papers. Willie and Parkhurst had finished their second tours. After three years, then cutting my fourth tour short, I'd become the old man. We were the last of the old-timers—everyone else in the team had less than a year in-country. And Mike had already gone home.

The lieutenant pulled out three neatly stapled batches of paper and handed one to each of us. As I read my orders to report to Da Nang for transport to the States, I felt a strange sense of detachment. Then anger about all that had happened, all that I'd done and all I'd been forced to do here washed over me. It made me dizzy. I sat down on the steps. I could picture Li's soft skin and silky hair, but I couldn't imagine watching her body swell with our child.

"You okay Sarge?" asked Willie. I looked at him as if I'd never seen him before. Recognition floated back. Yes. Private First Class Williams, our tunnel rat. Afraid of nothing. I'd watched him face situations that would terrify other men, including me. Right now he looked just vaguely familiar.

"Yeah, I'm okay. How about you, Parkhurst?" I asked.

Parkhurst looked up and stared, eyes unfocused, like someone who has just awakened. "Man, I'm ready to go home," he said. "Back to the World."

I remembered when he had joined the team. He had been pudgy then, a red-cheeked school-boy. Now he looked lean, gaunt, tired.

Lieutenant Jaimeson interrupted our reverie. "You gotta turn in your rifles," he said.

We looked at each other, shocked. Our M-16s, never further away than arms-reach twenty-four hours a day, had become an extension of our bodies. I unslung my carbine version of the M-16, and looked down at it. It had meant staying alive. There were places where the silvery metal showed through the tough military coating. Each individual nick and dent had its own story. The dent in the upper receiver from the time I banged it on the truck. Once I plugged the flash suppressor with mud and it bulged when I fired it. I'd stripped and cleaned this rifle a thousand times; it had almost become part of my body. This was another amputation. I glared at him.

"You know we have no M-16 replacements, or I wouldn't ask." He sighed. "Goddamn the paper-pushing REMFs!"

Hearing that kind of language from Lieutenant Jaimeson was shocking. He'd always been such a Mr. Milktoast we almost thought of him as an REMF.

"All right, Lieutenant," I said, removing the magazine and clearing the live round from the chamber. "But I don't like it. Goddam army, can't even give us enough rifles to go around." I handed it to him, along with the bandoliers of ammo I carried slung across my chest. Parkhurst and Willie grudgingly followed suit, removing the loaded magazines and clearing the live rounds from the chambers.

Lieutenant Jaimeson looked startled. "Christ! All of them were loaded?"

"Nothin' more worthless than an unloaded rifle," Willie said scornfully. "You can get yer ass shot off out here, y'know. S' what they tell me." Jaimeson turned red.

"Okay, let's get outside," I said, not knowing what kind of trouble the lieutenant could still cause us. Lieutenants were something I wouldn't miss. Jaimeson hadn't been too bad, though. We shook hands.

"I got more bad news," I told Parkhurst and Willie after we climbed the stairs. Lieutenant said that due to the usual clerical error, the chopper's only going to take us to a fire base. We'll have to hitch a ride to Da Nang to catch our freedom bird. But it's gonna be a real civilian airliner that'll take us home. It doesn't matter how we make it, just as long as we all do," I said.

"Goddam clerks," said Parkhurst, "Can't even get us out of here without screwin' it up!"

"You can always wait for the next flight. Go first class. Have a drink while you fly in comfort," Willie said.

Parkhurst snorted.

"Well, ladies, make up your minds. Looks like our ride is here," I said, hearing the faint whop-whop-whop of the chopper's blades. We climbed in—the last time we would ever board a chopper.

The hop offered a view of azure-blue sky and green foliage, spread over the land like a blanket. I looked at Willie. He sat on his helmet to protect his privates from bullets that might penetrate the chopper's belly. His head tipped back, he'd fallen asleep with his mouth open.

Whenever we found a tunnel, which wasn't often, Willie would get a feverish look like the Grim Reaper. He would shuck off his web belt with all its canteens, pouches and attachments. He wore a "tunnel harness" of his own design, which held a .45 cal. Government Model pistol under the left arm. Behind the right shoulder he had fitted a holster for a cut-down 12 gauge pump shotgun. When he stood, the muzzle pointed up. Crawling in a tunnel, it pointed forward, nudging his ear. After checking his shotgun for obstructions and functioning, Willie loaded the magazine with two rounds from his hoarded supply of commercial 12 gauge number four buckshot. He chambered a round, then recharged the magazine. Securing the shotgun in its place, he donned the harness and strapped it around his skinny chest. It looked strange, but he could reach the big pistol, or pull the shotgun up over his shoulder and into his hands while lying on his belly in an eighteen inch tunnel. That made it a creation of genius. A headlamp completed the ensemble.

I'd once commented as he geared up that the safety on the shotgun had not been engaged. "Yeah, I know, Sarge," he said, tapping his flashlight to be sure it worked. "They shoot first an' ask questions later down there!" he said, and dove head-first into the tunnel. I watched his "umbilical cord," the rope that, we hoped, could be used to pull him out, as it disappeared into the tunnel.

I looked over at Parkhurst. He'd been my corporal since Tony went home. Now he leaned back against the bulkhead, staring out at nothing. It looked like a case of thousand-yard-stare, the escape route taken by the mind when things get to be too much. Parkhurst had been one of the best support personnel

I'd ever had. He organized everything from weekend passes in Saigon for the whole team to insertions into areas where we never officially went. His attention to detail bordered on obsessive, or spectacular, I couldn't decide which. And he had a way of listening that encouraged people to talk. Parkhurst always talked to anyone we were going to trade with or ask for favors. It was hard to tell him no. He could be a fighter, alert, aggressive, capable. But now he was bone weary. He could have easily made sergeant, but over the months his enthusiasm flagged. He had no desire for promotion. He only wanted to go home and forget. Vietnam—and Laos and Cambodia—had become too big a burden.

In a way, I envied him. It seemed a century ago, before the army, when I still had Sarah, with her deep, almost debilitating gentleness. She cried for hurt animals and once for a dead bird we found. I thought about the two years we'd gone steady in high school, our secret letter campaign when she moved, our engagement. Sweet Sarah Stearn. I could still see her face with those flashing blue eyes. I had gone to Miami before I went in the army to tell her I was going, and to say goodbye. She was supposed to be staying with a girlfriend, but she'd stayed in a motel with me. I could remember how hurt she was when I told her I had joined the army. At first I wrote to her often, talking about what we would do when I got out. Her letters, smuggled from home, became sisterly, which was anything but what I wanted. Then one of the photos she sent showed her wearing a headband, a tie-died T-shirt and no bra. She was looking up at some bearded long-hair with the same adoring look she used to have for me. Soon after that, I got the Dear John.

I thought of Li. I stared out over the green canopy, closed my eyes, and felt tears on my face. No one would notice. No one could hear over the roar of the chopper. If they did, they'd pretend they didn't. I held on to a cargo strap and cried, sobbing, gulping deep breaths to soothe the ache in my chest. Looking down at the trees for the last time, I wondered what it would be like to let go, to just slide out the door. The image of Li as I last saw her was clear in my mind's eye, as it would be for the rest of my life. I had to keep on keeping on, just as I'd done so many times, on so many missions, struggling to keep going. Putting one foot in front of the other, however impossible it seemed. Maybe there was a chance Li and Rose would get passports and we could find them in France, I thought, not really believing it, wondering if I'd ever know if I had a son. Or a daughter with her mother's beauty.

I glanced at Parkhurst, who seemed to know I was struggling with something. He smiled wanly, and his eyes once again focused on something only he could see.

The chopper dropped toward the trees, and I could see the base. After we landed, we were directed to a line of trucks. A figure in greasy fatigues waved at us, scowled, pointed to a truck that was indistinguishable from the others.

"Get in back," he growled. He had an attitude, but he'd take us to the base where we'd go back to the World. I didn't care about anything else.

I didn't realize how tense we were until we climbed up in the back of the truck. Staying alive had shredded our nerves. We'd all seen guys who were short get wounded or killed. Now all three of us were short. Mere hours to stay alive.

Our outposts had been wrapped in loops of sharp-edged wire, booby-trapped with explosives, tin cans, and anything else that would make noise if the enemy tried to come through. The perimeter was sentried by men with machine guns. Outside the wire, we'd cleared off everything that grew leaves. It was hard to adjust to the lack of security here.

"Look at the goddam brush outside the wire," Parkhurst said.

"Wire? There hardly is any!" Willie noted.

"You guys ready?" we heard the driver's gravelly voice ask. Without waiting for an answer, he yanked open the door and slipped in behind the wheel, started the machine, and backed out into the road with a roar and a jerk.

The three of us occupied the back of a truck which was rated to hold two and one-half tons of men and gear. We huddled in the front corners, the expanse of truck looking vast, as if the machine was performing a lesser task, so far below its capabilities it somehow resented it, and found every rock and pothole in the road to get even. As if the jouncing shook loose random memories, I thought of home. School parties, "boondockers" out in the forest at night, drinking beer, classrooms and cruising around, tumbled out pell-mell. Home was like something I'd read about somewhere, but couldn't remember very well.

It was a time I lived without the automatic attack mode from the least sign of a threat. Could I fit into that world again? I felt hurt, deep in my chest, that maybe I would be like this always.

I worried that I'd never make it home, that Li would make it to France, and I wouldn't be there. I thought about the child again, a child which would be of her and of me. I wondered what the child would look like. A girl with her mother's good looks would have a choice of suitors. It would be difficult for a boy. Oriental boys weren't as likely to be accepted if they were of mixed parentage. It would be hard for him. Real hard.

The driver increased our speed where the road was straight. There were so many rattles it sounded like we were being fired on. I felt naked sitting in the back of the truck without my rifle, my paranoia expanding by the minute, fear having a strange effect on my senses.

I had that feeling again, the one that seemed to precede change, everything standing out clearly, like the images in a 3D movie. I could see every single leaf on each tree and plant, the tendrils of each vine. The smell of decaying foliage, ripe and moist, ever present, was pungent in my nostrils, malodorous as death. I expected to see Charlie in the trees at the side of the road and to hear the sound of AK-47 automatic fire at any minute. But it didn't happen. Maybe this was an omen for good things to come.

"God, would a cold beer go good right now," I said as the truck slowed for a stretch of road that was partly flooded. "When we get home, I want a half-dozen cases of cold beer. All at once." This was something we never had in the field. We got a "hot meal" every ten days or so, depending on where we were. We didn't care much about a hot meal when the mercury and the humidity both pushed a hundred, and we had no use for the can of beer that was almost as hot.

Parkhurst laughed. "Remember what we used to do with the beer?"

We had discovered our beer made a great target. One day after our hot meal I'd picked up my can of hot beer and paced off the distance to the edge of the clearing, set the beer on a convenient tree limb. When the rest of the team realized what I was going to do, they scrambled for wallets to make bets. I raised my M-16 and gently squeezed the trigger. The results were spectacular.

The beer exploded violently into a mist of foam, round and symmetrical, like a draft beer with a head on it twenty feet wide. Everyone laughed.

"Hey, Sarge," someone said. "Look at the can!" The can had burst at the seams, now a flat rectangle with the round top and bottom still attached. A small bullet hole just below the center of the square showed where it went in. I had inadvertently placed the seam of the can directly away from the path of my bullet. When it hit the can, the pressure blew the seam open before the bullet could make a hole through the other side. The top and bottom stuck out like misplaced wheels on some kid's toy. From then on we looked forward to our beer.

The heat pounded us so hard that cold beer—anything cold, for that matter—was hard to imagine. Without a canopy on the back of our truck, our helmets absorbed the sun's heat. Brain ovens. The air, heavy and hard to breathe, plastered the uniforms to our bodies. Our empty canteens served only to remind us of our thirst. It seemed as if days passed in the hours we rattled around in that truck, stuck in some sort of purgatory, never to make it home. Then I smelled the air base: the kerosene aroma of jet fuel, the sour smell of burning shit.

I found the assault on my olfactory senses oddly welcome. Fifty-five gallon drum-halves, which held the contents of the latrines, were pulled out when they were full, mixed with diesel fuel, then burned. The stench was overpowering, but it meant the safety of the base was close, and our departure from this slice of hell would come soon.

Then Willie yelled, "Sniper! In the trees!"

Collectively we hit the deck of the truck. Something struck me hard on my left side. Oh, God, I'm hit, I thought. I get where I can smell shit from the base and I get hit. Then whatever it was that delivered the numbing blow to my ribs moved. I looked down. "Parkhurst, get your goddamn foot out of my ribs!" I yelled. In that great-big truck, we were still falling all over each other.

"You guys okay?" Willie asked, lying flat on his face. "We got incoming?"

"I'm not hit," Parkhurst said.

"I'm okay," I said.

The truck was still moving.

"Willie," I said, "Look out and see what's going on!"

Willie peeked out from under his helmet through the wooden slats that formed the sides of the truck. "I don't see nothin'."

Suddenly the truck jerked, the wheels locked up. With a dizzying lurch, it skidded to a halt, one wheel off in the ditch at the side of the road.

"Out, out, move, move!" I yelled, and vaulted over the tailgate. Willie and Parkhurst followed fast, and we dropped into the ditch. I automatically looked for Mike, but he was a civilian by now, back in the World.

"Now what the hell are we gonna do," Willie muttered, "throw rocks?"

I looked up to see our driver walk calmly around the front of the truck. When he saw us crouched, up to our butts in the muddy water in the ditch, the look on his face was one of utter bafflement.

"What the hell you guys doin' down there?" he said.

"Get down! Sniper in the trees!" Parkhurst yelled.

Alarmed, the driver dropped into a crouch and turned to look. "Christ, I hope not," he said, scanning the side of the road to see if he'd missed something. "There's no one in those trees!" he said. We looked at each other, mystified. "Then why did you stop?" I asked.

"Something in the road. I thought it was a mine. It wasn't."

We got out of the ditch and climbed back into the truck.

"Never seen such a jumpy bunch," he said with a smirk.

"Just drive," I told him. "Shut the fuck up and drive."

I felt out of breath from the false alarm, and started to cough. Try as I might, I couldn't get my breath. Whatever was in my chest didn't want to come up. After a particularly violent spasm, I spat out a mouthful of thick, yellow phlegm.

"Jeezus, Sarge," Parkhurst said. "You okay?"

"Yeah. I think so. I've been coughing this shit up since that time we chased Charlie through that area they sprayed with defoliant."

"That was a long time ago. Couple 'a months?" Parkhurst asked.

"Six. About six months. I told Jaimeson, but he never got back with us."

The trees in the area where they had sprayed defoliant were all reduced to ragged, bare-branch skeletons. Whatever was sprayed on them didn't have a very strong smell. It reminded me of a faint whiff of car exhaust.

The day after we went through the sprayed area, Tony knocked on the doorway of my quarters. He had a boot in his hand. He set it on my bunk, then sat on a wooden ammo case and pulled off one of the boots he was wearing.

"What the hell are you doing?" I asked.

"Look at this," he said. "This is the boot I was wearing when we went through the area that had been sprayed." He rubbed the edge of the sole on the ammo case. It left a heavy black mark. When he rubbed the black mark with his finger, it made a little rubber ball that was slightly sticky.

"Now watch this." He rubbed the boot he had just taken off next to the black mark. It made almost no mark at all. "You cleaned your rifle since then? Notice anything unusual?"

"Yeah, now that you mention it," I said. "I got something on the fore end, something sticky. You don't mean..."

Tony took my rifle by the black plastic fore end and squeezed it for a few seconds. He held it out at arm's length, and when he relaxed his grip, the rifle hung suspended, as if glued to his hand. "We got some of that shit they sprayed on our rifles, and that's why it's sticking," he said.

I told him I'd let Lieutenant Jaimeson know about it.

The next day my chest hurt. I headed for Mack's end of the digs.

"Hey, Mack," I said, and started to cough. I spit out a big gob of ugly, yellow-looking stuff.

"You too?" Mack asked.

"What do you mean?"

"So far today, Tony, Skeeter, and now you are coughing like you got the flu. Who else went on that little excursion with you?"

"Evans was the other one. Don't tell me he's been here too?" I asked.

"Not yet," Mack said, handing me some pills. "One every six hours. These will break up that phlegm. Drink a lot of water with those. Wanna make a bet Evans shows up?"

"No. Guess I'd better find him, then let Jaimeson know something's wrong. Really wrong." Now there wasn't much doubt that the four of us—Tony,

Skeeter, Evans, and myself—had breathed something bad into our lungs. And sinuses, judging by the strength of my headache. Maybe it's just temporary, I thought.

Two weeks later we'd heard nothing about our chest problems. Since we seemed to be getting better, we didn't pursue it.

By now I felt like I had a continual cold, coughing up that same yellow stuff. I attributed it to nerves over the trouble Colonel Fowles was causing, trying to prosecute us, and our unsuccessful attempt to get passports for Rose and Li. Nerves and pressure, I rationalized.

Fifteen minutes later we were craning our necks to see the base as we drove up to the gate. It seemed obvious that we were on the same side as the guards at the gate, but they looked us over as though maybe we were VC disguised in American bodies.

"C'mon, dammit, hurry up!" Willie said, "You wanna frisk us?" His comment earned us a scowl from the Marine lance corporal. We weren't exactly powder-room fresh when we left, and by now we were so muddy and sweaty he probably smelled us about the time we smelled the base. Our driver didn't know where to take us and had to have the instructions repeated several times. We stretched and rubbed sore backs and asses, our patience no less chafed. Finally we were allowed to enter, and the truck stopped at a nondescript olive-drab building somewhere in the maw of the base.

"Wonder where they got that nice shade of green!" Willie said.

"If it moves, salute it. If it don't, paint it," Parkhurst said.

As we piled out, a butter-bars lieutenant in a clean, starched uniform strutted out of the building. He yelled at us to "form up," as if this was some close order drill we signed up for. His shiny brass name tag read "MILLS." On each collar he wore the insignia of his rank, a single butter-colored bar. Since we were going home, the three of us didn't pay any attention to this offensive bantam rooster. Our orders were cut, and whatever happened, he didn't have enough rank to change them.

"It's moving," Parkhurst said. "Anyone remember how to salute?"

"Maybe we should paint it," I offered.

Willie was staring at the perimeter. "Damn," he said to no one in particular,

"*That* tree line is even closer!"

We all turned to look.

"Sure is," I said, feeling uneasy. "Wonder what idiot is responsible for that?"

That was too much for Lieutenant Mills. Our comments started him off on a tirade about discipline.

"You better listen up, soldiers! When I give an order for you to fall in, I want to see you standing in line at attention! I don't know what the hell kind of discipline you're used to, but you all stink, not to mention you look like hell!"

"Yeah, how 'bout that?" Willie said. "Whassa matta you, Parkhurst? Jus' like this base, you smell like shit! You even look like shit!"

Butter-bars was several inches taller and a good twenty flabby pounds heavier than any of us. He stepped forward and shoved his nose a few inches from mine, continuing his tirade about discipline and order and what the hell kind of sergeant was I after all? I was close to boiling. When he started punctuating his message by stabbing my chest with his finger, my patience evaporated after the second stab. I grabbed the lieutenant's finger and bent it back. Grasping Lieutenant Mill's arm just above his wrist, I pushed down on both, sheer pain encouraging the flabby body attached to the finger to move down. The result was that the lieutenant ended up on his knees in front of me.

"Touch me again, you son of a bitch, I'll kick your ass." I smiled sweetly. I let go of him and he bounced to his feet, shaking his hand.

"You're going to the stockade!" he yelled at me. "Just wait until I get the MPs! You can't touch an officer!"

At that moment this sorry ass became the whole damn army, all the misfortunes it had heaped upon me, not the least of which was to deprive me of my occupation and the woman I loved. I drew back a fist and hit butter-bars in the face. I could see each stage of the blow. My fist, fingers held tight so they wouldn't break, sailed through the air. It landed on his nose, which flattened out on his face, and his eyes screwed themselves shut. The eyebrows shot up in surprise. I felt his upper lip yield to his teeth from the pressure of my knuckles. His lower lip stuck out under my fist, along with his jaw. For a split-second he looked like he was trying to bite my hand. His arms flailed as he went over backwards and a fine spray of blood flew from his lip.

The lieutenant, dazed, lay flat on his back in the dirt. Then he sat up, and blood gushed out of his nose, soiling the front of his starched uniform. With an effort, he got to his feet and stood there, wobbly and quiet.

I could almost hear the proceedings at the court martial. "...did willfully attack Lieutenant Mills, who in the course of his duties..." I thought about Mike, and knew if he could have seen what I'd done, he'd approve. Then my reverie was interrupted by a voice that was quite different from butter-bars'.

"Tenn-n-n-hutt!" it commanded.

Unlike Mills,' the timbre of that voice carried authority, demanded obedience. We snapped to attention. From behind us appeared a captain. He was slim, not tall, and looked to be in superb physical condition. His movements had the grace of a man with fast, sure reflexes. I'd experienced other eyes that bored into me like a drill bit, but his exploded through me, seeing everything within, as if it had been diagramed. Nothing could hide from those eyes. He sized up all of us with one raking glance.

It was butter-bar's misfortune to speak first. "Captain," he said, "these men..."

"At ease!" the captain barked.

But it seemed Lieutenant Mills was having a hard time following orders himself.

"But sir, these men..."

"Dismissed, Lieutenant! You are *dismissed*! I saw *everything* that happened," the captain snapped, "And I saw you trip and fall on your face in the dirt!"

"He—he hit me!" the lieutenant blurted out. He pointed his injured finger at me, then dropped his hand to his side where his finger was safe.

"Why Lieutenant," the captain said dryly, "I was watching all the time, and I didn't see anyone hit you. Did you men see anyone hit the lieutenant?"

"No, *Sir*," we replied, almost in unison.

"Listen up, *Lieutenant*," the captain said, pronouncing the rank as though it was something distasteful. "These men have seen more fighting than your goddamn precious pink little ass will ever comprehend! And if I ever catch you ordering anyone around the way you did these men, I'll see to it that you have a permanent position on point on every patrol out of my firebase for as long as you last—which won't be long."

He let Mills shrivel for a few seconds under his fierce look.

"You got that, *Lieutenant*?"

Mills' "Yes, Sir," was almost inaudible.

"Now get out of here and get cleaned up!" The captain watched him walk away a few paces, then called out, "Lieutenant?"

Mills turned around, stood at attention. "Yes, Sir?"

"Be more careful in the future. I don't want to see you trip again. Dismissed."

"Yes, Sir!" The lieutenant saluted and marched off.

We were still standing at attention. And smiling. That was a mistake.

The captain turned, and though his silence was terrible, it was mild compared to his look, which figuratively flayed us alive. Our smiles disappeared.

He walked up to me like the lieutenant had done, and barked, "Think that was funny? You want to take a swing at me, Sergeant?"

"No, Sir!" I said. I was standing ramrod straight at attention, eyes focused on nothing. I could feel the blood run out of my face at the mere question.

The captain backed off and looked at the three of us. "You ever fuck up?" he asked. "Well? You three ever do something dumb—besides this?"

In unison, we replied. "Yes, Sir!"

"That officer did something dumb today. Maybe he'll be a better officer now. You know I could have you in the stockade for striking an officer?" He paused again, and we noticed he was looking at all three of us, not just me. The silence hung heavy as a jailhouse door. Then, in a more relaxed voice he asked, "You men going home?"

"Yes, Sir!" we replied, again in unison.

"Think you can get home without striking any more officers? Even if they are assholes?"

"Yes, Sir." We breathed a sigh of relief.

"Okay. Just remember, for every one of us, there are a hundred rear-echelon mother fuckers who have no idea what it's like out there."

He paused again and studied each of us, one at a time. I looked at the medals and campaign ribbons on his chest.

"Carry on," he said in a low voice.

We saluted, each of us attempting to deliver a perfect salute. He was one of us. In that short time we had discovered he was a fair and capable officer.

"Jeezus, Sarge, that was kinda' stupid," Parkhurst said.

"Yeah, it was," I admitted. My face bent into a smile. "But God, it felt good."

Everyone smiled.

I glanced out past the wire, an old habit. I would have to learn that back in the World there would be no need for a guarded perimeter. No wire. I wondered how long it would take to quit looking for it.

CHAPTER THIRTY SIX

Homecoming

When the wheels of the big plane screeched down on the runway, we all came unglued. We were back home, on United States soil once again.

With the magic that is known only to non-coms and enlisted men, several bottles appeared out of nowhere and passed from hand to hand as the aircraft reversed its engines and slowed at the end of the runway. The men shouted and cheered, toasted everything they could think of. Home. The USA. Women.

We'd just spent a day-and-a-half with layovers on this Freedom Bird. As we approached the California coast, everyone had peered out the tiny windows on one side, crowded five or six deep, trying to get that first glimpse of American soil.

"Look, there's the coast!" someone hollered.

"No, you dumb shit, that's the edge of a cloud. We're above the clouds, you can't see the coast," Marc said. We had met Marc on the plane, our expert on California. He had visited San Francisco twice.

The plane dropped through the clouds, and the San Francisco Bay came into view.

"Look! Look! There's the Golden Gate!" shouted Willie.

"Nah," Marc said, "that's the Bay Bridge. You can't see the Golden Gate from here." No one questioned his authority, so the Bay Bridge it was.

With the first glimpse of home, my heart felt the absence of the one I wanted to share this moment with. Feeling my eyes sting, I donned my mask of ferocity and looked to see if anyone saw what I'd just felt. They were all looking out the windows.

We walked up the concourse from the gate where we deplaned, deliciously experiencing the land of freedom. Everyone looked so tall and well fed. Some stared at our uniforms, but most were indifferent.

The big change seemed to be the young people. Their dress had changed. They looked sloppy and dirty. Some looked as if they'd abandoned personal hygiene altogether. Most of the time we'd looked and smelled a lot worse, but not by choice. When we had facilities, we used them. We felt privileged to get a shower. A bath, a luxury. A clean uniform, a miracle.

I got my first hint about how things had changed when I spied a bumper sticker on a battered suitcase, a takeoff on the old slogan, "Get U.S. out of U.N." It had been changed to "Get U.S. out of Vietnam." Oh well, I thought. Among other things, we fought for their right to disagree.

The sight of a young man wearing the American flag sewn to the seat of his pants brought us to a dead halt. The flag had been cut to fit.

Confused and wary of the flag-wearer, we approached the metal detectors in silence. A group of young men and women had just come in from the other side. We passed each other in the middle of the concourse, separated by the red velvet ropes airports use to control foot traffic. They pinned us with venomous looks, and sounding like robots, recited their slogans.

"Make love, not war," shouted a girl with matted hair.

"Jeezus, who'd want to touch her?" Willie said.

"Not until she's been dosed with flea and tick powder, de-loused, and washed," Parkhurst commented.

"War is murder," said a man with long hair and a beard. Maybe some of them had an idea what they were saying, but most of them sounded like a tape played over and over, losing its acoustic quality, becoming distorted.

We hadn't been told that something like this might happen. We knew some people were against the war, but assumed it wasn't much different from other wars. We would have passed by their group without comment if it hadn't been for the one who called out to me.

"Baby killer!" He yelled, moving against the velvet rope.

I stopped and looked at him across the barrier, a blond kid over six feet tall. He wore a blue tie-died T-shirt and faded levis. His dirty long hair was caught up in a pony tail. An unsuccessful effort to grow a beard left fuzz on his face. He looked about eighteen, I guessed. When it dawned on me that he had singled me out, directed his expletive at me, it left me speechless. I turned away, and he yelled, "YOU, soldier boy!"

I looked back just in time to hear him hawk up a gob of phlegm and spit it at me. I felt it hit my face, slide down wet and gooey. For a few seconds, my astonishment kept me from realizing what had happened. I could see him standing there with a smug look on his face, as if he had scored a point for his side. He wasn't spitting bullets. Worse.

Without thinking, I let the strap of my bag slide off my shoulder. I launched myself at him, sailing over the red velvet rope. I tackled his marshmallow-soft body and lifted him off his feet. We landed on the well-waxed airport floor and slid several feet to the wall, coming to a stop under a water fountain.

I squeezed his throat with both hands. In the periphery of my senses, I heard Parkhurst and Willie calling my name, and heard the screams of the girls in the kid's group. This was a new, unexpected foe that had ambushed me, taken over for the enemy I'd left half-way around the world. My attack mode took charge, still programmed to keep me alive, to kill before something killed me. I shook the kid up and down, banging his head on the floor as my thumbs pressed deeper and deeper into his windpipe, seeking the fragile hyoid bone in his throat. It would snap without much pressure, collapsing his windpipe, asphyxiating him.

For a split second, everything stopped. I looked down at the terror in his eyes and released the pressure on his windpipe. Yeah, I realized, he shouldn't have spit on me. But he didn't deserve to die because of it. I relaxed my grip on his throat just as strong hands locked tight on my wrists and arms, yanked my fingers away. As they jerked me to my feet, I yelled out, "You fucking traitor!"

Like iron filings around the poles of a magnet, the two groups gathered. My buddies took my duffel and walked me away from the kid. His friends bent over him where he lay on the floor. Two Port Authority police officers came on the run in response to the screaming. One went to the kid, the other officer started toward me.

I burned with anger and it showed in my eyes. Wisely the officer decided not to talk to me. "Hey, Jay!" she said to the officer surrounded by friends of fuzz face. "Call the captain!"

By now we had attracted a crowd that blocked the concourse. "Uh, fellas, if you wouldn't mind, please move against the wall, so people can get by," the officer politely asked.

The blond kid still lay sprawled on the floor. I began to wonder if I had killed him after all. Regret for the whole incident set in fast. How could I spend all that time dodging bullets and avoiding booby traps and fail to dodge this kid's spittle?

A Port Authority officer wearing captain's bars walked past the metal detector and headed our way. Dark skinned, in his mid-forties. A big man. I guessed he weighed one-hundred-ninety pounds. He appeared to be in good physical condition in spite of a small beer-belly. He talked to the other two officers. They alternately pointed at me and at the blond kid. Much to my relief, I saw the kid sit up and lean against the wall, attended by his friends. He'd become a hero. Almost posthumously.

The captain talked to him briefly, then walked over to us.

"Oh shit, guys," I said, "I've been home for thirty minutes and I'm going to spend the night in the stockade. Maybe end up doing time in a federal prison."

The captain introduced himself and asked if I would mind telling him what happened.

"The kid spit on me. I reacted as the army trained me to react if someone attacked me," I said, filling in what details I could remember. "These guys pulled me off of him."

"Well, that's pretty much the same story he told us," he said, jerking a thumb in the direction of the kid. "Do you want to press charges?"

"Do I...huh?" I asked, thinking that I must sound as if it had been *my* head that got beaten on the floor instead of the kid's. Surely I hadn't heard him correctly.

"He assaulted you when he spit on you. Do you want me to arrest him for assault?" the captain asked.

Relief flowed through me, made my knees weak. I had to sit down on my duffel bag. "No. No charges. I don't want to press charges. I'd like to settle it so neither of us can...uh...file something later on."

"Okay," he said. "Did you guys just come home? From 'Nam?" he asked, squatting down next to me.

"Yeah. The three of us."

"I've got a son there," he said. He told us his son's name and his outfit, but we didn't know either one.

"I'll fix it so that kid can't bother you about this," he said. "And I'll tell him that if he comes back to the airport, he'll have an assault charge as well as public disturbance filed against him. Would you like me to do that?"

"Yes," I said, "I would. And thanks. Thanks a lot."

He smiled. "No problem. Glad to be able to be of help to someone in uniform. I guess things have changed a lot since you left. Now you know what to look out for."

We picked up our bags.

He smiled. "Welcome home!"

CHAPTER THIRTY SEVEN

Political Diagnosis

My lungs felt worse once I got home. I had spells when I couldn't get my breath, and the yellow stuff I coughed up was sometimes mixed with blood. Sometimes it was so thick I almost choked. I called the VA Medical Center in San Francisco for an appointment. Much to my surprise, I was told I would have to wait almost two weeks to see a doctor.

I stayed in a cheap motel until the day of my appointment, then took a taxi to the VA and checked in. After technicians took two X-rays and drew several blood samples, I was led to an examination room, told to strip to my shorts, and wait. Finally a doctor showed up, a young looking guy. He poked and prodded, looked at my chart, then poked and prodded some more.

When he put his ice cold stethoscope on the bare skin of my chest, I almost jumped off the examining table. "Jeezus, that's cold!"

"Sorry," he said, and put it on my bare back. I jumped again.

"Cough," he said. I did. He moved the stethoscope. "Cough," he said. I coughed. The stethoscope moved, I coughed. We played that game all over my back, then he started on my front. I was getting hoarse from all the coughing.

"What do you think, Doc?" I asked. "Did that defoliant mess up my lungs?"

"Let me listen to your lungs again," he said. "There's a problem, but I'm not sure what it is. The VA is doing a study on fungi in the lungs that some of our servicemen contracted in Vietnam. I'll probably recommend you be included in that group. It's at the VA's Fairmount Center, just outside of Washington, D. C. You may be there for several months. I'll know for sure when your blood tests come back."

"Yeah, but did the defoliant mess up my lungs?"

"They'll be able to tell you at Fairmount," he said. "Stop at the desk. I'll have a prescription waiting for you." With that, he scurried out of the room.

I didn't have much faith in this doctor's prognosis. Either he didn't know what was wrong, or he wasn't telling me something. I thought about tying his stethoscope in a knot around his neck. No, I told myself. The time for fighting is over. But I smiled at the image.

When my blood tests came back, I received a call advising me I would be treated at the Fairmount Center. I would receive an allowance for housing if treated on an outpatient basis. I could pick up my plane ticket at the VA.

Great, I thought. An all expense paid trip to Washington, D.C. Maybe it was defoliant, not fungus. Maybe they had some idea what the defoliant did to lungs. Or maybe they did, but weren't telling anyone.

The Fairmount Center was housed in an ugly building made of cast cement. The poking, prodding and X-rays seemed to be the standard admission ceremony, and a repeat of what the VA did in San Francisco. I had to don a gown that left my ass hanging out. Then I was led to a ward with two dozen beds, most of them full. I didn't see a doctor again until the following day.

Just before lunch, a harried-looking man with a gray-streaked black beard stopped and picked up my chart. He opened it and frowned. I wondered if military doctors were taught to frown whenever they look at a patient's chart.

"Well, doctor, does it look like I've got a problem? It started when we got into an area where they sprayed defoliant."

He gave me such a sour look he reminded me of Lieutenant Jaimeson and his perpetual antacid tablets. "There is no indication that you have problems from a herbicide," he said.

Christ, I thought, maybe I should ask him if he's related to a certain doctor in 'Nam. "Then what's the matter with my lungs?" I asked.

"You seem to have some kind of fungal infection," he said. "Everyone in this

342

ward does. We're trying to determine just which fungi, so we can treat it."

"But doctor, I..."

He dropped my chart into the holder and almost ran down the ward. He wasn't sticking around for questions. Maybe I should ask if he went to school with Dr. Samuels, I thought.

"Shit, this is all too familiar."

I asked my doctor how the chain of command worked, asked to talk to whoever held the next-highest rank. After a week, I'd gotten nowhere. I'd been down this road too, and I had no intention of letting them get away with it again. But I didn't think I'd have to worry about them trying to amputate a lung. Then again...

I found out from my fellow ward-mates that they all had been in areas where herbicide had been sprayed from airplanes. Their symptoms were a lot like mine. They had ruled out the hand-held sprayers we used around the wire, since the aerial spraying dumped a lot more of the defoliant. Everyone seemed to think that made the exposure more concentrated.

"You think this is a damn cover-up?" I said to my nearest neighbor. "Think they're afraid to admit that the defoliant was so harmful?"

"Hell, yes, they are. And harmful? More like deadly," he said. His name was John. Everyone called him Big John. He must have weighed three hundred pounds, and looked like two hundred ninety-nine of it was muscle. "They're just screwing us over. No one seems to know which of the fucking defoliants are the worst."

"What do you mean, which of the defoliants?" I asked. "Isn't it all Agent Orange?"

"Oh, no," he said. "Agent Orange is the most common, but they had Agent Blue, Agent Yellow, and Agent Green. As far as I know, there could be others. Some of them were experimental. No one has done any tests to see what they do to people. Except maybe on us."

"Well that's great," I said.

That afternoon, one of the nurses told me Dr. Dorn wanted to see me. He told me I had been classified as an outpatient, and gave me a schedule for physical and respiratory therapy. I wondered if they wanted me out of the hospital most of the time so I wouldn't ask questions and question answers.

I found an apartment, but not close enough to the hospital to walk every day, so I bought a used bicycle. For the next three months, I came in according to my schedule and breathed some kind of cool, mentholated steam. And got an injection without knowing what it was or what it was supposed to do. The bicycle seemed to be the most helpful therapy. But what did I know?

I sent word to Dr. Dorn that I wanted a 'real' doctor, not a VA doctor. I didn't know where he ranked in our chain of command. Far above us guinea-pig peons, but maybe not high enough to approve my request. One day when I showed up to breathe the cool steam, one of the orderlies told me Dr. Dorn wanted to see me in his office.

The clutter offended me. This guy's a doctor? I thought. Bulging file folders, books, and old paper coffee cups covered every surface. The floor-to-ceiling bookshelves across two walls were haphazardly arranged and full of stacks of papers as well as books. The doctor, busy writing something when I came in, didn't look up.

I didn't like being ignored, so I pulled up a chair in front of his desk and sat down. He still didn't look up. I took a sheaf of papers from one of the piles on his desk and leafed through it. Maybe it had something to do with soldiers hospitalized for exposure to defoliants that the hospital tried to pass off as fungi.

"Put that down!" he barked.

I tossed the papers onto another pile on his desk. "Hi. I'm Doug Walker," I said with my best phony smile. "You wanted to see me?"

"Yes. You're being discharged."

That I didn't expect. "You mean I'm healed?"

"No. You're being given a one-hundred percent disability, approved by Dr. Van Graff. I have a requisition for an oxygen tank and a prescription for refills and medication. I'm afraid we can't do anything more for your condition."

"So what's wrong with me?" I asked.

He studied the folder on his desk. "You have an acute bronchial inflammation that is caused by a fungus typically found in tropical regions. It is incurable and irreversible."

"What about the defoliant? What did that do to me?"

He went through the motions of studying the folder again. "There is no clinical indication of symptoms or effects from anything like that." He smiled, an empty smile, without feeling. His lips made a mere slit in his face. "I can assure you that the defoliants they used in Vietnam were pretty tame."

"Oh, come on, Doc. They could curl up and dry out the leaves on a tree until they fell off and the tree died. That has to have some effect on lungs."

"You've been examined by our specialists who find no evidence of herbicide …"

"Well what if I think they're wrong? There were four of us who did five mile runs every day in 'Nam, then couldn't run fifty yards after we got mixed up with that stuff. How about having an outside specialist check us out?" I knew if I was "awarded" a disability, the VA would not treat me for what really happened to my lungs. I didn't want that.

"Look, what can it hurt for a second opinion? I thought that was standard in the medical profession."

"Absolutely not! There is nothing wrong with your lungs!" His terse reply was accompanied by a reddening face and clenched fists. He glared at me.

I had been doing my best to hold my temper, but he looked like he was ready to attack. My resolve ran out and I snapped. "You're a damn fool if you think that's what's wrong," I said, my voice hard, eyes drilling into him. "Who the hell told you *that* fairy tale?"

"There's no need to be nasty," he said. He sounded worried.

I rose and glared down at him. "I haven't even begun to be nasty," I said in a low, cold voice.

"I know. I've seen your service record." He pushed his chair further back from his desk.

"Then you know what happened to that butcher of a doctor in 'Nam. You'd better get me a *real* doctor. I want an opinion other than the VA's. You call me then and not before."

We stared at each other. He looked away, his hands fluttering over his papers and books. Finally he reached for the phone. "Okay, okay. I will. It will have to be approved. I'll call Dr. Van Graff right now."

I stood, leaning over him, listening to his call. Somehow it seemed too easy.

"You can see him now?" I heard him say, looking relieved. "Dr. Van Graff can see you now. Do you know where his office is?"

"Tell him I'll be right there," I said. I turned on my heel and walked out the door, closing it a bit harder than I intended to. Quite a bit.

Van Graff's office occupied a corner with windows and was much larger than Dr. Dorn's. His desktop had been cleared off. A thick manilla folder was placed squarely in the center. Mine.

"Sit down," he said without ceremony. I sat. "You threatened Dr. Dorn." He leaned his elbows on the desk, laced his fingers and stared at me.

I laughed. "A good offense is the best defense, doc. And you're on the offense."

"You told him you'd do to him what you were going to do to that doctor in Vietnam."

"That's not what I said. And since you taped our conversation, you *know* that's not true." It was a shot in the dark, but by the look on his face, I knew I'd hit the jackpot. "Are you taping our little chat now?"

Van Graff looked uncomfortable. "You are being discharged. There is nothing further we can do to help you. You have a fungal infection. There is no sign of any chemical damage to your lungs. I have arranged for you to have a full disability pension, over eighteen hundred dollars a month. If you have other health needs, the Veteran's Administration will help any time. Now, I need you to sign these papers, here and here." He slid two sets of papers across his desk.

I could see the shadows cast by the blinds across the desk top. They looked like prison bars. Maybe a reminder I didn't want to do something that would put me in prison. Something like the thoughts that ran through my mind. I leaned forward, put my hands next to the two documents. I smiled at him. "Eighteen hundred? A month?"

He looked relieved. "Yes. Now if you'll just sign..."

He took a gold pen from his pocket, held it out to me. I took the pen, let my smile fade. Who does this son-of-a-bitch think he is? I stood, bent the pen in half and back until it snapped. I dropped the pieces of pen on his desk and wadded the papers into a ball. I tossed them across his desk.

"You think you can buy me off? You think I'm gonna push some damn oxygen tank around with me for the rest of my life? You think I'm going to be quiet, when there are God knows how many soldiers who've had the same problem?"

Van Graff jumped to his feet, smoothed out the disability papers. "You'd better take what you can get!" he yelled. "You know as well as I do you can barely walk. Look at your own therapy reports! You couldn't even walk for ten minutes without being exhausted!"

"Doc, I do believe you're yelling at me," I said. That explained why I never got more than a light warm-up in therapy. I could walk a lot longer than that. "Yeah, walking's a bitch. That's why I ride a bicycle here from my apartment. About two and a half miles, each way. What do you think of that, doc?"

Dr. Van Graff looked like he'd just lost the debate and might get kicked off the team. These bastards didn't want to get to the real cause of my problem, never intended to do anything but shut me up with a monthly check.

"What are you hiding? Do you think you can make everyone who got into that stuff go away with a check? What are you going to do with the other twenty guys in my ward? Do we all disappear? And the worst of all, you think you can buy my integrity for a *disability check*! It looks like *you* are the one who is for sale. I am not."

He said nothing, a confirmation in my mind that everyone of us in that ward were going away, one way or the other, according to their plan. Whatever the reason for the coverup, it went higher up the food chain than Van Graff.

"I want you to provide me a medical opinion by a doctor outside the VA system. A *real* doctor!"

"What the hell makes you think you can come in here and tell everyone what to do? Now take this settlement and sign it, or you'll get nothing!"

I tried to hold my temper, but the obvious cover-up was too much. I yelled at Van Graff like a Drill Sergeant yelling at a boot camp rookie. "Oh, so who's threatening who? I wonder what the *Washington Post* would pay for a story from a vet who got into something no one's talking about," I thundered, "a chemical defoliant that eats out your lungs, and a conspiracy in the VA to cover it up!"

Van Graff looked like he'd shrunk six inches. Then the voice of his secretary, peering around his office door, broke the silence.

"Are you all right, doctor?" she asked, her voice trembling a little.

"Call security," the doctor squeaked.

"Oh, hell yes, call security. Tell them I'm on the way to the newspaper. Maybe as well as the cover-up at the VA, they'll be interested in where we've been off and on for three years. Like in places the president said there were no American troops!" I leaned across his desk. "Think they could get some mileage out of that? How do you think the administration would like that? Maybe I'll tell them *you* suggested I talk to them."

Dr. Graff sat down hard in his chair. "No," he said. "They won't be interested. Who would believe someone who claimed to be a Vietnam vet, but couldn't even prove he'd ever been in the army? Or at this hospital?"

"What are you talking about?" I asked. "I've got my DD214 and my honorable discharge certificate! I can sure as hell prove I served in the army!"

"So you think. Get out before Security takes you out in a bucket!"

CHAPTER THIRTY EIGHT

Missing In Action In The USA

Over the next few days I tried to decide what to do. I called the *Washington Post* and asked who would be interested in a story about a cover-up in the VA. They gave me the name and number of one of their reporters. I started to call him several times, but I couldn't make myself do it. I thought the newspaper was a liberal rag. Somehow this problem was something that needed to be resolved within the family, not by splashing it across the pages of an unfriendly paper, to the detriment of the United States Army. Then my feelings would flip-flop. I'd feel as if I'd been treated shamefully, along with a lot of other guys, and think there would be no resolution unless someone did something. I worried about what Van Graff was up to. I felt like this wasn't the last time I'd hear from him.

I found a park with some bike trails and went for a ride each day. The riding continued to be therapeutic for lungs and attitude. At my apartment building, there was no place to lock up my bike. After each ride, I carried it up to the small balcony outside my apartment. One day as I leaned the bike up against the outside rail, I saw a black sedan pull into the parking lot and stop next to a FIRE LANE—NO PARKING sign. I wondered who the driver was who had such an inflated sense of self-importance.

I usually made a glass of iced tea to cool off before I shed my sweats and showered. The doorbell rang before I could take a sip of my tea. A finger of fear traced my spine. I knew it was the guys in the black sedan. Maybe they'll go away, I thought. It rang again.

I set my glass of tea on the coffee table. "Who is it?" I shouted through the door.

"We'd like to talk to you, Mr. Walker."

Not taking the time to look through the peep hole, I unhooked the chain, opened the door. Two men in blazers, slacks, white shirts and ties. "FBI, Mr. Walker. May we come in?" asked one of them. He wore a skinny tie and had a crew cut.

When I hesitated, he shoved the door open, hard, then stuck his credentials in my face.

"What do you want?" I asked, backing up. These guys were the ultimate muscle. My throat went dry and my belly tightened up.

"Sit down," said the FBI agent.

Thoroughly intimidated, I sat.

"I'm Agent Simmons. This is Agent Brown,"

Brown was a few years older, had a wide tie and a sour look.

"I'm former Sergeant First Class Walker," I said, swallowing compulsively. "Let me guess. You're from the FBI. My government is here to help me," my voice said. You smart-ass punk, my mind said. A dangerous punk, it added.

"Don't try to be cute. We know who you are. We know a lot about you. *And* your family," Agent Simmons said.

"What?"

"You were recently discharged from the VA hospital," Agent Brown said.

"Quite a commotion you caused," Agent Simmons said.

I couldn't believe yelling at Van Graff could get me investigated by the FBI. "*That's* what this is all about?" I asked.

Agent Simmons pulled a notebook from his jacket pocket. "Your father and mother, Douglas, Senior, and Dorothy Mae, live at 946 Mountain Drive, Payson, Arizona. They have a mortgage balance of seventeen-thousand, five-hundred forty dollars. Their fire insurance won't cover the cost of replacing their house, should it burn. Much less the contents."

He looked up. "Your father earns fourteen-thousand dollars a year as a teacher. He has a contract that is renewed every year." He looked at me. "Usually it is renewed." Back to his notes. "Your mother is a housewife. Sells her own handmade jewelry. Doesn't declare it as taxable. "

"What does this have to do with my parents?" I demanded, feeling my face get hot and my stomach grow cold with fear. I clenched my fists.

"It would be inadvisable for you to become angry, Mr. Walker," Agent Simmons said.

"That's *Sergeant* Walker to you, *Agent* Simmons."

"We know you're so dissatisfied with the VA hospital here you threatened to go to one of our newspapers."

"I thought the *Post* would love to hear what was happening to us after we served –"

"You served *nothing*," Agent Simmons snapped.

"I've got papers." I jumped to my feet, tore down the hallway after the box with my discharge papers. But when I slid open the mirrored closet doors, the box wasn't there. Frantically I raked blankets and clothing off the shelf, rummaged through the shoes and other things on the floor. The box had disappeared. All it had in it were copies. I still felt violated. They'd burglarized my apartment. My own government.

I went back to the living room. Anger increased the hurt of air moving in and out of my damaged lungs. "You bastards," I gasped as I dropped back onto the couch. "How can you do this?"

"We don't know what you're talking about," Agent Simmons said. He looked like a snake, eyes dead, but glittery at the same time.

"It's been nice chatting with you," Agent Brown said. "Don't get up. We can find our way out."

They turned and walked toward the door. They had turned their backs, showing how impotent they thought I'd become. The big glass of iced tea I'd made was sitting on the coffee table. I grabbed it, and with all the strength I could muster, I flung it at them. *"You bastards!"* I yelled. The glass exploded against the wall next to the door, like a bomb. Shards of glass, ice cubes, and iced tea splattered all over them, the wall and the floor. In unison they spun, hands going for the small .38 cal. revolvers holstered on their belts. In a flash I found myself staring into the darkness of both muzzles.

"Go ahead! Shoot me!" I screamed. "Go ahead!" I peeled off my sweatshirt, spread my arms. "Go on! Want me to kneel so you can do it Gestapo style? Shall I turn my back?"

Agent Brown holstered his .38.

Agent Simmons' face was contorted and deep red. He hesitated, then holstered his revolver. After he wiped the tea from his face with a handkerchief, he pointed a finger at me that shook with rage. "You watch yourself, mister, or..."

"Or what?" I taunted. On the way out, he slammed the door.

I felt cold, though I was soaked with sweat. My hands shook. I had no idea what to do, except keep my mouth shut and see if I could locate some of the guys from the team. I wondered if they'd received the same treatment.

I stood in the shower, turning the water from hot to cold. All the time we spent in 'Nam, the things we did, the sacrifices we made for our country. Now my country had scared the hell out of me. Intimidated me. Lied about how I'd served, lied about my disability. That scared me more than all the shooting and fighting I'd done. Scared me more than all my time in 'Nam.

Maybe it was my fault they were treating me this way, I thought. Somehow I was always attacking. Did I really need to defend myself all the time? Had I become "attack" when I didn't need to? What did these guys really want? I had changed so much I couldn't recognize myself. I wanted the old me back. Had I given up so much of the lifestyle I'd grown up with, the home-town kid I used to be, that he was gone forever?

But the VA refused to treat me, and these goons threatened me and my family. What should I have done? The most demoralizing blow was to become non-existent according to the army. It hit me harder than their physical threats. I couldn't believe they could erase all my records until I called the hospital. I asked for information on my treatment and date of my next appointment. I got transferred to a records clerk. "May I have your patient number?" she asked.

I gave her the number and listened as she punched keys.

"I'm sorry, that number is not valid. Are you sure it is correct?" She read it back.

"Yes, it's correct," I said. "Could you search for my records by my serial number?" I asked. I spoke my serial number slowly and clearly.

"I'm sorry, that number is not in our files. Has it been over five years since you were treated here?" she asked.

"No. I guess I'll have to come in," I said. "Thanks for your help." I hung up, an odd, vacant feeling in the pit of my stomach. I felt like I had been kicked out of a club I'd belonged to all my life.

For days, I walked and rode the trails in the park at all hours. I drank by myself. I was alone. I frequented several bars, felt angry at the patrons who were having a good time. One night, after several drinks, a bartender I didn't know handed me a card. *Vietnam Vets*, it said. *Vets Helping Vets*. I almost threw it away. Certainly I didn't feel the least bit thankful, thinking the bartender had no business meddling in my affairs. Several days later, it dawned on me that I must have looked pretty hopeless to him. Maybe he, too, spent time in 'Nam.

I was more than a little defensive on my first trip to the address on the card. Yet the organization's staff, all vets, set me at ease. Among other things, they provided a locating service. I gave them names of several guys from the team. Maybe together we could battle the Veteran's Administration, the U. S. Army and the FBI. I wondered if I'd ever find them, or if, according to the Army, they no longer existed. Maybe we were we all missing in action in the USA.

CHAPTER THIRTY NINE

Bobbie

She hung onto the cart, stood on her tiptoes to reach a can of tomato juice from the top of the display. Big, half-gallon size cans. When I came around the corner, my cart bumped hers, and she stumbled into the stack of cans, which fell in an avalanche to the floor. Two cans tumbled into my basket, the glass of bright red tomato juice printed on the label turning over and over in mid-air without spilling a drop.

"Ow! Dammit!" she yelled, as a can hit her foot, carving a crescent-shaped wound in her instep. She stepped back, stumbling over the pile of cans behind her. One arm flailed in mid-air, the other reached for the cart as she fell backwards. I stretched out my arm in a futile effort to catch her. As she hit the floor her head snapped back, making an ugly sound as it struck the tile-covered cement. She was out cold.

My clash with the Veteran's Administration had become a replay of David and Goliath. Except this time, it looked like David's sling was frayed. I had been just a number, but now, by a few keystrokes on someone's computer, I wasn't even that. I no longer existed. I could use my fists on assholes who spit on me and called me a murderer for serving my country, but I found myself out-matched by the V.A.

I decided I didn't need them and thought about moving to Florida, where the winters were supposed to be mild. But that was too close to Washington, D.C., for comfort. I packed my duffle bag and caught a flight to Phoenix, Arizona. Distance and moderate winters.

I'd been there six months, and had been drunk so often that getting off the booze began to look like it might not happen. Booze warded off the dreams, the nights of waking up in a puddle of cold sweat. It provided relief from the utter loneliness I suffered at night. Half awake, I would reach out for Li.

But the fear of losing my independence to booze sat in my belly like a bowl of bad beans. I could do it, I told myself. I *had* to do it. I'd been sober now for three days. I'd even quit smoking. So far, I could deal with the craving for alcohol and cigarettes.

Now I had to decide what I could do for this girl, who lay unconscious on the floor. She needed help, and it was my fault.

"Hey, someone get over here," I yelled. Pushing the carts to one side, I knelt by her. The bleeding from her foot was minor. She had a lump on the back of her head, maybe a concussion, which could be serious. I straightened her legs, then slipped my arm under her shoulders and eased her head down on my rolled up jacket. My heart beat loud and fast. This girl is familiar, I thought , wondering where a sudden desire to watch over her came from.

I took her hand to straighten her arm. It felt pleasantly warm. More than warm. Some kind of heat, or energy, came from her. Like a cosmic heating pad. It seemed like it came from her, anyway. I had never experienced anything like this. Somehow, I knew this girl. But from where? I smiled. What a terrible line.

Two grocery clerks came up the aisle at a run.

"What happened?" asked one.

"I told Wally we shouldn't stack those so high," said the other.

"Call an ambulance," I told him. Neither of them moved.

"Call a goddamn ambulance! Now! Move it!" My sergeant's voice. They went back down the aisle at a run.

"She just knocked herself out," I said to myself.

"*Who* just knocked her out?" a voice said, jarring me out of my fascination. I looked up to see a man with dark hair and glasses. He wore an apron like the two clerks. The name tag on the apron read, "HI, I'M WALLY, HOW MAY I HELP YOU?"

"She tripped when the cans that you stacked up too high fell over. When she fell, she hit her head on the floor. So in a way, you did, Wally," I answered. "Got a first-aid kit? She's bleeding." Wally looked at her foot, turned pale, and departed.

I hesitated, then gently pulled up her eyelids. Blue eyes, neither pupil dilated. She'll be all right, I thought. She's just unconscious. My hand went back to her face, gently tracing her eyebrows, the tip of her nose. It turned up just the slightest bit, not a pug nose, but just enough to be charming. My fingertips tingled. I took a clean handkerchief from my pocket and pressed it against the cut on her foot.

I watched as she lay there, eyes closed. A beautiful face. Creamy complexion, black hair, and long eyelashes. Her feet were small and her ankles slim and shapely. I found myself wanting to protect her. Hold her. Hold *her*, not just her body.

She was dressed in a man's blue cotton work shirt, sleeves rolled up, and tucked into baggy khakis. A belt at least a foot too long drew the pants tight on her small waist. The belt had been doubled back and shoved through the loops. She couldn't have been over five feet, four inches, I thought. She doesn't weigh much either. Her husband's clothes? I wondered. I looked at her left hand. She didn't wear a ring. That's good, I thought—then wondered what kind of fantasy I was building.

As the paramedics came through the door and headed our way, Wally arrived with the first- aid kit. Good thing no one had been bleeding to death.

A team of paramedics is the only thing that I have seen that works even better in real life than on TV. And these two lived up to my expectations. One checked her pupils with a flashlight, the other started to bandage the cut on her foot. The first one asked me if I saw what happened.

"Yeah, I did," I said.

He stopped his examination and looked at me, as if to say, "Well?"

"This display of tomato juice fell over on her. One of the cans cut her foot. She fell and hit her head on the floor," I said, leaving out the part about me running into her and knocking her into the display.

"Hey, this Patrick's sister?" the foot-bandager asked the eye-examiner.

"I think so," he said.

"You know her brother?" I asked.

"Yeah, he works out of our station. Nights."

Maybe they were her brother's clothes.

The young woman moaned and opened her eyes, closed them briefly, then opened them again. She tried to sit up, moaned, and touched the lump on the back of her head.

"Easy, ma'am," the paramedic said. "You got yourself knocked out falling over some cans of tomato juice."

She looked at me. "You!" She settled back onto my rolled up jacket. "You shoved me!" She pointed her finger. Then her blue eyes looked into mine. "I know you," she said. "But who...?"

"Take it easy," the paramedic said as he wrapped a blood pressure cuff around her arm.

"Get that thing off me! I'm fine! I don't need your help! I'm a nurse!"

"Ma'am, I need to take your blood pressure before we take you to the hospital. So please just..."

"I'm not going to the hospital," she said, forcing herself into a sitting position. "I have to get home and..." Her eyes rolled back and she passed out again. The paramedic caught her as she slumped down on the floor.

A young blonde woman came around the corner, pushing a shopping cart. She looked at the paramedics and the young woman on the floor.

"Oh God! Bobbie!" She cried. She was well dressed, an excess of gold jewelry hanging from neck and wrists. She dropped to the floor next to the wounded nurse. "Bobbie, are you all right? What happened?"

"Are you related to her?" the paramedic asked.

"No, she's a good friend," the woman replied. "My best friend."

Bobbie groaned again, opened her eyes. "Sue Ann!" She reached out and found the young woman's hand, held it tightly, as if the connection would keep her conscious.

"What happened?" Sue Ann asked, as the paramedics lifted Bobbie onto a gurney.

"I keep passing out." She closed her eyes again and her eyelids fluttered. "My car! Sue Ann, my car! Take my keys, they're in my purse!" she pleaded as they wheeled her out to the waiting ambulance.

I decided I'd had enough excitement for the day. I picked up my jacket and started to walk back to my apartment. Then I realized she might need me if the store tried to stick her with the medical bills. I wrote my name and address on a piece of paper and walked back to where Sue Ann stood watching the ambulance disappear.

"Here, give her this. In case the store tries to make her pay for the ambulance."

Sue Ann took the scrap of paper. "I need to get her car home. I've got company coming, and I still have to shop. Would you drive it for me?"

"I've got things to do," I said. "It'll be okay in the lot for a while." I knew it would probably get stripped overnight. And that would be my fault, too.

"Please?"

"Oh...okay. I'll drive her car, then you can bring me back here?" I asked.

"Okay, I will."

I followed Sue Ann to Bobbie's apartment, less than a half-mile away. Sue Ann pulled into the parking lot and drove down a row of covered parking spaces. She stopped, pointed at an empty space with a number stenciled on the wall. I pulled in and locked the car.

I always marvel how people will talk rapidly with a little prodding. Almost without drawing a breath, when they are uncomfortable. Sue Ann didn't know me and felt nervous about giving me a ride, so when I got in, I gave her my brightest smile. "Done," I said.

"Thanks. I couldn't think of anyone to call. Since Bobbie broke up with Wayne, she hasn't been seeing anyone at all."

"They broke up?" I wondered who Wayne might be.

"Yes. He gave her a black eye, so she rented this apartment and moved out. He finally left her alone."

"Do you know her brother?" I asked. "Patrick?"

"I know him very well," she said. "Patrick's all that's left of her family, you know. Bobbie and I went to the same high school. Between taking care of her father and her drunken grandfather, she practically raised Patrick. He's a paramedic now. She never had time to date in high school. She worked two or three part-time jobs to make ends meet. For the family."

Sue Ann told me how Bobbie's mother had died when Bobbie was young.

She said her father, now dead, started to drink, and beat her and her mother.

"Why'd she put up with it?" I asked, frowning.

"She didn't, not always. She would run away, stay gone for days, leaving no one to cook and clean. So he quit hitting her. I know, because she would come over and stay with me. I would sneak her into my bedroom at night. Now that her dad's gone, all she does is work."

"Where's that?"

"You don't know she works at St. Joseph's?" Sue Ann turned and looked at me suspiciously. "She's a nurse, you know. Been there for three years."

"Oh, that's right. So she's still there." I almost blew it. Why nursing? I thought. Another rescuer, like her brother?

"She tried to sober up her grandfather, who she loved more than anyone. He died while she was attending nursing school." Sue Ann got quiet for a moment, then cautiously gave me a look out of the corner of her eye. "I thought you knew Bobbie. Why are you asking all the questions? You *are* her friend, aren't you?"

I almost told Sue Ann she was a gossipy bitch, but I wanted to know more about Bobbie, so I tried to get the gossip flowing again.

"So she's living by herself now?" I asked.

"You know, you really have a lot of nerve, asking me all these questions. I thought you were Bobbie's friend! Do you even know her?"

I smiled at her discomfort, which instantly grew. "No," I said. "I don't. Never seen her before tonight." Sue Ann flinched. The car lurched over the center line.

"Get out of my car! Get out!" she yelled as she cut the wheel and pulled to the curb. I opened the door and stepped out.

"I'm gonna tell Bobbie you were so nosy!" she shouted as she pulled away, the door still open.

I laughed. I wondered if she would tell Bobbie about all the answers she gave me. Then I remembered I had Bobbie's keys. She wouldn't be needing them until tomorrow. I'd take them back then.

I hadn't thought about booze or cigarettes for over an hour. Now the cravings attacked full force. Pain speared my guts, doubling me over. Home, I thought. Gotta get home.

The supermarket next to my apartment had its own little restaurant where I ate breakfast most of the time. When I walked in the next morning, Bobbie sat in a booth next to the wall, her back to the door. Never sit where you can't see the door, I thought. All warriors know that. I stood under the "Order Here" sign, waiting for the tired-looking woman in the almost-clean uniform to take my order, and watched Bobbie. After I ordered I walked over to her booth.

"Mind if I sit down?" I asked. She looked up, startled, and knocked her knife to the floor. Both of us reached to pick it up. Her fingers brushed the back of my hand. Our eyes met. For a moment, bent over the knife on the floor, we seemed unable to move. I could feel her touch spread through my body. She took her hand away and the spell was gone like a faint breeze. I set the knife back on the table.

"You can sit down if you want," she said. "I'm almost finished."

"You okay?"

"Oh, yes. Two stitches in my foot, but it won't hardly leave a scar."

"It's my fault. I didn't mean to hurt you."

"It's okay. I know you didn't. They stacked those cans too high."

"Eat here often?"

"No. Not very often." Her eyes found mine again. They were the vivid blue of the sky just after sunset. A deep, cerulean blue. She stared, and I couldn't look away. Then the waitress set my breakfast on the table, and both of us looked down at the watery eggs and pale pancakes, relieved by the distraction.

I went about the business of applying butter and syrup to my pancakes. She had finished hers, but she made no move to leave.

"Do you eat here every day?" she asked.

"Breakfast, most of the time. When I eat breakfast," I replied.

"I have to go," she said, and stood up, still staring at me. I wanted to see her again.

"I have your keys. Would you have dinner with me tonight? I could meet you at J. B.'s. I'll bring your keys. It's just around the corner." I ran the words together. Maybe if I kept talking, she wouldn't have a chance to say no.

"Tonight," she said.

I didn't know if it was a question or a statement. "Seven o'clock? J. B.'s?"

"Okay, I'll meet you there. At seven," she said, still staring. "We'll go dutch."

She turned and walked away without looking back. She had been gone for some time before I stopped looking out the door where she vanished. My breakfast grew cold, but my appetite had vanished. I threw the cold mess into a trash can and stepped outside, wondering if I had replaced one addiction with another. Bobbie. Then the image of Li in her silk robe came at me so fast I almost stumbled. Guilt pelted me like fiery hailstones. I wanted a drink. Instead, I went to the bank to withdraw some cash from savings.

I hadn't opened a checking account. I knew the liquor store would take my checks if I did, and that made it too easy to buy booze. I checked the balance, which was still higher than it had ever been in my whole life. I'd brought home a lot of bonus pay, souvenir money, and still had what Mike shared with me. I withdrew fifty dollars.

I arrived at J. B.'s twenty minutes early and sat holding the paper, pretending to read. I could have been holding it upside-down for all I knew. What if she doesn't show up? My stomach did flip-flops, partly because I still hadn't had a drink.

When I saw her coming through the door, I felt like I'd found a missing part of me. This is not happening, I told myself. Then our eyes met. From some other perspective I saw myself get up, watched as I held out my hand. She smiled and placed her hand in mine. It buzzed like a battery. When she looked up, I knew we both felt it.

Dinner turned out to be a disaster. I wanted to ask her about herself, but I found out very little. She asked a thousand questions about me. I answered in generalities. I told her I had been in Vietnam for almost four years and had been home for about six months. I watched her every movement as she sat across from me. She was petite, bright-eyed and lovely.

"So, now you know all about me. What about you?" I asked. "All you've told me is that you're a nurse and you work at St. Joe's. What do you like to do on your days off?"

"I didn't tell you that I'm a nurse. Or where I work. Sue Ann told you that," she said, one eyebrow raised. "She called me this morning. She was very upset with you, mostly because you asked a lot of questions about me."

"Which Sue Ann answered," I said. "All of them." I felt as if I had been caught with my hand in the cookie jar. Bobbie didn't seem upset, though.

"Yes, I guess she did." Bobbie laughed. Her eyes sparkled. For a few moments neither of us said anything. Then she looked at her watch.

"It's late. When your shift starts at 5:30 in the morning, this is late. I have to go." She reached in her purse for her wallet. I picked up the bill.

"Why don't you let me get it?"

"No. We agreed."

She took my arm as we walked out of J.B.'s. She stopped when we reached the sidewalk. I asked her if I could walk her back to her apartment. "Not tonight," she said, looking up at me with unnerving directness.

"I have your keys," I said, fishing in my pocket.

"Thank you for taking my car home," she said. "And for dinner." She stood on her tiptoes and gave me a kiss on the cheek. "You can call me, if you want," she said, slipping a piece of paper into my hand. Then she turned and walked rapidly away. I watched to see if she would look back. She didn't.

I looked at the folded piece of paper. What if it didn't have the phone number, just said something like, "Ha, ha, fooled you." I unfolded it. A phone number, written in a neat hand, appeared below her first name. Smiling, I slipped the note into my wallet.

I slept in the next day. That afternoon I walked to the restaurant again for an early dinner. I wanted a drink badly and had no appetite. I couldn't eat a whole meal, so I choked down a cup of coffee and a donut. It settled sour in my belly. As I walked back to my apartment I had the feeling that something had gone wrong. It was the old familiar feeling from 'Nam. Paying careful attention to it saved my life more than once. When I put my key in the door, I found out what had happened. The lock wouldn't open. My landlord had changed it.

About a month ago, I kicked out the freeloading druggies that had attached themselves to me like so many leeches. But it was too late to make peace with the landlord. I'd had one loud party too many. The cops had been there several times. I argued with the landlord about moving out. Since he wanted me to move, I told him I wanted my damage deposit applied to my last month's rent. He refused, and I decided not to pay. He thought changing the locks would be checkmate.

I felt bone-weary, but the energy of anger took over. That son-of-a-bitch! If he'd decided to keep my five hundred bucks, I'd leave something for him to spend it on. I stepped back and kicked the door as hard as I could. The wood splintered off the door frame and the door banged open. I figured I'd have just a few minutes before the cops arrived.

I'd left a partly full bottle of Myer's Dark Rum in a kitchen cabinet. I took a hard pull on it. I started jamming things into my duffel bag. I realized that I would have to leave my almost new TV and stereo. Karla, who lived across the pool area, would be glad to take them. She had three kids, was divorced, and was on welfare. I ran over and banged on her door. It only took a few minutes to explain, and Karla and her kids moved their new electronic legacy from my apartment to theirs. I had eaten at Karla's table frequently. It felt good to give some payback.

I emptied the bottle, tossed my duffel bag over the wall of the small, barren enclosure that made my apartment a "patio garden" apartment. I pulled myself up, then dropped to the ground on the other side. So much for sobriety.

A large irrigation canal bordered the parking lot. I walked along the bank, realizing I now lived on the street.

"Chr-r-r-rist," I said aloud, "When did everything turn to shit? What's happening to me, what the hell am I gonna do now?" I wanted to scream at the top of my lungs. Maybe if I made enough noise, the universe would set things right. I had no nowhere to live. The craving for alcohol frightened me. Had I become an alcoholic? If so, an attractive woman like Bobbie would never look at me twice.

I knew of a place by the canal bank with some eucalyptus trees and thick oleander hedges growing between the trunks. A private hiding place. We had used it from time to time, my so-called-friends with their drugs, me with my booze. I headed there, tired and shaking from the fourth day without alcohol. Almost without alcohol.

Over the months since returning from 'Nam, I'd quit trying to understand what had happened to people's attitudes about the war and Vietnam vets. Being regarded as a hero had never been on my wish list. But why didn't most people at least see me as one of the good guys?

Now that I'd been home for a while, it was hard to understand why we'd done some of the things we did in 'Nam. Or what meaning it had. At the time, I thought I knew. It had become so difficult, so goddamned hard, to understand anything. I felt like I'd been used up and tossed out. I needed some new way to function, to find ground zero and start over.

I reached my hiding place. A wino, asleep on a cardboard refrigerator carton, opened his bleary eyes and looked up at me. By reflex, I evaluated him for threat potential. He came up a zero. The big guy was wasted.

"Beat it," I said. "Get the hell outta here." I wanted the place to myself.

"C'mon, man," he said. "There's plenty of room. Here. Have a pull." He held up a bottle of cheap wine.

Something inside me snapped. I kicked the bottle, sending it flying. He yelped and pulled back his hand, scrambled unsteadily to his feet, fear in his eyes.

"Now get the fuck outta here! *Now!*" I yelled, and took a step toward him. He turned and stumbled off. I sat down on the duffel bag, shaking all over. For a while I watched to see if the bum came back. I'd beat him senseless if he did. I found a bottle of aspirin in my bag, munched four of them, then took out a blanket. Sweating and shivering, I didn't know what was wrong with me. I thought about going to the VA hospital, then laughed. No fuckin' way. Not when I didn't exist.

I thought about the bum. The possibility that I could end up like that horrified me. Or was it too late? I had to do something, but didn't know what or how. I lay on the eucalyptus leaves, wrapped in my blanket, my head on my duffel bag. When the sun set, I felt chilled. I slipped in and out of sleep. Then the nightmares came back.

We huddled in the jungle outside a village. I knew we'd get in a firefight as soon as we approached. With the unmistakable sound of AK-47's, the shooting started. We couldn't see the village in the dusk, or where the shots came from. As we broke through the undergrowth, we saw the their escape route. We began to fire at the figures running from the village. They wore black pajamas and conical hats and returned our fire. As they ran toward us, we cut them down. Then we fired on the village. The night became quiet, and we advanced. Someone started torching the roofs. I passed by bodies, all babies and children, dressed in black pajamas—unarmed, dead. I ran from one to another in the waning light, looking carefully for any sign of life. I picked up a few of them, turned them over. Limbs blown off, guts spilling out, heads missing. I kept on, looking for any sign of someone salvageable in the carnage. Some, dead eyes still open, stared accusingly at me. Covered with blood and feces and the smell of death, I kept searching through the bodies.

I awoke to the sound of screaming. My own. The sun had gone down, the temperature had dropped. Still, I was drenched with sweat. I had the shakes so bad I couldn't get the lid off of my aspirin bottle. I shook out the blanket and changed into dry clothes. I desperately needed help. At the free clinic, I thought. But I would need a ride. Maybe Bobbie would take me.

Sweating, my muscles cramped, I got to my feet. I shouldered the duffel bag as soon as the world quit wobbling. My feet felt like they were encased in cement overshoes, but at least I could walk. I made my way along the canal to Bobbie's apartment complex, looked for her name on the mailboxes. Only the apartment numbers adorned the boxes. No names. I couldn't find her. I slumped down against the wall and held my head in my hands. Then I remembered when I had parked her car, the apartment numbers were stenciled on the wall.

I climbed the stairs toward her apartment, still sweating, breathing hard, trying to hurry. The last three steps seemed almost insurmountable. The building changed shapes as I staggered to her door and rang the bell.

She stood there, her shiny black hair brushed back, wearing a jogging outfit, a silvery-lavender color. My vision played tricks on me. When she moved, it glimmered and changed hues. Then I saw her through a hole in the center of a black cloud closing around me.

In the months to come, she would tell people that I just "dropped in on her," which is exactly what I did.

"I need a ride..." I said. Then everything turned black as I fell forward across her threshold.

CHAPTER FORTY

Almost Heaven

When I opened my eyes, I found myself in a soft bed. The room was almost dark. I had no idea where I was. I discovered I was wearing only my shorts. I eased one foot out of bed and felt carpet on the floor, further signaling this could not be the hospital. I had an urgent need to relieve my near-to-bursting bladder.

Moving slowly to keep the room from swaying, I got up. I pulled on my Levis, which I could see in the dim light over a chair next to the bed. I made it to the door and peered into the hall. The john had to be close. To the right I could hear voices arguing, and I suspected that the argument involved me. I turned left. The first door turned out to be the bathroom. I sat down on the commode, and the room quit swaying.

I moved gingerly down the hall, and paused at the end to listen before announcing my presence. I thought I might be discovered when my stomach rumbled with hunger. The hallway opened into the living room, and I could hear their words.

"Dammit, Patrick, I don't care if you don't think it makes sense." It was Bobbie's voice. "You're right. It *doesn't* make sense, but I know it's right. It *feels* right. So go ahead. Be a male chauvinist. Call it whatever you want. Make fun of me when I say it's intuition."

"Look, you don't know who this guy is, you don't know if he's some addict or pusher—"

Bobbie interrupted him. "We checked him over for needle tracks, his

366

whole body, last night. You even have the blood tests! How can you keep on with this bullshit?"

Blood tests? How the hell...? I looked at my left arm and sure enough, a needle mark. A blood test? I remembered my general condition last night. I couldn't blame them for thinking I might be an addict.

"He could be anyone, a rapist or murderer. You've taken him in! He should have gone to County Hospital! What's the matter with you, anyway?"

"If anyone knows what happens at County, it's you! The horror stories you've told me. And you still say we should take him there! How *can* you!"

"I can, easily, because I've seen lots of bums like this. I pick them up all the time! That's what I do for a living, remember? I try to keep their wasted bodies alive until I can get them to a hospital! He's probably a vet, and when vets go off the deep end, they're the absolute worst!" Neither one of them spoke for a moment. Then Patrick's voice, lower, softer, continued.

"I know what you went through with grandad. Dad too, for that matter. There's no doubt in my mind that I'd be burned out on drugs or in prison by now if it hadn't been for you. I care about you. I love you. You were like a mother to me as well as a sister. I don't want anything to happen to you! That's why, when we don't know who this guy is, and..."

"Look, Patrick, I know you're afraid for me. I can't explain what I feel. If you try to understand it with your head...you just can't. I feel like he's my other half. I want to find out why. For *me*. Somehow I know I can help him. I am *going* to do this."

"Christ, Bobbie, there's no way you could know anything about him. Get sensible about men for a change! You're gonna get hurt—again—if you hang onto this guy!"

I stepped around the corner and said, "Good evening."

Bobbie and Patrick showed a strong family resemblance, the same black hair and light complexion, blue eyes. With his slim and muscular build, Patrick might have been a weight lifter, maybe a boxer. He was tall, six-feet, weighed fifteen or twenty pounds more than I did—none of it fat. He frowned constantly.

His presence produced the same ingrained reaction as when I found the wino in my hiding place. I sized him up, decided on the most likely way I could take him out if he made a move toward me, although I had no reason to think he might. He would be a formidable opponent. But if he did, Uncle Sam's finest training wouldn't help me. Not right now. Just standing there took most of my strength.

Bobbie broke the silence. She stood and grabbed the afghan that covered the back of the couch where they had been sitting. "You shouldn't get chilled," she said. She stepped in front of Patrick and draped it around my shoulders.

When I felt her arms around me, arranging the afghan, I felt completely disarmed, unable to move. I could smell her perfume, the hint of some special soap. I felt her touch, and the energy, like electricity, coming from her. It eliminated everything in the room from my consciousness. Except her. I looked down into her eyes. She didn't flinch, didn't show any judgment. I felt that she could see into my soul, which filled me with both relief and fright. I tried to regain a hold on the tough me, the soldier adept at crisis and combat. I couldn't find him. This small woman reached her arms around me, pulled the afghan about my shoulders—and scared me speechless.

"Bobbie, for Chrissakes, you—" Patrick began to say. She cut him off.

"Goodby, Patrick. I'll call you."

He made no move to leave.

"I said, *Goodby, Patrick!*" She turned, gave him a fierce look.

"All right, I'm going."

"Let's sit on the couch," Bobbie said to me.

I wobbled over, and she took me in her arms. Half sitting, half lying on the couch, I put my head on her shoulder. As I lay in her arms, my fears faded. I felt a guarded, uneasy feeling. Almost safe, but not quite. I started to fall asleep again. Could we be good for each other? I wondered.

The dreams started again. We came out of the trees a few hundred yards from the shabby collection of huts and started taking fire immediately. They were expecting us. We split into two groups, moving in opposite directions around the clearing. When we stopped, we raked the huts from both sides with full-auto fire. No one behind those flimsy walls could still be alive. Three of us crept through the grass and lobbed hand grenades through the windows to be sure. A wall blew out. Pieces of meat and bone blew everywhere. The stench of blood, shit, and piss choked us. We entered the hut. One body had been nearly decapitated, the skull cap blown off, the eyes staring accusingly at me. The bodies had no age or sex, but one bloody chest, torn away from a torso, had a small bloodstained breast on it. I ran outside, puking.

We were all running. I heard an explosion. A huge fireball was about to catch me. I sprinted frantically. I couldn't get away. I sucked air in tortured gasps, my lungs raw, my legs in pain. Things blew past me, pieces of flesh, a helmeted head with a raw, bleeding skull, an arm, a leg, guts, more limbs, splattering me with blood and juice.

Through the dark terror of the dream, I heard her voice.

"I'm here, it's okay," Bobbie said. "You're safe. I'm here." I began to babble about the dream, about the bodies, the smell, death, everything I had never been able to tell another living soul. The words poured out of me, thirsting for a sympathetic listener.

The voice that warned me when something was about to go wrong now encouraged me to trust this girl. To keep talking. I could feel my tension ease, like stepping down into a warm tub, sinking into the water.

Later, when I opened my eyes, Bobbie smiled at me. "Hungry?" she asked.

I stretched. "Starved." She sat with her back to the sliding glass doors. The lights from the street shone around her silhouette, giving her a preternatural appearance.

"Let's eat," she said, and slipped her arm from under my shoulders, gently laying me back on the couch.

"Where're my clothes?" I asked.

"In the bedroom closet. I washed and ironed them."

"Maybe I'll put on a shirt," I said, smiling.

A few minutes later I came out of the bedroom wearing a clean shirt.

"Better?" I asked. When she turned, her glossy black hair whirled around her head, revealing a white throat and ear. I wanted to put my hand against her cheek.

"Well, I guess," she said, looking me over. "But you looked sexier in just your Levis." She turned back to the stove. Once again I was out of my league.

Whatever happened would be her call. I sat on the couch and watched her move from the kitchen to the table, setting out different things. I felt vulnerable, and didn't like it.

"Dinner's ready."

I stared at the table, unable to remember when I'd seen anything like it. Place mats, real china plates, cups with saucers, not mugs, a knife, spoon, two forks, and a water glass next to the salad bowl, which set on its own small plate. I stared at the cloth napkins in silver napkin rings, touched them to see if they were real.

"Is something wrong?" she asked, frowning. "Did I forget something?"

"Oh, no," I said. "It's just that I haven't seen a table set like this for...a long time. It's beautiful. So...civilized!"

"That's something you need more of, wild man," she said, and turned back into the kitchen.

Before I could digest that, she came back with a dish of chicken in a sauce of some sort, and a vegetable I had never seen before. Between bites of the chicken I poked at the mystery vegetable. "What's this?" I asked.

"Okra," she said. "Full of iron for anemic people."

It tasted slimy. I hated the feel of it in my mouth. I pushed it away.

"Eat your okra," she said. "You need it."

All at once the specter of a control trip raised its head. She wanted power over me. I reacted the same way I did with the wino and with Patrick.

I glared at her.

Raising one eyebrow, she said, "Well?" as if talking to a recalcitrant child.

CT, my nurse in 'Nam, could handle the toughest vets, even those whose mental state had been a whole lot worse than mine. But with me, Bobbie had even more command.

I choked down my slimy okra.

After she'd cleared the table and put the dishes in the dishwasher, we sat on the couch. I could have helped, but I didn't offer. We sat facing each other, two steaming mugs of hot chocolate resting on the coffee table.

"Why did you take me in?" I asked, still suspicious.

She sipped her hot chocolate. "Well, I couldn't very well just shove you out of the doorway and close the door, could I?"

"You could have done what Patrick said, called an ambulance. Been rid of me."

We sipped our hot chocolate. She said nothing. "He thought you should have sent me to County hospital. Why didn't you?"

"Patrick is a paramedic. He knows a lot about County that isn't common knowledge. If I'd called an ambulance, that's where you probably would have ended up if we couldn't find some sort of insurance card on you. And I wouldn't think of sending someone to the Veteran's hospital, unless I had no choice. It's even worse than County."

"There's something you aren't telling me," I said.

She stared at me, as if she had to make a decision. "You might think this is a little strange."

"Try me," I said.

She sipped her hot chocolate.

"My grandad had the gift of reading people. I got it from him. He always talked about his treasure. He said he planned to give it to me. When I was a little girl, I would sit next to him outside the general store in our little town, and he would tell me what people thought, and often what they would buy. Sometimes we could see what they had when they came out of the store. He just knew. We used to laugh about it. Our secret. He was my best friend.

"Grandad died just after my twelfth birthday. He was an alcoholic, so everyone else thought that his talk of treasure had been just the rambling of a drunk. Six months after he died, I started dreaming about him. It happened several times a week, for months. One night while I was dreaming, I asked what he wanted. He told me he wanted to give me his treasure. After that, the dreams quit coming. I'd almost forgotten. But certain things about people started popping into my mind. Not everything, or with everyone. But certain people. I knew their thoughts. I knew if they lied."

"That's interesting," I said. "In 'Nam, sometimes we knew things that were going to happen, with no logical explanation. We just felt like we needed to do something. Get off the trail. Double-time it out of there. It didn't take long to learn to listen. Saved our lives more than once."

"I can understand that," she said. "My brother has no faith in anything he can't explain. But I know that what I feel about people is right. I knew about you in the first few seconds I saw you, before I hit my head on the floor. I felt a familiarity, a...kind of kinship...with you. And on the way to the hospital, I saw more than that."

"What was it?" I asked, feeling curious, but guarded.

She hesitated. "Well—do you believe we live more than once?"

"I thought about that a lot, after I got to 'Nam, and learned what some of these people believe. It doesn't make sense to me that we can get it right in one lifetime. If we don't get another chance—maybe several—it would seem most of us are going to hell. Is that what you mean?"

She didn't answer; instead, she looked at me as if she was considering whether I could understand.

"It happened when the ambulance took me to the hospital," she said. I was only half conscious. I could see a fall or winter scene. Evening. I'd been locked in a box car. You helped me escape. We fled from an army of soldiers. There were swastikas. We crossed a border somewhere." She took a sip of her chocolate.

"I think we became lovers. Eventually you went back to help someone else and never came back. You'd been killed."

"I got a feeling I knew you, too. While you lay there on the floor, I wanted to watch over you...to kind of...protect you." I shrugged. "I didn't understand why. I guess it was a little late for that, though."

"After I woke up in the hospital's ER that night, I was afraid that I would never see you again. I wasn't sure where to find you. You mentioned your 'five star' breakfast spot to Sue Ann. That's how I found you, and why I went out with you. And why I took you into my home." She got the slightest hint of a smile on her lips and cocked her head to the side. "Think I'm crazy?"

"No, I don't. But in case you are, I'm glad."

She looked up. "Really?"

"Really. Like I said, I know about feelings that can't be explained. From 'Nam."

"Would you tell me about 'Nam?"

I shook my head. But told her about my dream. Some of it, anyway.

"You have to, sometime. Tell it to someone. Maybe not the worst parts, but start somewhere. For your own sake."

She leaned back on the couch, held out her arms. I moved into them.

As if they had their own life, the words tumbled out. Once I started talking, I couldn't stop.

"Sometimes my guts got so tight from fear that I had cramps," I told her. "My nerves frayed, every shadow looked like a hidden slope-eye, every crack of a branch the sound of an AK-47. One time my best friend and I knew we had walked into an ambush. We lost four men there, including him. I couldn't save him. Once my team wouldn't take orders, and that really scared me."

Thoughts I'd pushed out of sight clamored to be heard. Before I could stop, I'd blurted out how I enjoyed killing Charlie, enjoyed getting even. How I had to stop thinking about those things, or I'd come unwound.

Her body felt so soft, her breast against my cheek. I remembered how I'd taken refuge from battle by making love to Li. Now I was in the arms of another beautiful woman. The thought of Li brought a wave of guilt over me. I pushed it away.

Bobbie pulled me against her. I took her chin in my hand, drew her toward me. Our lips met. Then I felt her hands on my chest, pushing me away.

"No! Oh, please don't!"

I remembered Li stiffening at my touch in the beginning, willing to serve me with her hands, but not with her body. "Why are you leading me on, doing things that make me think you want me, then getting all pissed off when I try to touch you?" Hurt and anger punctuated my words.

"Men! You're all alike! Or on second thought, you're not! *You* take first prize for being the biggest jackass of all! You collapse on my doorstep. I take you in, feed you and care for you, get in a fight with my brother because of you, and you're going to reward me by grabbing my breast and maybe 'allowing' me to have sex with you? What do you think I am, one of your bar-room pickups who can't wait to go to bed with you? What's wrong with *me*? How *dare* you! What's wrong with *YOU*?"

She drew her arm back and slapped my face. I could taste blood in my mouth. She broke into tears and ran into the bathroom. I sat there, numb. What had happened? My mind had gone blank.

I stood and stumbled down the hall into the bedroom. I tried not to hear the sobs. Part of me expected her to follow, beg forgiveness, fall into bed with me. I was angry about the hand the universe had dealt me, about the war and its aftermath. I sat on the bed, sure she would come to me eventually.

I felt her presence, rather than heard her. I turned to look up at her face, her eyes large and tragic. She held her unbuttoned blouse closed with one hand. I felt an urge to dominate her and break what I imagined to be her power and control over me. I put away all thoughts of Li.

She reached out and gently placed her hand on my shoulder. I could see her silhouette in the dark, and watched as her hand loosed her blouse. As it fell open, her breath came fast and shallow. I drew her to me, took her in my arms and kissed her again and again. She returned my kisses, her teeth yielding to my tongue. She stroked my chest, slipped her arm around my neck. The taste and smell of her overwhelmed my senses, made me drunk with desire for her. I allowed my passion to take charge. I undressed her roughly, rapidly, and pulled her under the blankets with me, finding her body beautiful, slim and muscular. Without much prelude I entered her. Afterward, I lay on my back next to her. She didn't move or say anything. I fell asleep.

She awakened me the next morning, standing at the door of the room, dressed in her nurse's uniform. "Your breakfast is ready. On the table," she said, her voice flat. The events of last night flooded back with bitter regret. Now that she had given in to me, maybe she didn't want me. Panicked at the thought that I had lost her, I jumped out of bed, still naked, and grabbed her arm before she could open the front door. She turned, stared, unseeing, her face a wooden mask.

"I have to go to work," she said.

On the table I found a breakfast of bacon, eggs, toast, a cup of coffee and a glass of orange juice. I slumped into a chair, unable to eat. I was disgusted with myself. I had found someone who cared for me. She took me in and I treated her like a cheap pick-up. I saw the Vietnamese village and the woman who was gang-raped by the soldiers, then given a gun to shoot herself.

I *always* screw it up, I thought.

What were my values now? I tried to remember the good things I'd done, but everything I could think of seemed frivolous, self-serving. Had I become a taker, not caring, much less giving? War demons began to taunt me, whispered that what I had done in 'Nam was wrong. Did I really fight for a righteous cause?

Something black began to bubble up inside me. I could take care of it all. I knew how. I dressed and went to the liquor store a few blocks away. The clerk perked up when he saw me. After all, I had been one of his best customers.

"Where you been?" he said. "Everything okay?"

"Sure." I forced a smile. "Gimme a bottle of Myers Dark. A fifth. And two packs of Marlboroughs." I paid for the rum and cigarettes without more small talk, and walked back to the apartment.

I opened the bottle and poured a glassful of the dark liquor. I took a good-sized swig, felt it burn its way down, then drained the glass and refilled it. I lit a cigarette, looked around for an ashtray, found none. I threw the match at the kitchen sink. Blowing smoke out of both nostrils, I turned back to the task at hand. I just had to get drunk enough to do it.

I needed the box from my duffel bag. I looked in the closet and found the bag on the floor, empty. I panicked. Where had my stuff gone? Had Bobbie found the box, hidden it where I couldn't find it?

Almost frantic, I searched the closet, finding only the clothes she had washed and hung up. I raked the hot end off of my cigarette on a pair of pants and burned a hole in the carpet. A speck of burning tobacco fell on my skin and I jumped.

I dropped onto the bed, fell back on the pillows, wondering what to do next. Had she given the box to Patrick for safekeeping? I sat up, dizzy from the rum, opened the top drawer of the dresser. Socks and underwear. I slammed it shut. In the second drawer I found a cigar box with some mementos. The loaded dice I bought in Saigon and never had the guts to use. An AK-47 round. Vietnamese coins.

Underneath the cigar box was the locked walnut case with my name engraved on the lid. I kept the key in my wallet. I took it out and opened the box. The hard-chromed Government Model Colt .45, cleaned and oiled, ready for use, lay on its velvet bed, next to a full box of ammo. It felt good in my hand, a tool that I knew well how to use. I put it back, took the box to the kitchen table.

I needed to write a note to Bobbie, tell her how sorry I felt, that things would be better this way. In her small desk with the top that folds down I found paper and a pen. But I needed a couple more slugs of rum first.

I poured more rum into the glass and lit another cigarette. I hadn't had anything to eat, and the alcohol went straight into my system. Feeling like the biggest shithead in the universe, I picked up the pen with a shaky hand. I would soon take care of all that.

I wrote my note. Reading it through took some squinting and a great deal of concentration. It sounded appropriate. I propped it against the full glass of orange juice, filled my rum glass again. My stomach hurt, so I drank more. I had trouble trying to fill the glass, slopping rum all over the table.

I reached for the box. It was locked. When I'd set the pistol back inside, I let the lid with its automatic lock snap shut.

With difficulty I managed to stand and search my pockets for the key. Not there. I took a step toward the hall and fell against the wall. Somehow I made it into the bedroom, where four identical keys were lined up on the bed. I wrapped my fingers around one of them, and they all disappeared. I staggered back to the table. When I managed to get the key in the lock, it wouldn't turn. The box fell to the floor. When I bent over to pick it up, I fell to the floor beside it.

"Goddamn box!" I yelled. I smashed it against the floor and the top popped off. The two magazines slid under the table. Cartridges scattered everywhere. I grabbed the pistol and tried to retrieve enough ammo to load one magazine. On the third try I got the magazine inserted. I reached up on the table for the glass, drained it for the last time. I had to pull back the slide on the .45, then release it to load a round. It slipped from my fingers, slammed forward, and there was a tremendous roar. My finger was in the trigger guard, and when the slide slammed forward, I accidentally pulled the trigger.

"Je-e-e-ezus-Christ!" I mumbled. I managed to get back up in the chair. A calm came over me. I had let Bobbie down. I had been unfaithful to Li. I would atone for that—and everything else.

I could see everything very clearly now, the scratches on the tabletop, the matte hard-chrome finish on the pistol—every little machining mark and nick. I took it in my hand, turned it around and put the muzzle in my mouth. The metal banged against my teeth. I could feel the outline of the slide as my mouth closed around it. I tasted the burned gunpowder and gun oil, felt the texture of the finish. The front sight rested firmly against the roof of my mouth, in perfect position. I closed my eyes and reached for the trigger with my thumb.

No matter how hard I concentrated, my thumb refused to pull the trigger.

I took the gun from my mouth and sat there, shame washing over me like something hot and sticky. The bottle still had a little rum left. I couldn't find the glass, so I drank it from the bottle, and dropped it on the floor. Broken glass went everywhere.

I picked up the pistol again, tried to put the muzzle in my mouth. I couldn't do it. The room began to melt and blend as I slid off the chair.

I'll never understand how a woman who weighs one-hundred-ten pounds could pick up a man who weighs one-hundred-seventy pounds and put him in bed. Bobbie did just that, then called Patrick and told him she had an emergency. She'd found me on the floor in the kitchen, lying on my side underneath the table. When she moved the chair, she saw the 45 in my hand the shards of the rum bottle. Then she saw the note.

I'm not sure what all they did to me, but it kept me alive. I know they took another blood sample. My blood alcohol was so high that statistically I was dead. And dehydrated. They gave me something intravenously, and an injection.

I woke up about three o'clock the next morning, feeling like I'd been hit by a truck, then beaten with a Louisville Slugger. I lay there, not moving anything but my eyes. Even that hurt. I still had an IV in my arm. In the dim light from the hallway, I saw Bobbie curled up asleep in the big easy chair next to my bed, still wearing her nurse's uniform,. I must have made some noise as I stirred. Instantly she was awake.

"Hello," she said with a tired smile. "How do you feel?"

"Awful," I said.

She sat on the side of the bed. "Do you want to live?" she asked. "Or are you going to try this again?"

Her voice had an edge to it. "I want to live," I said, solemnly. Meekly.

"I want you to live, too. We'll talk tonight, after I get home from work."

When I awoke later, the IV was gone. I sat up, and my head felt like someone had driven a spike a through it. I lay back down.

"Bobbie?" I called out. No answer. When the spectacle I'd made of myself came back, I cringed, feeling a combination of humiliation and shame. I lay there and thought about life and death, the lives I had taken and seen taken, the violence of death in war. All the times we worked so hard to come back alive. Now, it seemed utterly incongruous that I could have attempted to end my life.

I tried not to fall asleep again, fearing the dreams would return. I did, but and there were no more dreams, only a much needed deep sleep. I woke up when I heard Bobbie open the front door.

I struggled out of bed, still weak, and found my jeans in the closet. I had to walk carefully to keep the floor from swaying. As I came out into the living room in my bare feet, I saw Bobbie sitting on the couch, her elbows on her knees and her face in her hands.

I had to walk slowly so I wouldn't fall over. I stood next to her for a moment, not sure what to do. She didn't move. Finally, tenuously, I said, "Hi."

She looked exhausted, smiled anyway, and held out a hand. I sat next to her, afraid to do more than hold her hand. "You look a lot better," she said. Always the nurse, I thought. No, she was more than that. A healer.

"I feel a lot better."

"Do you really want to live?" she asked.

"Yes. I want to be with you. I...I guess that's why I couldn't do it."

"I want you to live, too." She had been looking into my eyes, but now she looked down at her hands, which were folded in her lap. "I had such strong feelings about you. The first thing I wanted us to find out was where we got this connection. I wanted to make love to you. I wanted it in that order, until last night. Then I wanted to...to have wild sex with you. I kept waking up last night, feeling that I'd helped mess things up. I've been asking for another chance—for us."

I wondered how she could possibly think *she* had messed up. I started to speak, but she silenced me.

"I know you have a lot of love in your heart. That's why I want to know if this time, you *really do* want to live. What I *don't* want is to come home some day and find that you've succeeded in doing what you couldn't do last night. I thought you'd shot yourself. I almost fainted. When I realized you were just drunk, I got *furious*." She looked up, eyes wide and anguished. "Am I important enough to you that you want to be with me?"

I nodded. "Yes," I croaked. "I do."

"Then we'll work it out." She sighed. "I'm so tired."

I held out my arms and we leaned back on the cushions. She put her head on my shoulder, drew her feet up under her. In less than two minutes she had fallen asleep.

I felt her completely relax, her breath coming slowly and regularly. Gently, I bent down and kissed the top of her head. I felt the energy she always seemed to have, like sitting next to an old-fashioned radiator in the winter.

It scared me to think she found something attractive in me. Not just physically, but spiritually—something good, in spite of the warrior that I was. I didn't know if I could cast off enough of the old bonds, change the reactions that had damned me so often. If not...

As I nodded off into a state of half-awareness, Li appeared in my mind. Her face showed the same love and concern she had for me when we parted. I knew we would share the love we had for each other always. It could not be altered, would never diminish—but in that moment, I knew it was unconstrained. We would never forget, nor would we ever be crippled with bonds from our love.

I vowed that this time would be different. I had another chance and I would not screw it up. I would make it work.

CHAPTER FORTY ONE

Healing

Over the next two months, I made inroads into my temper. I had to learn to think what the effect of everything I did would be on Bobbie.

I tried to do things that would be helpful. Little things. Like drying the dishes and silverware with a dishtowel like she did, so there would be no water spots. Wiping the baseboards with a dust cloth after vacuuming. Cleaning the bathtub. Putting the seat down. I was developing a regular domestic style. I kept it up because she let me know she appreciated it.

I hadn't spent much of the cash I brought home. Several times I offered to share rent and utilities. I wanted to do something to contribute. She wouldn't take the money. "Save it. You may need it later on," she always told me. Finally I asked if she thought that something was going to happen to me.

"No," she said. "But right now, I make plenty of money. You've been buying groceries and taking me out. All that leaves is rent, electric, and a few clothes once in a while."

I could never seem to find much at the grocery store that she would eat. I took her out often, and she ate such small portions I wondered how she could stay healthy. She liked wine, but where I could drink the whole bottle, she thought having two glasses of wine constituted a night of heavy drinking. Three, if I could tempt her, and she turned into a tiger when we got home. I always tried for three.

Tonight, Bobbie and I had reservations at seven at the Lobster Pot. It was an upscale restaurant, superb food, quiet, and a good place to talk. When she wasn't home by six o'clock, I started to get edgy. By six-thirty, I'd started to pace the floor. Twenty minutes later I grabbed a jacket and my .45, convinced that something had happened to her. Wild images of catastrophe ran through my mind, sending me into a state of near-panic. Kidnappers. Someone shooting up the hospital. A car wreck. Or losing her to another guy. I'd kill the sonofabitch.

As I reached for the doorknob, someone pounded on the door, sending my heart rate into triple digits. I froze.

"Doug! It's me, I forgot my key!"

Relief surged through me, then anger. Didn't she know I'd worry about her? Of course she did. I yanked open the door and she flung herself at me, arms around my neck, standing on her tip-toes. She let go of my neck and looked up with a big smile.

"Guess what?" she said. "I got promoted!"

"Why didn't you call me? Didn't you know I'd be worried sick about you?" I barked.

I regretted my words as soon as I said them. She shriveled from the rebuke and tears welled up in her eyes. She ran down the hallway to our bedroom and slammed the door so hard it sounded like a claymore going off.

"Wait!" I said, "I didn't mean to..."

The realization of what I'd done dropped on me like a dead weight. I leaned against the wall, slid down to the floor. She had come home so full of joy and enthusiasm, so happy to see me. And I had managed to destroy her good feelings. She's the best thing in my life, I thought. If I lose her, it will be because I'm so goddamn stupid. It always seemed that having something good meant I would feel the pain of its loss. Was this part of my legacy from 'Nam?

When I heard the bedroom door open, I sat there on the floor, head down, elbows on my knees. I didn't know if I could face her.

"Doug?" she said. "Uh...Doug?"

I looked up. She held out her hand, her face laden with worry and concern—for me. Even after what I'd done to her. I felt utterly worthless. How could she still care?

She reached for my hand, pulled until I got up. She wiped the tears from my face with a tissue, then put her arms around my waist. Suddenly she pulled back. "Uh, could you put that thing somewhere else?" I pulled my .45 from my waistband, put it on the end table.

"I'm sorry I was late. You kind of surprised me," she said. "I didn't think you would be so worried. I had to stay late and talk to my new supervisor.

"I'm sorry too," I said. "I'm so sorry about what I said, and a lot of other things." I tried to talk fast because I knew my voice would crack if I didn't. It cracked anyway. "You're just so important to me that if something happened and I lost you..."

"You can be so insecure sometimes, yet so sure and utterly fearless at others. I don't understand what makes you tick," she said.

"I don't either. I'm kind of a nut case. After something like this, I feel like Dr. Jekyll and Mr. Hyde. I wanted very much to...to do something nice for you, take you somewhere nice, have a good time tonight."

I was showing my vulnerability, and had to create a distraction. "If you don't mind being seen with a testy old nut case," I said, as I crossed my eyes and made a face.

"You know, I'm beginning to understand a few things about you. If we talk about you, somehow you manage to change the subject, like you just did. And a lot of your joking around means the subject is one you don't want to talk about. It's too close. Or it hurts too much."

"Yeah, well." I couldn't deny it. "Uh...you're right. How did you figure that out?"

She raised her eyebrows and rolled her eyes. "Do you think I'm dumb just because I'm so in love with you?"

"I love you, too," I rasped out. "I ..."

She laid her head against my chest. "Oh, Doug. You've never said that before. Do you really?"

I tried to think of something humorous to say, couldn't. "It's kind of crazy," I said. "Yes...I do love you. It's just that I can't see any reason for you to love me." In the back of my mind a voice said, *If she really knew who you are and what you've done, she wouldn't even like you.* I couldn't come up with a good argument against that.

Bobbie put her hand against my cheek. "But that's still not all of the problem," she said.

"No. It's kind of like if I have you, have your love, and if, for some reason,

I lose you…I couldn't go on. I…" *You had to leave Li, the mother of your child,* said a little voice inside my head. *And look what happened to Dan when you left him down there on that creek bank!*

A part of me spoke up in my defense. *But that's not the same! It's what he wanted! He told me to go… I'm not going to leave Bobbie.* One part of me tried to placate another part of me. *Maybe you're trying to push Bobbie away! Like you left Dan…and left Li…left them,* the first voice said. My world collapsed into hurt and despair. Oh, Dan, God, I wish you were here. I wish we could talk about the things that happened.

I thought about Bobbie's gentleness. Her hand still rested against my cheek. I reached up and put mine over hers. Could I ever talk to her? She'd see I was a monster and run.

She mopped my face again with a tissue, turning my head so I had to look into her eyes.

"Isn't that what you're mostly afraid of? That you have a pattern of losing someone after you get close to them? First there was Sarah, before you even joined the army. Then Dan. That was his name, wasn't it? And several other guys in your team?

"Yeah. Mostly Dan." And Li, I thought. Would I lose Bobbie if I told her about Li?

"Tell me what happened to Dan," she said.

"I can't." I could see Dan running across the rice paddy, taking a burst from an AK-47, getting up, going down for good.

"Yes, you can."

"It still hurts too much."

I sat on the couch, head down. She sat across from me on the coffee table and took my hands. "Tell me about it," she said, softly.

I told her about the mission, about the bad military intelligence we had been given on the NVA. My voice held out until I came to the part where Dan told me he wanted to stay behind, that it was his white horse. My throat closed up, but I croaked out the words, how he insisted I leave him, how I escaped up the ridge. That he saved my life.

I told her about the NVA soldiers I killed, trying to secure his escape. To my surprise, she didn't shrink from me.

I told her about watching Dan die.

Slowly I got to my feet, sapped of energy. My legs wouldn't move. I closed my eyes and wept, wondering if the anguish would ever stop. Bobbie stood on her tip-toes with her arms around me. She held me tight. I sagged into her embrace without thinking she might not be able to support my weight. The telling had left me completely wrung out.

"Dear God, I miss him so much," I said. "We were best friends. We grew up together, stuck it out together in high school." I felt embarrassed. "I seem to be crying half the time any more. That's not very macho."

Bobbie handed me another tissue, raised one eyebrow. "No, not very macho. But it's very good," she said. "Doug. Look at me." She put her hands on my face. "Look at me. You need to see someone. A professional. Remember that lady we met at John and Melanie's party? She seemed nice. Dr. Davis. You talked to her for quite a while."

Oh God, I thought. That's all I need. I slipped my arms around her waist and pulled her close. "I'm hungry." I grabbed a tissue and wiped my nose. "Takes a lot of energy to make all those tears."

"You just did it again!" she said, pulling away.

"Am I so transparent to you?" I asked, surprised. "I can't even see it myself. Well, sometimes I can."

"Yes, Doug. You are. Transparent as glass."

"Sometimes I feel so weak, like such a weenie."

"No," she said. "You're anything but that."

Bobbie sat me down at the kitchen table and opened the refrigerator. I got up to help.

"Sit!" she ordered. I sat. We ate leftovers, washed down with a bottle of Chablis.

"We should have called and cancelled our reservations," I said.

"I already did. Pass the wine, please."

I watched as she filled her glass again.

"Yes, she said. This is number three."

"Oh. I wasn't counting."

"Of course not."

We took the rest of the Chablis and sat on the couch.

"Who is Lee?" she asked.

I felt panicky that she knew anything about Li. I had never mentioned her, and I could think of no one who knew about that part of my life. I sat up and took her by the shoulders.

"Who told you about Li?" I asked.

"Ow, that hurts," she said, squirming out of my grip.

"Tell me. Who told you?"

"*You* told me," she said as she rubbed her shoulders. She sounded like I had unfairly accused her of something. "Anyone ever mention that you talk in your sleep?"

"Yes," I admitted. *Now what am I gonna do, tape my mouth shut every night?*

"You talk about some pretty awful stuff. And you use words I've never heard you use around me."

Bobbie got up and sat on the coffee table, facing me. "Doug, you've talked about someone else a lot. Cried for someone. Is that Lee?"

"Yes," I said. But it's a...woman's name. It's spelled 'L-i.' She was...special."

"More than special. She was someone you loved. Deeply."

I nodded. "She was half French, half Vietnamese. And you're right, I loved her very deeply."

It didn't seem that Bobbie felt as if she'd just discovered the "other woman." There was nothing accusing, or jealous, in her tone of voice or the way she acted. I was surprised and a little ashamed that I thought she might be.

"Tell me about her? Please?"

"Well...it's kind of a long story. Are you sure you want me to?" I asked.

"I'm not upset about her," she said. But I would like to know. I think it will help me understand you a lot better."

I thought about some of the things Mike and I had learned living with the girls. The responsibility for someone totally dependent on us. Bittersweet memories that stung; others that took me to deep love and laughter. I decided Bobbie would understand this part of my life—and the way it ended.

I talked about Li, Mike, and Rose for over an hour. Bobbie didn't move, except to take my hand. When I told her Li was carrying my child, she moved close to me, put her head on my shoulder. I could feel the wetness of her tears as I told her the last of the story.

"I don't believe I'll ever see her again," I said. "Or my child. But she will never be far away from me."

After we sat there for a while, I realized how good it felt to be able to tell someone what had happened. Someone caring and understanding. I felt immensely relieved.

Without saying a word, Bobbie got up and went in the bathroom. I could hear the water running, and soon she came out with a wet washcloth held to her face. She sat down next to me.

"Doug, I don't know what to say." Another tear traveled down her face. "Except that I do understand you more. I'm glad you trusted me enough to tell me. Thank you."

Suddenly the silence became deafening. "Tell me about your promotion," I said. wondering if she'd noticed I'd changed the subject.

We talked about her new job, how she had some ideas to improve the nursing procedures. "That, of course, will generate some resistance," she said. "Any time something changes, some of the people don't like it." She turned, curled up against my side.

"You know what I'd like to do now?" she said.

"Let me rub your back, and then..."

"Certainly," she said. "Especially the 'and then' part."

The wine had its predictable effect. After the 'and then' part, we fell asleep, arms and legs entwined.

Early in the morning one of the dreams came back. This time I remembered. It had been about the firefight and the cache of supplies we found. Most of the dream happened the way it really did. Except for the crispy critters.

In the dream, we used one of the two barrels of gasoline to soak the materiel. We poured half the other barrel into each tunnel entrance. At the same time, we threw blocks of C-4 explosive into the entrances and lit the gas-soaked materiel on fire. The explosion shook the ground.

We were moving out of the depression when one of the guys yelled, "Hey, look! There's another tunnel, and two of them just crawled out of it!"

I had slung my M-16 over my shoulder. I whirled around, drew my .45. Two writhing bodies, one on its knees, one lying on its side, were reaching for me. Both were burned black—their hair and ears had been burned off, lips burned away. Their eye sockets were empty.

"Goddamn," Tony said. "They can't still be alive. They're crispy critters!"

They were barely recognizable as human forms. Then they stood and walked toward me, hands held out, flesh sloughing off. A continuous moaning sound rasped through their raw, putrid-smelling flesh. I pointed my .45 at the closest one and pulled the trigger. The pistol produced only a metallic click when the hammer fell. I racked the slide, pulled the trigger again with the same result. Frantically I dropped the magazine, grabbed a loaded one from the pouch on my belt. I slammed it home, worked the slide. Before I could pull the trigger, another explosion rocked the entire depression. Both creatures were blown on top of me. I kept screaming, trying to push them off, but their flesh came off in my hands.

"Mike!" I yelled, over and over. "Mike! Help me!"

Then, half awake, I sat up in bed. I felt arms around my chest. A frightened Bobbie tried to hold and comfort me. But I thought the arms belonged to the burned creatures. I shoved her so hard she fell off the bed.

Before, the dream had been only the feeling of someone burned coming after me. This time it played through in gloriously gruesome technicolor.

I crawled over the bed to where Bobbie had landed on the floor. "Are you okay? I'm so sorry! I didn't know it was you!"

She sat up on the side of the bed, took my hand. She looked scared. "You were yelling for help. Who is Mike? Was he your other sergeant?"

"Yeah. I needed him to help me. The burned things knocked me down. I couldn't get them off." I frowned. "But that's not what happened. The dream was different this time." I wiped the sweat off my forehead. My t-shirt, even my shorts were soaked with sweat.

"I'll get you some dry underwear," she said.

"Nothing like that's ever happened before," I said.

"You *are* going to see someone about it. You ARE going to!" she said. "*Understand?*"

"Yeah. You're right. I guess I need to."

CHAPTER FORTY TWO

Dr. Davis

Dr. Beverly Davis looked up when I walked in. She placed a folder in the center of her desk. Mine, I guessed.

"Good morning, Doug."

"Yeah. G' morning," I growled.

She indicated the big recliner across from her desk. I dropped into it. The lever at the side of the chair reminded me of the emergency brake on an antique car. It's not going to slow down the ride *I'm* on, I thought.

The wall behind her desk had framed certificates hung from the ceiling down to the credenza. Okay, I thought, reading the letters after her name. So she's a shrink. I tried to forget the titles and letters. Only a sicko needed a shrink. I was no sicko.

We talked about where I was born, where I was raised. My life when I was a kid. As we talked, I kept waiting for her to blame me or criticize me for something or tell me I hadn't tried hard enough. The hour sped past. Before I knew it, she was asking me if I could come at the same time next week.

"How did your session go?" Bobbie asked when I got home.

"It didn't go like I thought it would," I said.

"Why not? Do you mind telling me?"

"I don't mind. It was strange. She asked me where I was born and grew up. What my family life had been like. She seemed accepting, not critical. All we did was chat. It went fast."

"Did you make another appointment with her?" she asked.

388

"Yes," I said. Bobbie looked relieved.

My life with Bobbie was changing. I sensed a growing tentativeness in her, a reserve. She seemed to be watching and waiting. I couldn't blame her. If I'd found her passed out next to a suicide note, I'd have been anxious every time she was out of my sight. Given my violent dreams and the volatile anger she'd put up with, I didn't want to create a crisis about anything else. Maybe, I thought, seeing a shrink would help us get back where we once were.

I started cooking Bobbie's breakfast each morning. It took two days to realize she couldn't eat three eggs. Just one. Over medium. She turned her nose up at my runny, sunny-side-up eggs. But we both liked crisp, almost burned bacon. I had to have coffee. Strong and black. She wanted orange juice. The natural kind, not re-constituted.

We had an argument over bread. One morning she spent twenty minutes explaining how my highly refined white bread had no natural nutrition. I thought I'd done a great job of masking my irritation about being told I shouldn't have white bread, my favorite since childhood.

"I think I'll stick with my white bread," I said. Then I made the mistake of grabbing a slice and spreading butter on it.

"That's dumb," she said. She got up, snatched up my new loaf of doughy white bread. She opened the wrapper and held it under the faucet, turned on the water, and dropped the thoroughly saturated loaf in the garbage.

"This egg is perfect," she said, taking a bite. "It's just right, sweetheart," she said with a smile, and finished her breakfast without another word.

I learned to eat whole wheat bread. Not just so-called wheat bread like brown-colored white bread, but the kind that had all sorts of seeds, nuts, berries, and whole grains baked into it. Chewy, chunky, crunchy stuff. I wouldn't have admitted it, but it tasted better than the old doughy white bread.

On my second visit, Dr. Davis asked what I liked to do. I told her I liked to hunt and shoot. I regaled her with tales of hunting trips and personal experiences of the effectiveness of the Colt 1911A1 Government Model on Viet Cong and NVA. I left convinced she had been enthralled with my tales. Later, I couldn't remember her sounding like she approved or disapproved of anything. She only listened.

"Well, did you like it better than last time?" asked Bobbie when I came home. I knew she wanted more than a casual answer.

"Yeah. I guess. We talked about hunting a lot. And guns. I sort of expected her to not to like my stories, but she didn't say anything negative. Come to think about it, she didn't approve, either. She just listens."

"That's what she's supposed to do."

"So how is that going to help?"

"She has to get to know you. Find out what you like. And why."

"So how does that help?"

"If I knew, sweetheart, you could just talk to me for all those hours. She reached up and put her arms around my neck. "Except we'd probably get distracted. Then they'd say we had an addiction."

I wondered if she felt this way because I'd been willing to try to change, to help our relationship. If so, I'd see Dr. Davis forever.

"I think I already have that addiction. With you."

"Oh really?" She said, slipping her hand down the front of my Levis. "Hmmm. It feels like you need some therapy. Lots and lots."

"I could use a good dose of therapy. But lots and lots may make the addiction worse. My body might quit before we ever get to lots and lots."

Bobbie stood on her tip-toes and rubbed her hips against me. "We can adjust the doses," she said.

My need for therapy had suddenly become urgent.

My third session with Dr. Davis felt much more informal. I found myself looking forward to seeing her. She asked me about shooting an M-16, which loosened up my tongue for more battle stories. It also elicited stories about my Thompson submachine gun and my very accurate long-range bolt action rifle. I told her about some of the firefights we'd been in and some of our narrow escapes. Before our session ended, I quit talking. I found myself resenting the long silence that followed.

"It feels unreal to think you want to hear all the things I've been telling you. And it feels unreal to find myself telling you about experiences I've never told anyone else about," I said.

"You spent a lot of time learning to use different kinds of weapons," she said.

I nodded, aware that she'd changed the subject. Like I'd been doing with Bobbie. "Anyone who's been listening would have found that obvious."

"You still feel good having a handgun," she said, keeping the conversation going in her direction. "Like the one you've been carrying a under your shirt since you've been seeing me."

That surprised me. I didn't think she noticed.

"That's okay, Doug. I don't think you will go off the deep end and shoot up my office. Or anywhere else, for that matter.

I shrugged. "Okay," I said, wondering just how this was helping.

The next week passed in a blur of the mundane tasks life imposes on everyone. But one of the tasks turned out not to be mundane. I took Bobbie's car for service. I stayed with the car and watched. I didn't know it at the time, but the kid doing the work was the owner. I pointed out he had missed two fittings when he did the lube job, and didn't check the differential.

"Well," he said, when I went into the office to pay the bill, "before you pay, you want to make certain the job was perfect?"

I looked up from the service ticket and gave him my best smile. "How would you like for me to make certain you can spit out your front teeth?" I asked.

He shrank back, took my check and tossed the receipt on the counter from arm's length. His bravado gone, he said nothing until I pulled out into the street. "Don't bring the car back here again!" he shouted.

I was in traffic and couldn't stop. I'd just go around the block and see if that smartass wants to do something about it, I thought. I'd punch him out. Then I realized I'd have to find another place to get Bobbie's car serviced if I did. Her approval rating of me would hit the basement when she found out.

My hair trigger was still proving to be a disaster.

The next day I sat on the couch staring blankly at the envelope I received in the morning mail. It was from from Stryder. My address had been scrawled on lined paper and taped to the envelope with see-through tape. The return address read, *Stryder, Gen Del, Arlington, Virginia.* It had been forwarded from my old apartment. The vets-helping-vets organization, whatever its name was, had found Stryder's address for me months ago. I'd written to him several times. I hadn't received a reply, so I quit writing.

I slit the top with my pocketknife and pulled out two sheets of lined paper. I struggled through his typing errors, trying not to let the letter summon that old gut-feeling of something-gone-wrong.

My mind went through a time-warp to the other side of the world. What had happened to everyone? Was anyone else still alive? Were we all doomed to blow our brains out, or live in a refrigerator carton? Maybe Dr. Davis had an answer for that one.

Stryder's letter left me with a lump in my throat. He said he'd been having trouble with his legs. How could someone like Stryder have trouble with his legs? *Stryder?*

I took a pad of lined paper and tried to write something. After several starts, I wrote 'From Sarge,' on a blank sheet. I took a hundred dollar bill out of my wallet and folded it into the page, stuck it in an envelope. This could be a favor or a curse, I thought.

The mail truck had stopped two doors up. I waited for it.

"How 'ya doin?" the postman asked.

"Oh, okay," I said, handing him the envelope.

He peered over the top of his glasses at it. "No return address?" he asked.

"Nah. We know how to reach each other."

I wanted to show Stryder's letter to Dr. Davis. His letter made me feel cynical and suspicious all over again. Maybe Dr. Davis has been making a fool out of me, I thought. I knew that was not rational. I couldn't pinpoint how, much less why she would do that. I had no reason to believe she had done anything but listen to all my stories. She'd made a few suggestions and asked some questions that stirred up old memories. Nothing else. I didn't want to tell her some of the things her questions stirred up. Yet something in my head wanted to get that stuff out, talk about it, confess. Do penance. Whatever. I began to wonder how bad I was messed up. It scared me.

When I got home that evening, I stared at the televison without having any idea what was on. "Oh, hell, I'm just not going to tell her about it," I said, thinking out loud.

"Tell who about what?" asked Bobbie, as she dried the dishes.

Great. Me and my big mouth. "That shrink. I'm not going there again." The words, unexpected, just fell out of my mouth. "It's expensive. I can't afford it."

Bobbie came into the living room, still wiping her hands on the dishtowel. She turned off the TV, and sat on the coffee table, facing me. I looked down.

"Doug, you promised." She made it sound like I'd taken an oath to God. When I looked up again, the desperation in her eyes caught me off guard.

"You haven't given it a chance," she said. "I'd bet the whole farm you haven't let her get any closer to you than you let me get the first six months we dated. You probably want to quit because you're beginning to feel you need to talk to her."

Even if I'd been tortured, I wouldn't admit how right she was. How could she know that, I wondered. "Look," I said, I just don't think..."

She stood suddenly, bent over me, a small thundercloud with big lightning bolts. "You'd better go! You just better be there!"

To my astonishment, she drew back her fist and smacked me in the middle of my chest. It didn't hurt, but it seemed to shatter something in her. She dropped down on the coffee table, crying. I sat up. "Bobbie, please, I want you to understand..."

She flared up like a fire doused with gas and shoved me back on the couch. "No! *You* better understand! I want you to keep seeing Dr. Davis, and I have a very selfish reason for it! I want you to do it for *me*! We're not going to even *have* a relationship if you don't! And I'll still love you, but I won't be able to live with you!" I reached out to her, half expecting her to fling my hand away and tell me to leave.

"I'm sorry," I said. "I'll go. For you, I'll keep on..."

"I want this to work, Doug," she interrupted, launching herself from the coffee table, tears coming afresh, "I really love you," she said, choking out the words. "I want you to do it for us," she said as she wrapped her arms around me, holding me so tight it was hard to breathe. I felt her fear as her tears soaked through my T-shirt. How could I deserve someone who cared so much? I was always making her cry. How many times could I be the cause of her tears before she gave up?

"I'll go. Since you think it will keep me from hurting you so much, I'll keep going. I want this to work too," I said. "I'll see Dr. Davis as long as you think I should. And...I do love you. Very much."

We leaned back on the couch cushions and held each other for a long time. It felt good to hold her, good to dare to believe she loved me—for who I was. Not for who I thought I was, but for who *she* thought I was, even after all the things I'd told her.

I turned her face toward me and kissed her. More than just passion and need for each other brought our lips together hard, exploring, giving new meaning to French kissing. I held her to me, close, tight, felt her pull me to her. An almost desperate need for each other took over, reluctantly waiting until we reached the bed. We thrust deep at each other, sometimes Bobbie on top, sometimes me.

Afterward, my every sense remained vivid, elated. We hadn't moved for a long time. At last Bobbie raised her head and looked toward the kitchen.

"How'd you like to take me out to dinner?" she asked.

"Does that have anything to do with that smoky smell? Like dinner burning?"

"It just might," she said, kissing me softly.

"Do you think we're going to have to have some more therapy?" I gasped.

She pulled back and gave me her mischievous look. "Absolutely not," she said.

I gave her a look of mock disappointment.

"Not on an empty stomach. But I think I'd like two—or maybe three—glasses of wine with dinner.

CHAPTER FORTY THREE

Mind Maintenance and Repair

I came home from another session with Dr. Davis, slamming the door as I came in.

"Doug? Is that you?" Bobbie asked from the shower.

Who did she think it would be, for Christ sakes. I got a hold on my temper. What the hell's the matter with me? I thought.

"Yes. It's me."

"How did your session go?" she asked. "Doug? Are you there?" she asked when I didn't reply.

I looked up when she came out of the shower, hair wet, wrapped up in a terry cloth robe three sizes too big.

"Not a good session," she said.

"No. But I'm trying not to give up. The last three times all she did was let me ramble on. This time I told her I want someone who I can care for who can love me. What a mistake. She got all over my case. Said I was too controlling. Overprotective." I noticed Bobbie was doing just what Dr. Davis usually did. Listening.

"Well, am I too controlling?" I asked.

"Sometimes," she said.

My mouth dropped. Could Bobbie and Dr. Davis be scheming against me? I wondered.

"She even asked if I was negligent as a team leader."

395

"What did you tell her?"

"I said I didn't think so. I don't, you know."

I felt my temper trying to take control again, and shut it off. I didn't want to have a fight with Bobbie. It wasn't her fault.

"She said my control trips were because I was afraid I'd lose someone, or I was afraid they'd get hurt. And, of course, that's you."

Bobbie sat in my lap and put her arms around my neck, which made it impossible for me to be angry. Now who's being manipulated, I wondered. But I loved every minute of it.

"You want to know what I think?" she asked.

"Yes, I do."

"You try to protect people from things they don't believe exist, whether they want to be protected or not. And you react. Remember what you told me about the kid who spit on you at the airport? You have a hair-trigger. You didn't act then, you reacted."

"You're right. As usual. But it's hard when someone does something stupid, not to..."

"Not to what? Not to throttle them, break their bones, shoot them? she asked, innocently.

"Especially if they did something to you. Dr. Davis asked me what I was doing tonight. I told her we were going out. You know what she said?"

"What?"

"Lay off the control trips. She said I needed some help with it."

"I'll help you." Bobbie snuggled tighter against my chest. "I think there's hope for you, even if you're more stubborn than...I don't know what. An old mule. A Missouri mule."

"I almost forgot. I got a letter from one of the guys. I gave a copy of it to Dr. Davis." I handed her the envelope.

1800hrs21august

Hey sarge you old sonofabitch how the hell are you. It made me glad to get you letter, good knowin your alive an doin ok. Havent hear from you since you were living in a bottle if you know what I mean! And im not gonna be much help w/what you want.

Your not the only one who didnt exist any longer. Theres a lot of guys whose records dissappeared. We are two of them. Bet everyone els is, our guys I mean. I tried to get my records. Got told the fire at somewhere destroyed my records Some record center burned up a lot of stuff all very cnvenient.

I thought the same as you did, theres some sort of record where we trained. Not so. I sent them a copy of my discharge, hounorable, model 1-A. and d214. Didnt hear from them. Wrote my fucking senator. Well guess what happened a couple weeks later? A BURGULAR broke into my home where I paid a hundred fifty a month to live and we didnt have a guard at the gate oh yes, didn't have a gate either so they got away with my duffel bag and then I didnt have anything to copy any more, no hounerable, no214. no goddam gi bill, no helath care. fuckem the county's programs just as good as far as bases we trained at having records they don't keep them after a while as it becomes part of your goddam serfice records an I know thats true becarse my senator who sits on the righthand of God told me so. you know my tyhping s not good as it used probably cause I use two fingers what looks like im flippin off the keys. Its called a huntin pecker but hell I never had hunted pecker I was always huntin PUSSY So anyhow wherever we went we never went there because of the convenient fire some goddam dickhed lit at theRecord Senter. yeah I know its center iwrote all the bases I could remem, same goddam story.it happened before me getting all fucked up on alcohol.

But I really did write both senators the second one said the first one told me what happened about the fire and my congressman said hell if they couldnt help, how did I think he could or please politely fuckoff and if your address is general delivery you probably wont vote. I should be here where you sent this for awhile the winters up north are bad if your livin in a carboard refrig box

Hey sarge, you remember what we know and don't want anyone to ever know? it must have taken a year for me to quit dreaming. you know they tell me I got sir osis of the liver. of the goddam brain would be worse. But that's all well thank god. What's worse is my feet, they got sores on them, an one o my legs. My sugars all fucked up, I can't walk so good these days of bein back in th USA, some asshole protester sed its my countrys fault

an I hit his soft ass for treason. Ha. I gotta get out of her, the public library,
they don't want you looking like me to stay around. stole their goddam pen
and paper ha, got thelast laugh. You cant know how friggin good it is to
hear your doin allright did you get off the bottle, you must have

your friend

s Stryder

remember you guys called me that?

CHAPTER FORTY FOUR

Change Can Come Too Late

When I got home, Bobbie looked up from where she sat at the kitchen table, a cup of hot coffee in front of her. Something was wrong.

"Hi, beautiful," I said.

She sighed, shook her head. "Sit down. Please."

I sat.

"I saw Dennis today."

"I don't think I know Dennis, do I?"

She sipped her coffee and rolled her eyes. "Dennis owns the station where I get my car serviced. Or used to."

"He would have missed several things..."

"Like his teeth?" she asked.

"Uh, well, he missed greasing some of the fittings..."

"Well, now he won't be greasing any of the fittings. He asked me to take my car somewhere else next time. He said something about you threatening to punch him in the mouth and break off his teeth."

"I just wanted to make sure he did a good job on your car," I said, realizing how lame it sounded.

She sipped her coffee again. "Doug, why can't you deal with people without threatening to kill or maim them?"

We didn't go out that night, and the next morning she left an hour early. "I'm having breakfast with Beverly," she said as she went out the door. No "Thanks for breakfast," since I didn't make it. I walked her to the door. If I got no "I love you," it would send my spirits spiraling into a pit of darkness. She turned toward me, pleading an unspoken request with her eyes, then stood on her tip-toes and kissed me lightly on the lips. "I love you," she said. She turned away, but not fast enough to keep me from seeing the tears.

If I didn't want to lose her, I'd better get myself straightened out, I thought. I wondered how many times I'd promised myself, and still hadn't done it. Maybe it's too late now. God, I hoped not.

The next morning Bobbie took my hand and looked up at me. "Are you going to see Dr. Davis?" she asked. My regular appointment was today.

"Yeah, I'm going. You bet," I said. "I don't know if it will help, but I'll keep trying."

I was rewarded with a hug, a smile, and an "I love you," as she left for work.

When I got to Dr. Davis' office, I wavered. Could I trust her? Then I thought about Bobbie. I'd better start trusting, in more ways than one.

"I had a bad dream," I told Dr. Davis. "I sat up in bed, yelling for help. Bobbie put her arms around me. I thought she was something from the dream. I didn't mean to, but I shoved her clear off the bed. She hit the wall, and fell on the floor. I'm worried I might do something worse. I've been having another dream, too, but it started before I left 'Nam. I don't know what they mean."

I told her about both dreams, then told her about trying to blow my brains out in Bobbie's kitchen.

"Another time, up in the mountains, I climbed out on the rocks at the edge of an escarpment that drops off almost five hundred feet. I had my .45. I thought I'd crawl down into a crevice and end it. No one would ever find me. Instead, I sat on top of the cliff, watching the sunset, thinking how beautiful it was. All my feelings went numb, and so did my mind. I hiked back to my car, my mind a blank. I couldn't think about anything except driving home."

"Doug, you've been in more danger since you got home than all the time you were in Vietnam," Dr. Davis said.

That stopped my clock. "You surprise me with some of the things you say. How could that be? There were people over there trying to kill me. A lot of them."

She smiled. "Sometimes you don't like what I say. But think about it. Since you've been home, you almost killed a kid in the airport, and you almost took your own life—twice."

It was a sobering thought.

"How did your session go?" Bobbie asked when I got home.

I sat down next to her. "She talked to me about being afraid of loss. A lot of what I do is because of the fear of loss."

"Wow," Bobbie said. "Too bad I didn't tell you that about a thousand times already."

"Okay, okay. You're right. She told me that the fear of loss creates anger. That I care so much, the loss will hurt. Or be debilitating. She pointed out almost all the things I feared would happen to me, or to someone I...uh... loved, never did. I'm not sure I agree with her completely, but she said trying to keep some imagined disaster from happening has actually caused some of the losses that hurt so much."

As soon as I said it, I knew that if I lost Bobbie, it would be for this reason. I would cause it to happen.

"That's a lot to digest," she said.

"Yeah, but I think I've found something that counteracts that stuff." I took her hand, turned it up, and gently kissed her palm.

At first, Bobbie didn't realize I wasn't kidding, that I meant what I said. Her eyes got moist. "I hope I'm the right medicine," she said.

"Well...it's starting to make sense, and the way Dr. Davis says things, it doesn't make me feel like I totally messed up...or that it's all my fault. She, uh, sounds a lot like you."

She gently nipped my neck. "Know what?" she asked.

"Tell me," I said.

"I think there's hope for you." She sat up and looked into my eyes. "I always have thought so, Doug."

Her faith in me bolstered my feeling that maybe, once again, I could become a member of the human race.

She cuddled up against me the way she always did, and tucked her feet up under her. I felt like she had let go of a large part of the watching I had been feeling. Maybe I was earning back her trust.

CHAPTER FORTY FIVE

Gone

Bobbie had been putting in a lot of overtime at the hospital. Part of her new job involved administrative paper work, which she tried to minimize and make easier for the nursing and emergency room staff. As she predicted, there were objections to everything.

She had been coming home late and uncharacteristically grumpy. I would fix dinner for her and keep the apartment clean while she worked long hours. I didn't do as good a job as she wanted, and eventually she started making caustic comments about my housekeeping.

"You left the pan from last night's meat loaf in the kitchen sink," she said. "It's going to be dried out and hard to get clean."

I almost said that I wouldn't make meat loaf any more, then saw how tired she looked. "I'm sorry, sweetheart. I'll wash it tomorrow."

"The kitchen floor needed to be mopped, too," she went on. "Probably those tissues are still in the bathroom because you didn't buy any toilet paper today."

I wrestled with my temper, wondering what had happened to make her so upset. It seemed like more than just overwork. Still, it hurt. The next morning I decided to take a break from my domestic role and left a note saying that there was a casserole in the oven left on warm. I called Vinnie, a fellow vet, and made arrangements to meet him at his favorite bar for a few beers. Later, he went home with one of the girls he knew at the bar. I came home alone.

None of the lights were on, and at first, I wasn't sure if Bobbie was there. I turned on the kitchen light. My note was still on the table. The casserole was still in the oven, which was still on. It had baked itself into the consistency of floor tile.

None of the other lights were on, including the night light in the hall. I stumbled over something, then reached for the night light, which had been turned off. The gym bag that I used to carry laundry to the washers downstairs was lying in the middle of the hallway. How did this get out here, I wondered. I'd left it on the bed. Did she throw it out into the hall?

Just as she was pretending to be asleep when I got in to bed, I pretended to be asleep the next morning when she left. She slammed the door so hard the latch jammed.

I wracked my brain, trying to understand what had gone wrong, just when I thought things were getting better. I had no idea, but I had no intention of putting up with it for another night. I called Vinnie and asked if he'd like to have company for a few days.

I left Bobbie another note, saying that I'd be at Vinnie's for a night or two. And that I didn't know what was wrong. I asked if we could talk, and signed it, "Much love, Doug."

Vinnie and I visited two of his favorite hangouts. I had a couple of beers, then reverted to Myers Dark Rum and soda. I drank more than I realized and I decided to call Bobbie and give her a piece of my mind. I called around nine o'clock, and got a busy signal. I watched the clock and called every half-hour until we left, just after midnight. Each time I got a busy signal.

The next morning, as I swilled coffee for my hangover, I decided it was a good thing she left the phone off the hook. I certainly would have said something I'd regret.

That night Vinnie and I went to the Last Call Saloon. I didn't really want to go, but didn't know what else to do. It turned out to be a worse dump than the one the night before. I ordered a double Myers and looked around. The place was full of cigarette smoke, which tempted me to break my two year record of no tobacco. Someone had turned the music up too loud, and I couldn't hear myself think. And I didn't hear the woman who sat down next to me at the bar.

"I said hello." She leaned close to me, giving me a whiff of several days' alcohol on her breath. "You look like you're all by yourself."

I leaned away from her alcoholic halitosis. "As a matter of fact, I'm waiting for my wife" I said. "She just won the WCW finals."

"What's WCW?" she asked.

"Women's Championship Wrestling. Heavyweight class. She's really jealous. She's on parole for assaulting the last broad that tried to pick me up."

"Fuck you," the woman said, and moved away.

"Jeezus," Vinnie said. "No one better mess with you tonight."

"Right. I'm sorry, Vinnie. This crap with Bobbie has me really uptight. For months now, I've been trying to be someone I'm not sure I am. I guess it's not working. I've been seeing a shrink, and most of that's been a load of bull shit." As I said the words, I knew I didn't believe them.

I pushed my glass toward the barkeeper. "One more," I said.

Vinnie headed for the dance floor. I sat at the bar by myself, guessing that my black mood telegraphed the message that it wouldn't be a good idea sit down next to me. I was so sure things were working out with Bobbie. I'd been doing everything Dr. Davis suggested. So now I hadn't seen Bobbie for two days and hade no idea what was going on.

Everything Dr. Davis had said now seemed wrong, I argued to myself. Except the part about fear. Yes, I had to admit I'd been afraid of loss. And now it looked like I'd lost my relationship. I wondered if there was another guy. I'd kill him. With premeditation, malice aforethought, calmly, rationally. Well, maybe not rationally.

Two business-types came in with their wives. Or dates. White shirts, cuff links, ties, suits, polished shoes. One wore shoes with that pattern of little holes across the toes; the other had loafers with tassels. I wondered what they were doing in a dump like this.

They talked about the day's business, some kind of merger, about fees and bonuses. Two more parasites, totally out of touch with what the world was all about.

I pictured myself doing what they did. It would be a recipe for successful suicide. Disgusting, I thought.

I ordered another drink and turned sideways at the bar. The women with the suits were very attractive, especially the one with dark hair. There was no ring on her left hand. Her low cut dress showed most of her breasts. I was wondering how sensually smooth her breasts might be when her date got up and walked toward me. The look on his face was an unhappy one.

"What are you staring at?" he asked.

"Sonny," I said, "I don't think you're man enough to find out."

He had such a fast right hook I almost didn't see it coming. I managed to lean back and take a glancing blow on the chin. I knew his left would follow, and it did. I blocked it, grabbed his arm with my other hand, and pushed myself forward, off the bar stool. He swung his right again, and connected with the side of my face. I dropped my weight toward the floor, swinging him over my shoulder. He landed hard.

"You sonofabitch," I yelled, and started to kick the edge of my boot into his larynx. Something hit me from behind and I crashed into a table and went down. It was Vinnie.

"Doug! Goddammit, Doug, stop!" he yelled. "He's down."

The other suit with the hole-pattern in his shoes got out of the booth. Before he had taken two steps, Vinnie was in front of him. "Sit down!" Vinnie roared. The suit shoved him aside.

"You take one more step, asshole, and you'll be lying next to your buddy," I told him in a low voice. I hoped he would stop. This altercation had become too familiar. I'd almost killed a man for hitting me this time, instead of spitting on me. Like the kid who spit on me, he deserved a lump on the head, but didn't deserve to die.

The suit stepped over his prone friend. "You're gonna pay for it, you fuh-h ..."

A dark form in the two-hundred-sixty pound-range appeared and shoved a long nightstick into the suit's solar plexus. It dropped him to the floor, next to his buddy. Not quite the way I thought it would work, but what the hell.

The owner of the nightstick had three stripes on his blue uniform shirt sleeve, and a gun on his hip. A police sergeant.

An ambulance arrived. The paramedics bent over the first suit where he lay on the floor. He had a lump on his head, but he insisted he didn't need to go to the hospital. That was a relief. Then they stood and looked at me.

"Let's take a look at your face," one of them said. "It's beginning to swell."

"My face is fine," I said.

"You better let us look at that," the other said.

I took a step back. "You guys are gonna need your own services if you don't leave me alone," I said.

"Okay, relax," the other one said. "If you'll just sign this waver..."

He handed me a printed form. I wadded it up into a ball and threw it over the bar.

"Get the fuck out of my sight," I said. A hand came from behind me and closed over my arm. Fortunately, I looked to see who it was before I took a swing at the owner. It was the police sergeant.

"We need to talk," he said. I allowed myself to be led away from the bar.

The week-day crowd at the Last Chance hadn't been large enough to spill over into the back room. The sergeant escorted me, Vinnie, the hole-pattern shoes guy, tassel-loafer guy, and the lady with the killer breath into the empty room. The bartender brought me a bar towel wrapped around some ice. I'd have black-and-blue marks tomorrow.

After separating all of us and questioning everyone, they took written statements. The cops let me and Vinnie go. The sergeant told me they had talked to two patrons in the bar who said the suit swung first. Halitosis lady and the bartender also agreed.

Vinnie and I went back to his apartment.

"Jesus, Doug, I thought you were going to kill that guy," he said.

"I *was*," I said. "I never thought I'd thank someone for knocking me to the floor in a bar, but thanks. I'm glad you did."

"Let's get some sleep," Vinnie said.

The next morning I slept in. When I looked at my watch, I realized Bobbie would be at work by now. It was too late to call her. I wanted to talk to her today. I'd go to the apartment this afternoon and wait until she came home.

I sat on the couch all afternoon, trying to understand what I was feeling. I realized the dark haired woman at the bar made me think of Li, which is why

I had been staring at her. I hadn't been angry at all last night. After the guy swung at me, my thoughts had become very calculating. I hadn't been out of control; nevertheless I didn't know how to keep it from happening again. I wasn't sure I wanted to. That was the biggest problem.

The longer I thought about my life, the less sure I felt about anything. I had been about to ask Bobbie to marry me. Now I didn't know. I wanted to live with someone, to share my day, my life, my bed—and my love. I wanted someone who wanted to share with me. Or did I? I was young, fit, and attractive to women. I could make a lot of pick-ups, then when something like whatever had happened with Bobbie came up, I could just tell them to leave. But that would be running away.

I wanted a job, a profession. The suits from last night made anything requiring that kind of dress code a definite no. But I wanted something to get into, a way to productively channel my energy and passions. Right now I felt stuck.

My gut told me I had to get away. Go on a trip.

The front door opened, and I heard Bobbie's voice. "Doug?" she asked, timidly.

"In here," I said.

"I'm so sorry I was cross and mean. I was—Oh my God, what happened to you?" Immediately she leaned over the black-and-blue welts on my face. "Oh, Doug! Are you okay? Let me get some ice," she said.

"No, no, I'm okay. This is from last night."

"Last night? Doug, where were you? I was so worried..."

"I left you a note that I'd be at Vinnie's," I said. "That's where I've been the last two nights. I tried to call the first night, but the phone was off the hook. I...kind of thought you didn't want to talk to me."

She sat next to me, looking very contrite. "Oh, I'm sorry. No, I hoped you'd call. I got home late. When I realized you weren't coming home the first night, I dragged the comforter into the living room and slept on the couch. Somehow I couldn't sleep in our bed without you. I knocked the phone off the hook with the comforter. I was frantic that you hadn't called, then I found the phone. When you didn't call last night, I was afraid something bad had happened. I was scared. I'm really sorry, Doug."

"I got in a fight last night. Almost killed a guy."

"Is that how you got these bruises?"

I told her what happened at the Last Chance. When I finished, she examined my wounds.

"I'm going to get some ice."

I started to object, but the nurse in her could not be deterred. That's not such a bad thing, I thought. She does care about me.

Gently Bobbie applied the small ice pack to my face. I couldn't tell whether it was the ice or her touch that felt better. Sometimes she could melt me into a pile of warm putty.

"So what's been happening to us?" I asked. "Why were you mad at me?"

She put down the ice pack and looked up at me like a misbehaved child who is truly repentant.

Part of me wanted to crush her to me, tell her how much I loved her, vow we would never be apart again. But another part of me wasn't so sure that's what I wanted.

"I haven't been feeling well," she said. "Some female stuff. I was taking hormones, and as if that wasn't enough, my period started. I'd been worried because it was late. All the overtime had worn me out. And all the bitching at work. You were so wonderful, Doug, cooking and cleaning. And...I took it all out on you. I'm so sorry..." She started to sob.

I took her in my arms, feeling how much I needed her to need me. I had a lump in my throat that almost choked me. We sat there for a long time, neither of us saying a word. Finally she sat up and looked at me. "What do you want to do, Doug?"

"I don't know. I think I've got to get away and take another look at myself." I looked into her eyes. "If I'm not really any different—if I haven't changed, I won't be any good for either of us. Last night raised some doubts that maybe I'll always be like that. Maybe I'm still a...killer."

"When do you want to go?" she asked.

"Maybe tomorrow," I said.

"I'll wait for you."

I knew she would, and that there was no one else. She would be here when I returned. Part of me felt ashamed that I could do this to her, but I had to go.

I decided to stay at Vinnie's for a few more days. He knew someone who had a Datsun pickup for sale. I had Vinnie's mechanic go over it bumper to bumper. He pronounced it in good mechanical condition. I bought it.

I asked Bobbie if she thought Dennis would check it out for me. "If he finds out it's yours, he'll probably do it for nothing," she said, laughing.

"Yeah, just so he can put water in the gas tank and iron filings in the crankcase.

I felt stuck between two worlds—one with Bobbie, one without. I wanted to be with her. I was afraid to be with her.

For two weeks, I drove around the country. I had been writing to my mom and dad, and it felt like the right time for a visit. I called them from a small town in Utah. Yes, they assured me, I would be welcome to come, and stay as long as possible.

Our reunion was tentative until we realized none of us held a grudge. Dad told me over and over how sorry he was about the way we parted. Each time he did, he got to the verge of weepiness. Finally, my inspiration struck. I told him it had given me a chance to develop the strength and character I'd gotten from him, to learn to deal with life and the challenges it presented. That seemed to give him a reason to forgive himself.

Three days later I called Bobbie from a small town in Missouri, the apogee of my wandering.

"I, uh...I was just wondering...do you think you would let me take you to dinner when I get back next week?"

"Well, hang on for a minute. Let me check my calendar."

Oh, great, I thought. Is she seeing someone?

"You said next week? I just happen to have some time. Either Monday, or Tuesday or Wednesday, or Thursday. Also Friday, Saturday and Sunday. The week after that looks about the same."

"You know who you remind me of?" I asked.

"Who?" she said.

"Me."

"Oh. That's pretty wonderful."

"I'm glad you think so. Why don't I call you when I get back in town?"

"Okay," she said. "Doug?"

"Yes?"

"I've missed you."

Dr. Davis had reminded me about the times in 'Nam when I knew something would happen, without any intellectual reason or explanation how I could know it. She told me to ask myself how I felt about Bobbie. Alone and on the road, without the distraction of all my fears, I knew I loved her. So much it scared me. Driving across the Texas panhandle, much of the road was straight as a string. I settled into a kind of near hypnosis as my intellect made the car function. The rest of my mind was free to look at what I wanted to do.

I would always love Li. Nothing could ever change that, or take it from me. I felt with certainty that I could encapsulate that love, and not feel guilty for any love I would have for someone else. With that resolve in my mind, I headed for home.

The next day I stopped for gas about two hours from home and called Bobbie. We said our hellos and how-are-yous, and the silence of who's-going-to-speak-next grew louder and louder.

"How about dinner?" I blurted out. "It will take me about two hours to get there."

"Only if the place serves wine," she said.

That sounded encouraging. "I'll find a place that does. See you in two hours," I said.

After a short stop at a grocery store where they sold cut flowers, I pulled into the parking lot at our apartment. I felt foolish wondering if I should just walk in or knock. I knocked. Bobbie opened the door. "It's so good to see you, Doug," she said.

I presented her with my almost-fresh bouquet.

"They're lovely," she said. "Come in."

Off she went to the kitchen for a tall glass and some water. She put the flowers on the table and turned around.

The light blue sweater she wore accentuated her breasts and small waist. Tight Levis showed off her legs. "You're beautiful," I said, as I put my arms around her.

"I'm hungry," she said. "And thirsty."

I asked for a bottle of wine before we ordered. Dinner was a success. We had more successes after we got home.

The next day Bobbie and I were sitting on the couch like we always had, the television on and neither of us paying any attention to it. "What would you think about being married to a photographer?" I asked.

Bobbie recovered first. "Is that a...proposal?" she asked.

I stuttered and stammered, then blurted out, "That isn't what I meant to say." Which wasn't what I meant to say, either.

"I would hope not," she said. "When I receive a proposal of marriage, I expect it to be from bended knee and somewhere there had better be a ring with a full carat rock."

My blunder stung her, and her attempt at humor didn't soften it. I knelt in front of her and took her hands. "Bobbie," I said, "I manage sometimes to say some stupid things. Tonight has got to be the worst. I've thought about marrying you very often. I guess that's why it slipped out that way."

"Doug, you can be so romantic. A really romantic dunderhead."

"And you have the darndest way of taking the awkwardness our of a situation," I said. We both laughed. A forced laugh.

"I shall consider us to have an agreement of non-engagement," she said.

I wanted to kick myself around the block. She couldn't hide her hurt feelings.

I got up that night without waking Bobbie, and sat on the couch, staring at the wall. I had wanted to marry her for some time, yet my fears and my sense of loyalty to Li had been insurmountable. Now I had faced them, and made my decision. Yet I wavered.

No decision is worse than the wrong decision. Face your fears, said a voice in my head.

I'll find a ring and propose tomorrow, I decided.

I was up, showered and dressed the next morning before Bobbie. I opened

411

the bathroom door while she was in the shower. "Omelettes will be ready in five minutes!" I said, as I pulled the shower curtain back a crack and peeked in. "Then again, it might be thirty minutes..."

"I'm too hungry to wait that long."

"At least you didn't say you had a headache," I said, feigning disappointment. She was out of the shower in four minutes.

"So where are you going so early?" she asked, as she washed down a bite of her omelette with orange juice.

"Oh, I almost forgot. Vinnie and his girlfriend want us to go to dinner tonight." I wondered if the distraction was enough to keep her from asking again.

"That's fine," she said. "Ooh, I'm going to be late for work." I opened the door for her. She stopped and put an arm around my neck. "Doug, I love you." I almost melted into a puddle.

"I love you, too, Bobbie. I'm so sorry I've hurt you."

She stared at me for a moment with her big brown eyes. "Love will heal everything," she said, and she was gone, leaving me with the certainty that I had made the right decision.

I started looking at rings as soon as the jewelry stores opened. I had a ring from her jewelry box I'd seen her wear on her ring finger. With a little luck, I could pull this off.

By noon, I felt frazzled and had a headache from looking at diamonds under the bright blue lights everyone used. What had seemed like a good idea had proven to be complicated.

I parked in front of a store next to the college. Collegian's Diamond Imports. Inside, there were no blue lights.

"The blue can cancel the undesirable yellow hue some diamonds have," the salesman explained when I asked.

"I want a wedding and engagement set with a full carat diamond," I told the him.

He showed me a variety of mountings with spaces for smaller diamonds around the center stone, then opened what he called a diamond wallet. Inside were unmounted diamonds, each one nestled in a folded slip of white paper. This was a totally different way to buy a diamond ring, and I found it appealing.

"I need this ring for a marriage proposal dinner this evening," I said.

He looked at the clock. "If all I have to do is mount the center stone, I could have it for you in two or three hours." He handed me a ring with smaller diamonds already mounted on the sides, then took a large diamond from its folded paper and placed it in the center. "This diamond weighs eighty-seven points—that's hundredths—of a carat. It would cost you a lot less," he said. "And the total weight would be more than a carat."

Bobbie said it better be a "full carat rock." I knew she would be delighted with anything, even a gold band.

"How much is the full carat rock?" I asked. He added it up, and I winced. I couldn't afford the bigger diamond. Still, the total weight with the smaller diamond would be over a carat.

"I'll have to write a check for this on Valley Bank. If that's not a problem, I'll pay you now."

"I'm sure we can get the check approved," he said. "Are you a vet?"

"Vietnam. Three years, six months, in-country." I wondered how he knew.

"We give a discount to vets. Fifteen percent. You originally asked for a full carat center stone. With your discount, you'd be within less than about a hundred dollars." He opened the diamond wallet again and set a full carat stone in the mounting.

"This one's a hundred and five points," he said. Frozen fire flashed around the room. A beautiful stone. A *big* one. It was perfect.

"I'll take it," I said.

By the time Bobbie got home from work, I had picked up the ring, a new blazer, and a white shirt. Never able to tie a tie, I bought a clip-on. Any tie was a huge concession.

"Don't take too long, sweetheart," I said. "We have reservations at six-thirty." Our reservations were for seven, but I thought our departure might get delayed. At six-fifteen, she came out of the bedroom looking radiant. She stopped stock still when she saw me wearing my new outfit.

"My heavens. You look like a cleaned-up version of the man I love," she said.

"Well the man you love, who I hope is the one I saw in the mirror tonight when I shaved, has something to talk to you about. Come and sit down for a minute."

The light in her eyes made me wonder if she knew what I was up to. She sat on the couch, and I knelt in front of her. As soon as I took her hand, she got all misty.

I looked into her eyes, feeling better about the words I was going to say than anything I'd ever said.

"Bobbie, I love you. I can't promise I'll never hurt you. You know I'm such a dunderhead at times. But I promise you that if you will do me the honor of becoming my wife, I will cherish you as long as I live. Will you marry me?"

I reached into my jacket pocket for the little black box that held the ring. When I opened the box, she gasped. I took it out and slipped it on her finger. It fit perfectly. "I have delivered a proposal on bended knee, with a one carat rock, as you specified. As a matter of fact, the total weight is one and one-quarter carats "

" Doug, It's beautiful! And it's so brilliant—and *huge*. Did you do all this today?"

"I did. Now my foot's going to sleep. Can I get up now?"

She laughed. "Oh, get up, silly. I was just kidding about the one carat rock."

"I wasn't taking any chances," I said.

She ooh-ed and aah-ed a few more times, holding her hand out where the setting sun caught the diamonds. "Oh, look!" She said, pointing to the tiny rainbow specks of light refracted onto the wall.

"Well?" I asked.

"Well what?" she said.

"I asked you if you would marry me. You haven't answered my question."

Her excitement faded and a look of uncertainty took its place. "All that time you were driving around the country, I didn't know if you wanted..."

I took her hands. "I've had a stack of baggage. A lot of unfounded fears. Driving around gave me the time to realize how much I love you and want to be with you. I'm more certain that I want to marry you than I am about anything."

We stood looking into each others' eyes. For the first time in my life it felt comfortable to lower the armor I always carried. The two of us together had infinitely more strength than we had apart.

"I will marry you Doug. I was beginning to think I'd be an old woman before you asked." She looked at the ring again. "Oh, Doug, thank you. It's... so beautiful." She put her arms around me and her tears washed mascara all over my new white shirt.

I discovered that our junior college offered a degree in photography. More than a dozen classes were scheduled in the fall semester, starting in two weeks. I picked up a catalogue and the class schedule, and read the course descriptions.

A new career was unfolding before me. I could leave the past behind and rebuild my life with someone I deeply loved, and who loved me.

We were married during the break between fall and spring semesters. Vinnie and his girlfriend attended, and one of my classmates did the photography. It was a simple ceremony that Bobbie and I wrote. Afterwards, we called my mom and dad, then her brother.

I took my finals early, since they consisted of examples of our darkroom work and composition. I had an abundance of prints to choose from. Bobbie got off work for eighteen days for our honeymoon. I didn't want to take the Datsun, since it was small and uncomfortable. Bobbie's car was no better. When Vinnie offered his four-wheel drive truck, I almost laughed. But Bobbie loved it.

Winter came late that year. We were able to travel through southern Utah and parts of northern Arizona before the first storm hit. We came home for a few days without telling anyone, then went south with a guide book and no particular destination.

We were happier than we'd ever been.

Spring semester flew by, then summer school. I had a gift for photographic composition, and worked to perfect it. I made straight A's.

Bobbie and I saw Dr. Davis, sometimes together, sometimes separately.

Dr. Davis had taught me a lot about making things work, but I still thought she was pushy. I didn't want to take a chance on messing something up, so I kept coming.

Bobbie hadn't been feeling well for several weeks. She went to see Dr. Wilson, her gynecologist, for some tests. I took her back for the results and was sitting in the waiting room, reading the same page of a dog-eared magazine for the third time when a nurse came through the door.

"Mr. Walker, would you come with me, please?" she asked. "The doctor would like to talk to you."

Bobbie sat in a chair across from the doctor's desk. She looked like she'd gone into shock. I sat next to her, pulled her into my arms. Her eyes, large and unusually bright, stared through me. "What is it?" I asked.

"Doug, I'm going to die," she said in a wavery voice. "Dr. Wilson says I have pancreatic cancer. I only have a month or two."

"I'm afraid that's right," Dr. Wilson said.

"No-o-o-o," I moaned. "We'll work on it. There has to be some way...some treatment..."

"I'm sorry, Doug," said Dr. Wilson. He went on to explain all the reasons why there was nothing that could be done.

Neither of us spoke as we drove home. Bobbie moved into the middle of the seat and leaned against me. I put my arm around her.

"I feel so helpless," she said. "I don't want to leave you."

I pulled into a parking lot and wiped my eyes. I promised myself this would be the last time she would see me cry.

I dropped out of school and stayed home with Bobbie. Anything I could get for her, anything I could do, I did. At first she fussed about it, then as she became weaker, we settled into the realization that we had very little time. We spent most of it sitting on the couch, wrapped in each other's arms. Touching—any contact—brought us a measure of solace as we tried to cram a lifetime into a few more weeks.

There were times I wanted to leave with her. I thought about the times I'd tried to take my life, but couldn't. I was going to lose her after all, and I knew I would have to stay. I would have to deal with it.

I left our apartment only to pick up Bobbie's medicines and to buy groceries. One of the nurses, retired from the hospital where Bobbie worked, stayed with her when I was gone.

I made an appointment with the oncologist, Dr. Richards, who Dr. Wilson had consulted.

"There's must be something," I pleaded. "Something new or..."

"I'm very sorry, Doug." He let out a long breath. "A situation like this is harder for me to cope with than anything I do. I can't begin to know how much it hurts both of you. I hope and pray that someday..."

Bobbie lost so much weight it hurt to look at her ravaged body. Her pain became so severe I had to carry her when she got out of bed. As she became weaker, she required medical care I couldn't provide. Dr. Wilson had her admitted to St. Joseph's Hospital. I wondered if he thought she would be more at home there, where she had worked. So many of her co-workers visited, expressing their hopes, offering their prayers, that the doctor limited her visits. She had a lot of friends who were saddened by her illness, and tried to keep tight control over their feelings. Often they ended up in tears—and were comforted by Bobbie. I had never seen the depth of her compassion, and I wondered how many other ways I hadn't really known her.

I stayed in her room night and day. Usually someone brought something for me to eat. One of the few times I went to the cafeteria, I looked up to see Angela, Bobbie's nursing supervisor when she had been working there, standing at my table.

"May I sit down?" she asked.

"Suit yourself," I said, not anxious to talk to her.

Angela sat down and leaned across the table. I felt like she was about to hit me.

"What's the matter with you, Doug?" she said. "Can't you see you need to pull yourself together for Bobbie? You look like hell. You're causing her a lot of anguish seeing you like this."

Anger rose up in me, wanting to deny it. Meddlesome broad, I thought, clenching my fist. Then I thought about how much Bobbie still worried over me, and I knew she was right. Did I get something to eat, Bobbie would ask, then she would want to know how I could sleep in the lumpy chair in her room. Once, a hint of a smile appeared when she asked if I had to iron my own shirt. In spite of her pain, she still cared about me. Angela was right. I had to do it for Bobbie.

I looked down at the floor, vowing that this woman would not see the anguish my guilt poured all over me.

"Yes," I said. "I'll do anything. But how do you know...?"

"I know because I've been a nurse for a long time," she said. "I also know because she told me."

"You talked to her? About me?"

"She called me," Angela said. "She asked if I'd talk to you. She said she's tried to get you to take better care of yourself, but you won't listen to her."

Something else I've screwed up, I thought. I hope it's not too late to fix it.

"Do you want to know what you can do to ease her burden?" she went on. "You can quit feeling sorry for yourself long enough to convince her you will eventually get over her death."

Angela's words stung. I remembered the night CT put me in a wheelchair and took me with her on rounds, bringing me back very humbled. "Looks like I'm getting another chance to learn that lesson," I said.

"What lesson is that?" Angela asked.

"Never mind."

"You two used to laugh a lot," she said. "And you used to tell funny stories. In a morbid way, sometimes. Like shooting a pot of rice out of a soldier's hands."

"Yeah, I remember that." I smiled. "Bobbie didn't like those stories. But she'd think about them, then she couldn't help but laugh. Then she'd get mad at me."

We fell silent. Angela stared at her fingernails while I stared into the past and all the death and pain in my life.

"Doug, our tears are not for the dying," she said. "They're for ourselves."

For a moment my sight blurred. I felt as though I might pass out. Then I met her gaze, and, for the first time, I saw her pain.

"You're right. I've been wallowing in self-pity. It's just that...I'll miss her... so terribly."

She nodded. "You and I have something in common. We both love her."

I reached out and took her hand. "Thanks," my voice croaked.

On the way back to Bobbie's room, I saw a sign that said "Chapel," and an arrow pointing down a short hallway. I didn't remember turning the corner, or opening the door. I sank into a small pew, two rows back from the altar. Sobs burst from my chest and tears soaked my handkerchief. Until now, I'd had a shred of hope she would recover. Now I accepted that she would be gone.

Every Sunday, when I was a youngster, our minister gave what he called a Youth Sermon. I remembered the one about how to talk to God—the same way you would talk to a loving father. That sounded like the God I knew from 'Nam.

"God, I don't quite know how to ask, but Bobbie and I need a lot of strength right now. We've done about as much as we can. We need some help." I remembered I should ask in Jesus' name, which I did.

I thought of Corporal Melvin Platt, and the peace of mind he had found when he lost his leg. "Help us both find the certainty and peace Mel found," I added.

When I got back to Bobbie's room, she was awake.

"Hello, lover," I said with a big smile. "I'm going home to clean up and get some clothes. Is there anything you want?"

"Yes," she said, "I gave Angie a list of things. Doug, after it's over..." she started to say. I put my finger against her lips.

"I'll be okay," I said. I bent over the bed and looked into her eyes. "It'll take time, but I'll always have your love to lean on...and your strength...for the rest of my life. And that will be a long time." I forced a smile.

"I love you, Doug. You're the best thing that ever happened to me."

I flinched. I thought of all the pain she had suffered because of me. I didn't understand how she could believe that, but she did. Knowing that gave me the strength I needed for the next few days. I felt tears running down my face, in spite of my vow.

"I love you, too, sweetheart." I turned and walked blindly out into the hallway.

On the way home, I thought about her words and knew that at last I'd done something right. Something that meant a lot to her.

When I returned from our apartment, I had the things Bobbie wanted, and three changes of clothes and toiletries for myself. I could use the shower in her room.

I would not let her down again.

Every day seemed to pass slowly, except when I marked an X on the calendar at night. Then I wondered how it had streaked by so fast. The few times I tried to spend a night in our apartment, the emptiness closed in. I called Vinnie and asked if I could stay with him for a few days.

"Sure," he said. "I'll give you a key. You can come and go whenever you want."

"I can't tell you how much I appreciate it," I said.

"Doug..." he said. Then paused. "You're my family. Anything you need..."

Several days later, Bobbie's pain medication quit working. For most of the day, I stood next to her bed, holding her hand. When the pain became intense, she would squeeze my hand. Between bouts of pain, I bathed her face with a cool cloth. I talked to her, although she did not always respond. I told her again and again how much I loved her, how wonderful she was.

I began to feel angry because her doctor hadn't ordered something else for her pain. I pushed her call button, trying to remind myself if I lost my temper, it would upset everyone, Bobbie most of all.

One of the nurses came into the room. "How is she, Doug?"

"She's hurting," I said. "I don't know if she's sleeping now, or if she's passed out."

"The doctor has been in surgery," the nurse said. "He prescribed something for her a few minutes ago. It shouldn't be long now."

"How did you know my name?" I asked.

"I met you at a party with Bobbie. I'm Mary Lou. I've worked with Bobbie for four years." She started to say something else, then changed her mind. She stepped to the other side of the bed, took Bobbie's hand in both of hers, and whispered something to her that I couldn't hear. She did an abrupt about-face, and left in a hurry.

A few minutes later, Mary Lou returned, pulling an IV rack with a bag of clear liquid.

"For pain?" I asked.

"Yes," she said. "It's pretty potent stuff. She will probably sleep—soundly. Doug," she said, anguish showing in her eyes, in her voice, "she may not wake up before...

After Mary Lou hooked up the IV, Bobbie's hand slipped out of mine and her face relaxed. Just for a moment I panicked. When I saw her chest rise and fall, I, too, resumed breathing, then fell exhausted into a chair.

"Why don't you go home and get some sleep, Doug?" Mary Lou asked. "We'll call you when..."

The 'when' made my heart skip a beat.

"Will you be here?" I asked.

"I'm here until four in the morning," she said.

"Is that any indication...?" I asked.

"It's uncertain, Doug, but it can't be very long."

I looked out the window, and to my surprise, it was dark.

"I'll be at Vinnie's. You have his number."

The walk to the parking garage, along with the cool night air, revived me enough to drive. Vinnie's place was only fifteen minutes from St. Joseph's, and the late evening traffic was almost non-existent. Nevertheless, I had to concentrate to keep the truck in my lane.

Something I had learned to pay attention to in 'Nam nagged at me. My energy was about to run out. My attention focused on the street to keep the truck in the right lane. I looked down at the speedometer and back up, looked for a traffic cop. Nothing. I tried to persuade myself that I was just tired. I didn't buy it, but the feeling persisted.

I pulled into Vinnie's driveway, unlocked the back door, and stumbled into the bedroom. I fell, fully clothed, onto the bed, sound asleep.

From the deep blackness of sleep, I felt someone shaking me.

"Doug, wake up," a voice said. Vinnie's. Then more shaking.

"What? What?" I said, still groggy.

I sat up and looked at Vinnie's face. It held so much hurt, for a moment I thought something had happened to him. Then I knew.

"Doug," he said, "It's the hospital." He held out the phone.

I mumbled something into the receiver. "Doug?" a voice asked. Mary Lou's voice.

"Yeah."

"Doug, you'd better come," she said.

I jumped up, dropped the phone, and would have knocked Vinnie over if he hadn't stepped back.

"Doug, wait," he yelled. "I'll come with you!"

I shot out the door and ran for my truck. Now I knew what the feeling I'd had earlier was all about.

I slid to a halt in a no parking zone in front of the hospital. I ran into the lobby, frantically pushed the elevator button. Nothing happened. I found the stairs, took them two at a time, and burst out onto the third floor. The doctor stopped me at the nurse's station.

"She's very weak, Doug. And she doesn't have much time," he said.

I bolted down the hall and into Bobbie's room. Mary Lou was there. She stepped away from the bed. I looked down at Bobbie. Her eyes were open. She smiled at me, then lifted her hand from her side a few inches.

I took her hand, and she squeezed mine gently. I felt pain surge through me, so much I thought I wouldn't be able to stand. I hurt more than I ever had, more than from the punji stake, Mike's death, or from losing Li. I was beyond tears. I felt a clarity I'd never experienced before.

"Hello, my love," I said, a little surprised to find I was smiling—that I *could* smile.

"I'm so glad you're here, Doug," she said. "I love you with all my heart."

"That's the most precious gift in the world," I said.

She raised her hand. "Take my ring with you. Please."

I looked at her ring finger. All this time she had been wearing it.

"Sure," I said.

As the ring slipped from her finger, her hand slipped from mine, and she was gone.

I had no idea how long I stood there, holding Bobbie's ring. Nor do I remember how I got into a hospital bed. When I raised my head, I saw Vinnie asleep in a chair against the wall. Then the weight of the world fell on me and I remembered. I heard a moan, then a long, deep, sorrowful wail. Mine.

Vinnie took me home—to his apartment. I spent the days sitting in front of the television. I didn't go out, didn't shave or change clothes. When Vinnie came home one afternoon, he turned off the television and pulled one of the chairs in front of me.

"Doug," he said.

My eyes were still focused on the blank television screen.

"Doug, dammit! Listen to me!"

I knew he was talking to me, but it didn't register. Then he stood and slapped my face. Hard. I snapped into action and threw a hard right at him. He must have been expecting it. I just grazed his chin.

"Doug!" he yelled, "it's me, Vinnie!"

When I realized who it was, that I had hit him, it overwhelmed me. "My God, Vinnie, are you okay?" I asked.

"Yeah—I guess," he said rubbing his chin. "I'm just glad I dodged that punch. Or most of it."

"I'm sorry. I didn't mean..." At that moment I thought about Bobbie. I put my face in my hands and wept.

When I managed to stop, Vinnie came out of the kitchen with a cup of steaming coffee, a sandwich thick with deli roast beef, and potato salad.

"I don't think you've eaten for several days," he said. "You better go slowly on this if you want to keep it down." He set the cup and plate on a TV tray next to me. It smelled like the nectar of the gods. Too heavy a meal for right now, I guessed, as I started to demolish it.

After several admonishments to eat slowly, Vinnie gave up. I finished the sandwich—and kept it down.

"Doug, you're not going to like this," Vinnie said. "But if you want to stay here with me, you have to do it. I made an appointment for you with Dr. Davis tomorrow at nine-thirty."

A cascade of emotions followed each other through my mind. I knew I needed to see her. I wanted to see her.

"Thanks, Vinnie. You've been a true friend. I appreciate what you've done for me." I sighed, wiped my nose on my handkerchief. You're right. I'll go see

Dr. Davis."

"I'm off tomorrow. I'm going to drive you," Vinnie said.

"Afraid I won't go?" I asked.

"No," he said, after a pause. His eyes said "Yes."

The next morning, Vinnie drove me to Dr. Davis' office.

"You can just drop me off," I said.

He scowled, shook his head. "I'm going with you."

When Dr. Davis called me into her office, Vinnie didn't get up.

"Vinnie, I'm going to be okay. I need to walk home—to your place, I mean—just to get some exercise and fresh air. Please don't wait for me."

Reluctantly he left.

My session with Dr. Davis helped immensely. She talked as much as I did, perhaps more, this time. I had already begun to experience some of the things many people feel when they lose a loved one. I had beat myself up, mentally, for causing Bobbie so much pain in our relationship. I thought of so many times I could have been more kind and loving. Today I had been wondering how she could possibly become so ill without me realizing it. If only I had done this, or that.

Dr. Davis helped find the tools to work through the myriad guilt trips my mind contrived. The one thing I found hard to understand was my own grief from losing Bobbie. I couldn't control it when I was alone, but managed to set it aside when someone was with me.

"Doug, in the past, you have taken things in your life that hurt and built armor plate around them," Dr. Davis said. Some of them you have worked your way through when you thought it was safe. Some, I've helped you with. And you still have some sealed away. That's what you've done with your hurt over losing Bobbie. Probably some time you will deal with it, hopefully when and where you can heal the wound.

"So now what are you going to do now?" she asked.

"Maybe it's odd that I know with such certainty what I want to do," I said. "You know, I was a wreck when I met Bobbie. I had no one else. She saved my life. Kept me from becoming a gutter-drunk. She believed in me, invested her love in me. I don't want her effort, her love to have failed. Which it will if

424

I slide back where I was.

"Before she died, we were getting along really well. It seemed we had the best of all possible worlds. I still want to be a success. I want a job I can get my teeth into and work myself to exhaustion sometimes because I want to. I want to be a photographer—an exceptional photographer."

CHAPTER FORTY SIX

Tony

The 1980 Prescott Frontier Days celebration had just begun, which would culminate in the parade and the rodeo over the 4th of July weekend. I grumbled to myself about the tourists as I drove around the block for the third time looking for a parking place.

I was about to step into the restaurant-micro brewery for lunch, when I saw Tony step up on the curb, not twenty feet away. We stared at each other. Our minds raced back over the years, gauging the changes time had wrought. As we crossed the distance between us, the years slipped away. We embraced in the middle of the sidewalk.

"Sarge?"

"Tony! What are you doing here?" I choked out. All the things we'd done together kaleidoscoped through my mind.

"I'm here on business. About to get some lunch before I drive back to L.A."

"Chow's pretty good here," I said, poking a thumb at my original destination.

"Jeezus, it's hard to believe it's you. Where've you been? What're you doing?" he said as we walked inside.

"Give me several days and I'll tell you. First, let's go quaff some suds."

"We'd like a booth in the bar," I told the hostess. "You *do* still drink beer, don't you, Tony? It's fresh, brewed on the premises." The way his face lit up answered my question.

As we ate, we exchanged details. Tony had two sons and a daughter. I stared at him, seeing the changes from the young soldier who was part of my team in 'Nam. His black hair had grown white at the temples, but he still had a full head of hair. Deep crow's feet ran out from the corners of his eyes.

"We've both changed," he said. "You used to be skinny."

I nodded. "Yeah, about fifty pounds skinnier." More like sixty.

"Me too," he said. "Remember all the five-mile runs we used to do?"

"God, do I ever. I'm starting to have some knee problems," I said.

"Yeah, me too. I had knee surgery three years ago. And the Doc put me on a diet."

"You look really good." I wondered if I lied with conviction.

Tony just smiled, the same way he used to when we got a crazy mission. "Yeah. Thanks anyway."

"Well, we're in pretty good shape, considering," I said.

"So how are you making a living?" he asked.

"I've been a freelance photographer. It was hard getting started—everyone with a camera thinks they're a photographer. I stuck with it and my images began to sell. I traveled all over the country, living in the camper on the back of my truck when I didn't have money for a motel.

"Do you know what's happened to everyone?" he asked.

I looked down at the mug of beer, picked it up and gulped down the rest of it, waved at the waitress. "You knew about Kennelley?" I asked.

He shook his head. "Not good?"

"No," I said. I told him about the phone call I got the day after Mike drove his car into the bridge abutment. Suicide at thirty-four years of age. They called it an accident. Tony looked sad and stared into the remnants of his beer.

"What a way to go."

"You know about Willie?" I asked.

"As in Willie our tunnel rat? Not good either?"

"No. He freaked out in a San Francisco bar, crawled onto a shelf inside the bar, and wouldn't come out. They had to dismantle the bar to get to him. I went to see him once, in the institution they stuck him in, but he didn't recognize me. I haven't gone back."

427

We were quiet as the waitress brought our lunch.

"There's one name you haven't mentioned," Tony said as I leaned back into the booth.

"Whose?" I asked, already knowing the answer. He spoke the one syllable that could still make me feel like I'd been kicked in the belly.

"Li," he said.

I looked down at my beer and watched the bubbles pop. The memories played as I closed my eyes and took a deep breath. The smell of her hair, her slim arms around my neck.

"We were trying to get them out as French citizens. We had to leave before we could get them passports. Forgeries, of course. We left them a lot of money. We thought we had made arrangements for the passports. They were supposed to fly to Paris—since their father was French—and call us. We were going to meet them there. Get married, and come home.

"I wrote to Li all the time, full of hope. I began to worry when she didn't write back. I wrote my congressional delegation, who were no help, probably because of my misplaced service records. The army really screwed me over. At first I had no service record at all. I sent a copy of my honorable discharge to my senator's office. Someone determined my records had been burned up in a fire. Then they were 'misplaced.' They were never found, and I didn't get much help."

"Jeezus, some reward for serving your country," Tony said.

"I tried everything I could think of, even going back to 'Nam. I made some contacts who could get me there illegally—but they warned me I wouldn't get any help from Uncle Sam if I got caught. I'd go to prison—or be executed. It would have cost a whole lot more than I had. Not the kind of thing you could go to the bank and borrow on.

"What I've wondered all this time is whether or not the guys we paid for birth certificates screwed us. Or if someone—maybe Major Fowles, or someone else who didn't like us—had tipped off some government official. They could have confiscated their bank account, seized the house, in spite of the way Cap'n Hank had it set up. I still don't want to think about those possibilities."

"Yeah. That's tough."

I looked down at my beer. "That's not all." The words came out low and strained. "She was carrying my child."

Tony reached out, put his hand on my arm. "And you don't know...?"

"Nothing...I tried to reach Cap'n Hank. You remember he had a bad heart?"

Tony shook his head. "Ah, no. Not him too?"

"Yeah. Not long after we left."

We'd been quiet for a while when Tony asked, "What happened with your service records?"

I shook my head. "I got into a shouting match with the head of the VA hospital when I got back. The one in Alexandria. Over the defoliant. I threatened to go to the *Washington Post* about it."

"Oh, I'll bet that got their attention."

"That's not the half of it. That's when I became a nonentity, no service records. No hospital records. When I came up with my DD214 and my certificate of honorable discharge, I went from no service records to lost service records. I ended up getting grilled by the FBI. They even changed some of the dates on my college transcripts. And that was three years after I got back. Those bastards scared me more than anything that happened in 'Nam."

"Why would they mess with your college records?"

I shrugged. "I guess they thought if it looked like I attended college over that period of time, I couldn't have been in Southeast Asia."

"How could they do that?" he asked.

"Hey, if they can give someone a whole new background in the witness protection program, it can't be that hard. It reminds me of some of the pilots I've talked to that flew for Air America. Their records were normal, then they had no service record for a year. Then they had an assignment and a promotion from lieutenant to major, or captain to colonel. Our own government. That's what's scary."

"You know," Tony said, "I went to the Vietnam War Memorial. None of the names of any of our guys are on it. We didn't exist. None of us died."

"Somehow I'm not surprised."

We drained the last of our beers.

"I found out there are things I just can't do any more, " I said. "When I'd been back a year or so, I happened on a bad car accident, people laying all over the pavement. I wanted to help, but when I got a whiff of it I almost puked. Never got out of my car. I'd driven half a block when a chopper landed on the highway. The red and white colors, instead of olive drab, confused me. I just couldn't deal with guts hanging out any more, or squirting stumps. Remember being in a chopper when the cargo bay was all slick with blood? So slick you wondered if you were going to slide out if the chopper jockey jinked? And the pain, the screams."

Tony frowned, his face turning pale. "Yeah. It's still hard to talk about," he said

"It seems to get easier, though, if you find someone you can talk to. Someone who will listen without condemning. I know a lot of guys who still can't talk about it. Kennelley couldn't. That's why he drove his car into a bridge abutment."

"You sure about that?"

"Yes. Can't prove it, but that's what happened."

Tony turned his mug around and around, making circles on the table from the condensation. We both studied them. "I had a real hard time for a while, sometimes dreaming about—well, stuff we did, and wondering, always wondering if we did the right thing," he said.

"I don't know if I look for forgiveness, or for some kind of understanding " I said. "Over the years it's begun to seem like there really is some kind of plan after all. For everything. Like, God..." I shrugged. "You remember those five mile runs—the ones with field packs and rifles? Remember how it felt when we finally stopped, and took off our packs? Like we were almost floating? Sometimes I float."

Tony nodded. "Yeah, we did what we felt was right. The road to hell is not paved with good intentions. I don't know what it *is* paved with, but not that. We fought for each other—to keep each other alive and unharmed. That was more important than anything."

"Yeah. We did a lot of brave, crazy things."

We sipped our dark beer, thinking of people and places long gone.

430

"So are you married now?" Tony asked.

"No," I said, looking down. "Not any more." I still felt the pain, although the years had blunted it. Talking about Bobbie still hurt.

"Hey, man, I think I asked about something else that...well, maybe you'd rather not talk about it."

"It's okay. I met Bobbie..." I told Tony about falling in love with her, how she changed me, our brief marriage, and the pancreatic cancer that took her.

"My God, Sarge, I'm so sorry to...I don't know what to say, except that I'm sorry for your loss. How long has it been?"

"Going on ten years. I loved Bobbie. More than I imagined. I thought that perhaps being with her, I would get over Li. But no one will ever take Li's place. Or hers." I pulled out a handkerchief and blew my nose.

"Sarge, I...."

"Tony, my friend, It's not Sarge any more. Just Doug."

"Jeezus, Sarge. Er, Doug. I'm so sorry. I don't know if I could take it if.."

"Yeah, you could. I hope to God you never have to. But you could."

I stood and pulled out my wallet. "I'll get it," I said.

"I'll put it on my charge card, if you'll let me buy. I can deduct it."

"What the hell, if we can stick the IRS for it, why not?"

We stood, and Tony reached out and enveloped me in a bear hug. I wrapped my arms around him and hugged him back.

"Some time I'd like to meet your family." I said.

He pulled a business card out of his wallet. "Call me. I'd love that. And you'd be surprised how much my wife knows about you. You'd be welcome in our home."

We walked out the door into a blaze of red, white, and blue. While we reminisced over our suds, the Rodeo Days decorations had been put up. Hundreds of American flags lined the street on both sides, swaying in the breeze.

Tony stiffened just slightly, as if coming to attention. I almost did the same.

CHAPTER FORTY SEVEN

All's Well That Ends

I saw the card stuck in the door as I cut across the yard. Salesman or bible-thumper? I wondered. My belly tightened up when I pulled it from where it was wedged under the screen. Lt. Col. R. E. Reid, it announced in bold letters. United States Army Investigative Division. Then a phone number. An eight-hundred number. I stared at the card, wondering why he needed an eight-hundred number. Would criminals call toll-free to confess? What did he want with me? Did he think I'd done something criminal? I turned it over.

LOOKING FOR FORMER SGT. 1ST CLASS D. B. WALKER. PLS CALL REGARDING AN OPERATION IN VIETNAM AROUND NOVEMBER, 1964

My guts tightened up, my breath came fast. I had to set down the groceries I was carrying to keep my knees from buckling. I fumbled for my door key. Inside, I fell into my easy chair and read the card again. After all these years, the bastards are going to come after us, I thought. I crumpled the card, dropped it in an ashtray, struck a match and lit it. I turned the pieces until the whole card was white ash. That won't be the last of it, I thought, wondering if I shouldn't have made such a rash decision. Maybe I should have called.

The next day I stayed late in my studio, making prints from negatives of some of the custom portraits I'd shot. I had Lieutenant Colonel R. E. Reid more on my mind than air-brushing a facial scar from a life-size portrait, and I ruined the print.

"Thank you, Colonel R. E. Reid. There goes fifty dollars in material, plus my time. How's your expense account, Colonel Reid?"

I threw it in the trash, cleaned up my equipment, and retreated to my office. I re-heated a cup of yesterday's coffee, stale and bitter, the way I felt about how my government had treated me—and a lot of other vets. That's not what my country would have wanted. This was not *my* country.

The walls of my office were covered with some of my best wildlife shots—Rocky Mountain Bighorn sheep, a full-curl Desert Mountain Bighorn, a mountain lion. Today they looked me in the eye, accusing me of—I didn't know what for sure. "Shut the hell up," I yelled at the inanimate images. "I know. I hate this, too. It's boring." The Kodiak bear, hanging over the desk, stared open-mouthed with fangs bared. He roared loud in my memory, huge paws and sharp claws raised. I felt a tingle pass over my scalp. I had a close call getting that shot. My guide pumped seven twelve-gauge slugs into him and he still rushed another ten yards. His twelve-hundred pound carcass came down hard almost on top of me. He sprayed me with blood-tinged slobbers as I lay where I'd fallen on my back, cradling my camera. But I felt more afraid right now, knowing Colonel Reid wanted to see me. Maybe there's not much to what he wants, I thought, not believing it one bit.

When I got home, I pulled the car around the back of the house without looking at the front door. I didn't want to see another card.

The next morning when I left for work, I went out the front door, then stopped short. Where the hell was my car? I remembered I'd parked around back. When I turned, I saw the card from yesterday, wedged in the doorframe, just like the other one. Same name, rank and phone number. I took a quick step sideways, like I'd found a viper ready to strike.

The day dragged by. Around eleven o'clock I punched my intercom button. "Hey, what do we have this afternoon?" I asked Cindy, my receptionist.

"Joanne Evans, black-and-white portrait, at three-thirty," she said, "one more at four-thirty."

"I'm going home. I've got some of my own stuff to airbrush. I'll be back about three. Take a long lunch hour if you want to—with pay—and come back about four.."

"Oh, great. I was going to go to the sale at Sears," she said.

On the drive home, I thought about the first few years I'd made my living as a freelance photographer. Traveling all over the country had been an escape. Which at the time, I needed. Living in the camper on the back of my truck, or in a motel when I had the money, gave me a feeling of anonymity. I yearned to have that lifestyle back again. Especially, now, the anonymity.

When I turned onto my street, I saw a dark-colored sedan parked in front of my house. It had government plates. I mentally calculated the total of my bank accounts and the equity in my house, wondering what attorneys charged these days.

I drove on by. The figure behind the wheel looked right at me. Hell, I thought, he must know who I am, what I drive. I stopped, turned around, and pulled in behind the house. He'll have to ring the bell if he wants to talk to me. Damned if I'll give him the satisfaction of catching me in my front yard.

I'd no sooner unlocked the back door when the doorbell rang. Anxious bastard, I thought. Let him wait. I set down my briefcase and hung up my coat. The bell rang again. Fear, frustration and helplessness chilled my blood. Would I be lodged in some stockade by this time next year? What for? I twisted for the deadbolt on the front door, pulled it open.

Lieutenant Colonel Reid looked every bit the professional soldier. He was taller than me, about six-foot-one, probably in his fifties. And he looked fit. He wore a rash of ribbons on the left side of his uniform jacket. He had a Purple Heart and a ribbon for time served in 'Nam. Another REMF? I wondered. So now he's headhunting for someone. The bastard.

"Sergeant Walker? Douglas Bradshaw Walker?" he asked, smiling. He offered his hand. When I didn't take it, his smile disappeared. Cut to the chase, I thought. Get the bullshit out of the way.

He frowned. I need to talk to you, Sergeant Walker. May I come in?"

"It's *Mister* Walker," I said.

"All right, *Mister* Walker it is. May I come in?"

I stepped back and opened the door, motioned to the couch. I'd always hated that couch. My five-foot, four-inch ex-significant other picked it out because her feet touched the floor when she sat on it. He'd have his knees under his chin.

434

He set his briefcase on the coffee table and took out a fat folder. "Mr. Walker, were you and your platoon engaged in an action on or around the Ho Chi Minh trail in Laos, on or about 12 November 1964?"

"Team. Not a platoon. An A-Team. Can't you guys get anything right?" I wondered if that, or anything else, mattered any more. Christ, is that what they're coming after me for? Or coming after all of us? Who the hell do they have for witnesses? Or are they going to smear Mike's reputation for shooting those two toasted Charlies in the head? I thought about Kennelley and the so-called accident when his car slammed into a bridge abutment. I felt myself scowl, giving Reid knife-blade looks.

"Ah, is that about the right date, Mr. Walker?"

"I think before I talk to you any more I'd better have an attorney. Now please go."

Lieutenant Colonel Reid looked surprised. "No, no, Mr. Walker –"

"Don't give me a hard time, this is my home and I'm ordering you to leave. Get out or I'll call the cops." I slipped my hand down the side of the chair cushion where I kept a .45 Colt Government model, loaded, cocked and locked. I flicked the safety off and started to stand with it when Lieutenant Colonel Reid took the wind out of my sails.

"You don't understand! I'm trying to correct some injustices done to you and the members of your platoon. Er, A-Team. You and others in your outfit were told your records had been lost, or burned up. I've found some records that I'm sure will be of great interest to you. Not just about your time in Vietnam, but concerning the condition you were treated for at the VA facility, and your disability. Please believe me. There's nothing of a criminal nature here. Except maybe on the part of the U.S. Army. More like an apology."

I stared at him, hearing but not believing. My grip on the pistol relaxed. I flicked the safety back on, pushed it back between the cushions. I rubbed my forehead, wondering if this was true.

"We found a recommendation for a unit citation, naming you and a Sergeant Kennelley as non-commissioned officers in charge of a team..."

"A-Team," I said.

"An A-Team that engaged a superior force of enemy troops, killing most of them, and destroying a large amount of materiel headed down the Ho Chi Minh Trail. The officer who submitted the recommendation was a Lieutenant J. E. Jaimeson."

He handed me a copy of the citation. Lieutenant Jaimeson's scrawl at the bottom of the last page looked familiar, even after all these years. My hands shook so hard I had to lay it flat on the table.

"... with a small reconnaissance team, engaged and inflicted an estimated ninety-five percent casualties on an enemy force consisting of more than two full platoons, destroying an estimated eight tons of the enemy's food and munitions that were en route down the Ho Chi Minh Trail..."

Along with these papers I found a citation for me, for the Silver Star. The room blurred and faces I hadn't seen for more than a decade marched down a trail on the wrong side of a red line on a map. Reid hadn't turned out to be a headhunter like I'd thought, but I'd be damned if I'd let him see my tears. I got an iron grip on my emotions, summoned up what anger I could find to mask my feelings.

"So?" I asked.

His face softened. "I don't think you understand. You've been a victim of an old policy of the U.S. Army, handed down, actually, by the executive branch. A quite paranoid executive branch during those years. Anyone who threatened the establishment no longer existed. We found these records, signed by your lieutenant. We also found this." He pulled a fat folder from his brief case. "You were in the VA hospital in, let's see, 1967. You were diagnosed with an incurable condition, awarded a one-hundred percent disability."

I nodded. The lump in my throat kept me from talking. I concentrated on keeping a blank look on my face, wary of what he might pullout of his briefcase next.

"I still don't think you understand. Your country owes you, more than it can ever pay in cash. It may help, though, to know that you have over four hundred thousand dollars, including interest, in disability payments owed you. But I'd guess that what's more important to you, the U.S. Army will have to acknowledge your service—that you did in fact serve in Vietnam."

His words didn't register. Even after all the years I wanted to hear them spoken by the U.S. Army, it seemed impossible it could be happening.

"There are others from your outfit, too," he continued.. "It started when someone who insisted on being called 'Stryder' kept calling and writing his senators...

Stryder. Loyal Stryder. Crazy Stryder. A damn good soldier. I felt a stab of fear for him. "Where is Stryder?" I asked, vaguely aware I had interrupted Reid. The look on his face told me Stryder was gone. "Tell me where he is, goddammit!"

"I'm sorry. He's dead."

The words hit me like the shock wave from a thousand pound bomb. Christ, there were getting to be more and more deaths, fewer of us left. Stryder, who never knew when to quit. Thank goodness.

"This guy kept on badgering anyone who would listen to him," Reid went on, pretending he didn't see the tears that finally forced themselves down my face. "He wrote letters to dozens of senators and as many congressmen, the members of the Armed Forces Committee, all sorts of veteran's groups, and started working the newspapers. All his correspondence he wrote on lined paper. He generated a lot of human interest—the GI who served his country, now disavowed, without benefits of any kind, living on the street. Finally he started getting some serious attention on the Hill. The U.S. Army, fearing an investigation would be a disaster, which it would have been, decided to cooperate. That's my private opinion, anyway.

"It looks like malnutrition and alcohol took their toll on Stryder. They found him dead in the refrigerator carton he lived in. An investigation ..."

He went on, but I didn't hear the rest. I could see a young kid, leading his Sergeant through the jungle. His grin, the almost-crazy glint in his eyes. Reid looked down at his briefcase, mostly, I guessed, to give me a few minutes to pull myself together. The phone must have rung, for I could hear Cindy leaving a message on the answering machine. "...so I told them something must have happened to you or you'd be here. I'm canceling your last appointments..."

"Do you know where he's buried?" I interrupted.

"Stryder? No. But I can find out. Why?"

"I want him to be burred in Arlington with honors. And I want the name of every man we lost added to The Wall."

Reid frowned. "I can probably arrange that. Look," he said "I saw a lot of action in 'Nam. Guys I got close to...well, some of them didn't make it. You can get *so* close in a hell-hole like that—like brothers. Even closer. I understand what you're feeling." He gathered his papers, snapped his briefcase closed. "How about if I come back next week? Wednesday? I've got to go back east tomorrow. I'll call you, if you'll give me your number. He held out a pen and the back of one of his cards.

After he'd gone I sat and watched ghosts from the past march through my memory once again. I called Cindy, asked her to cancel all my appointments and take a four-day weekend with pay.

My CAR-15, the civilian model of the rifle I carried in 'Nam, stood in its corner of my gun safe. I took the rifle and two loaded magazines, and my .45 Government Model with two full magazines. I slipped a blanket and a canteen into my day pack, and drove out of the city.

After I'd hiked to the deserted lookout point where I did much of my thinking, I relaxed.

The sun set, fired the clouds with colors—of battle, of blood and mortar bursts, bomb blasts and muzzle flashes. Colors of flowers, the Fourth of July—and colors of peace.

Finally, it would end. I pulled a flask of single-malt Scotch from my pack. "For Strider," I said to the heavens. "And all the other guys." The liquor burned its way down and I wept.

CHAPTER FORTY EIGHT

Cap'n Hank

"Goddammit, I'd like to see you long enough to blow the foam off a few beers!" said the voice on the phone.

The voice sounded familiar, I thought. "Sounds great," I said. "You buying?"

"I will if you let me wear my purple heart," the mystery voice said. That made the connection.

"Cap'n Hank? Cap'n Hank! Jeezus Christ! Is that you? They told us you were *dead!* Where the hell have you been all this time? You'll never believe how glad I am to hear your voice! We thought your heart quit on you right after we came home! "

"It's beating well enough I can still drink you under the table," he said.

I laughed. "And you're still full of it. You never could! Where the hell are you?"

"I just got out of Walter Reid. Had more surgery. Just after you guys left, I got flown back to the World. They thought I was going to die. But I fooled them."

"You can't believe how glad I am to hear from you. You want to come here for some beers, or you want me to come there?"

"I'd like to come there. I have some information I'd like to pass along in person. It's important."

"Great," I said, wondering what it was. "When?"

"I took a chance. I've got a flight booked into Sky Harbor in Phoenix tomorrow. Any possibility that would work for you?"

"You bet it will. I'll make it work. I'll pick you up. What airline, which flight?"

"I can rent a car," he said.

"Jeezus, Cap, you're family! Hell no, I'll come and get you." I jotted down his flight information.

I buzzed Cindy and told her I wouldn't be in the next day.

Cap'n Hank's flight wasn't due until a little after nine. I wanted to beat the morning rush, then have some time for myself. The two hour drive gave me time to ponder a multitude of people and events from 'Nam. My memory cascaded out of control, recalling times happy and not-so-happy.

I turned on the airport off ramp, and found the parking garage. Inside the terminal, I found a snack bar that offered a coffee special for a mere two dollars. Refills were one dollar. I could eat well for a day in 'Nam for less than the refill. Some bargain.

With three hours to kill, I engaged in one of my favorite pastimes—people watching—but the concourse was almost deserted. I thought about Anne. Anne with an "e." I wondered where she was now. Probably married with four kids, I guessed. I thought briefly, painfully, about the time I brought JR's body home. And I began to wonder what Cap'n Hank was going to tell me.

"Shit," I said to the empty concourse. Colonel Reid's visits were the first of any kind of good news. Which way's this gonna go?

A crowd of de-planing passengers headed down the concourse. I sat at the snack bar and watched. So many of them looked angry at the world. Or frightened. Maybe they knew how they felt about the world. I didn't know how I felt any more.

When the public address system announced the arrival of Cap'n Hank's flight, I walked down the concourse to the gate. I saw him as he made his way through the passengers that were hugging family or loved ones.

"Cap'n Hank! Over here!" I called. He turned and came toward me, pushing an oxygen bottle like the one the VA had told me I'd have to have for the rest of my life. He looked better than I thought he would. His hair was mostly

440

gray, but he still had a military bearing and stood straight. I wondered if he still had four needle-sharp pencils in his inside pocket.

"Hey, Sarge! How are you?" He opened his arms and gave me a hug. "You look great!"

"Yeah, so do you. What's with the oxygen tank?"

"I'll need it for another week or so. It's just to make it a little easier on my heart while it heals up."

"You got baggage?" I asked. He nodded.

We retrieved his suitcase and I carried it to the car. The entrance to the interstate was just ahead. I wondered if he was hungry. "You want something to eat?" I asked.

"I'm so goddam hungry, I could bite the head off a rat!" He laughed at the assessment of his gastronomical condition. "Remember, you taught me to say that?"

"Uh, yeah. I think so. What do you want to eat?"

"Well, I've heard so much about Mexican food. Never tried it. Do you know of a place that serves good Mexican food?"

"I just happen to know of five or six. We'll try the one on top of the list."

We pulled into the parking lot at El Macayo in central Phoenix just before the lunch hour rush started. Cap'n Hank was taken with the serapes and sombreros which were a part of the decor.

"I'd like to get one of those," he said.

"One what?"

"One of those big hats." He pointed.

"They're called sombreros." I smiled, imagining him under one of the giant sombreros.

The hostess led us to a booth. I asked her to tell our waitress we wanted two beers. "Draft okay, Cap?"

"Sure," he said.

We made small talk for a while. He asked me what I was doing, and about my family. I told him about my reconciliation with mom and dad, and my photographic business. We drank two more beers, then Cap'n Hank frowned.

"I'm kind of surprised you aren't married," he said.

It felt like Cap'n Hank was leading up to something. I thought about Bobbie and felt the inevitable pain in my chest. "I was married, about ten years ago. She died of cancer. I haven't been able to get close to anyone since then."

"Oh my God," Cap'n Hank said. "I'm very sorry." He gulped the rest of his beer. "Well, I've got some news for you. I didn't know whether or not to tell you because I didn't know if it would be welcome, or painful. I wanted to tell you in person. I guess I still don't know."

"It's Li, isn't it?" I asked. Before he could answer, I got up, crossed the room to the bar. "Do you have Glenmorangie, Sherry Cask?" I asked the bartender. If he was going to tell me what I thought he was, I'd need some fortification.

"I have the fifteen year old," he said.

"Two doubles. Please ask my waitress to bring another round in a few minutes."

I took the drinks to our booth. "Single-malt. Very smooth," I said. I gulped half of it, thinking it was a waste of fine sipping Scotch. "Go ahead. Tell me," I said.

"I got a letter from Li."

"So she's alive." It was a statement, more than a question. A terrible relief. All along, I had known she was alive. Without a doubt.

"Yes. She tracked me down through the U.S. Army and Harvard Law Alumni Association. It's taken quite some time. I decided to write to her before I talked to you. Partly, to make sure she was still at the address she sent. When she replied, I enlisted the aid of a few of my retired JAG cronies to have someone visit her. Someone who, of course, still does us favors in the new Vietnam. Then I called you."

I didn't think I could move my body, except my elbow. I threw back the rest of my double, picked up the second one.

There was no question about what I wanted.

Epilogue

Silhouetted against the deep sunset colors, palms and cypress framed a photo too wild to capture. Beyond the porch of our hut, the land sloped gently down to the water. The road on our spit of land was barely above the water level. The monsoons had started.

Li and I had been married at the American Embassy in Bangkok. Our little slice of Eden in the jungle of Thailand had served as a retreat for us. Here, in the joy of our reunion, our love had grown even stronger. Together we would live out the rest of our lives. But not here. Regardless of everything, I loved my country. We would live in the U.S.A.

Li turned from her flower boxes, her labor of love, trying to grow blooms that birds and bugs would not find delectable. Her profile cast a shadow as she climbed the stairs and sat next to me in the old fashioned swing. We sat silently, listening to the sounds of the birds as the sun set into the thatch of trees.

"Have you taken your lung medicine yet?" she finally asked, resting her hand on my thigh.

I put my arm around her, pulled her close. Pitch from the trees and dirt stained her small hands. Scarred and rough, they showed the ravages of time, the post-war years washing dishes, laundry, and scrubbing floors in Ho Chi Minh City. When she lost our child to dengue fever.

"Yes, love. I took my pills, but you're the medicine that gives me strength and keeps me going. I felt her slender body relax. Slowly I pulled the pins from her hair, watched it spill past her shoulders, silver and black in the last of the twilight.

My country had come through for me.